Praise for the worl

Break...

This was a lovely, feel-good romance with minimal angst and lots of sweet moments of sapphic love and family... With an enemies to defence partners to friends to lovers evolution of the main characters' relationship, it was fun to see how Adrienne and KJ's relationship grew without the overly-angsty moments that sapphic romance novels can be filled with.

I strongly recommend it to those who love hockey, and those who know nothing about it.

-Gillian F., NetGalley

Demon in the Machine

...is an exquisite steampunk and paranormal mashup permeated with action, mystery and romance! This book had my heart thundering in my chest on so many levels! One of the many things I love about MacTague's writing is her ability to create strong, complex and "real" characters and the wonderful dynamic she develops between them. This book is no exception! All great steampunk features wonderful gadgets and contraptions and this novel is rife with such inventions as multifunctional goggles, powerful jump suits enabling the scaling of tall buildings and, of course, the new horseless carriage. My favourite aspect is how MacTague adds her own flair to these gadgets in terms of how they are powered. I also love how she brilliantly captures the atmosphere; the romance, etiquette and manners of the Victorian era and then pumps it full of grotesque imps and demons! However, what really draws me in to Lise's novels is her fantastic characterization. So, if you enjoy layered, well realized and imperfect but enticing characters, then this book is definitely for you!

MacTague is really suited to steampunk! She excels at writing stories with strong women and Briar and Isabella are no exception. *Demon in the Machine* is a wonderful mélange of mystery, steampunk, paranormal and romance that is appealing on so many levels!

-The Lesbian Review

Five Moons Rising

MacTague completely knocks it out of the park with this one, one of the best lesbian paranormals I've read. This book blew me away. Not just for the imagination MacTague demonstrated around the different creatures that haunt the darkness and the work Malice and her colleagues have to undertake to defeat the rogue ones, but also because of the underlying themes and threads that hit on so many subjects. Family, commitment, what it means to belong, what it means to trust–MacTague covers them all and in writing that's so powerful it took my breath away at times.

It's another winner from MacTague, who is rapidly becoming one of my all-time favorite lesfic authors.

-Rainbow Book Reviews

This book is absolutely brilliant. It is filled with memorable characters and a plot that will keep you coming back to it even when you know you should be working or sleeping or doing something else. MacTague really got into her head and gave us a beautiful account of what it would be like to be a werewolf. It was so wonderfully done that I now have a massive book crush.

-The Lesbian Review

Vortex of Crimson

MacTague does it again… a fantastic end to the saga that has seen Jak and Torrin fight all sorts of battles, both physical and emotional. I love how MacTague mixes in the action scenes and conspiracy theories alongside the touching and sometimes angsty romance between Jak and Torrin. Neither the action nor the romance ever takes over completely, the balance is always spot on.

-Rainbow Book Reviews

Heights of Green

What a rip-roaring sequel this is to *Depths of Blue*! There are layers within layers in this book, and the subtle ways they are revealed is brilliant in its execution. It's clear something is going on, but MacTague teases this out, strand by strand, and brings it all to a stunning ending. There's politics, intrigue, action, and lots of emotion. Both Jak and

Torrin's actions and reactions are explored in just the right amount of detail alongside the story itself, and it's a fantastic blend. The book finishes on a great cliffhanger, ready for book three, and I can't wait to get started on that.

-Rainbow Book Reviews

The ending had me standing on my feet. Reading it had me pumped and the teaser at the end did nothing to slow my heart rate down. The way Jak's and Torrin's journeys split apart and then come back together had me turning pages so fast I got a digital paper cut and those SOBs hurt! But it was worth it.

-The Lesbian Review

Depths of Blue

I thoroughly enjoyed the story and the characters that Lise MacTague has drawn in *Depths of Blue*. The world building is top-notch and the backstories of the characters are told in such a way as to move the story along and not in a pedantic, expository way. I would recommend anyone who likes a good sci-fi book give this a try.

-Lesbian Reading Room

This is a proper sci-fi/action/adventure story with two very strong female leads and I absolutely loved it! Both Torrin and Jak are kickass women, and that was such a refreshing change—there's no tough butch here rescuing a weak femme damsel in distress. They can both look after themselves and they therefore have a lovely tension between them from the start. This is part one of a trilogy and I cannot wait to get into book two—I love MacTague's story-telling, her narrative and descriptive skills, and the universe she's created. Excellent lesbian sci-fi, of which there isn't enough, so this is a brilliant addition to that genre.

-Rainbow Book Reviews

...absolutely a must-read novel. Lise MacTague has a really refreshing take on this genre. Her world is well created and different enough to make it interesting. Her story moves at a good pace, lingering only on important moments. Her characters are both gorgeously written, full of insecurities and real.

-The Lesbian Review

…I rather enjoyed going along on its smooth, well-trod road full of tropes like: mistaken identities, space opera-ish drama, mounting sexual tension, women passing as men in the army, big patriarchal bad guys, and that-thin-line-between-love-and-hate. Oh, and some pretty steamy sex scenes.

-*Casey the Canadian Lesbrarian*

WINTER'S
MOONS

About the Author

Lise writes speculative and romantic lesbian fiction (often in the same book) in all sorts of different flavors. She has written one contemporary hockey romance, a space opera trilogy, one steampunk novel (but she'd love to write more), and a mess of paranormal urban fantasy. She grew up in Canada, but left Winnipeg for warmer climes. After flitting around the US, she settled in North Carolina where the winters suit her quite well, thank you very much. These days, there isn't nearly enough hockey in her life. She makes up for that lack by cramming writing in around her wife and kids, work, and building video game props in the garage, with the occasional break for D&D and podcasting. Find some free short stories and more about what she's up to at lisemactague.com.

WINTER'S
MOONS

LISE MACTAGUE

BELLA
BOOKS
2022

Bella Books, Inc.
P.O. Box 10543
Tallahassee, FL 32302

First Edition - 2022

Editor: Medora MacDougall
Cover Designer: Kayla Mancuso

ISBN: 978-1-64247-418-3

Acknowledgments

I need to start by thanking my alpha and beta readers: Lynn, Amy, Joy, Nyssa, and Mildred. I appreciate you taking a crack at my stories when they're still raw. These stories would be much poorer without your assistance. Thank you especially to KD Williamson, Stephanie Goldman, Jax Meyer, and Ashly Rodriguez for being excellent sensitivity readers while I was seeking to depict main characters outside of my personal frame of reference. Any errors of characterization are my own.

As always, a huge thanks has to go to my editor, Medora MacDougall. I look forward to working with you every time. Your comments keep me thinking and clarifying. Now if only I could shed the weird Canadian Englishisms that creep into my prose.

Thank you to everyone on the Bella crew for continuing to pick up my stories, even when they get...complicated. Thank you for giving me the space to stray into the world of sidequels, and to fully flesh out Cassidy's story. There is so much to be told in this side of the storyline, and my linear-thinking brain really appreciated the opportunity to write it out chronologically, instead of having the story play out off the page.

To my readers: thank you so much! I'm always thrilled to hear when one of my stories has made an impression, whether it's through a review, or someone who reaches out directly. The stories keep coming, but it's your reactions and feedback that keep me from sticking them in a drawer and forgetting about them.

Thank you to Margaret Snow for lending me a name. Snow has turned out to be one of my favorite characters so far, and I'm thrilled to have such a perfect name for her.

And finally, but never lastly, to my wife and kids (Lynn, Whit, and Ce), thank you for your continued support. Thank you for putting up with the endless "what if" questions and speculations on what character X would do in situation Y. I've filled a lot of road trips with strange forays into my brain, and you all still talk to me, despite knowing what goes on in there. Lynn, thank you for being my love, my best friend, my project partner, my sounding board, and so much more. I love you so very much, and I can't imagine my life without you and the kids in it.

Dedication

To everyone who struggles with impostor syndrome. I see you. I feel you. You *are* good enough and you *can* do this.

CHAPTER ONE

The wolven was young, Snow could tell from the way she held herself: unsure, as if the weight of her wolf hadn't yet settled completely. The girl still hadn't picked up on her presence, which might not have been a fair benchmark. Snow had spent most of her life learning to draw in on herself, staying off the radar of humans and wolven alike. There were advantages to being overlooked.

Take her current situation. What was the youngster doing, loitering near this warehouse-looking building in the middle of an industrial neighborhood? Did she also know Ruri? If so, why wasn't she going in?

Snow raised her head and inhaled deeply, tasting the cold wind. The smells of the city, exhaust, human sweat, the occasional mild reek of garbage or sewage, were shot through with traces of Lake Michigan, even this far from the beach. Underneath it all was an unfamiliar scent, one that raised her hackles, though she wasn't quite sure why. It was enough to warn her away from rushing into the building, even though it held the wolven who could clear up the circumstances surrounding her brother's death.

Dean... Snow shook her head, trying to rid herself of the image of the baby-faced boy he'd been. He'd worshiped her, had cleaved to her side like a shadow. When the time had come, he'd requested that she be the one to turn him, to allow him to join her and their deceased mother as wolven. A smile drifted across her face. No one had ever asked her to catalyze the change before that and none since. Some of her traits were undesirable. Luckily for Dean, her lack of dominance had not been transferred along to him. He might still be alive if it had.

Snow frowned at the lit windows of the squat building where Ruri was said to be living. There was no trace of her, only the young wolven. If this really was Ruri's home, there should have been some trace. Hell, the corner where Snow loitered unnoticed would have been a prime area for scent marking, and though the unique markers of Ruri's scent were all over it, they were older than they should have been. Either someone had lied to her, or there was something else going on, something she didn't understand. Her lips curled in a soundless snarl at the idea.

Her source had been adamant that Ruri was living in this area but had been cagey about why she'd left the North Side Pack. Still, the vamp had insisted the wolven hadn't gone far. At the time, Snow hadn't thought too much about it. Vampires loved to hold back their little tidbits. She and Carla, the vampire Lord of Chicago, had been doing occasional business for the better part of a century. She could see no advantage for the leader of Chicago's vampire community to betray her now. Besides, if Carla had wanted to sell her out, Snow would be hanging upside down from a meat hook. Her blood—the blood of any wolven—was too highly prized to be wasted on pooling onto the uncaring pavement of a somewhat smelly alley.

The girl pushed herself away from the wall where she'd been watching the brick building.

Snow started forward, then froze. She hadn't meant to move, but her wolf knew something was amiss. She snarled at Snow to keep moving, to stop this youngling, this cub, before it was too late. Snow held still. She hadn't gotten this far by jumping into situations she didn't understand.

The young wolven's head whipped around to stare right at her. Odd-colored eyes glared at her, one a brilliant crimson, the other electric blue. Snow would have put money on the young wolven's teeth having already lengthened. Her hair was light brown, but with an odd dapple, so it looked like she was standing in the shade beneath trees on a moonlit night. For a second, the same strange effect shaded across the pale skin of her face.

Ah, hell. Snow forced herself to relax. The cub was quick, both in reactions and to shift. She would have to be careful with those instincts. They would mark her out as inhuman almost as quickly as dropping to all fours and calling the wolf to her would. An easy smile crossed Snow's face. She opened her posture, keeping her hands where the wolven could see her.

"Howdy," she said, making no attempt to raise her voice, knowing the cub would hear her half a block away.

The wolven's eyes hardened from surprise into suspicion. "Who are you? What are you doing here?"

Snow held up her hands, palms forward. "I'm passing through, that's all. I didn't peg this as anyone's territory." She allowed her gaze to slide away from the wolven.

"And you just happen to be where I ended up?" The wolven snorted. "That's hard to believe."

"I came to visit a friend," Snow said, "but I don't think she's home."

A gust of wind brought with it the sourness of disappointment. "I don't smell her either," the wolven said quietly. "Someone is moving around up there, but I don't think it's them."

"Them?" Snow cocked her head. "There's more than one up there?"

"Which one are you here to see?" The wolven left her post and started purposefully toward her.

Her presence washed over Snow like a wave. It threatened to pull her under. From half a block away, she hadn't been able to get a read on exactly how dominant this one was, but it was plenty. She was very new to have such power behind her.

"Ruri," Snow said, the answer pulled from her by the wolven's presence. She snapped her mouth shut. A polite redirect of the conversation had been on her lips, but her wolf was eager to please this one.

"Ah." She stopped in front of Snow, looking her up and down while her nostrils flared.

Snow shifted, putting her shoulder forward. If the wolven attacked, she wouldn't find it easy to go right for Snow's soft belly, and Snow was already poised to flee if necessary. The wolven's scent pushed in on her, filling her nostrils, inviting Snow to come with her, to be held safe at her side among her pack.

"Alpha?" Snow whispered. It was ridiculous. Her youth was painted across her. The youngest cub would know this one was very new indeed, yet all the markers of the head of a pack came with her. The head of a familiar pack, one that was as close as Snow had to family—or had been until Dean was taken. "Of the North Side Pack." Her voice flattened as she spoke the name. This was who she'd come to see Ruri about. This was Five Moons.

* * *

Cassidy nodded. "Yeah." It was strange. If those words had come with that tone from another wolven, especially not one of her pack, Cassidy Nolan's back would have stiffened. She would have lifted her chin and done her best to stare down whoever had dared to disbelieve her, and her wolf would have snarled, ready to fight to defend her position.

That wasn't happening. The spirit of the wolf inside her grumbled a bit but didn't seem too put out by this stranger. That was also odd. They'd caught her watching them, and yet the wolf was unconcerned.

"I mean no disrespect," the strange wolven said. A hint of a Southern accent was buried under a clipped Midwestern cadence. "I was surprised. You're awful young to be Alpha." She shrugged and glanced off into the shadows. Dark hazel eyes held shards of silver, though she didn't seem to be on the edge of changing.

Cassidy watched her closely, not worrying about the other wolven's response to her forwardness. Deep brown hair faded to auburn at the tips; when she turned her head, the cloud of loosely kinked curls lifted and fell in waves. Her sepia skin reminded Cassidy of an old photograph, or maybe it was the feeling that this wolven was caught slightly out of time. Her clothing wasn't quite right for present day, a trait Cassidy had noticed among the wolves who called her Alpha. They would hold on to favored pieces of clothing or styles. This wolven had that same look. She'd been around for a while.

"Is there a minimum age?" Cassidy asked. She tried to inject a bit of humor into the query, but she still wondered. There might be an advantage in talking to a wolven who wasn't part of her pack. She couldn't ask her packmates such questions. They didn't need to know the reservations she held. The pack had been through so much in the past months.

She'd been through so much. And now her sister wasn't answering her calls, hadn't for a couple of weeks, now when she needed her most.

"How do you know Ruri?" Cassidy turned back to watch Mary's building.

"I knew her when she was your pack's Beta." A whiff of sadness tickled Cassidy's nostrils, with its unmistakable blue tones. "I heard she broke with the North Side Pack. I thought I'd look her up on my way through town."

"Sure." Why did Ruri make this woman so sad? "I'm Cassidy."

"Snow." The woman made eye contact for a moment. Her eyes still held hints of silver, but they'd started to recede as Cassidy continued not to show aggression.

"How do you know it's not Ruri up there?"

"Doesn't smell right. The only hints I get of our kind are old."

"Me too." Cassidy shoved her hands deep into her pockets and considered the building. Someone was home and moving around on the third floor, where Mary kept her living quarters. It was where she'd expected her sister and her sister's girlfriend to be. "I don't smell blood."

Snow cast her a startled look. "Why would there be blood?"

"If someone was up there without Ruri and my sister's permission, they'd be bleeding."

"Ah." Snow chewed on her lip. "I imagine that's true."

Cassidy barked a quiet laugh. "They wouldn't know what hit them." She lifted her head and inhaled again. "I don't smell much of Ruri or Mary." Not that Mary had much of a smell. The absence of Ruri's unique fragrance was more concerning. She wasn't sure if she would smell Mary from across the street, but Ruri should have stood out like a golden beacon in the scent landscape.

Did Mary break up with Ruri? She shook her head. That would be a huge error in judgment on her sister's part. Not that she was showing the clearest thoughts these days, not for the last…five years was it? *When did the government turn Mary into a Hunter?* Cassidy hadn't thought to ask about the actual timeline. Too worried about the actual answer, she supposed.

"I need to go up there." She took a step toward the building but stopped when a warm hand wrapped around her elbow. "What the—" She spun, glaring at Snow. "That's not a good…" Cassidy trailed off. Her wolf hadn't reacted. She was so accustomed to the other half of her soul twitching at the slightest sound that her lack of reaction was far more shocking than the most frenzied outburst would have been. "…idea," she concluded belatedly.

"You shouldn't go up there." Snow snatched her hand back and looked down, her words a fierce contrast to the deference of her body language. "Something isn't right. The smells are all off."

"Off? All I get is the usual crap Chicago smells." Cassidy inhaled reflexively. "It's not even as bad as normal. There's something floral."

"In Chicago. In February." Snow glanced up at her from the corner of her eye. "That's the weirdest part of it all."

"Huh." Cassidy scowled up at the lit window. "All the more reason to check then." She stepped toward the street.

Snow hesitated, then followed her. "I'm coming with you."

"Pretty sure I can handle myself." The wolf twined around her core in agreement. The two of them could handle pretty much anything anyone tried to throw at them. Her skin started to prickle in anticipation of an excuse to shift.

"Just in case." Snow lengthened her stride until she was abreast of Cassidy. A mirthless grin flashed across her lips. "I'm not going to be the one to lose the third North Side Alpha in less than six months."

"You're not one of mine," Cassidy said. "I can't make you stay back."

"Oh, you probably could." Snow sounded almost cheerful. "I'd be happier if you didn't try."

"If you say so." There was something about her, this wolven who wasn't of her pack but didn't set off the alarms she expected from an outsider. "How are you in a fight?" Gauging Snow's wolf was difficult. The woman was definitely wolven, but her presence didn't expand around her like the others Cassidy had met. It was like their identities extended beyond their skin, some more than others. There was no one in her pack whose self was so compact.

"You don't have to worry about me." Silver flashed in Snow's eyes again. The glints intensified until her eyes shone nearly white.

Cassidy grinned. "Excellent." She knew her own eyes were glowing to match Snow's. "Let's see what's waiting at my sister's place."

CHAPTER TWO

Snow picked her way after Five Moons. With unconscious ease, they navigated the piles of ice and snow the plows had shoved to the periphery of the street. The Alpha of the North Side Pack was at one enough with her wolf to have the unmistakable movement of the wolven in human form. It wasn't flawless, but this Alpha didn't lack confidence.

They stopped at a grey metal side door. Five Moons—it was impossible to think of her as Cassidy—produced a key and fit it to the lock. She lifted up on the handle and turned the key. It was obvious she'd been here before. She had mentioned that this was her sister's place, so that fit. Was this sister also wolven? That would make sense, except for the glaring lack of strong wolven scents.

The door opened, revealing a dark space beyond. Faint traces of Ruri's scent wafted out with the change in air pressure, but there weren't enough. If Snow was going by her nose, she would have said that Ruri had spent some time here a couple of weeks ago. There was no trace of another wolven's scent. The pieces weren't lining up.

Her wolf shifted nervously inside her. They lingered in the doorway, scoping out what they could see of the darkened interior.

"Maybe we should—" Snow cut off as Five Moons stepped blithely into the shadows "—wait," she finished to herself. She lifted her nose, sniffing the air again. Along with old aromas of wolven, she smelled oil and gasoline, shot through with metal. This was a garage, one that included a workspace, not simply vehicle storage.

Five Moons was a lighter shape in the gloom. Wolven eyes were better in darkness than humans', but even they couldn't see through pitch-black conditions like these. There were no windows on the front of the building. The only light was what little came in through the door. Snow listened closely, trying to determine what Five Moons was doing and if she was in danger.

There was some rustling in one corner, then the lights came on. They weren't enough to dispel the darkest shadows, but they revealed an empty space where a car would have been parked. From the oil spots on the floor, the vehicle wasn't new. Along one wall were two cages of chain-link fence. One held the type of tools Snow expected to see in a working garage. The other, the one Five Moons was stepping out of, held a small table with a laptop on it. Shelves along the back were filled with sleek black boxes. Snow cocked her head. Those were out of place. Almost as out of place as the trace of flowers with the same bouquet she and Five Moons had picked up outside.

"Are you coming?" Five Moons asked. She didn't raise her voice; she didn't have to. The words came easily to Snow's ears.

"I guess so." Snow stepped fully into the room, allowing the door to close behind her. The click of the latch in the frame made her wolf twitch. They were shut in a room with a strange wolven and a stranger situation. *I get it*, Snow thought to her wolf. *But we need to know. Dean deserves this much.* He'd deserved so much more, but he wasn't going to get it.

The wolf subsided, but not completely. She didn't like where they were. Snow couldn't blame her. She wasn't any more comfortable.

Five Moons was poking around the space. She lingered at the spot where a car had been parked, squatting and running her fingertips over the oil spots.

"Doesn't seem like they've been home for a while," Five Moons said. She rocked back onto her heels and considered the stained concrete floor.

"Maybe the car is in the shop?" Snow ventured. She moved toward Five Moons but not too close. It never paid to venture into the personal space envelope of a stranger, and Alphas claimed bigger envelopes than most. Often, they seemed to be trying to claim the whole world. Snow supposed that was what made them Alphas.

"It would have to be pretty messed up for Mary not to fix it herself," Five Moons said. "Also doesn't explain why she's not answering her phone."

"Ah." Snow filed the sister's name away for later. She shrugged, trying not to show her mounting anxiety. "Cars break down, though."

"They do." Five Moons looked up at the ceiling. She worried at her lower lip. Her eyes still glowed electric blue and unsettling crimson. "Does it smell to you like anyone has been here lately?"

"Not really?" Snow sniffed again. The scents were impossibly muddled. There was that old trace of wolven, then newer traces of flowers, and something that seemed like an approximation of human but which made the hairs on the back of her neck stand on end. "Do you have a heavy fae population here?"

"Fae?" Five Moons cut her such a look that Snow almost stepped back. "I don't know what you're talking about. Like fairies? There's Boystown." Disapproval dimmed her eyes. "No one calls them that anymore."

Snow shook her head. "Like real fae. The things the stories are based upon." All legends had roots, and she was beginning to wonder what was coming up in Chicago.

"Then no." Five Moons bounced to her feet. "I've never heard of such a thing."

"If you had a fae problem, you wouldn't have to ask."

"Then why bring it up?"

"This is reminding me of stories I've heard." Snow looked around, trying to peer more deeply into the darkest corners of the garage. It didn't feel like they were being watched, but she was starting to doubt her senses.

Five Moons grunted. "Stories. I don't have time for all that."

"There are truths in tales."

"If you say so." Five Moons looked up at the ceiling again. "I think we've learned all we can down here. I'm going up. You coming?"

* * *

Snow glanced obliquely at Cassidy after the question. She was certainly giving it a lot of thought. Cassidy could almost see the wheels turning in her brain.

"I'll go on ahead if you don't want to," Cassidy offered. She frowned. The wolven was a stranger to her, a lone wolf who hadn't bothered to announce herself to Cassidy and her pack. Sure, Mary Alice's home was technically outside the boundaries claimed by the

North Side Pack, but they were close enough that Snow should have at least stopped by. That was what wolven protocol dictated, or so she understood. Many of the intricacies of wolven relationships, not only within the pack, but also to the wolven not of the pack, were lost on her. It didn't help that she still had so many questions and not many people to answer them.

But this wolven felt different than those she called her own. Maybe it was that she was the first lone wolf Cassidy had encountered. Aside from Ruri—who Cassidy privately considered part of her pack, even if she wasn't officially a member—Cassidy hadn't had much opportunity to talk to outsiders. None of it explained the lack of threat she felt from this one.

Snow shook her head. "I'm coming." She glanced around the lower level. "This place makes me nervous. The whole situation makes me nervous."

"I hear you," Cassidy said. "I'm not reading that Mary and Ruri are home, but if they aren't, who is that upstairs?"

Snow swallowed, the movement of the muscles in her throat visible even from ten feet away. "So how do we go in, Alpha?"

"I'm not your Alpha," Cassidy said. "What do you think?"

Snow shrugged. "I'm not one for direct confrontation if I can avoid it. I think your instincts are going to be better in this situation than mine."

Cassidy considered it. She hadn't heard from Mary for a few weeks. Someone was making a nuisance of themselves around the edges of her territory. She clenched her fists. Nuisance she could have handled, but not when the second wolven in two weeks had just gone missing. One might have been bad luck or circumstances, but her Beta was on edge over this new disappearance. It felt good to have some confirmation that her anxiety wasn't misplaced. More confirmation would be better. If that wasn't Ruri upstairs, maybe whoever it was had information on where her sister and Ruri were. She needed Ruri; she needed Mary more.

"We have to go up there," she said, "but I don't want to scare anyone off. I'm a quick shift, if it turns into a fight. How about you?"

Snow shook her head. The skin over her cheeks shaded into russet, and a sudden whiff of shame burned Cassidy's nostrils. "I'm pretty slow."

"Fair enough," Cassidy said. She held out her hands to show she meant no harm by what she was about to say. "Then transform now. I'll go in first and you skulk back. If things go sideways, I'm trusting you to have my back while I change to furform."

"You'd trust me with that?" Snow's eyebrows arched high over eyes that still shone silver.

"You could have attacked me already. I haven't exactly been keeping my guard up with you." *Not that you should be admitting that.* Cassidy's wolf rolled over without concern. She didn't see Snow as a potential threat, never mind an enemy.

"All right." Snow shrugged out of her jacket, then reached for the bottom of her shirt before pulling it up over her head.

"Okay." It was Cassidy's turn for her cheeks to burst into flames as she spun around to watch the far wall. The casual nudity of the wolven of her pack was something she'd come to terms with, but it felt odd to be watching a complete stranger strip. Her wolf snorted in her ear, and a feeling of mild amusement crept through Cassidy, as if her wolf found her remaining modesty hilarious in its ridiculousness.

Her wolf's entertainment was echoed by the stranger's quiet chuckle.

Cassidy waited through the sounds of her clothing being removed and placed on the floor. She heard the sound of Snow's palms being placed against the ground, then the wolven inhaled deeply.

The transformation took longer than she'd expected. Snow's groans and pants sounded like she was in genuine agony. Cassidy knew she was fast and that the wolven of her pack could vary in the amount of time it took them to express their wolves to the outside of their skin, but Snow's transformation took longer than even the weakest member of the North Side Pack. Maybe that was why Cassidy's wolf didn't consider her a threat.

After what seemed like an eternity, Snow's pain noises were replaced by the panting of a wolf. She padded over to Cassidy and shoved a cold nose into her palm.

Cassidy looked down at the silver wolf. There was no other way to describe the color. There were no wolves with a similar coloration in her pack. The long outer fur was white, but beneath it was a dark grey. When the wolf moved, the color seemed to shift with her. It was beautiful, matching her eyes and name perfectly. But there was no time to admire Snow's furform.

The wolf's paws were nearly soundless as they made their way across the concrete floor. For a moment, Cassidy considered sending the elevator up empty but discarded the idea. They'd been reasonably quiet so far, and no one had come to investigate. Either they were still undiscovered or whoever was up in Mary's living quarters was setting a nasty surprise for them. The elevator wouldn't change either of those scenarios. No, it was better to make their way stealthily up the stairs.

Cassidy had disabled the silent alarm, so there was no chance that Mary's employers would come running. The alarm had been set. So whoever was here had known how to deal with it.

She eased open the door to the stairwell. Quickly, but silently, she made her way up to the second floor. Snow ghosted along in her wake, with barely the scrape of a toenail on metal to betray her presence. Metal stairs didn't creak like wood, but there was more noise from each footfall than Cassidy would have liked. The smell of Snow's wolf was comforting. Much like the aroma of Snow's skinform, only more potent. Cassidy spared a glance behind her at the second-floor landing to make sure Snow was still close by. The wolf panted up at Cassidy, carefully avoiding direct eye contact.

Cassidy nodded down at her. One more flight to go. She moved deliberately, taking her time so not even the slightest sound could give them away. It took longer to mount the second flight, and every step closer to the door at the top of the stairs twisted the tension in her muscles ever tighter. By the time they reached the top landing, Cassidy's wolf snarled within her chest, demanding to be released. They had no enemy, no one to confront, but that didn't matter at all to the raging wolf.

She warred with herself in front of the door to the third floor. Only pointing out that the wolf wasn't going to be able to unlock the door kept her aggressive other half somewhat contained. She took a deep breath as the wolf refused to back down. Snow leaned against her hip, her shoulder warm through Cassidy's jeans. The contact got through in a way that Cassidy's reasoning hadn't. The wolf retreated with a faint huff, allowing Cassidy to unclench her fists long enough to pull the key out of her pocket.

She unlocked the door as quietly as she could and held her breath as she pushed it open.

The yawning emptiness of the third floor greeted her. Mary's living area took up only a small portion of the overall space. A light was on in the area that Cassidy recognized as a sort of living room. The massive metal box where Cassidy had spent the better part of a month—of a lifetime—was long gone. Cassidy took a few steps to the side so she could see around the privacy screens that made up the "walls" of that space.

A familiar figure looked up from the sofa, the light on the side table illuminating her.

"Oh, hi, Cassidy," Mary said. "What's up?"

CHAPTER THREE

Cassidy stared at the woman on the couch. Mary was holding a battered paperback and smiling at her like she hadn't dropped off the face of the earth when Cassidy needed her most.

"What do you mean, what's up?" A vein throbbed in her forehead, pulsing as she struggled not to unload on her sister. "Is your phone broken? I've been trying to get hold of you for days and days now. Mom started calling me, even though she thinks I'm in Honduras."

A low whine from the stairwell startled both of them. Snow's silver fur was very visible through the opening. She stared intently at Cassidy, the first time she'd looked her in the eyes since they'd met.

"What's that?" The smile didn't drop from Mary's face. "Do you have a new puppy?"

"Puppy?" The wolf's snarl lifted Cassidy's lip. "Since when do you call us dogs?"

"You?" The smile was marred by a quizzical crease between Mary's eyebrows. "I don't understand." She pointed toward the doorway. "Who's your new pet, silly?"

"Pet?" This was only getting worse. Cassidy's mouth gaped open as she tried to figure out what had happened with her sister. "Oh my god. You and Ruri broke up." She stalked toward Mary. "What did you do? I can't believe you'd drive her off like that."

Mary laughed, a high breathy sound that stopped Cassidy in her tracks. Her sister had never made that particular noise. "Ruri and I are just fine. She's in the kitchen." Mary stood up. "Ruri, darling, we have a visitor."

Cassidy stepped back. Something was very wrong. The smell of flowers filled her nostrils, promising to choke her under an avalanche of petals. The cloying aroma intensified as Ruri walked through the gap between the privacy screens.

"Hi, Cassidy," Ruri chirped. She waved vigorously. "Who's your new friend?"

"So you don't know her?" Cassidy asked. She brought a hand up to her nose, trying to block out the floral scent that was making it harder and harder to think properly. Her wolf paced within her, scoring the underside of her skin with claws that felt like they would shred her open if she didn't relinquish control now. The wolf had never cared too much for Mary but was prepared to tolerate her for Cassidy's sake. She'd never had any such problem with Ruri. "I don't understand," Cassidy whispered.

She backed away two more steps, then the backs of her legs collided with something warm, furry, and immovable. A sharp pain on the back of her arm sent her wolf into a frenzy. She whirled, a tornado of teeth and claws that erupted their way through Cassidy's skin. She collapsed to her knees. By the time her hands hit the ground, the bones had snapped and rearranged themselves. Fur and fluids sluiced from her skin as she watched muscles writhe fingers into paws. Her mouth burst with salty liquid as her muzzle lengthened and sharp teeth emerged through her gums.

Her very human scream of shock and pain twisted into a canine howl of rage. The stupidly gawking faces of her sister and Ruri morphed into something she didn't understand. Her wolf didn't give her a chance to think about it; they leaped toward the bundles of sticks that stood where Mary and Ruri had been moments before. At her side, Snow also charged. Where Cassidy and her wolf went high, Snow stayed low; she snapped at brittle twigs, breaking them into small pieces that fell from her mouth to lie unmoving on the ground.

Cassidy's wolf was intent on the red string that held the bundle together. Cassidy tried not to think about how this tightly woven bundle tried to avoid their teeth and claws. The wolf was too fast. They snagged one end of the string in their jaws and pulled. The string loosened, then caught in the knot that bound it. They yanked at it, then shook their head side to side. The string frayed under the pressure of their teeth. Confident in their triumph, they jerked their head away from the bundle. The red string broke, but the knot stayed intact. The bundle tried to slip away, but they wouldn't be denied. With a frantic lunge and snap, their sharp teeth severed the string where it wrapped around the twigs.

Sticks large and small fell with a clatter to the concrete floor. Satisfied that the bundle was no longer a threat, they turned to offer aid to Snow. Her bundle was still intact, though much reduced. Snow circled and lunged, shattering mouthful after mouthful of twigs. Moments later, the bundle lost cohesion and crumpled. Too many sticks had been broken and the red string slipped off them, fluttering to the ground to land lightly on the messy pile.

Silence permeated the third floor as the two wolven stood frozen, sides heaving as they listened for more of those things. Cassidy's wolf was starting to calm as the scent of flowers began to dissipate. Cassidy pushed herself back to the fore, and the wolf melted away. Moments later, Cassidy stood, her feet bare against the cold floor.

"What the hell was that?"

* * *

The Alpha's question echoed through the space. Snow's wolf reluctantly returned control of her body. She was very conscious of how much longer it took her to shed her wolf form than it had Five Moons. A minute or more later, Snow crouched on the ground.

She licked her lips and looked up at the angry Alpha. "You have a fae problem."

Five Moons' eyes flared red and blue, a flash that reminded Snow incongruously of the lights of a police car. Maybe it made sense. Human police had always represented danger to their kind. There were no cops for the wolven. They policed themselves.

Snow pushed herself to her feet. Her knees wobbled a bit, but she locked them before she could show intolerable weakness to an unknown wolf. "Which one was your sister?"

"You couldn't tell?" Five Moons glared at her. "I thought you knew Ruri."

"All I saw were the sticks." She looked down at the broken twigs. "I take it you saw something else." Watching the Alpha carry on a conversation with the moving bundles had been unnerving, to say the least.

"My sister." Five Moons indicated the pile by the couch. "Ruri was in the kitchen." She raked her fingers through her hair. "They looked normal. Didn't act right and smelled worse, though." She gave a humorless bark that was probably supposed to be a laugh. "Freaked my wolf right out."

"Mine too." Snow shook her head. "I've heard stories. I think they were changelings. Someone used them to replace your sister and Ruri."

"That's weird."

"Very weird. Fae don't like cities. There's too much iron, it's in pretty much everything, in one form or another. They can't abide its touch. You don't find many this far into an urban center. And this was a major working. The stories I heard about people being switched for these things were all pretty old." She glanced over at Five Moons. "I sort of see why they might replace Ruri. Former Beta of one of the most powerful wolven packs in the Midwest, that makes sense. But why involve your sister?"

Five Moons stared at her, eyes wide with incredulity. "You mean you don't know?" Before Snow could answer, Five Moons shook her head and continued, "Of course you don't. No wolven simply walks up to the Hunter's home to talk."

"Hunter?" Snow asked, her voice faint. "Your sister is Chicago's Hunter?" Her voice raised in pitch as Snow tried and failed to modulate it. "Malice is your sister? How the hell is Malice your sister? And what does this have to do with Dean's death? Did you get him killed?"

"We need to talk," Five Moons said. "Like really talk. You're coming back to the hotel with me."

CHAPTER FOUR

Snow stared at Five Moons' left shoulder. "I don't think so," she said. "I came here to talk to Ruri. Came to talk about you." She tried to keep the venom out of her voice.

"Me?"

"I have to know what happened to him. To Dean."

"Dean." The Alpha's response was flat. "He was a…casualty."

"Of?" Snow pushed back at the dodge to her question. All she'd had on her brother's death were rumors. It wasn't enough. "No one knows how he met his end. Some say it was the Hunter, others a lone wolf." She lifted her gaze to meet that of the defiant wolven in front of her. "Still others say it was Five Moons who came for him."

"The Hunter?" Five Moons disregarded Snow's direct gaze, looking instead at the pile of sticks that had been masquerading as her sister. She shook her head. "We should go. I don't think it's safe."

"We're safe enough," Snow said. "We took care of the changelings."

The Alpha shook her head in an emphatic negative. "The silent alarm. I don't know if it's been set off. If it has, Mary's—Malice's employers will be sending someone to check on her. We can't be here when they arrive." She skinned off the remnants of the clothing she'd been wearing before the change took her. "Follow me. I can get us back to the den without being seen."

Snow shook her head. "Why would I go with you when I don't know if you killed him yet?"

"Me?" The Alpha's eyes clouded in confusion. She leaned down, placing her palms against the concrete.

"Five Moons."

"Why are you calling me that? That's not my name." She took a deep breath.

Snow cocked her head at the wolven woman. What exactly was going on here? She'd come to discover her brother's fate and to avenge it if warranted. On one point, the rumors all agreed: an Alpha named Five Moons had taken over her brother's pack after the usurper who killed him was eliminated. She'd assumed they were a new Alpha who'd come by the strange name as a result of how they'd assumed the leadership role of the North Side Pack. This Alpha knew too much about the Hunter and how she operated and not enough about herself. How could she not know that the other packs were calling her Five Moons? Her nostrils widened slightly. She smelled a story here, and unless Snow missed her guess, it was still unfolding.

Cassidy stared at her, waiting for an answer. She stepped closer to Snow, who backed up.

"It's your Alpha name. All Alphas have a name they're called outside their pack. Dean's was Velvet. Yours is Five Moons."

"That's not what I would have picked."

"Alphas don't usually claim their own names. They're bestowed, either by the pack or by other packs in the area. It's usually descriptive of how the Alpha is perceived by others, but sometimes it comes about for other reasons." Snow was willing to bet this was one of those situations. Where had the name come from? And how did it relate to her brother?

She dropped to all fours. "Lead on, Alpha of the North Side Pack. We can talk about Dean and how you came to replace him in front of the remains of his pack."

The Alpha snorted. "I'll settle for not ending up in the government's hands. We can talk about whatever you want when we're out of here. Hell, we can even have tea."

"I'd like that." Snow ignored the sarcasm and opened her mind. *Come back, sister.* Pressure grew in her muscles as her wolf's presence rushed from the back of her mind to the fore. Sharpened teeth burst into her mouth, followed by the pop of claws through the flesh of her fingertips. She welcomed the ripple of fur across muscles that reshaped around her bones. By the time Snow stood among the effluvia of her change, the Alpha was over by the open window.

Now that she wasn't a blur of fur and teeth, Snow took a moment to peruse the Alpha. Her mismatched eyes blazed red and blue in her face, but that wasn't the strangest thing about her. No, her pelt was a crazy patchwork of colorations and patterns. Red and brown fur dappled across her shoulders, while white and grey fur lay in brindled stripes along her back half, almost to her hindquarters and tail. Her legs shaded down to golden paws in front, but the hind paws were an inky black. Snow had met many wolven as she ranged across the continent, but she'd never seen one like this one. The mismatched eyes were uncommon, but paired with the fur… Her mind shuddered away from the implications.

The Alpha looked back at her, then hopped out the window.

The drop wasn't too far, about a story to the roof of the building next door. She didn't hesitate and followed on the wolven's heels. They streaked across the flat roof toward the edge. Five Moons ran along the gutter, keeping an eye on the ground below. A two-story drop would be possible in a pinch, but even with their enhanced healing abilities, it would slow them down.

A low rhythmic thumping sound pulled Snow's attention from the Alpha. The noise was coming from the other side of the building, but it was distinctive. A helicopter was coming their way.

She snapped her jaws shut on a yelp when a steel band closed around one of her forelegs. Five Moons kept her jaws clamped on Snow's leg and wrenched her back, sending her toppling off the roof. She twisted in the air, trying to get her paws around before she hit the pavement in the alley. She almost managed but couldn't bite back the yip of pain when she hit, her shoulder taking the brunt of the landing. There was no snapping of bones, and she rolled, coming up to glare at Five Moons who landed on all fours next to them.

She didn't dare snarl at Five Moons. Her restraint was wasted, however, as the Alpha had her attention on the skies. She scuttled toward the nearest wall, and Snow followed suit. No sense in staying exposed to those above.

Five Moons glanced over at her with approval. She lifted her nose to the sky, then took off down the alley.

Snow collected stories, but she did her best to stay out of them. They were hers to take in, to savor, to barter and trade in kind. Five Moons could have asked before sweeping her up in one. She ran soundlessly behind the Alpha in her crazed coat and hoped she didn't regret sticking around.

* * *

Cassidy let her mind wander, trusting her wolf to keep them headed toward home. Once they'd hit the river with its tree cover, scant though it was in places, she'd stepped aside and let her other half guide them. Her mind's eye kept returning to the sight of twigs wrapped with string moving about as if alive. Surely she was in some sort of nightmare, though nothing else about the situation was dreamlike: not the stab of pain in her front paws as they had absorbed a two-story drop, not the scents of the city that coiled around her in a languid vortex of sickly brown and grey. She sneaked a glance at the silver wolf who paced them. She kept up with Cassidy's wolf well enough; they'd only had to slow their pace a bit from their usual ground-devouring lope.

Striking white eyes caught and held hers as they ran, and Cassidy was almost forced to drop the gaze before the other wolf looked away first. Was she a lone wolf or did she belong to another Alpha? Cassidy had yet to deal with a loner. Since the mess with MacTavish taking out the old Alpha, lone wolves had been keeping well clear of her pack. She supposed it made sense and was just as glad. Loners freaked the hell out of Luther, and Cassidy liked her Beta better when he wasn't on edge. Naomi probably would have been better equipped to handle strange wolven.

And Dean. How did he figure in to all of this? She knew very little about her predecessor. What she'd heard about him was positive, and he was undoubtedly a far better example to emulate than MacTavish. She didn't really consider the deranged loner to have been a real Alpha. None of the other wolven seemed to, not even those who had been part of the odd group he'd held together through sheer force of will.

So what was Snow's story? And what had been going on at Mary's place? How could her sister have been walking around one second and become a bundle of twigs the next? For that matter, how had the sticks been moving under their own power? Surely that's what had been going on. Or was it?

The river's scents shifted slightly, and Cassidy's eyes sharpened. The wolf took the spur away from the river, following a thin strip of green overgrowth, then they were cresting a tumbled concrete barrier. Their claws caught and dug into the roughness of the rubble on the other side, and they emerged into the backyard of the hotel. Cassidy skidded to a stop on old concrete that had started to crumble on the edges. The hotel towered over them, a mass of pale brick and masonry that wouldn't have looked out of place in a 1920s' gangster movie.

Home. The wolf settled back on her haunches and allowed herself to be shouldered out of the way as Cassidy reached for her humanity and wrapped it around herself. The burdens and cares of being human washed over her, leaving the freedom the wolf offered behind, offering only skin and two legs in its wake. The cold winter air cut at her, made all the chillier for the fluid that clung to her nudity. She paced to the back door and threw it open, grabbing for a couple of coats and two Gatorades. They'd done enough shifting that some fluid replacement was called for. Her stomach grumbled, and she made a mental note to get something to eat sooner than later. Shrugging on a jacket, she walked over to where the silver wolf was quaking and waited as the wolven's silver fur slowly receded to reveal warm, brown skin.

From the amount of time her change took, this new wolven wasn't especially strong, not as the pack measured things. Cassidy wasn't always sure what constituted strength to them, only that she had it. As far as she'd been able to make out, it boiled down to the ease with which she could switch her forms, the fact that she didn't take any crap, and an edge over the others while in wolf form.

The not taking crap was new. It wasn't that she'd been a pushover when she was human, but she'd definitely been more laid-back. Maybe not where Mary was concerned, but if someone had told her that they never fought with their siblings, she would have known that person was a liar. Maybe it was that her packmates felt like a sort of family. There was a certain familiarity to them, one that had developed after not too long. She could almost feel them sometimes, like dappled points of light against her skin. This new wolven had some of that, but as if the light was coming from much further away.

She sighed. So much of what she was trying to figure out felt like she was pushing her way through a dark field where bramble-filled vegetation threatened to trip her. If she fell, the thorns would tear her apart before she hit the ground. But she had no way of knowing what she was doing and no one to admit that to. The closest was Naomi. Luther was her Beta. He should have been the one for her to lean on, or so she assumed, but he held a barrier between them. She'd found herself leaning on Ruri for advice to complement Luther's, but they'd been out of contact for a bit now. Naomi listened and didn't judge. There was none of the measuring from her that she felt from some of the other wolven in the pack, but even Naomi would have to be concerned when her Alpha admitted her weakness.

The woman coughed, then clambered from all fours to stand in front of Cassidy. Her dark Afro was plastered to her scalp, and she ran her hands through it almost negligently to return life to the curls.

"Here." Cassidy thrust the jacket out toward the woman.

Their eyes met and she nodded once with thanks but didn't say anything. Instead, she shrugged into the coat and gathered it around her, averting her gaze once again. Not that Cassidy would forget her eyes. The sight of the forthright hazel gaze set off by some of the thickest black lashes she'd ever seen was going to linger.

She passed over the second Gatorade then gestured over her shoulder. "Let's get inside. We can find you some clothes." *And someone to tell me what the hell I should do with the lone wolf who was dropped in my lap.*

CHAPTER FIVE

"Follow me," Five Moons said. Snow stared after her, then took a long swig from the bottle of Gatorade and complied. All of this traipsing around in the other wolven's wake was getting old. This wasn't her Alpha. She didn't have one, which suited her needs and way of life just fine.

"About Dean," Snow ventured after they'd made their way into the hotel. It was much as she remembered from her last visit with her brother. That had been a decade or so earlier, if her memory was correct. The years started to blur together after only a few decades, and it had been far more than that since she left Dean with the North Side Pack as it was known even then.

"We'll get there," the Alpha said. "I need to…" Her voice trailed off and the scent of uncertainty wafted from her. On its heels came spiky anger.

That's not a good sign. Snow slowed a bit to open more distance between them.

They passed through a long hall and into the open common area at the front of the building. A couple of wolven lounged on couches arranged in a square. Snow inhaled surreptitiously, trying to gauge how many wolven made this place their home. There weren't nearly enough scents.

"How many did you lose?" she breathed.

Five Moons shot her a sharp look. Shame pooled through the anger. "Too many," she said. "I did what I could." Resolve replaced the anger. She believed the assertion.

"So Ruri isn't around, I imagine." It seemed unlikely since there was a fae copy of her with the Hunter.

"No." Five Moons raised her voice. "Someone get Luther," she said to the two wolven. "Oh, and Naomi."

"Yeah, okay." A shaggy-haired wolven Snow had never met rolled to his feet.

Finally, a name Snow recognized. "Would you tell Luther that Snow is here for a visit?"

The wolven cut his gaze over to Five Moons, who nodded.

"We'll be in my rooms."

"Yes, Alpha." He loped off, leaving the other wolven to watch them closely, eyes narrowed. Snow had met him a number of times before, but Jonah was as wary of her as if they'd never crossed paths. Another bad sign.

Her rooms. The Alpha apparently didn't see her as a threat then. That was good. Snow bore her no ill will, as long as she truly had nothing to do with Dean's death.

"I'm in the penthouse," Five Moons said. "I trust that won't be an issue."

The Alpha wasn't asking. She led the way to a corner stairwell, then trotted up the steps two at a time. Snow paced her easily but made sure to maintain the distance between them. The hotel had an elevator, but no one ever took it. The last time she'd been here, it was being used as a mobile closet for cleaning supplies—Ruri's idea.

The penthouse, was it? Dean had preferred to keep his quarters on the ground floor, closest to the doors if someone dared to come through them with hostile intent. Snow tried to withhold judgment on Five Moons' decision to take the top of the building. There was probably a good reason. It wasn't Five Moons' fault Snow couldn't think of one.

When they reached the top of the stairwell, Five Moons shouldered open the heavy door into the short hall, then pushed through another door. It wasn't locked, which Snow took as the first point in Five Moons' favor. The Alpha trusted her pack, which meant they must trust her.

By the set of her shoulders, however, Five Moons didn't hold the same confidence in Snow. That was also good. A strange lone wolf showing up without warning just outside an Alpha's territory was about as unsettling as it could get. Snow had considered stopping by and announcing herself and her intentions. It was what their customs dictated, after all, and a good idea beyond that. If she was a known quantity, there was less chance that she'd be set upon by wolven who were only protecting their autonomy. However, if she'd done that she wouldn't have been able to get a read on the Alpha who had taken over her brother's pack. This was an Alpha whose origins no one knew. Also unknown was the relationship she had to the rogue loner who'd taken out Dean.

Rumors abounded, of course. Snow had plenty of experience teasing truth from fiction in the tales she gathered, but the stakes had never been this high.

Five Moons opened the door to her rooms, then waited for Snow to enter first. It was a power move, one that forced Snow not only to enter a strange space that could be filled with who knew how many wolven, but it also forced her to pass within close proximity of the Alpha.

Snow hesitated out of reach.

"Well, come on," Five Moons said. "I don't have all day. Believe it or not, there are more important things going on than who you are and what you're doing in my territory." She glared at Snow, her eyes gaining the brilliance in their depths that signaled the onset of the change. She grinned, displaying teeth that had already grown slightly sharper. "I won't bite."

"Promise?" Snow asked. She slipped past the Alpha before she could answer, giving her as much room as possible without obviously hugging the far edge of the frame.

The room beyond was simple, yet comfortable. Overstuffed furniture lined the living room. It was well-worn and frayed around the seams, but no more than one might expect from a group of wolven. The smells of multiple wolves filled the space, overlapping to the point where she was unable to pick out the scents even of wolven familiar to her. With a pang, she realized she was still trying to find Dean's scent. A whine climbed out of her throat before she could force it down.

"So what were you doing outside Mary's home?" Five Moons asked as she rooted through the ottoman in front of one of the couches. She pulled out a stack of clothes and eyed Snow critically, then dropped one article back in and pulled out another. She waved a hand at the other furniture.

Snow wasn't ready to settle just yet. She hadn't gotten a feel for the space. Her wolf demanded she pace the room, getting to know its corners and openings, but the Alpha wanted her seated. She sat and tried to cover her discomfort by taking a long pull from the bottle in her hand.

Five Moons waited for her to finish her drink before tossing her a pair of pants, a T-shirt, and sweatshirt.

"I told you already. I was looking for Ruri," Snow said quietly. "We've known each other for a long time." She pulled up the pants under her coat. The fit was pretty good, but they'd been worn soft and smelled faintly of Five Moons under a patina of detergent.

"And why did you want to see her?"

"I told you that too." Snow shucked the coat and pulled the shirt over her head, glaring at Five Moons through the cloth where she knew the Alpha couldn't see her.

"Humor me."

Snow's lips stretched into a grim approximation of a smile. "I wanted to find out about the wolven who took over the North Side Pack."

Five Moons inhaled. She was trying to gauge whether or not Snow was lying. It made sense, now that they were away from the odd mélange of smells in the Hunter's lair.

"What is this about the fae?" Five Moons asked. "How do you know about them?"

"I've heard stories from other packs." Snow shrugged. "It's the only thing that makes sense. How else do piles of sticks come alive and move around? How do they take on the appearance of others? Last time I checked, that doesn't happen on its own."

"The fae, though." The North Side Alpha shook her head. "That's so hard to believe."

"What's this about the fae?" A rough voice, gravelly with age and fatigue pulled their attention to the doorway. A squat white man, skin tanned by years of exposure to wind and sun leaned against the doorframe. His skin was unwrinkled, despite centuries of dealing with the elements, but his stance and the shadows in his steel-colored eyes betrayed his age. Long brown hair, only a few shades lighter than Snow's own, was pulled back into a low ponytail from which tendrils had escaped and curled in a rough halo around his face. Beyond his eyes, the only touch of time on Luther's face were the traces of white at the edges of the chin scruff that was too short to be called a beard, but too long for five o'clock shadow.

"Luther!" Snow stood to greet the wolven but stopped when Five Moons stared right at her.

"You know this wolven?" the Alpha said to Luther.

He nodded. "Snow has been coming around for a long time, though it's been a while." He cocked his head at her. "Ten years, give or take?"

She smiled. "Something around there."

"I'm not surprised to see you." He came the rest of the way into the room. A female wolven entered behind him. She was familiar, a more recent addition to Dean's—to the North Side Pack, name of Nancy or Nadine. Snow had only met her one other time, on her last visit with her brother.

"And why is that?" Five Moons asked.

"Dean was—" His face twisted with grief.

"Dean was my brother," Snow said before Luther could get the words out. It didn't feel right for someone else to announce it to the new Alpha. She should know where Snow stood. Now that she knew Luther was still around, she was reasonably certain this new Alpha wasn't the type to have usurped Dean.

"Ah." Five Moons nodded slowly. "If I'd known he had any siblings, I'd have kept a lookout for them." She glanced at Luther and the other wolven.

"I appreciate that."

"What was this about fae?" the female wolven asked. She perched on the edge of one of the couches, arms crossed in front of her chest. Her dark skin was a touch lighter than Snow's. Her black hair had something of the 1980s to it, with its asymmetrical Afro that accentuated high cheekbones and full, almost pouty dark lips. There was nothing soft about her eyes, however. The dark brown, nearly black orbs glittered as they held Snow's. There was a hint of recognition there, but her guard was as high as it could be.

"Thanks, Naomi," Five Moons said. "I'd like to know more about that as well."

"You don't see their workings much," Snow said. "Especially not this deep into such a big city. That was definitely their handiwork, though. They've taken Ruri and the Hunter and replaced them with impostors." She grinned, remembering how she and Five Moons had destroyed the changelings. Violence wasn't her first instinct, but the idea that someone could have tried to replace wolven with such cheap copies offended her deeply. "Those have been handled."

"So where are they?" Five Moons sat forward, her fingers laced together, the knuckles white. "Where are Ruri and Mary Alice?"

"Mary Alice?" Snow asked.

"The Hunter," Luther said, his voice resigned.

"Ah." She'd only heard Chicago's Hunter referred to as the Hunter or Malice. She risked a look over at Five Moons. "I don't know."

"I see." The air grew still around them as the Alpha's anger seemed to fill the room. Luther crossed the room away from her, toward the windows that looked out toward the river. Naomi looked at her Alpha. Her face and scent betrayed no fear, but her easy lounge against the arm of the couch stiffened.

"Sorry," Snow said. She cast her tone low. "I haven't dealt with the fae before, not firsthand. From what I've heard, they're more common in rural areas. It's weird to find traces this obvious in the middle of a city as big as Chicago. I don't know how the fae who cast the spell managed with so much iron and steel around them. The metals sicken or weaken them, which should make that kind of magic difficult to pull off. Or so I've gathered."

"Is it possible this 'spell' was cast somewhere else?" Five Moons asked.

"That makes more sense than it being worked here."

"Then I know where they are." Five Moons stood. "Luther, I'm heading to Wisconsin."

Luther turned away from the view. "Respectfully, Alpha, I think that's a bad idea. We still don't know what happened to Harold and Blair. We need you here to find our packmates."

A stench of equal parts rage and despair seethed from Five Moons. She balled her hands into fists in her lap. Small rivulets of blood trickled from her hands as claws bit into the soft skin of her palms. Beneath the turbulent top notes lurked the stale scent of indecision.

"I can't just—" She stopped herself and turned her head to stare at Snow. "Why don't you wait outside? I need to talk to my wolves." Her voice was soft, but each word hammered at Snow, demanding her acquiescence.

Snow was on her feet before she knew she had moved. "I'll be down in the lobby then?"

"That'll do." Five Moons turned her attention back to Luther. "Don't go far. I have more questions for you."

"All right." Snow backed away from the cozy arrangement of comfortable furniture. There was no way she was going to turn her back on a wolven as agitated as Five Moons. The Alpha seemed to be holding herself together, but the mix of emotions she was betraying were dangerous. She didn't envy Luther his position as the pack's Beta.

Tales be damned, she thought as she slipped out the door. Even with the door closed, she could still feel the Alpha's emotions beating at her. If this was what it was like to be swept up in a story with Five Moons, maybe she'd be better off leaving, no matter what the Alpha had instructed. Five Moons could try ordering her around, but she wasn't Snow's Alpha.

Snow didn't do Alphas. She sighed. Her head wanted her to leave, but the wolf disagreed. There was something else here, something deep, something important. They'd stick around a little longer, as long as she felt the situation hadn't completely disintegrated.

CHAPTER SIX

Cassidy waited a few moments to be sure Snow was gone. Though Snow wasn't one of her wolven, she still stood out, a muted star amongst the constellation of wolven that orbited Cassidy. As soon as she'd faded even further from Cassidy's internal starscape, she turned to Luther and Naomi.

"So she's the old Alpha's sister."

"She is," Luther said. "She used to come by every so often to check in with Dean. She was the only lone wolf he didn't insist on performing the ceremony on."

"Shit, the ceremony." Cassidy stared at the closed door to her suite. "I'll have to do that."

"Sooner than later." Luther nodded, relief that he wasn't going to have to talk her into it written across his face. "An excellent idea. Don't be surprised if much of the pack stays away, however."

"Bad memories," Naomi said. "But we should get something of Snow's to pass around. If our packmates decide not to come, they need to be able to recognize her scent. If you want her alive, that is."

Cassidy's eyes sharpened on Naomi. She wasn't her Beta, Luther held that role firmly, but there were times when Luther was far more conservative than perhaps the situation required. She'd gotten used to bouncing ideas off Naomi as well, especially when she'd had an argument with her Beta. Naomi's point of view was a useful counterpoint, and she'd become a regular fixture in Cassidy's very small inner circle. Her occasional bloodthirstiness still came as a surprise to Cassidy. Not that she disagreed, but it was still easy to forget that these people weren't exactly human. And that neither was she.

"There's no reason not to. Not yet, at any rate." She could be ruthless too, when the situation called for it. "Is there any way she could be related to Harold and Blair's disappearances?"

Luther cocked his head. "Nothing's impossible, but I'd be shocked. Snow keeps to herself. As far as I know, she keeps moving. Doesn't belong to any pack but spends time with a lot of different ones."

"Really?" Cassidy sat up. "That's unusual, right?"

Naomi waggled one hand back and forth. "It is and it isn't. Lots of loners live in proximity to other packs. They don't usually bounce around so much. We tend to be a little territorial."

"Tell me about it," Cassidy said. "So what's her deal, then?"

"She collects news and stories," Luther said. "Brings them around to the packs. She's one of the only ways we know what's happening in other places, to other wolven. Before her, that kind of information was brokered through the vampires. Their prices were high, but they've come down a lot over the past hundred years."

"That's how long she's been doing this?"

Luther nodded.

"Hmm." Maybe Snow could help her out. It was only a matter of time before her pack figured out that Cassidy had no idea what she was doing and turned on her. She'd heard about what happened to Alphas who went up against stronger challengers. She cared for the wolven who called her Alpha and would do everything she could for them, but she wasn't sure that she was their best option. She didn't want to find out by dying.

Can you trust her? The question was a good one. She was still very much an unknown quantity. Her wolf didn't mind her, which was a point in Cassidy's book.

"So, tell me what the deal is with the fae," she said.

Naomi shrugged. "I only have what I've heard."

"That's becoming quite the refrain," Cassidy said, her voice dry.

Luther looked uncomfortable. "Same here. Maybe a bit more than Naomi, but nothing concrete. Humans used to be more concerned about them, but that faded decades ago. Centuries ago in some places."

"So are they a real thing, then?" She wasn't sure if she wanted the answer to be yes or no. A yes was something, but how did you track a story?

"I believe so," Luther said. "I mean, we're stories to humans too, and we exist."

Cassidy leaned back in her chair and stared at the ceiling. If only Mary had left some better indication of where she was going. All she knew was it somewhere in Wisconsin, and that was only because Ruri had casually mentioned it. A whole state was a big place when you didn't know what you were looking for, but it made more sense as somewhere her sister and her sister's mate could have run afoul of these fae if what Snow said about them disliking urban areas was true.

"Dammit." She was truly stuck. There was no place to look, and it made no sense to send someone and waste their time while weakening the pack further. She wouldn't have minded wasting her own time, but there were things closer to home that needed her attention. Besides, she could still feel Ruri's star pulsing dimly among the rest of the wolven she'd collected to her.

"Alpha?" Luther asked.

"It's nothing," Cassidy said. "What's our progress on our missing packmates?"

Naomi slid from her perch to plop down heavily on the couch. "Not a damn thing to report." She sighed. "Blair seems to have gone missing near the edges of our territory, just like Harold. We talked to her coworkers and confirmed that she left work. Beth was able to track her scent to just inside our territory before the traces dried up."

"And nothing about what might have happened."

"No scent, no blood smears, no scuff marks. The whole area was clean."

"No scents?" Cassidy looked over at Naomi. "That could mean vamps, right?"

"It could. The Hunter doesn't leave much of a smell behind either."

"It wasn't Mary."

"We don't know that for sure," Luther said, his voice studiedly neutral.

Cassidy pinned him with a glare. "It wasn't. Not only has she been missing for weeks, but I saw Snow tear apart something that was supposed to look like her. She's gone." The last was delivered in as flat a tone as Cassidy could manage as the idea that something could have actually happened to her sister finally started to sink in.

"If she wanted to do this under the radar, a disappearance would make a great cover."

Cassidy was on her feet and in Luther's face before he could blink. She stood there, her presence beating at him while her wolf scratched to be allowed free to grab the scruff of this threat to their dominance.

A good shake would put him in his place. Cassidy allowed enough of the wolf through that she could feel her teeth lengthen. She parted her lips in a silent snarl.

Luther stared at her for a moment, before dropping his eyes and looking down and to the side, exposing the column of his neck. She and the wolf considered it before deciding that forcing him to back down in front of another was punishment enough.

"So we'll table that line of thought," Naomi said. "Vamps could be behind this, though I'm not sure what they'd get out of picking up two of ours."

"Don't vamps love to snack on wolven?" Cassidy asked. "Maybe they're getting tired of their usual fare. Maybe they think I'm too weak to push back."

"Could be." Naomi's face grew thoughtful. "But why now? Usually they have lone wolves who are willing to give up blood for free in exchange for some cash and a place to stay."

"Loners trade with vampires?"

"More regularly than we do," Luther said quietly. "Dean had some lines of communication open with them, but they haven't been reestablished."

"Maybe it's time to change that." Cassidy looked down as if she could see Snow through the floor. She had only the barest feel for the lone wolf, enough to know she was still within the hotel, but not much more than that. "Let's start small. Send the lone wolf to one pack, see if she can get them to meet with us. I don't care who it is, but let's at least see if the other wolven have noticed anything off within their borders." She sighed. "We'll do this according to your traditions. Bring her to the ballroom, and let the others know that we have a lone wolf to take care of. And that their attendance is optional."

* * *

Why am I still here? Snow's knee jiggled furiously as she looked around the hotel lobby. The two wolven who had been hanging out there had left as soon as she appeared. Even knowing the pack was coming out of a recent turbulent period, their skittishness still stung. Dean's pack was as close as she'd gotten to having a pack of her own since their mama's. They'd left after Mama was killed. Not that Snow wanted in on the pack life—on that she and her wolf were in perfect agreement—but it would be nice to have somewhere that felt like she belonged.

She leaned against the edge of the sofa, conscious of the smell of strange wolven wafting up to mix with hers. She wrinkled her nose. Wherever she belonged wouldn't be crowded. She thought about her van, the Volkswagen bus she'd been babying along since the sixties. She was going to have to pick that up before it got towed.

Waiting had never been her strong suit, and before long, Snow was pacing the length of the lobby and back. Was there any point in sticking around? The Alpha didn't trust her, not that Snow could blame her. She'd pretty flagrantly ignored centuries of tradition and protocol by refusing to present herself. On the other hand, if Luther was willing to stand at Five Moons' side, then she couldn't be too bad. As much as Snow wondered how much longer Luther would be around, he had a strong sense of justice. That was a big tick in the column for Five Moons not having been the one who murdered her brother. It was too bad those two wolven had scuttled off when she showed up in the lobby. Having a chat with some of the pack would have been helpful.

Her stomach growled, reminding her that she'd expended a lot of energy in the past few hours. Her bottle of Gatorade was empty, so she wasn't as parched as she might be, but there had been nothing for her to blunt the edge of her hunger. Maybe she could snag something to eat. Wolven could be exceedingly territorial about their food stores, so she'd have to be careful about it. Lucky for her, she was used to being surreptitious.

Snow glanced about to see if anyone was around. There was a flicker of movement up the grand staircase to the second floor. Someone was watching her, someone who wasn't keen on being spotted themselves. These wolven were skittish. And their numbers were far fewer than she remembered. If half of those who remained had been around the last time she'd been through, Snow would have been shocked. The lobby didn't smell deserted, but it was missing the vibrant mix of wolven scents it should have carried.

And the Alpha wasn't exactly stable herself. Not in a deranged psychopath kind of way, but she seemed strangely unsure for someone who'd risen as high as she had in the pack structure. That in itself was intriguing and hinted at strange undercurrents to the story unfolding here.

The story. If she was smart she would extricate herself from this one before she got too entangled. She pushed away from the couch and headed toward the front doors. Five Moons wasn't *her* Alpha. Did it really matter that she'd told Snow to stick around?

She hesitated.

"Snow?" Luther's gravelly voice filtered down the stairs, his descending footsteps following behind a second later.

She turned and put on a distant smile. "What is it?"

"Cassidy was wondering if you'd do her a favor." He stopped on the bottom step of the grand staircase. Whether it was conscious or not, the decision put his head above hers.

Feeling her lips twist into a wry smile at his dominance games, Snow cocked her head. "And what do I get out of it?"

"We'd owe you," he said. "The pack would."

"I need to know what the favor is before I'll agree to anything." Her mama hadn't raised a fool, after all.

"We need an emissary to the South Shore Pack. Cassidy wants to talk to their Alpha, but we never reopened lines of communication after Dean was taken down by MacTavish."

MacTavish, that was another confirmation of the rumors. Snow narrowed her eyes. "I'll go, but not for your Alpha's favor. I'll go if you fill me in on everything that happened from when Dean went down to where we are now."

He thought about it a moment, then nodded. "I can do that. Before that, though, there's the matter of the ceremony."

"Ah, yes. I'd wondered." She brushed lint off the front of her sweatshirt. "Best to get this over with, I guess."

CHAPTER SEVEN

The ballroom was nearly empty. Cassidy stood on the small stage, flanked on either side by Naomi and Luther in their wolf forms. She was still in skinform as she stared down at the woman in front of the stage. When she spared a glance at the small group of wolven who had turned out to witness the lone wolf ceremony, she could see the turbulent red of fear wafting from them in waves.

The wolven in attendance were all stronger, which made a certain amount of sense. The stronger wolven and those who were more dominant were more likely to range widely within their territory. They were the ones with jobs on the edges of the pack's claimed boundaries, the ones who helped keep an eye on those who came and went. They'd be most likely to run into a lone wolf. So it was strange to see them clustered together, somehow managing to have someone facing in each direction while also watching the stage. She knew exactly who had come to watch and who had decided to stay away. It was interesting. None of MacTavish's former wolven had come down; these were all Dean's packmates. Perhaps they were more comfortable since most of them would have known Snow.

The only one who didn't stink of fear was the lone wolf. Wisps of blue came off her, chased occasionally by a thread of orange. Mostly sadness, with a bit of anger thrown in. The emotions made perfect sense for the situation. If their situations were reversed, Cassidy probably would have been closer to the rage end of the spectrum.

Snow looked past her, not meeting her gaze. To the others, it likely seemed as though their eyes were locked together. It was a neat trick, and Cassidy filed it away for later. There was something about this wolven. She managed to sidestep the constant push and pull of dominance and submission that went on in the pack. Of their small band, only Cassidy's relative position never changed. Even Luther's and Naomi's dominance occasionally waxed and waned between them. Never enough for Luther to lose his Beta position or for Cassidy to consider bestowing it upon Naomi, but it was there. Snow didn't do any of that. She wasn't a pushover, that much was already clear. It was more that she simply refused to participate in the shifting relationships that made up the pack's structure below Cassidy. How did she do it?

"It's time," Cassidy said. She'd been thoroughly briefed on what was supposed to happen, but honestly, she was a bit lost. Parts of it made sense and others were so at odds with how a new person would have been introduced to a group in human society. Anxiety rose within her for a moment, but she pushed it down. She would do this, and it would be done right and properly. It was important to her pack, and she wouldn't fail them at something so simple. Her wolf rubbed against her in approval, managing to feel like she was standing at Cassidy's back. If something happened, if it all went awry as it had the last time, she would take over in a flash. There would be no repeat of the former Alpha's demise.

Snow's eyes snapped to hers for a moment, then she bowed her head and walked along the front of the stage to the stairs, never looking up, even as she made her way across the stage and knelt before Cassidy.

"Alpha," Snow said. "I beg leave to pass through your territory." Her voice was cool, almost disinterested. She bent her head to the side, exposing her neck.

Cassidy stepped forward, into the lone wolf's personal space. With her own wolven, that space was welcoming, pulling her in and warming her to her toes. Snow's did not. For a moment, Cassidy wondered if Snow wasn't a given name, but a nickname bestowed because of her cool personal presence. It intrigued her, and she wondered if she could warm the space that Snow held.

"Don't." The lone wolf's voice was pitched so low only her ears would pick it up. Her eyes locked to Cassidy's with such fierceness that her wolf bristled.

With a start, Cassidy realized she'd been trying to do...something. She wasn't sure quite what it was, but she felt her own sense of self pushing out toward Snow. She snatched it back, and Snow relaxed perceptibly. When she looked away, Cassidy's wolf conceded as well.

Cassidy leaned in toward Snow, making sure she wasn't bleeding any of herself out into the lone wolf's space. She placed her nose to the warm skin of Snow's neck. The motion should have been intimate, but it wasn't. She breathed deep, getting to know Snow's scent. It was as cool as that sense of her personal space was, but not cold. There was a sense of distance to it, but also the knowledge that she was not passionless—more, perhaps, that she chose when and who to bestow that intimacy to.

"I know you," Cassidy said and stepped back.

Luther and Naomi paced forward, flanking her to either side. As one, their massive wolf heads leaned in. As they approached, Snow turned her arms outward, the veins in the paler skin of her wrists visible and exposed. The wolven pressed cold noses to either arm and sniffed audibly. After a moment and a few deep inhalations, they too stepped back.

"They know you." Cassidy reached a hand forward. "If you have a token that may be distributed among those of the pack that they may also know you, you will surrender it now." That form was ancient or so she'd been told. Snow's eyes sharpened at the requirement.

She lifted her arms, gesturing to say, "This is all I have." It was borrowed, but her scent would already have permeated deep into the fabric. Cassidy stared at the lone wolf, her face impassive. After a moment, Snow shrugged out of her sweatshirt, leaving her clad in a T-shirt that hadn't been hers at the beginning of the day. "Will this do?"

Cassidy took the sweatshirt and brought it to her face and inhaled. Snow's scent exploded around her. She closed her eyes to take it in, trying to separate the whorls of grey and blue with slivers of silver that glimmered through in spangling streaks from the rest of the room's scents. It was as if she was taking in the translation of Snow's wolf form into smell.

"This will be fine." She lowered her hand. "We will pass it to our pack, that they will know you when you meet them."

"Thank you, Alpha," Snow murmured, her eyes lowered again.

Cassidy licked her lips and looked out at the huddle of wolven who eyed the stage and the corners of the room warily.

"I guess that's pretty much all of it," she said. Those words weren't part of the forms Luther and Naomi had drilled into her, but since she had everyone together, they might as well get a few other orders of business taken care of. "You can go," Cassidy said to Snow. "Or stick around, if you want."

Snow nodded and hurried down the stage steps, but stopped not far from the bottom. She glanced at the pack members clustered near the opposite wall, then chose to loiter near the stage, carefully not watching them. Cassidy would have bet real money that if Snow had been in furform, her ears would have stayed swiveled toward the group of wolven even as her eyes looked away.

She cleared her throat. "So, you know we've had a couple of pack members go missing the past few weeks, Blair most recently."

That got their attention. Cassidy's skin prickled from the intensity of their eyes upon her. It was a little intimidating to suddenly be the focus of that group.

"I don't have any good news on that front." She sighed. "We're looking for them, but so far there's very little to show for it."

One of the wolven lifted his head and looked her in the eyes. "Is it possible they left on their own?" Oliver asked. Hope lightened his voice.

She shook her head. "I don't think that's the case. Neither of them came to me, and they left their belongings behind." She paused. "I can still feel them, but I don't know where they are. I don't know why they're gone."

The group shifted, almost as one.

"Anyway, it's time to implement the buddy system." Cassidy dropped her voice by half an octave. She needed to project authority right now. She shifted her feet farther apart and raised her chin. The widened stance helped her project the confidence she knew these wolven needed to hear from their Alpha. "No one from the pack goes anywhere outside the den alone. If you're heading to work, you go with a group and a group meets you on the way home. I don't want to lose anyone just because they let their guard down. I'm counting on all of you in attendance to let those who aren't here know and to volunteer to accompany our meeker packmates. Is that clear?"

"Yes, Alpha," the group chorused. A couple of the wolven had looked ready to protest when she'd instructed them to buddy up, but they'd subsided when she'd appealed to their protective natures. If only she'd known that particular tactic back when she'd still been in school. Some group projects would have gone a lot more smoothly.

School. Cassidy turned her head so she wasn't looking out at the people who were depending on her. She missed being in university so much. She'd had no one to handle there except herself. Not that she was trying to shirk this particular responsibility, but it wasn't one she'd chosen. No one else had been able to step up, so it had dropped in her lap instead. At least Naomi and Luther were giving her a hand with things. There was still so much she didn't know.

"That's it, then," she said. "Let everyone know. Let's not lose anyone else. I need volunteers to keep looking for Blair and Harold. In pairs of course. Spread that around too. Anyone who's interested can come by my rooms or let Luther know." She hesitated, but the gathered wolves kept watching her. "You can all go now."

The wolven dispersed, at least enough to trickle through the open doors.

"You can go too." Luther and Naomi looked up at her, then back at each other.

Luther nodded his shaggy head once, then leaped off the stage to land impossibly lightly on the floor below. Naomi sat, watching her closely. When Cassidy moved to walk down the stairs, Naomi came with her.

"Some of your wolven went missing?" Snow asked. She pushed away from the wall and crossed the floor to Cassidy's side.

"That's what I said a moment ago."

"At the same time?" Snow showed no sign of being put off by Cassidy's brusque response.

"No. One went a couple weeks ago. The other disappeared yesterday." She was starting to give up on Harold, but there was still time to find Blair, or so she hoped. Cassidy should have been out looking for her, not stuck inside doing ceremonial bullshit.

"Huh."

"Why do you ask?"

"You're not the only pack I've heard of who's had members vanish." Snow's brow furrowed. "No one wants to talk about it, not really. What I've heard has been mostly whispers and rationalization. Like maybe they'd cut out and hadn't told anyone. It's been going on out west for at least a year, maybe two, but mostly in smaller cities and towns."

"That isn't good."

"No, it isn't." Snow was watching her expectantly, like Cassidy had some secret knowledge to impart, but she didn't. She was as confused and frustrated as anyone else.

"You shouldn't go anywhere alone either," Cassidy said.

Snow's eyebrows climbed halfway up her forehead. "I'll keep it in mind." The chill of Snow's scent intensified until Cassidy wondered if flakes might come sifting down from the ceiling.

"It's dangerous out there right now, and I don't know why." Cassidy clenched her fists. "If I can't stop it from happening to my people, then I sure as hell can't stop it from happening to you."

The declaration thawed something inside the prickly wolven, and she quirked a half-smile Cassidy's way. "I don't recall asking for your help. I know the deal. I've been a lone wolf for longer than you've been alive, I wager."

Cassidy stiffened her spine indignantly at the implication that she didn't know what she was doing. "Fine. Go out and get yourself disappeared or killed. You better not take any of mine down with you." The words were out of her mouth before she could fully contemplate them.

Snow's brows snapped down into an impressive scowl. "I'm not the one asking for favors, Alpha." In her mouth, the title sounded like an epithet. "Look to yourself before you accuse others of failing your own wolven. You're their protector, aren't you?"

"I ought to—" Cassidy clamped her teeth down on the words that threatened to spill out. This wasn't what she wanted. Snow was a potential ally, and she had precious few of those right now. Cassidy had become so reactive since she was changed. She had two modes, it seemed: laid-back and on the attack. She couldn't relax enough to get to laid-back, not right now, but the lone wolf didn't really deserve her aggression, not when she was doing so little to provoke Cassidy.

"That's what I thought." Even though Snow looked away, she still managed to watch Cassidy from the corner of her eye. "I have an errand to run. Alpha." She inclined her head, then was gone.

It was a while before the air around Cassidy thawed.

CHAPTER EIGHT

Snow's eyes still burned, though the tears had stopped twenty minutes before. The open window wasn't helping, but she hated having them closed all the way, even when she was on the freeway. Concrete hummed under the tires of her little van. It was well after rush hour, so she could actually open it up.

Luther had filled her in on the events of the previous October while giving her a ride to where she'd parked her car. His dispassionate tone had done little to camouflage the pain she'd smelled on him as he recounted the tale of the rogue Alpha who had somehow insinuated his wolves into their pack, then used them to overthrow the North Side Pack's rightful Alpha. He'd talked at length about how Dean had been covertly dosed with wolfsbane and left defenseless before the lone wolf ceremony with MacTavish. How Ruri had stood by as the loner had killed Dean. How she'd run, leaving MacTavish's wolves, wolves they'd brought into their pack thinking they'd been abandoned, to wreak havoc on those who couldn't protect themselves. As Dean's Beta, her responsibility had been to those he'd protected, especially when he was no longer able to do so. The stink of his fury at Ruri's abandonment on the heels of Dean's death had been strong enough to taste.

It explained why she'd seen the Ruri-changeling at the Hunter's den, though it didn't shed any light on where Ruri and the Hunter were now. It also didn't explain why Five Moons seemed closer to this supposed betrayer than she was to her own sister. Something wasn't quite right there.

A wolven taking a Hunter as a mate. Now she'd heard everything. It was funny how the whole Romeo and Juliet storyline seemed so romantic, up until it was being played out in your own community with someone who hunted down you and your kind. Still, it sounded like the Hunter had done what she could to mitigate MacTavish's sins. She was hazy on exactly why Malice had gotten involved. Five Moons must have figured into the equation somehow. Luther had been cagey on the details there and had refused to be pinned down on it, despite her subtle probing.

Fresh tears threatened to well up as she considered how Dean had met his end. He'd been defenseless, unable to change, while those he'd trusted had ripped apart those loyal to him. Could there be a worse way for an Alpha to go? At least in an Alpha challenge, everything was up front. The possibility of death was in the open and acknowledged by all. That's what an Alpha signed up for. To guide the pack, to protect it, and to put themselves in harm's way for the good of the pack members. That was what Dean had believed. MacTavish had apparently disagreed.

She'd heard about MacTavish. Stories of a strong wolven who could force others into a one-sided bond with him had been making their way around the wolven communities of the Pacific Northwest for years. Everyone knew of a pack that had lost wolven to him, but there was no hard proof, not until he'd showed up and decided that her little brother's pack was ripe for the taking.

The van's metal steering wheel creaked under her grip. Snow loosened her grip before she bent it out of shape. Why had MacTavish picked North Side?

She'd discovered what she'd come looking for. It should have been time to go. She'd gotten a full meal, and the energy lost to two back-to-back changes had been replenished. She was in a good place to move on, but that didn't feel right. Maybe it was some lingering attachment to Dean's pack, even without him helming it. She still didn't know if they were in good hands. Five Moons had taken back the pack, Snow owed Cassidy her thanks for that, but was the new Alpha a good fit for the wolven who sheltered in her shadow?

She kept driving toward the South Shore Pack's territory. She'd given her word to Luther. He'd delivered, and now she would as well. Besides, there were secrets yet to discover.

As she continued down the freeway, she considered how best to announce herself. Coming into a pack's claimed land was always tricky. She'd spent a bit of time with the South Shore Pack, but her trips to Chicago always took her to visit Dean. While she'd dropped in on the other Chicago-area packs on occasion, she hadn't spent long getting to know those wolven. For the most part. There were some exceptions, some indiscretions she preferred not to think too hard on.

South Shore was a rougher neighborhood, though it had been getting quieter over the past couple of decades. Some of that might have been due to the pack's influence. Hammer, their Alpha, was a massive wolven who preferred order to chaos. Snow had seen firsthand how a pack could make changes that were felt even in human circles that had no idea of the beings living in their midst. Her mama's pack had influenced the human community around them, but not for the better, and it had ended with Snow and Dean losing her as the neighborhood descended into bootlegging and rum-running.

Beyond that, South Shore's pack was on the smaller side. They seemed rougher among themselves than Dean had permitted among his wolven, but those were the main differences.

A physical challenge was to be avoided, so Snow's best bet was to find an area that smelled of frequent wolven activity and arrange to be discovered. Confronting them at their den could be misconstrued as an attack, and Snow preferred never to engage in combat.

The side streets were quiet, the streetlights shining pools of radiance down below leafless trees. Her breath steamed in the car as she crept down the street with both windows open as far as they would go. So far, she'd encountered no trace of wolven. She swept her head from side to side, probing the crisp air for even the faintest whiff.

Brick houses and low apartment buildings inched past her. Most of the windows were dark, but occasionally warm light spilled from inside onto the tired snow heaped up over dead grass and spindly shrubs. Winter was nearing its end, and even the snow seemed ready for spring to come.

The pack had held a den toward the heart of the neighborhood, near 73rd and Jeffrey. There was no reason to assume they were still there. Many packs were nomadic and would move from den to den within their territory. It helped keep the neighborhood humans from getting too twitchy. These days they weren't met by mobs bearing torches and pitchforks. Instead, as one group of humans moved out, they would be replaced by those who did not make for good neighbors. It was best to keep moving, or accept that the area around the den would become rundown and filled with desperate and unpredictable types. The South Shore Pack followed such tactics, but if they still maintained ties to their former base of operations, she might be able to track them to where they were now.

Sure enough, as she neared Jeffrey Boulevard on 73rd, she tasted her first trace of wolven. It was barely perceptible, but it was there. For a moment, she considered getting out of the car to track it but decided against it. The van would offer her some protection against getting jumped. If she lost the trail, she could circle back around and pick it up again. For now, she was better off being cautious. She'd approached dozens of packs over the years and had only had to defend herself against physical aggression a handful of times.

She stuck her head out the window and took a deep breath, trying to get a feel for the direction in which the scent was stronger. It seemed like the trail got denser toward the lake. She grinned a bit. Only back in Chicago a few days, and she was already using Lake Michigan as a landmark.

It was a good thing it was as late as it was. If someone caught her with her head hanging out the window, driving at a snail's pace down the street, they would think she was casing the neighborhood for sure. So far, most of the vehicles she'd passed had been parked. The occasional exception with occupants paid her no attention.

The scent picked up in strength a few blocks past Jeffrey, and more notes of wolven began to appear. There was definitely more activity this way. Still more wolven traces joined up with the stream and headed down Clyde Avenue. The buildings got smaller, with fewer duplexes and apartments and more single-family bungalows. They were still mostly brick, however, a sight that was a little strange after the last few years spent in Albuquerque with its stucco and siding.

She crept along, the mingled scents of wolven becoming more intense and more varied until they converged on a house of cream-colored brick that stood out from the other red brick homes on the block. The building had been added onto multiple times. It seemed that someone had done their best to turn what had probably been a fairly typical bungalow into a multi-family home. Yes, that was something that would suit the needs of a pack of wolven just fine. The street was parked up, with cars lining both sides. Banks of snow narrowed the road until her van barely fit through in places. Halfway down the block, Snow found an open spot.

Without too much trouble, even given the icy edges of the road, she parked the van. She rolled both windows up until they were barely cracked, then settled in to be discovered.

* * *

"So what do you think of Snow?" Cassidy asked. She fiddled with the edge of her seat belt.

"Don't know much about her, really," Naomi said. She peered through the windshield at the stoplight. "Our packmates seem to know her pretty well, the ones that have been around a while, anyway. Hell of a coincidence."

"Coincidence?" Cassidy was pretty sure she knew what Naomi was hinting at but wanted to hear her say it out loud.

"That she shows up right after another member of our pack goes missing. Weird stuff happened before MacTavish made his last way through town too." The light changed and Naomi eased them forward.

"Different weird stuff, right?" Cassidy stared out the passenger side window. She didn't remember anyone mentioning unexplained disappearances in connection with the rogue Alpha's takeover of the pack. "I'm parked down that street."

Naomi turned the wheel. "Yeah, you could say that. We had a rash of wolven who'd been turned against their will. It's happened a few times before, so we didn't think a whole lot about it, but looking back…Well, a lot of those wolven went for MacTavish." She looked thoughtful. "Not all of them."

"This seems like a pretty different situation. And Snow is known to the pack."

"So was MacTavish."

"Message received. I'll be careful around her."

"Don't worry." Naomi's face twisted into a humorless grin, her teeth a quick white flash against dark skin that disappeared as quickly as it came on. "You won't be alone on that one." She brought the car to a stop next to Cassidy's beater. "You need anything else?"

Cassidy shook her head, then slipped out the door. "Thanks for the lift. I'll see you back at the hotel. At the den." Maybe one day she'd start using wolven terms without having to think about them.

Naomi pursed her lips. "Alone? What about the buddy system?"

"You're here now."

"And I won't be once I drop you off. Seems to me I should be sticking around."

"I'm picking up the car and heading back. Are you suggesting we leave your car here and both drive back in mine?" It wasn't the point, and Cassidy knew it. Her wolf was starting to bristle at being challenged, even if Naomi was simply trying to keep to the rules Cassidy herself had set.

"Of course not." From the sideways glance the other wolven shot her, she wasn't buying Cassidy's attempt at derailing.

So be it. Cassidy sat up straight and allowed her presence to fill the car's interior. She glared at Naomi, daring her to push the matter further.

"Alpha..." Naomi licked her lips. She took a deep breath and stared out the windshield, carefully not looking Cassidy in the eye.

"It's a quick errand," Cassidy said quietly. "I get my car and get out. Unless you really think whoever is testing us will do so right outside Malice's home."

"Probably not."

"They'd be insane to try it." Cassidy allowed her restless wolf to surface a bit. "They'd be insane to try me."

"Yes, Alpha." Naomi's shoulders relaxed a bit. She wasn't completely convinced, but she'd been diverted from a full-on challenge.

"Good." Cassidy reached over and gripped the other wolven's shoulder. She was pleased that Naomi cared about enforcing her rule, if not that she was trying it with her Alpha. It was a difficult concept to convey through touch, but more tension bled from Naomi's frame.

"I'll see you soon," Naomi said when she dropped Cassidy next to her car.

"Yes you will." Cassidy waved.

Naomi nodded and kept on down the narrow side street without any further comment.

By luck or the regard of some obscure god, she'd managed to avoid picking up any parking tickets. Ostensibly, she was only here to get her car and head back to the hotel, but not without swinging by Mary's place first. Luther would have crapped a brick if she'd told him her plan. Naomi, while less uptight than Luther, would have also been unhappy. At least Naomi seemed to understand that Mary was her sister, even if she was the big bad Hunter of Chicago. Maybe one day Luther could come to some understanding of Cassidy's inability to completely sever ties with her.

He seemed to think that because she had the pack now, her ties to her biological family shouldn't matter, but Cassidy couldn't bring herself to pull away completely. Holding Mary at arm's length the past few months had come naturally. Sure, she had a really good reason to be pissed at her sister. Mary was the one who'd decided to deal with Cassidy being turned into a werewolf against her will by locking her in a metal box for far too long. She'd also been busy.

Between that and Cassidy picking up a wolf pack to take care of despite only having become wolven herself last October, a little cooling-off period between them was more than a good idea. It was necessary. That didn't mean she intended to go no-contact forever, but she needed to know she could do this on her own. It felt wrong to be reaching out to her sister for help while also trying to prove to the wolven of her pack that she could keep them safe.

How's that working out for you? The voice in the back of her head sounded especially snide today. Try though she might, she simply wasn't feeling comfortable. It felt like she was wearing a sweater that was three sizes too large, and every time she tried to roll up the sleeves and get to work, they came undone, flopping all over the task she was trying to accomplish and making it that much more difficult. She had no doubt that a more experienced leader would have figured out what was going on after the first packmate had gone missing. And now a second one was in the wind. Either they were taking off with no word and none of their belongings because of what a hash she was making of their pack or something much darker was unfolding. And to think the better of the two options was that she sucked at being Alpha.

Cassidy sighed and jammed her hands deeper into her pockets. The evening was chilly. It didn't bother her as much as it used to, but why put herself through the discomfort if it wasn't necessary. The wolf rubbed against the underside of the skin on her arms, reminding her that she had access to a thick pelt.

The area was deserted. Even during the day it was pretty quiet, but right now, she might as well have been the only one left alive on Earth. A few months ago, she would have worried about being out by herself so late. A mirthless grin stretched her face. She almost wished someone would try to jump her. It would be nice to take her bad mood out on some deserving asshole.

Sadly, no one was foolish enough to approach her. She made her way to Mary's place in a somewhat circuitous route from the last time she'd been there. She might not have been some Special Ops supersoldier, but she knew a little bit about keeping herself safe.

That's odd, she thought as she turned the corner. There was a large real estate sign tacked to the front of the building. "For Lease" it proclaimed in large red letters.

Cassidy quickened her steps. When the front door was locked even though she hadn't locked it behind her on the way in the previous night, she wasn't surprised. For a moment, she considered yanking the doorknob out of the door. It probably still wouldn't have opened, but she'd have felt better.

Her wolf paced inside her as she considered her options. A quick climb up the side of the building would get her through one of the windows on the third floor. Broken windows weren't noticed so quickly when they were higher up. She glanced around. The street was still empty. She decided to head around to the back anyway.

The alley looked much the same as it had when she and Snow had run down it. Was it only the previous day? Cassidy shook her head.

She quickly pulled off her shoes and socks and stashed them on the sill of a window that had been bricked over years before. She shook her hands to loosen them up. Wiggling her toes against the ice-cold concrete beneath her feet, she concentrated on letting the wolf to the surface of her skin, but only in the places she wished.

Her hands and feet spiked with pain, then itched abominably as fur broke the surface. Liquid rolled off her skin slowly, not the sudden gush it produced when she went for a full change. When her nails popped off, pushed by claws that split her skin, she winced. Her jaw ached, and she clenched her teeth, fighting against the emergence of the wolf there. *We only need hands and feet*, she thought fiercely at her wolf.

The wolf laughed. *Claws* and *teeth*, she responded with a fierceness that Cassidy felt in her gut. *What use is one without the other?*

What use indeed? Mary's home was now unknown territory. Maybe more weaponry wasn't such a bad idea.

Cassidy let her mouth fall open, to make room for her rapidly lengthening teeth. When she felt the muscles in her jaw shift, she stiffened and pushed back. *Teeth only*, she thought. *If someone sees us…*

Her jaw continued to cramp for a moment while the wolf considered Cassidy's point, then the ache receded.

Cassidy released her breath in an explosion of vapor that wreathed her head for a moment before dissipating ahead of the chill breeze from the lake. The wolf had stopped trying to push herself all the way to the fore. Her feet were no longer cold. Strangely elongated paws that retained some of the shape of her human feet insulated her nicely. Her hands were covered in fur, the effect of paws mostly missing, except for thick pads on her palms and the tips of her fingers. The thick claws on her wolfish hands and feet were exactly what she needed to gain purchase on the side of the building.

She backed up a few yards, then took off at a run, launching herself as high as she could. With that single bound, she managed to clear most of the first story. Her claws punched holes in the concrete that sheathed the back of the building. She paused, bouncing against the wall, testing the purchase of her clawed hands and feet. They held well.

Cassidy grinned. This was a new one for her, but she liked the feel of it. She pushed off with one foot as she released one hand, then jammed her claws in place against the wall. They slid in relatively easily, a small cascade of sand sifting out from around the sharp appendages. This was going to be a snap. It took her a few tries to get the rhythm of it, but when she did, she scaled the remaining story and a half of Mary's home with ease. By the time she reached the ledge of the windows that marched along the third floor, she hadn't even broken a sweat.

Hooked into place at the windows' ledge, Cassidy pushed lightly at the frosted glass. The window didn't budge. She scooted down the row a bit and tried again. Still no movement. She tried again and again, but each window was locked up tight.

By the fifth window, Cassidy and her wolf had lost patience. She made a fist, then looked away as she punched through the glass before her. The window shattered inward, broken shards tinkling to the concrete floor inside Mary's living quarters. She froze, listening for sounds of movement inside.

Cassidy's ears itched as the wolf tried to force herself to the surface.

"Not now," Cassidy said out loud. She shook her head once. "Let me listen." The tightness to her skin receded.

She waited one heartbeat, then another, and still another, but there were no sounds from within.

Cassidy pulled herself over the windowsill and into Mary's living quarters. She sidestepped to avoid the broken glass on the ground. The pads on her feet were tough right now, but something that sharp could still go right through them.

She looked up, allowing her eyes a moment to adjust to the relative darkness of the large room. She needn't have bothered. It was empty, echoingly so. Not a single item remained.

CHAPTER NINE

Each step Cassidy took reverberated painfully back to her. She gentled her stride as she worked her way through the floor that had been her sister's living area. Whoever had emptied it had gone further than simply taking out Mary's furniture and things. She wrinkled her nose at the smell of harsh chemicals. The concrete floors had been sanded and sealed, almost obliterating any sign that someone had been living there. Cassidy took some grim pleasure that whoever had done this hadn't been able to totally erase the scratches where the metal box had been. It had been her home for days.

For a moment, she felt those metal walls around her again. Try as she might, she hadn't been able to get out, not even after throwing herself at the door over and over again until she lay in a bruised heap at the bottom. Her wolf had come to her, had tried to show her the way, but Cassidy had been so terrified by what was going on that it had taken her a long time to listen. There had been more than one wolf whispering at her. Each had counseled different actions, some too gruesome to consider, and she couldn't get them to stop.

Cassidy became aware that she was crouching, her hands over her ears. How much time had she spent like that over the days her sister had held her captive? Without Ruri to guide her through the change, she would have lost herself, of that she was certain. Not much else made sense these days, but she knew she owed her sanity, and probably her life, to Ruri. Mary hadn't been any help at all. All she'd done was try to move the problem out of sight. And now she'd taken Ruri out of the picture.

That Cassidy couldn't reach out to either of them now when things were spinning off the rails made her all the more conscious of how poorly she was doing as Alpha. The wolf swirled within her, wrapping herself around Cassidy's core and lending her support. Ruri might not be there, but the wolf was.

Cassidy shook her head. She'd hated that box, but it wasn't right that all evidence of the worst time in her life could be so easily obliterated. She squatted and ran her fingertips over the shallow grooves.

There was no question about who had done this. The government wasn't going to leave anything that might expose them to questions about the occupation of the person who'd lived here—or, more importantly—who had bankrolled her.

Cassidy sat back on her heels. Her eyes prickled with tears that she refused to let fall. She missed Mary. Missed her sister. No matter what had happened between them, they were still family. Blood. The wolf settled herself around Cassidy's core, offering her warmth and support. The comfort opened something inside Cassidy, and suddenly she was sobbing into her palms.

So much had been taken from her already, and losing Mary was more than she could bear.

But Mary wasn't gone. She sniffled loudly, trying not to hear the sound bounce back to her ears again. Mary wasn't gone. She was merely not there. Two weeks wasn't that long to be out of contact with somebody. She'd been worse than that around the end of the semester.

Except that Mary had always had time for her calls. The number of times Mary had missed a call and hadn't reached out as soon as possible was one Cassidy could count on one hand. Dread spun up again inside her, threatening to take hold, but her wolf stood in the way. She had confidence in the Hunter. The Hunter was Cassidy's kin, after all, and the wolf held complete and unshakable faith in her.

It helped. Not completely, but a bit. Cassidy wouldn't believe Mary was gone for good until she saw her sister's body. Two weeks was too early to be this worked up.

She pushed herself up and continued prowling the length and breadth of the third floor. There was nothing. Finding information on where Mary had been headed in her capacity as Hunter had always been a long shot. Now, it was an impossibility. Her sister's employer had been thorough, meticulously so. Obsessively so. It wasn't fair. She had hoped against hope that even if Mary wasn't there to help her, something in her belongings might shed some light on where she'd gone. The government was ripping that from her too.

The second floor was as empty.

Where did her art go? Cassidy surveyed the space that had been crammed with materials, tools, and half-finished sculptures. They'd left the partitions between the different areas; those looked original to the building or as near as that it made no difference. Mary hadn't put them up, which was apparently all that mattered. A quick walkthrough proved the space was as deserted as the one above.

She swallowed hard and made her way down to ground level. Sure enough, the garage area was also barren. The chain-link cages were gone, Mary's tools and equipment with them.

Cassidy stood in the middle of the space and turned slowly to take it in. Nothing, nothing, and more nothing. How was it so easy to wipe out somebody's existence?

Her head snapped up. What had Mary's employers told Mom? Would they tell her anything? If the government didn't tell Mom, should she?

She laughed, the sound echoing harshly in the empty room. "What are you going to tell her? 'Hey, Mom. Mary's place was completely cleared out, she might be dead, but don't worry, she's probably not. How do I know? Well, that's a fun one!'" The words sounded so much worse out loud than they had in her head. No, better to leave that one alone until she had to confront it head-on. There were other problems to handle.

Like what she would do when their mom called again wondering why she hadn't heard from Mary lately.

Her wolf nudged her, the implication clear. It was time to drop the issue. She couldn't do anything about it now; the time for worrying would come later.

Cassidy headed for the door. She threw it open and took a moment to inhale the wonderful mystery stench of the city. It never truly went dark, was never really empty, and tonight was no exception. What she needed was a run. Her wolf twisted and snarled within her, demanding to be released and set upon their foes, not that Cassidy had any idea who those might be.

Neither of them were going to get what they wanted. A run sounded good, but it was better that they track Blair's last moves instead, before her scent disappeared completely. She would look into it on the way back home. No need to pull anyone else in on the search. She wanted to do this one alone, where no one could see her when she failed to uncover anything helpful.

She stabbed awkwardly at the screen of her phone, trying to avoid scratching the glass with her nails while disabling the lock and pulling up her phone app. She pressed down on Mary's name and waited for it to go right to voice mail.

"Hey, Mary. Just to let you know, your place is emptied out. Looks like your bosses have written you off. Mom doesn't know you're missing, but I'm sure you'll show up real soon to let her know you're okay. Right?" The anger was rising in her again, and her wolf's agitation with it. She took a deep breath. "Look, Mary. Just let me know you're not dead in a ditch somewhere, okay? I miss you. Plus, I could really use your help. Just call. Please."

* * *

The loud tap on her window was designed to startle Snow out of her slumber. She opened her eyes slowly, despite the racing of her heart. Someone was at the driver's side window. From the smell, they were wolven in human form. Wolven didn't usually wear hoodies in furform.

She turned slowly toward them, her eyes fixed on their sweatshirt collar. "How long've you been watching me?"

The wolven shrugged. "Long enough. What's your business, loner?" Their gender was impossible to place by their voice, not that Snow particularly cared. Male wolven tended to be larger than the females, but each was as deadly as the next.

"I'm here to see Hammer."

"Why should the Alpha see you? Planning on sticking around for a while?"

"Yes, but not here." Snow lifted her eyes for a moment. "I'm here on the behalf of Five Moons and the North Side Pack."

"Oh, are you now?" A spike of anger flared through the figure's scent. "Then I guarantee he'll want to see you." The wolven pulled on the door handle, which didn't move.

"I'm coming out," Snow said. "You don't need to mess with my car. I'm the messenger, that's all."

"Sure, sure." The figure stepped back.

Snow waited a second, then pushed the door open and stepped out onto the street. The sky was beginning to lighten in the east. It couldn't be called a sunrise, not with clouds forming a low blanket over the city, but it was something. The neighborhood was stirring to life around them, with humans scraping the night's layer of frost from their windshields and cars pulling away from curbs. They drew a couple of sideways glances, but nothing more than that.

The wolven stayed out of arm's reach, which was a relief. If they were worried about being attacked by her, then she had some space to breathe and hopefully enough room to turn if it came to that.

"House is that way." They pointed behind her.

"I know." Snow stalked down the street looking for a break in the snowbank, content to have the surly wolven following along in her wake. Just because she chose not to partake in her kind's power games didn't mean she didn't know how they were played. The situation was tenser than she'd assumed. Keeping these wolven off-balance would be key to keeping her hide whole.

Once on the sidewalk, she made a beeline toward the house. More wolven loitered on the wooden stoop. It might have looked casual, except not many humans hung out in below-freezing temperatures when the sky was barely turning toward dawn. The group watched her closely. She spied more than one set of bright eyes as she walked up to the stairs.

"She's here to see Hammer," her escort said.

"Good luck," a light-skinned female wolven said. "He doesn't like surprise visitors."

"He'll see me," Snow said. "North Side wants to talk."

One of the watchers whistled long and low. "That'll get his attention."

They moved to let her pass. She lifted her head, though she wanted to drop it under the weight of their stares. A few of the faces were familiar, though they watched her with the same intensity as the strangers. South Shore had done some recruiting.

The attempt at bravado didn't seem to impress them much, but no one crowded her too closely, a favored wolven dominance tactic. Instead, she thought she detected some scents of anxiety and concern. Despite the facade of unconcern, the South Shore Pack was on edge.

One of them opened the front door, then stood back so she could precede them up the stairs and into the house. The move appeared to be courteous, but it meant all those jumpy wolven would be at her back.

"After you," Snow said. She waited for one of them to move, but no one did. The half dozen wolven stares felt nearly tangible on her skin. She waited a few agonizing heartbeats. Her wolf wanted to go ahead, to keep these wolven from having an excuse to come at them. Snow wasn't going to give them the satisfaction of knowing how cowed they actually were.

Finally, having decided she'd made her point, Snow took a step into the house. The front room was well lit. Comfortable furniture was crammed into nearly every available space, leaving only a narrow path that wound between overstuffed chairs and sofas. They looked well-used, accustomed to the stresses a pack of wolven would inflict upon them. Patches covered obvious rents in the original upholstery. It should have looked junky, but instead it looked like a home.

There was no sign of Hammer, so she threaded her way between the mismatched living room sets and deeper into the house. What had been a formal dining room at one time had been replaced by a long table without chairs, the type you might see at a wedding buffet. The tablecloth that ran the length was a little more stained, and the spots of red were more likely blood than red wine, but that was it. She smelled nothing to indicate the cloth wasn't regularly cleaned.

Two closed doors led out of the room, as well as an open door through which was clearly a kitchen.

A loud thud from behind the door to the right pulled at her attention. She felt a wolven coming up behind her, so she moved, heading toward the sound. Snow snatched her hand away as the one closing on her tried to grab her.

She pushed open the door and lunged through it, turning to snarl at the one who had tried to stop her.

A tall wolven woman with ebony skin and black hair buzzed tight to her scalp loomed at her. Her eyes blazed orange against the darkness, and her teeth were lengthening.

"What are you—" Snow pushed the words out past her own sharpened teeth.

The wolven shouldered her to the side and lunged into the room.

A massive male wolven lay on the floor. A small wolf with charcoal-grey fur worried at his ankle, while a little girl with her hair done up in braids held in place with colorful barrettes wrapped her arms around the much bigger wolven's neck in an almost comical attempt at a headlock. The dark tan skin of her arms looked light against the man's warm umber skin, where it wasn't covered by a short dense beard.

He was making a show at trying to escape the hold when the wolven woman swooped in and snatched up the girl. In a blur, she was down by the wolven man's feet, corralling the young wolf who wasn't too interested in giving up their prey. The wolven woman snatched the little one by the scruff and hauled them away, shoving both children behind her.

"I'm no threat," Snow said, raising her hands to show the lack of claws.

"We'll see about that." The deep voice came from the floor. The massive wolven flowed to his feet.

"She's from Five Moons," the wolven woman said. "Says she needs to talk to you."

Hammer grinned, his teeth white against the black beard that covered the lower half of his face. It flowed halfway down his chest, a dense mat of curly hair.

"I do," Snow said. "Need to talk to you. The North Side Pack wants to talk."

"Interesting to see you running messages, Snow." Hammer slouched back onto the arm of an office chair. He was going to great lengths to appear casual, but his presence filled the space, shoving his dominance toward her. "Didn't think you did the pack life, not after you turned me down flat fifty years ago. What's the new Alpha have that I don't?" There was nothing sexual about the questions. Hammer had been shocked when she'd chosen to remain on her own. His pack had been tempting, but she'd steered mostly clear of it since then.

"She's not my Alpha," Snow said. "I have no Alpha. I'm doing this as a service."

"I hope you were well compensated." He cocked his head. "Still the lone wolf, are you? Or do you belong to yet another pack who wants to intrude on my borders?" He loomed forward, somehow managing to press into her personal space, even from across the room. When she didn't say anything, he continued, "I'm sorry about Velvet. He was a decent sort, for an Alpha."

"Thank you." Snow met his eyes. Their dark brown hadn't taken on any of the color of his wolf form. "That means a lot."

Hammer waved a hand, his stance suddenly much more open. "I know what it's like to lose family. You don't have to be littermates to be close." He glanced over at the children who were watching from behind the woman who had snatched them up.

At their Alpha's relaxation, the wolven woman also became less tense. The cubs didn't let up with their fearless stares. Snow was aware of more wolven filtering in through the open door at her back.

"So what does North Side's new Alpha want with me?" Hammer asked. "Five Moons has had months to reach out, but she's only doing it after my pack members vanish. Are they with her?"

"No." Snow grimaced. She'd been hoping that the other area packs would be unaffected, but apparently that had been wishful thinking. "She's having the same problem. She wants to know what you might know about it." She should have known better.

"Is that so?" Hammer scrubbed at his chin through his beard. "I don't like the sound of that at all. What do you think?" He looked over at the wolven who had fetched Snow from her car.

"Timing is convenient," the wolven replied. "Can we trust Five Moons? Can we trust this one?" They glared at Snow.

"I don't have any stake in this." Snow shrugged. "They gave me some information, and in return I said I'd see if you wanted to talk. If you don't, I'll let her know. Either way, it's the same to me. I got what I came for."

Funnily, her disinterest in the outcome of the errand seemed to be what swayed them. "Eh, maybe meeting isn't a bad idea. It should be somewhere neutral, though. I don't trust outsiders on our turf when our pack is getting picked off."

"Agreed," Hammer said. "Tell Five Moons we'll meet. She brings three wolven and we meet at…"

"Make it the vamps' problem," one of the wolven watching said. "No one would try anything with them around."

"And what's that going to cost?" Snow asked. "You know they don't do anything for free."

"Do you really think they'll pass on the opportunity to eavesdrop on this conversation?" Hammer grinned, his teeth sharp in the low light of the desk lamps. "I don't think so. Run along to Five Moons. Tell her we'll meet at Faint right after dusk in three days, before the club opens."

"I can do that." Snow turned to head out of the room.

"Oh, and tell the North Side Alpha that I expect her to arrange things with Carla," Hammer called after her. "She put this party together. She can reserve the dance hall."

Snow lifted her hand in acknowledgment. It was fair enough, as long as she didn't end up being the one to make the trip down to Faint. One visit a decade to the vamps was her limit, and she'd already hit that.

CHAPTER TEN

Snow stepped carefully through the front door of the North Side Pack's den. The front lobby was empty and still. Would the building ever regain the energy it had contained when Dean had been in charge? She looked around. There was no one to meet her. Someone should have been stationed to watch the entry. That was half the reason for a pack: everyone had a job, a purpose to help keep the pack functional and healthy.

She was supposed to report to Five Moons. After that, it was time to go. Or was it? Her initial goal had been to find out how Dean had died. She'd done that. He'd died terribly, watching his pack be torn apart by those he'd welcomed into it.

Her further goal had been to make sure the pack would continue. Five Moons had seemed to be on her way to getting things handled, but as she made her way through the empty lobby, doubts swirled through her mind.

Sure, there were pressures on the Alpha, but that should have meant more attention being paid to the den's weak spots, not less. And there was always pressure on an Alpha. That was the whole gig. If Five Moons wasn't equal to the task, she should step aside.

Snow kept her ears open as she mounted the grand staircase. There were some sounds of movement down the halls, so the place wasn't completely deserted. She put her shoulders back, carried her head high, and made no attempt to muffle the sound of her footsteps. The pack should all know who she was by her scent, even those who hadn't made it to the lone wolf ceremony. Looking like she had something to hide would only raise unwarranted suspicions.

No one came out of their rooms to check on her as she made her way toward the penthouse stairs. There were rustles as wolven moved behind doors, likely in response to her presence. Her wolf whined within her, deeply concerned about the behavior of these wolven.

It's not our problem to solve, Snow thought to the sister of her soul. She pushed open the door to the stairwell, then loped upward, taking the steps two at a time. Before long, she stood in front of the door to Five Moons' rooms. It was cracked open. A low murmur of voices spilled out into the hall.

She paused, pondering how best to handle the obstacle. Simple was best. She knocked lightly.

The talking ceased immediately.

"Come on in, Snow," Five Moons said.

Snow pushed the door open just enough to squeeze through. Five Moons was stretched out on one sofa, clad only in a pair of loose shorts and a baggy tank top.

Snow already knew the two wolven who lay entwined on the other couch in an easy tangle of limbs. She remembered them from previous visits with Dean's pack. From the anxiety that permeated the room, Alicia and Jamieson's touch was for comfort. There wasn't even the faintest whiff of sexual arousal; instead a nearly visible miasma of concern filled the space. A third wolven lounged in an overstuffed chair, his feet up on the sofa where his two packmates lay.

"Am I interrupting?" Snow asked.

The Alpha shook her head in a short chop. "Just confirming that we have nothing, nothing, and more nothing to go on in Blair's disappearance. Exactly like Harold's."

"Sorry, Alpha," Alicia murmured. Her embrace around Jamieson tightened.

"It's not your fault." Five Moons waved a dismissive hand in their direction. "I wish I'd found something."

"So, you went looking yourself?" Snow asked. Dean would have done the same. Except… She cocked her head. "And you definitely went out with a buddy."

Five Moons stood and addressed her wolves. "Thanks for the update. I'll take things from here."

"Yes, Alpha." The male wolven who Snow didn't know gave her a wide berth on his way out of the room.

Alicia and Jamieson stopped to wrap their arms around their Alpha. Five Moons closed her eyes and pulled them to her. They buried their heads in the crook of her neck, taking a deep breath while their Alpha held them close. The moment didn't last long; it didn't need to. When they stepped away from Five Moons, they smelled more relaxed than they had when Snow joined the little group. Oddly, the Alpha smelled more agitated.

Jamieson quietly shut the door after himself.

"So that buddy system is working well, I take it." No Alpha was above their own rules. At least Dean hadn't operated that way.

Five Moons smirked and stretched. "Of course."

Snow didn't have to smell the Alpha to know she was lying. "Mm hmm."

"Nothing happened." Five Moons settled herself back onto the couch. "I can take care of myself."

"All Alphas think so."

A flash of anger muddled with anxiety reached Snow's nose, though Five Moons' face stayed smooth. "What do you have for me from the South Shore Pack?"

"They're willing to meet."

"Thank god," Five Moons said.

"I don't know how thankful you'll be after you hear the kicker. And the chaser."

Five Moons arched an eyebrow at her choice of words. "Which do I want to know first?"

"Well, the kicker is they'll meet you, but they want neutral ground." When the Alpha didn't say anything, Snow continued, "The meet is at Faint in three days."

"Faint?" Five Moons surged to her feet. "The vampire nightclub? Where the Lord of Chicago pulls the strings of humans and wolven alike to dance for her?"

"So you've had dealings with her, then."

Five Moons shook her head, dashing Snow's relief that she wouldn't have to open a channel with the vamps also.

"I hear things," the Alpha said. "Luther doesn't like her. Naomi thinks she's a necessary evil, and it could be a lot worse."

"They're not wrong. Carla Sangre is dangerous, manipulative, and never to be trusted. She's also much better an option as Lord than many other vamps would be."

"Great." Five Moons dropped back to the couch. "If that's the kicker, what's the chaser?"

"South Shore is missing wolven also."

"Ah. That figures."

"I'm pretty sure it's the only reason they're willing to talk. You should really consider normalizing relations with the other Alphas in the area."

"I know." The Alpha scrubbed her hands over her face. The funk of anxiety flowed from her, spiky and stuttering.

Snow wrinkled her nose. "Do you know how to do that?" she asked gently.

Anger sliced apart the scent of concern. "Of course I do. I know what I'm doing."

"Okay." Snow held up her hands in an attempt to mollify the Alpha. "I'm sure you're doing your best."

"My best?" Five Moons was back on her feet, looming directly into Snow's personal space. "Are you saying my best isn't good enough?"

Snow looked away from the Alpha, trying to defuse the anger that was ratcheting steadily up into rage.

Five Moons stared down at her. Snow felt the heat of her gaze on the exposed side of her neck. She bit her lip as she froze in place. Her wolf counseled stillness. They needed to keep the Alpha's attention on how meek they were, how quiet and docile. They weren't a threat, could never be one.

Both wolven jumped when the cell phone on the end table buzzed loudly. Snow barely stifled a sharp yip.

Five Moons didn't bother to conceal a snarl of frustration. She strode over to the table and snatched up the phone.

"Who the hell—" Her words cut off when she peered at the screen. All the aggression she'd been holding on to drained out of her, and she collapsed to the couch cushions as if her rage had been the only thing holding her up. She closed her eyes, took a deep breath then lifted the phone to her ear.

"Hi, Mom."

* * *

"Cassidy Anne Nolan," Sophia Nolan said pleasantly into her ear. The use of her full name was made even worse by the calm tone.

"How are things?" Cassidy asked brightly. She could fake unconcern also.

"I'm surprised you picked up."

"The satellites must be lined up today. The connection is really clear."

"Indeed." Sophia bit the end off her agreement. The silence stretched thin until Cassidy had to break it.

"Are you calling about Mary?"

"I'm calling about you, dear." Mom's voice warmed a handful of degrees. "But since you mention it, do you know why your sister hasn't seen fit to call her mom for weeks now?"

"I'm sure she's fine, Mom," Cassidy said with as much enthusiasm as she could muster. It came out sounding a little demented, so she dialed back the cheer. "She's a big girl."

"You don't think it's strange at all?"

She did, actually. Mary's disappearance had been eating at her for days now, but what could she say? Their mom didn't need to worry about what her daughter was up to on a top-secret government mission to the wilds of Wisconsin. Cassidy was positive Mary wasn't dead, not when someone had gone to the trouble of leaving a couple of shitty replacements at her place. Though, the place had been cleaned out afterward, which had implications she preferred not to dwell upon.

"So you *do* think it's strange," Mom said when she didn't immediately respond.

"No." Cassidy tried to make herself believe the simple statement and for her mom to believe it also.

"Liar."

"Mom."

"Don't you 'Mom' me. I'm your mother, and I'm allowed to be concerned about the well-being of my eldest daughter when she drops off the face of the earth. Especially since she's the only one who calls me anymore."

"That's not fair," Cassidy said. "You know my situation doesn't allow me to chat as often as I'd like." She sighed. "Look, I didn't want to tell you, but since you're being paranoid about it..."

"It's not paranoia to know something's wrong with one of my babies."

"Mary has a girlfriend." *Sorry, Mary,* Cassidy said to her sister wherever she was. If Mary was all right, she was going to kill Cassidy when she found out she'd been ratted out, but Cassidy couldn't stand the weight of her mom's disappointment on top of everything else she had going on.

"She what—" Her mom sputtered to a stop. "Oh!"

"So maybe it's not some big nefarious thing that she's been hard to reach. I bet they're on a romantic getaway together. Mary said something about heading to the woods with Ruri." That part at least was true.

"A girlfriend?" Sophia practically trilled the word. "Why am I always the last one to find out?"

"Because you'd get on her case about it," Cassidy said. "You know she plays the dating cards close to her chest."

"I suppose. Thank you for telling me. I wish you'd told me sooner so I could have stopped worrying."

"Yeah, well. I didn't want to narc on my only sister."

"I suppose I can give you that one."

"Thanks, Mom. You're the best."

"Only mom you're ever gonna have. Are you all right, sweetie? You sound stressed."

"Oh, you know me," Cassidy said airily. "I'm fine, just trying to get my fieldwork handled, that's all."

"Well, don't work yourself to death. I'm sure you have a lot of credits to catch up on, after changing your major yet again." Her tone was neutral, too much so to not be covering up some disapproval.

Cassidy cringed. Her sister had come up with that little story as cover for her real situation. She was the one who'd told Sophia that Cassidy had shifted the focus of her studies once again—from finance to behavioral biology. The decision had been a little out of left field, but not as shocking as it would have been for her to find out her daughter was a werewolf. It wasn't a major Cassidy would have chosen for herself, but it allowed her to be unavailable and had enough truths sprinkled throughout to be plausible. Cassidy had started out majoring in fashion, before shifting her focus to French. She'd settled on a finance major last year and was just starting to get into some interesting classes when she'd gotten pulled into the world of the wolven.

"You got it. Oh wait, hold on." Cassidy pulled the phone down from her ear, then covered the mouthpiece. "What's that?" she asked to the mostly empty living room. She was conscious of Snow trying to watch her without seeming like she was doing so. Curiosity gave her scent a light blue tone that was shot through with flickers of surprised red.

"I have to go," Cassidy said back into the phone. "My prof wants to talk about tomorrow's trip."

"Oh." Her mom made no attempt to soften her disappointment. "I understand. Give me a call when you can, all right?"

"I will." Cassidy squeezed the phone, being careful not to crack it in half. "I love you, Mom."

"I love you too, Cassie-bean."

Cassidy smiled as she thumbed the phone app closed.

"Is everything all right?" Snow asked cautiously.

"Of course it is." Cassidy's smile turned brittle around the edges. To her dismay, her attempt at a sunny disposition crumbled and the anguish she'd been sitting on poured out behind it. "Oh no," she sobbed through the tears that soaked her face. "You can't see...you can't...it's..." What was it? Her wolf twined around her core, adding her warmth and support. Snow's presence didn't bother her at all.

The edge of the couch dipped as Snow joined her.

"Stop," Cassidy choked out. "I don't want—" She couldn't continue. She had no idea what she didn't want. Had no clue what she wanted. "I'm so tired of keeping my head above water. I'm paddling with everything I have just to keep from drowning. I can't reach out to anyone. I don't know who's trying to help and who wants to hold me under." The more Cassidy thought about the situation with its complications piled on top of complications, the more her wolf's twining started to resemble pacing. They were caged. Trapped in a situation not of their making with no way to undo it.

Snow didn't say anything, but she laid a hand on Cassidy's shoulder. In a second, Cassidy was melting into the hesitant touch. The contact felt so good. She'd been holding herself away from the rest of the pack, afraid they'd divine her shortcomings. The only time she'd allowed herself the luxury of another's touch had been in the care of one of her wolven when they needed reassurance or when she coupled with one of them. Luther was her most frequent companion. He didn't ask questions about where her head was. Some of the others did, especially the occasional female wolven she dallied with.

When Cassidy didn't turn on her, Snow wrapped both arms loosely around her. Her embrace seemed to say it was there for Cassidy as long as she wanted it. Cassidy snorted out a watery laugh. If Snow knew how badly she needed this, she might not have offered.

CHAPTER ELEVEN

Snow held the Alpha close as the terrible tension started to drain from her frame. The terror and heartbreak slowly receded from her scent as well. This wolven had been skirting the edge of a breakdown, Snow was certain of it. That she'd managed to hide it so well from her pack was impressive and terrifying. Either the North Side Pack was more broken than Snow believed, or Cassidy was exceedingly skilled at deception. For the life of her, Snow couldn't decide which was worse. It wasn't that she detected any malice in the Alpha, but with someone that skilled at dissembling, would she?

Cassidy let out a long shuddering sigh. She wrapped her arms around Snow and squeezed once before sliding away from the embrace.

Snow wished she hadn't left. It had been a long time since she'd held that kind of contact with another wolven. Cassidy wasn't the only one starved for wolven touch. Still, better that it stop there than that the touch shift into something sexual, as so frequently happened among their kind.

"Better?" Snow asked. She watched the Alpha's face closely.

"Yeah," the Alpha said. "That really hit...something."

"I know what you mean." There had been no trace of deceit in Cassidy's response, and her scent hadn't wavered. She seemed sincere.

Snow was simply going to have to believe she was what she said she was. "How long has this been going on?"

Cassidy looked up at her. "Which 'this' are you talking about?" She laughed, a short harsh bark of a sound. "There's a lot to choose from."

"Let's start with the hardest parts," Snow said. At Cassidy's grimace, she grinned. "Get the worst out of the way. What comes after won't seem so hard after that."

"If you say so." Cassidy frowned.

"How long have you been wolven?"

The Alpha shot her a look. That hadn't been the question she'd been expecting. "It's been four months. Maybe." She stared into space. "Since before Halloween."

"That recent?" Snow settled herself back into the couch and considered the other wolven. The tank top and shorts revealed a lot of pale skin. It was mostly free of marks, which would have been unusual in an Alpha. Physical remnants of violence faded more easily on wolven, and from Alphas most of all, but they picked up so many. Snow could only see three marks that marred Cassidy's skin. She hadn't been Alpha for very long, so that made a certain amount of sense.

"Wait, Dean died at the beginning of October." She stared at Cassidy with mounting horror. "You've been Alpha about as long as you've been wolven."

Cassidy shrugged. "Yeah, that's about right. Is that bad?"

"I take it you didn't exactly grow up among us."

"I learned about your existence the same time I was turned."

"Oh no." Snow stared at the Alpha who didn't know enough about the wolven or her own situation to understand why it was so dire. "If you don't mind me asking…" She paused, unsure how the question would be taken. Dean hadn't cared a lick if a wolven was born or made. Given that he'd grown up in their mother's pack as a human and had been turned when he was of an age to request it, he hadn't seen the difference. Not everyone was as open-minded as he'd been. What wolven prejudices had Five Moons picked up already?

"Ask what?" Cassidy inquired when the silence had gone on too long.

"How did you come to be one of us? To be wolven."

"That's a story and a half." Cassidy massaged the distorted crescent moon bite mark that stood out on her shoulder. "I'm surprised you haven't heard it. You're a collector, aren't you?"

"Not many stories about you yet, I'm afraid. Just that you came out of nowhere to take over after Dean's killer was eliminated. And that the other packs call you Five Moons."

"The name gives it away." She traced a bite on her thigh, then leaned over and indicated one on the opposite calf. The marks were strange. They looked more placed than received in battle. There was a thread connecting them, but Snow couldn't quite grasp it. There might be one explanation, but it was too far beyond the realm of possibility to contemplate.

When Snow said nothing, Cassidy sighed. "I invited a cute boy over to study. I thought maybe we'd work on our classwork, then get to studying each other, if you know what I mean. He showed up with a group." Cassidy's voice turned clinical. She wrapped her arms around her knees and pulled them close to her chest. Anxiety suffused her scent.

Snow's wolf let out a whine and demanded they get close to the Alpha again. She agreed and shifted forward to place a hand lightly on Cassidy's foot. Snow didn't want to crowd the other wolven, but she needed Cassidy to know she wasn't alone in this memory.

Cassidy started at the touch but didn't pull back. She gave Snow a wan smile. "They chased me through the apartment. I hid in a closet and called my sister. It took a while for them to find me. Now I know they were playing. There's no way they didn't know exactly where I was."

Snow squeezed her foot. "They're not here now. No one is going to hurt you."

"No, they're all dead. Mary and the others saw to that." She grinned fiercely. "I saw to a bit of that myself."

"Good."

"Yeah." She sat up straighter, her arms still clasped around her legs. "They dragged me out of the closet and onto the bed. Then they started to shift and change. I'd never seen anything like that. They waited until I could see them. They wanted me to be terrified. I thought I was going to die."

The anxiety that had filled the room like a noxious cloud was being replaced by remembered terror. Snow placed her other hand on Cassidy's foot, warming the chill flesh with her body heat.

"The first bite hurt more than I'd expected. Their faces were gone, replaced by muzzles, teeth, and eyes that burned. The teeth punched through my skin as if it wasn't really there. Then there was another bite, and another. I passed out before I could feel all of them."

"How many?" Snow asked in a whisper. She already knew the answer.

"Five bites for five moons," Cassidy said simply. "I woke up at Mary's house. I don't remember much. There was a bed at first, then I was inside a box. Then Ruri was there. She saved me from the wolves inside me and brought me to the one who's with me now. The one who I am."

"That's not..." Snow struggled to find the words for what Five Moons had gone through. "...normal. None of that should have happened. You shouldn't have survived."

"I nearly didn't, from what Ruri said. From what others have said since."

"Most people don't survive more than one bite. Hell, a lot of people don't survive even a single bite. The change isn't automatic. Surviving two bites is nearly unheard of. Five should have been a death sentence."

"It was supposed to be."

"And how did you end up in that situation?"

"My sister," Cassidy said simply. "She made waves with the pack after MacTavish took over. He wanted revenge, I guess. I was it. I was supposed to die a long slow death without Mary being able to do anything to stop it. Maybe she was even supposed to give me the killing blow. My survival wasn't a part of his plan. Not that he was ever going to get away with it. Mary would have killed him either way. Still, I'm glad I made it, not just because I happen to like living. If I'd died, Mary probably would have wiped out the pack. I'm happy it didn't come to that."

"Damn." Snow stared at the livid half-moon mark on Cassidy's calf. "That explains a lot."

"About how messed up I am?"

"Actually, yes." Snow patted Cassidy's foot reassuringly. "It's not your fault, but you kind of are."

"Gee, thanks."

"You probably shouldn't be Alpha," Snow said carefully. She pulled her hands back.

"I know." Cassidy's face flashed between hurt and angry, but her scent settled on despair.

"That doesn't mean you're not doing a decent job, even though the situation is about as awful as it gets." Every word was true. Snow had been tallying up a list of the Alpha's shortcomings, tutting at the lack of planning and the obvious places she was falling down as the leader of this pack. Of course she was. Cassidy was definitely strong enough to be an Alpha. That she'd survived the horrific circumstances that changed her into one of the wolven was testament to that. Her origin story explained a lot about that strength. While the stories of wolven turned from two bite marks were few and mostly didn't end well, those wolves tended to be more powerful. Sometimes, they were even created that way on purpose, but those who initiated it were betraying a shocking lack of concern for the one being turned. In Cassidy's case, that had been the point.

Still, in a decade or two, she would be an excellent Alpha, and that was a ridiculously short amount of time in which to become one.

"You don't have the background. Alphas aren't taught, not really. Sometimes a Beta might be groomed to take over from an Alpha, but that's as close as it gets. No, they're part of a pack; if they aren't born into one, they join it. They learn what it's like to be a member. They take on more responsibility. They figure out what safety looks like for the pack. Then one day, they challenge the Alpha, or they split off with wolven who're looking for a change. Your situation is unprecedented. You can't be blamed for that."

"I don't know about all that," Cassidy said quietly. She stared past Snow through the windows that looked out onto the city. "I do know that I'm in over my head. I feel like I'm drowning, but if I sink, everyone around me will be dragged down too. So I'm trying to keep my head above water and wondering if that's all there is. Does every Alpha feel like they're seconds away from being discovered as a fraud?"

"Not in the least." Snow smiled. "Dean was an amazing Alpha. He was so good at it. Almost zen, you know? Like he just had to let what he needed to do wash over him, then he'd do it."

"Is that why they called him Velvet?"

Snow shook her head. "It's because he had this smooth, easygoing exterior, but underneath it he was as hard as he had to be. He wasn't above taking someone out, and the wolven knew that. He was like a velvet glove over an iron fist, but in the best possible way. I wish you could have known him."

"Me too," Cassidy said quietly. "There's so much I want to ask him. Like is Luther ever going to unwind enough to let me run things without considering every single other angle? Or is there something I can do to get Beth more comfortable with me? And what do I do when my wolven disappear and I have no idea what's going on with them?"

"MacTavish has a lot to answer for," Snow said. "It's too bad he's dead. I'd happily bring him back if it meant we could take him out slowly again."

"He went out plenty badly," Cassidy said. "At least from what Mary told me, anyway."

"That's something, I guess."

"So, do you want the pack?" Cassidy asked. "You know them. You know what to do." She warmed to the idea and met Snow's eyes. "You'd be so much better at it than I am. I could see how things are really supposed to run, instead of jury-rigging things from one disaster to the next."

"Oh no." Snow held up her hands. "No, no, no, no." She shook her head for emphasis. "And still no. Have I mentioned no?"

"Why not?" Snow's emphatic answer had deflated Cassidy a bit, but she still had to push. That was Alphas for you.

"I am *not* Alpha material. I never have been, I never will be."

"Why not?" Cassidy cocked her head. "If you're as old as Dean, then you've been around. Haven't you done all that soaking up what the pack is supposed to be like?"

"Child, I could write you a book on what healthy pack structure looks like, but that won't help me run one. Check with your wolf. How strong does she think I am?"

The Alpha's eyes grew vague for a moment, then sharpened. "She's not worried about you at all. She seemed surprised I had to ask. She likes you, though."

"I'm not surprised. I'm not dominant. For most wolven, I don't even register on their radars. I will never be a threat, and I'm fine with it. I don't want to be in charge."

"I don't either," Cassidy said.

"But you could be," Snow snapped back. "There's the difference."

"I don't understand."

"I know you don't." Snow took a deep breath. Cassidy was pressing her buttons, but it wasn't her fault. "Look, MacTavish was bad news."

Cassidy snorted. "Obviously."

"He wasn't bad news because of what he did here. He wasn't even bad news because of how he did it, though that was exceedingly messed up. He was bad news because of why he did it." Snow looked up to see if Cassidy understood.

"Okay?"

She didn't. Snow tried another tack. "There are people who want to be in charge who shouldn't be. They shouldn't be running things because they see being in control as the end goal. They want to be in charge because they want to be in charge. Not because they want to help out those under them or because they see a better way of doing things. Being top dog"—her lip curled at the slur—"is the whole point. That doesn't help anyone. MacTavish was one of those."

"That makes a certain amount of sense."

"Good. We can speculate on what exactly his character flaws were that led to that, but suffice it to say, he wanted it but shouldn't have had it." Snow nodded. "You say you don't want to be in charge. That's fine. I think you're saying that because you're ill-prepared and out of your depth. But you keep stepping up to do it. You are Alpha material, or you will be one day."

"Okay." Cassidy seemed to take some solace from that statement.

"I neither want to be Alpha nor do I have the capacity. You might not want to be saddled with it, but you have the force of will to back up what you want done. I don't have that. I redirect, I mollify, I make sure I never get backed into a corner, because I'm not coming out of it if someone decides that's where they want me to be. And I'm okay with that. I know how to navigate this world being who I am. Not everyone wants to be on top, you know."

"I know. Ruri always says she's happy not being Alpha."

Snow gestured with one hand. "Perfect example. Most wolven are happy with where they stand in the pack. I'm happy being outside the pack."

"Why? I thought all wolven wanted that pack life. Even MacTavish wanted to be part of one. At least, that's why the others say he stole ours. Tried to, anyway."

"MacTavish was a psychopath. There was nothing in him that wanted to be part of a pack. He wanted to dominate one, that was all."

"So we leave him out of it. What about you?"

"Not all wolven want to be in packs, all right? Some are happier on their own. Some come together for short periods, then break apart. Some of us bounce between packs. Not everyone wants the same things. For me, I get tired of playing dominance games. I don't have time for them, I'm not interested in them. Being part of a pack means measuring yourself constantly against the others and where you place. It's exhausting, and I just don't care."

"Fair enough." Cassidy paused. "So what is dominance?"

"What is dominance?" Snow stared at the Alpha. "What is—" She shook her head. "You really are a cub in the woods."

"Not my fault, remember?" Cassidy said. "But I want to know. Maybe I'm not ready to be Alpha, but I'm what the North Side Pack has. I want to do a good job. I'm hoping you can help."

"You want me to help you run this place." Snow's voice was flat, and she made no effort to warm it.

"No, because you don't want that, and I get it. I'm hoping I can talk you into hanging around a little longer. You can let me know where I'm screwing up. Like it or not, this pack needs someone in charge, and I'm it. We're in a bind, and I need a hand." She gazed solemnly at Snow, looking her straight in the eye. "Please."

Well, I'll be damned, Snow thought. Maybe this baby Alpha was closer to running things than she'd thought. Five Moons was asking with quiet dignity. She was making no attempt to bring her wolf to bear. There was nothing of her innate dominance in the request.

"So, what? You want some sort of an advisor, is that it?"

"That's it." Cassidy held out her hand. "No more, no less."

"And what do I get out of it?"

"I guess we could pay you," Cassidy said, her hand still out. "The pack isn't exactly flush, but we could find some money somewhere. You'd get rooms here, and we'd feed you regularly, just like any other pack member. Other than that, I'd pretty much have to owe you."

"That could work." It was silly to even consider the offer, but Snow stared at Five Moons' extended hand. The smart move would have been to say she wasn't interested and head out of town before rush hour started.

She took Cassidy's hand. "I'll see what I can do for now. No promises."

"None needed." Cassidy closed her fingers carefully around Snow's hand and shook it once, then let go. "I suppose the first thing I should get is your take on what to do about this meeting you managed to set up in a vampire den."

CHAPTER TWELVE

Cassidy had never been inside Faint before. Even before she'd become part of the world of the wolven, though, she'd heard of the club. It had been farther from school than she'd wanted to trek, but some of her friends had been down a few times. They'd come back with stories about how decadent and over the top the atmosphere was. While that definitely hadn't been her scene then, these days she was certainly indulging the hedonistic side of her nature in a way she had never contemplated when she'd been fully human.

The doors weren't open to the public and wouldn't be for a few hours, so the atmosphere was probably much more muted than it would normally be. There was a sense of emptiness and longing, as if the building wasn't complete without the dancers and revelers that would fill it. Not that the halls were empty. Strange creatures who looked human but felt anything but passed their little group with looks from sideways glances to open stares. Cassidy tried to keep her nose from twitching. These things might have looked human, but most of them had no smell at all. They blended into the scent background. There was no way to tell what they were feeling. A few were actually human, and they smelled everywhere from terrified to euphoric.

Snow had warned her about the vampires' thralls. Humans were the vamps' favorite food source, both for blood and for whatever contact high they got from human emotions. They also recruited from among humans. The vamps let the occasional human into their circle, whether it was to get some use out of them or with an eye to eventually turning them. If the human didn't work out, they had a tendency to disappear and resurface somewhere else, with no memory of how they got there or about their time with the vampires. That was if they reappeared at all. Some never returned, though not in the kinds of numbers that might invite attention. Cassidy supposed that was where Mary came in.

The thralls that wandered the halls seemed divided by purpose. Some were highly aroused and to such a degree that a bright green miasma seemed to follow them. Others had the purposeful walk of someone who had a task to discharge. Both groups made Cassidy uncomfortable.

The scents of her companions were much easier to parse. Luther was miserable. His scent had started out at a high state of anxiety but had taken on a flare of anger almost immediately. Naomi's scent shaded a bit toward concern, but it was mostly a steely blue aroma of determination. Snow smelled more at ease. She was watchful, certainly, but there was nothing here that sent red spikes of worry through her.

That made sense, since Snow was the only one of them who'd been to visit the Lord of Chicago before. Cassidy tried to calm her racing pulse, to follow Snow's example. At least the others had dealt with vampires before. This was Cassidy's first experience. She would have loved to have spoken with Mary before the meeting. She was certain her sister would have had plenty of pointers for dealing with Carla Sangre.

Three days later, and the only difference in the gridlocked mess of her life was that they were going to talk to someone else about it. Mary was still missing, but now her voice mail box was full. Blair and Harold were still gone, and a couple of her wolven had reported being followed by shadowy figures.

The previous day, Carlos had left his job at the County Clerk's office. He'd noticed a tail as he made his way across Madison Street to wait for Zoya to get off work at the Bank of America Building. He'd kept to large groups of people, which hadn't been difficult since downtown had been emptying out at that time. The tail was gone when he and Zoya had left. At least it showed that the buddy system was working. It also demonstrated that they still weren't safe. And of course neither Carlos nor Zoya had gotten a look at the tail. Carlos had described it as a sense of someone following, a recurring scent among the crowd, but beyond that it was human, he'd had nothing.

Those she'd set to continue the search for Blair and Harold had found nothing new, though they were straying farther from North Side territory. They'd done a bit of checking downtown after Carlos's experience, but that had been a dead end as well. What they needed was a cop or a private investigator, someone with experience tracking those who were lost. What they had were a handful of white-collar workers, some service and retail employees, and a sprinkling of wolven with backgrounds in various trades, led by a college dropout. If she'd known what was coming, she would have majored in criminal justice instead of finance.

Snow led the way deeper into the nightclub. It was larger than it looked from the outside. Cassidy wondered how many of the buildings on either side of the nightclub were actually part of it. The sumptuous decoration of the public areas had given way to wood paneling that screamed money in a way that the common areas hadn't. The communal areas had whispered of sensation and temptation. When the dark decor extended to back rooms where it wasn't needed to keep up the appearances, Cassidy knew that whoever ran this place didn't have to watch their budget.

"We're almost there," Snow murmured as they mounted a wide set of stairs.

Cassidy's feet sank into the plush wine-red carpet with each soundless step. Two pale faces stared down at them from the top of the stairs. Cassidy blinked and caught a blur of movement as two figures joined them, one on each side of the steps. With each stair they climbed, another pair of vampires appeared to flank them. By the time they reached the top, every other step was bookended by a pair of vampires who watched them soundlessly.

They were surrounded by the creatures, yet Cassidy could only smell those she'd brought with her. The anxiety in Naomi's scent had heightened, and Luther smelled like he was a step away from full-on rage. His scent pulsed with an angry red that was riling up her own wolf. She didn't have to look at him to know his eyes were glowing. Oddly, Snow smelled more or less the same as she always did.

She looked over in Cassidy's direction, not quite making eye contact, then yawned.

The face of the vampire nearest to them cracked into momentary anger, before settling back into a blank stare.

Cassidy couldn't help smirking. She considered trying to make her face as smooth as those of the vampires but decided against it. Better to go into this looking like this was a joke than to let them know the kind of impact their display was having.

Snow stopped at the landing at the top of the stairs. A massive door of dark wood stood closed before them.

"What do we—" Cassidy's whisper to Snow was cut off as the door swung open on soundless hinges. The room beyond was dark, save for a dim light toward the back.

Her jaw ached as her wolf demanded some means to defend them when they ventured into this dark place that smelled of blood and pain. Cassidy sniffed again. There were other notes in the air, notes that pulled at different parts of her. Her teeth lengthened at the blood, but beneath it was the smell of sex and release. Her fingers twitched and her nostrils flared again, trying to bring more of that to her, to cover up the jagged pain scents that floated along with the remnants of pleasure. If she'd been in wolf form, she would have sneezed to clear her snout of the olfactory intrusion. She settled for a quick wipe of her nose with the back of her hand, then started forward.

The room was large. A massive carved wooden desk sat in a pool of light cast by the heavily shaded lamp upon it. Behind it was a wingback chair, swiveled away from them. The leather gleamed in the lamp's light. More furniture dotted the room, arranged in small vignettes. A chaise longue sat behind a fur rug, grizzly bear if Cassidy had been forced to guess. In the opposite corner was a heavily carved screen that might have been ivory. It certainly seemed old enough to be so. The scene was one from Greek mythology. It seemed to involve Medusa, though she was the one holding Perseus's severed head. The fish tank was the strangest touch. It took up much of the same wall as the screen. Red lights illuminated it from the bottom. Flickers of movement in front of the lights gave it a juddering strobe effect. Cassidy wondered what kind of fish the vampire lord kept.

"Snow." The single syllable held more promise than it had any right to. Something in Cassidy tightened, but Snow betrayed no reaction.

The leather chair turned around to display a woman with curly auburn hair in strong contrast to skin so pale it was nearly translucent. In the low light, her skin glowed. Between the dark red flash from the depths of her black eyes and the utter lack of scent, Cassidy knew this was a vampire. She was the mold upon which all female vampire movie castings had been pulled.

"Cassidy is it?" the woman asked. She pushed herself out of the chair and moved toward them. To say that she was graceful was an understatement. With both hands outstretched toward her as if Cassidy was a long-missed friend, she flowed like water around the edge of the desk and up to her.

Cassidy's pulse pounded in her ears. Her wolf was torn between attacking the vampire out of hand and wanting the woman to rub both hands through the fur of her belly. Of their belly. For a moment, Cassidy was in complete agreement. Then she shook her head. They were here for a reason.

"Snow," the woman said, this time her tone was teasing. "You didn't tell me how attractive your new Alpha is."

"She's not my Alpha," Snow said quietly. "How she looks isn't relevant and wouldn't be even if she was."

"Oh, Snow. Snow, Snow, Snow. Looks are always relevant."

Snow sighed. "Cassidy, that's Carla Sangre, the *vampire* Lord of Chicago." She emphasized the word "vampire," as if to say she might be someone's lord, but she wasn't Snow's.

She wasn't Cassidy's either. "Carla." Cassidy inclined her head. "I'm pleased to meet you." She hesitated, not sure if this was a handshake scenario or not.

"And I am most pleased to meet you." Carla reached out and took Cassidy's hand between both of hers. "I must say, if I'd known more about you, I would have made certain to reach out sooner. Much sooner."

"We reached out to you." Cassidy wondered at the coolness of the hands around hers.

"That you did. I'm so glad you took me up on my invitation to meet before that boor Hammer shows up."

"I suppose I should thank you for allowing us to meet on your turf."

"Turf." Carla's laugh was light and tinkling in a way that had to have been affected. "How charming."

"Yes. Well."

"And of course, there's the matter of payment," Carla said, her voice sharpening to a sly edge. "As the one to make the arrangements, you make the deposit, as it were."

"Snow mentioned there would be some options." She really didn't want to give up her blood to this thing. As alluring as Carla was, below the surface that promised everything, Cassidy knew that there were depths that would take and take until she had nothing left to give. She was sure part of her would love it even as it stripped away everything that made Cassidy who she was and replaced it with adoration. Her stomach lurched, and the promise evaporated. She pulled back her hand.

Carla didn't miss the way she swallowed hard before she reclaimed her hand. She looked toward the screen. "Send for Evan, if you would." Her smile turned brittle as she turned her gaze back on Cassidy. "Faint provides for all discerning tastes."

"My apologies if you felt offended," Cassidy said carefully. She didn't want to commit too much to an actual apology. She had the feeling Carla would press that advantage much further than it ought to go.

"So, payment." Carla smiled, exposing two needle-pointed teeth. Had they been so sharp before? Cassidy couldn't remember. "I can take payment in blood." She held up a hand when Cassidy started to protest. "We are vampires, after all. If you didn't know what that meant, you should have done your research before coming to visit." Her lips affected an insincere pout. "Of course, it's difficult to do so when your main source of information is out of town and for so long. A shame really. You'd been so close to this point."

Carla was suddenly standing behind Cassidy, leaning in, her lips at Cassidy's ear. "Sisters," she whispered in a waft of cool air that drifted across Cassidy's earlobe.

She closed her eyes against the sensation that traveled down her spine and pooled in her belly. Goose bumps were chased by heat.

"Not so uninterested, it would seem," Carla said quietly. "Maybe Evan won't be necessary after all. A shame. He'll be so disappointed. But I'm not."

The fog the vampire created in Cassidy's brain cleared. She lurched forward, away from Carla. "What did you say about my sister?" Cassidy whirled around to face her. "What do you know of Mary?" She stepped toward the vampire, allowing her wolf to creep in around the edges of her skin. "You need to tell me what you know." Her voice distorted as her muzzle lengthened.

"I need to do no such thing." Carla moved away from her more quickly than Cassidy could track. She appeared on Cassidy's other side. "Not without proper payment. You haven't even paid me for the pleasure of hosting you. We can settle up for the first, then discuss the second." She grinned up at Cassidy, her teeth on full display. "I can promise you that payment will have its own rewards. Just know, if you don't pay in blood for the one favor, you will pay for the other. And blood is the lightest payment plan we offer." Carla leaned in toward her.

Cassidy licked her lips as she struggled to come to a decision. She had to meet with Hammer and the South Shore Pack, but she also needed to find out what she could about her sister.

"The blood doesn't have to come only from you," Carla breathed, so quietly Cassidy wasn't sure if the others could hear. "There are privileges to being in charge. You don't have to bear the price on your body alone."

Cassidy glanced over her shoulder at Luther, Naomi, and Snow.

CHAPTER THIRTEEN

Snow could easily read the turmoil on the Alpha's face, and likely the others in the room could as well. Cassidy wanted to take the vampire up on her offer. The scent of indecision oozed off her in waves. There was no way she should have even been tempted.

Will it undermine her if I step in? Snow watched the Alpha out of the corner of her eye. She turned her head slightly to see what emotions Luther and Naomi were betraying. Both of them stared straight ahead, as if pretending not to see the dilemma their leader was caught in.

"I can't do that," Cassidy finally said. "You'll get our payment for the grace of hosting this meeting. Nothing more." The last was said through gritted teeth.

"What a pity," Carla said. "Have you decided on the mode?"

"I'll take the favor," Cassidy said. "Or rather, offer it. I'm not ready to barter with my bodily fluids."

"You make that sound downright unpleasant." The vampire frowned artfully at them. "I assure you it will be anything but."

The sound of a door opening distracted their group, but the vampire didn't even glance in its direction.

"Excuse me," came a deep voice from behind the decorative screen on the far side of the room. A burly man made his way out past it. His face lit up at the sight of Carla. "Mistress," he exclaimed, then bowed low. "You wished to see me?"

Snow caught a flicker of movement between the sections of the screen after the man moved past it. For a moment, a dark eye caught hers and held it. She couldn't make out much more than the fact that the eye was a deep black, so deep she was sure she could drown in it, even from the other side of the room. The owner was female, on that Snow would have bet good money, and her skin was dark, much darker than Snow's own. Since when did Carla have others sitting in on her meetings? Snow couldn't recall Carla ever having done that when they'd met in the past. The screen had been there during their most recent meeting, when Snow had first come to town looking for information about Dean, but she hadn't noticed anyone behind it. With vampires, would she have?

"Evan," Carla said, gesturing for him to cross the room toward her.

Snow glanced away from the screen for a second, but when she looked back, there was no sign of anyone there. She glanced toward Cassidy and the others, but they were all watching Carla and the newcomer.

From the absent scent trace, the man was a vampire. He was much newer than Carla. If it hadn't been for the lack of smell to him and the way he sometimes moved a little too quickly, Snow wouldn't have guessed he was anything other than human. He still maintained a hint of a tan. Snow squinted at his left hand. Yes, there was the telltale phantom white band of a wedding ring. He'd worn that until he was turned, most likely.

He was reasonably attractive, Snow supposed. His blazer gapped open to reveal a bare chest that appeared to have been sculpted out of alabaster flesh. The barest bit of chest hair sprinkled across his pectorals, more accentuating than obscuring them.

"Say hello to Cassidy Nolan," Carla purred. She wrapped a hand around Evan's upper arm. Together they took a step toward the Alpha. "She's deciding on the terms of her payment. I thought you might be more to her taste than I."

"I see." Evan grinned broadly, the expression looking somehow wholesome next to Carla's wicked-edged leer. "I would be happy to accept payment on your behalf, mistress." His smile darkened. "I promise to make it more joy than burden." There was the vampire in him. He might be new, but he was still dangerous.

"I believe the Alpha has already made the terms clear," Luther said. His voice was studiedly neutral.

"She deserves the opportunity to change her mind," Evan said. "It is a woman's prerogative."

Snow managed to hold down a gag. Next to her, Naomi swallowed a quiet choke.

"I haven't changed my mind," Cassidy said. "I owe Ms. Sangre a favor."

It was an understandable choice. Snow would have taken blood. That was over much more quickly, and she took a certain joy in ruining Carla's anticipation for feeding on her. Snow didn't respond the way the vampire lord preferred, not that Carla would admit it. Nor would she pass up the opportunity to drink freely given wolven blood. Favors were tricky. They were the main currency between the various factions of non-humans in Chicago and in many other cities as well. There was always the risk that someone might refuse to make good on a favor, but word of that trespass tended to spread quickly. Snow preferred not to have favors hanging over her head. Those owed to the vampires tended to be more trouble than they were worth.

"Of course," Carla said.

Evan looked disappointed. He licked his lips even as he shrugged.

"What do you know about missing wolven?" Snow asked. The vampire had played coy when she'd asked earlier. That had been three days ago, though. It was perfectly reasonable to ask again and much more tactically sound to do so in front of allies.

Carla's eyes sharpened and she shot Snow a hard look.

"Yes," Cassidy said "Maybe you can tell us more about that. I'd be willing to talk about different payment for that information."

"Have you been losing vampires?" Luther asked.

"Let's walk and talk," Carla said. "I've received word that your appointment is here."

Unless the rumors about vampire telepathy were true, Carla had received no such message.

"Maybe the person behind the screen would like to weigh in," Snow said.

"There's no time." As Carla spoke, the door through which they'd entered opened. "This way." She swept out of the room. Evan waited politely for everyone to exit. He made eyes especially at Cassidy, who seemed not to notice.

Snow would have given a lot to find out who had been sitting in on their little gathering. Carla knew the woman had been there.

"There was someone behind the screen?" Cassidy whispered as they left through the open door.

Snow nodded.

"Hmm." Cassidy stared off into the middle distance. "I don't like this place," she finally said.

"That's not a nice thing to say." Snow glanced around them meaningfully. "It has its charms. You never know who's about." Or who could hear. Vampire hearing was plenty sharp, if not as good as that of the wolven. Snow would have put her hearing up against that of a vamp, but they could get so close without being noticed.

"That's true, I suppose." Cassidy nodded. "We'll talk later."

Carla appeared between them and slid an arm through the crook of Cassidy's elbow. "Talk about what?" she asked.

"Talk about people going missing," Cassidy said.

"I don't like to think about it," Carla said. "Nasty business."

"So you have lost your people?" Snow asked.

Carla shrugged. "Fledglings strike out on their own all the time."

It wasn't an answer. "Then what do you know about wolven disappearances?"

"I know that information has a price, and this tidbit is expensive indeed."

"So what?" Cassidy said. "More blood?"

Carla's demure smile widened into something disturbingly sharklike. "If you're offering."

"There are other forms of payment than blood or favors," Snow said. "Information is a good one."

"I suppose," Carla said. "What do you know, young Alpha?"

"Not much," Cassidy admitted. "I've lost two people in the past couple of weeks."

"You're giving the milk away for free if you tell her that without an agreement in place," Snow said. She plastered on a bland grin. "Careful what you say and to who."

"You're so suspicious," Carla said to Snow. She turned her attention back to Cassidy. "That isn't the most valuable morsel, but it's not worth nothing. For that, I can tell you that your pack isn't the only one to have lost members."

Which they already knew. Or at least Snow did. There were packs out west who'd seen wolven disappear. Snow was the one who'd passed that information on to Carla. She sighed.

"You know what," Cassidy said. "I think I'm good. We'll figure this out on our own if we have to."

"Suit yourself," Carla murmured. She traced the back of Cassidy's hand with her fingertips. "We're here." They drew up in front of a pair of double doors at one of the club's many private rooms. "Try not to kill each other, all right, kitten?" She gripped Cassidy's hand and leaned forward. "Don't forget that you owe me a favor. I look forward to collecting."

"O-okay," Cassidy said. She stood straight, trying to act like Carla wasn't freaking her out. "I got it."

"Good." Almost quicker than Snow could see, Carla's hand flicked out, her sharpened nails laying open the back of Cassidy's hand. Blood welled up in the shallow cuts, and Carla ran her fingers over the rents. She lifted her hands to her lips before anyone could stop her. "Sublime," she said.

"You didn't earn that," Snow said. She glared at the vampire.

"I'm about to," Carla said. She looked around. "Watch your backs. There is more going on here than you know. The hand that reaches out in friendship can just as easily plant a dagger between your ribs." She stared Cassidy directly in the eyes, then flicked a glance over at Snow. "Both of you." She backed up, now holding Snow's gaze, then turned and swept away down the hall and around a corner.

"That was cryptic as fuck," Cassidy said.

"And not especially helpful." Snow shook her head. "Talk about telling us something we already knew."

"Are you ready, Alpha?" Luther asked from next to the door.

"I guess I have to be," Cassidy said. "Wish me luck," she said to Snow.

"You won't need it if you remember what we told you."

"Yeah, well." With a crooked grin, Cassidy stepped toward the closed doors.

* * *

Cassidy took a deep breath and held it as Naomi and Luther each opened one of the double doors before them. Snow stood off to the side, doing her best to look like she wasn't with them but had merely managed to show up at the same place and time. Part of Cassidy really wanted to tug at her, to pull Snow into her orbit. It would have been so easy. The lone wolf shone in that web that seemed to live only inside her head. But if it was only in her head, why could she make things happen when she plucked at the wolven who showed up in it? She didn't like to; it felt too much like coercion. Snow wasn't quite a part of it; she stood to one side, slipping between the other points like a rogue planetoid.

Maybe it was that there were gaps in the collection. Ruri's point of light was so dim it was easy to overlook. Blair's and Harold's lights were as muted, but at least they hadn't gone out completely.

She was holding her breath, trying to work up the nerve to get going. There was nothing else to do but keep moving. She exhaled and strode forward, head held high. Snow came in a few yards behind her. On her heels, Luther and Naomi closed the doors.

The room was dominated by the presence of the huge wolven who stood in the center of the floor, arms crossed and facing mostly away from her. At his side were three more wolven, two women and a man. The entourage watched her group closely. She glanced their way long enough to get a feel for them, then focused on the South Shore Pack's Alpha.

He was tall, topping her by at least a foot, if not a foot and a half, with long dreadlocks that were pulled back into a loose tail that draped halfway down his back. His dark brown skin was lighter than the charcoal-grey suit he wore, but not by much. And he still gave no indication that he'd bothered to take note of her presence.

Cassidy rolled her eyes, and it was only then that she saw the catwalk around the edges of the room's high ceilings. She should have noticed that first, but the other Alpha's presence had blinded her to that very obvious, very dangerous feature.

She turned in place, trusting in her feel for the room to tell her if the Alpha or his wolven attacked. Luther glanced up, as did Naomi. Snow kept her gaze fixed on a point on the wooden floor.

"Heh," the Alpha said, barely loudly enough for her to hear.

Cassidy finished giving the walkway a close look. Nobody was hiding out on it, which she couldn't have known without looking. The vampires' lack of smell was a bigger hindrance than she'd anticipated. Apparently, she was acclimating to her wolven senses. Not being able to trust her sense of smell was leaving her feeling very exposed.

Her inspection had taken longer than it needed to. When she finally faced him again, the Alpha was looking right at her.

"You've got some stones," he rumbled, his voice coming from somewhere deep in his chest.

Cassidy smirked. "Don't need them," she said. "They're far too delicate and only get in the way."

Snow's muffled snicker wasn't the only one. A wolven woman on Hammer's left quickly dropped her half-grin when the Alpha shot a look over his shoulder.

"Gumption doesn't make you a proper Alpha," he said, taking a step toward her.

"My pack says otherwise, Hammer," Cassidy responded. She also took a step toward the center of the floor.

"What's your name, little girl?" Hammer sneered. "You can't be the one they call Five Moons."

"Is that so?" Despite having only recently discovered the name she'd been given by those outside the pack, Cassidy found herself unaccountably enraged by his refusal to use it. She stepped forward again, and before her foot hit the ground, the tips of her fingers were already split open by hard claws. Her muzzle lengthened as needle-sharp teeth shoved into her mouth. Her skin itched for a moment, then burned in brief agony with the eruption of fur through it. Fluids soaked into her clothing.

Hammer laughed, his already deep voice dropping further in register as similar changes wracked his body. They paced toward each other, and by the time they stood in the center of the room, their muzzles bare inches apart, they were balanced on back legs more suited to wolves than to humans. The seams on the shoulders of his suit had split, revealing dark fur that gleamed with moisture beneath.

Cassidy's wolf demanded full release. She was certain they could take him. This wolf might be huge, but they were fast, they were cunning, and they would outlast him in all the ways that counted. Cassidy snarled, allowing her wolf's rage to fill her, but holding on to the barest control. Hammer growled right back and lunged forward. Cassidy whipped her head out of the way and shifted to one side. The other Alpha's teeth clashed together where her muzzle had been the moment before.

She swiped forward, driving her claw-tipped hand through the fabric pulled taut over his rib cage. Before she could tear his flesh into the same ribbons as his suit coat, Hammer eeled away from her and lashed out with a wicked backhand that caught her across the ear. Pain sent spangles of light across her vision as she pivoted away.

The others had said this would be a formality, posturing that would occur as their wolves sized the other one up. The thought skated dimly across Cassidy's consciousness. It didn't matter what the other wolven had said. The blow had been very real, and she knew the wrong move would result not only in her own death, but possibly the deaths of those who'd come with her.

By the time she blinked the spots free of her vision, he was already in her face. Cassidy instinctively straightened her arms, trying to shove him away as he snapped at her with wicked teeth. Hammer's reach exceeded hers, and she had to struggle to keep him from closing the remaining distance while dodging his bites. If he got his jaws around an arm or closed them over her shoulder, she would end up with broken bones to go with the lacerated skin.

Cassidy's arms were tiring from keeping the other wolven at bay. *Might as well give him what he wants.* She stopped pushing against him, allowing his weight to topple forward into her. The growl that ripped from his throat was rough with triumph, but it tore into a higher register as she lifted her back legs, using the claws on her back feet to rip through his shirt and into his soft underbelly.

Hammer roared and rolled away from her, giving her the chance to scramble to her feet. Fire scored the top of her shoulder. He'd gotten a bite in before she'd clawed him. It had come so fast Cassidy hadn't noticed it. Blood flowed down her upper arm, dripping from her elbow to land on the floor with rhythmic splats.

The other Alpha bounced to his feet. He shook out his claws and made a point of licking her blood from his teeth before closing in again.

She shifted, trying to get around him, but now he was the one who pivoted with her. God, but he was fast. Her wolf insisted they were quicker, but Cassidy wasn't sure that this was the time or place to put that to the test. Not while they were in a literal den of vampires.

The vampires.

Cassidy flicked a look up toward the catwalk, then stepped back. She risked another look above, then stepped farther back as she glared upward.

CHAPTER FOURTEEN

When she peeled away, Hammer also looked up.

"Slippery bastards," he growled, the words surprisingly easy to understand despite the current shape of his mouth.

As soon as his eyes flicked up, Cassidy struck. She came in low and hard, hooking her arm around his midsection while planting one of her feet behind one of his. His center of gravity was different from a human's and he was much bigger than she was. She hadn't sparred against anyone who could assume betweenform, and he didn't go down as quickly as she'd hoped.

Hammer grabbed her shoulders as he toppled, the claws on both hands digging through her jacket and the fur beneath it. He ground his claws into the wound he'd already opened. Cassidy's vision darkened momentarily from the pain as she collapsed with him, but she was able to stay on top. Before his back hit the ground, she was swarming up his torso. The air left his lungs in a quiet huff, but she already had her teeth wrapped around his neck.

He stiffened for a second, then went slack. His chest rose and fell in rhythmic pants Cassidy quickly recognized as laughter.

She loosened her grip on his neck and pulled back cautiously. When he made no effort to move against her, she backed away completely, sliding off his chest and getting her feet under her. She risked a glance at Hammer's wolven. They came forward but ignored her. Instead, they reached down and helped their Alpha to his feet.

He took the assistance with surprising grace. His eyes cut her way once, but then he returned his attention to his wolven, clasping them to him and murmuring comforting words into their ears. The display was affecting, and Cassidy found herself retreating to the comfort of her group.

Naomi snaked an arm around her waist, and Luther hugged her from behind, resting his chin on her shoulder. Cassidy breathed them in, banishing the smell of strange wolven from her nostrils and allowing their scents to obliterate Hammer's on her body and clothes. The adrenaline from their confrontation was turning into a different type of energy, one that was twisting Cassidy's insides in a way that wasn't at all unpleasant.

"Well met, Alpha," Hammer said from across the floor. "I'm glad to see the new North Side Pack has a worthy protector."

Cassidy nodded toward him. He'd resumed skinform, though his suit was now crumpled and shredded. Even the damp spots did nothing to lessen the impressiveness of his physique. She allowed her wolf to shift away from the outer parts of her skin, leaving it sticking to her clothing as the fluids of her transformation had nowhere to go. The wolf was happy to leave. They'd made their point, and the wolf would be waiting in case anything untoward happened, but she seemed convinced that the threat wouldn't come from Hammer.

"Can we actually talk now?" Cassidy asked. She stepped away from the embrace of her pack, but not before realizing that her hand was being held and not by Luther or Naomi. She spared a glance to the side as Snow relaxed her grip and withdrew.

"Of course." Hammer gestured to the edge of the room to the large booths that ringed it. "You choose."

Cassidy strode to the nearest booth. The table would have comfortably seated ten humans. Hammer alone took up enough space for two, but there was still plenty of room for each of their groups to occupy a side. One of his wolven slid in first, then he followed, leaving the other two to take up the side between him and the booth's opening.

Her wolven hesitated as they moved to fill in. After a few moments, Cassidy inclined her head to Snow, indicating she should be the one deepest in the booth. It was the most protected position, if somewhat limited. Snow looked her in the eyes for a second, then slid in without comment. Cassidy mirrored Hammer's position across the table, with Naomi to her left and Luther taking up the most vulnerable spot on the end.

"That was a nice trick," Hammer said. "I should have known any successor to Velvet would be as canny as he was."

Cassidy shrugged. It didn't seem quite safe to take his compliment at face value. "Let's get to why we're here."

"And why are we here?" Hammer asked. "I got your message. Velvet used to send Raquel when he wanted to meet. Is she…"

"MacTavish took her out," Luther said quietly. "She died when he took over."

"Ah." He lowered his head, and his scent took on a hint of sadness. "I'm sorry to hear that. We howled for your losses when we heard of them."

"But you made no effort to reach out to us," Naomi said accusingly.

Cassidy placed a hand on Naomi's arm.

One of Hammer's wolven spoke up. "A lot happened, and we didn't recognize the one who came out on top." She was a short woman, even seated. Tan skin and long black hair marked her as Latina. Her cheeks were round with dimples that looked like they saw regular use, but her brown eyes were hard. "MacTavish was no longer a threat, but we didn't know who this Five Moons was. Was she one of the rogue Alpha's, and if not, where did she come from?"

"MacTavish had nothing on me," Cassidy said. "I never met him, though he was responsible for me becoming wolven."

Luther nodded. "He set his dogs on her."

"And then we took care of him." Naomi grinned.

"No one reached out to us," Hammer said.

"That's my fault," Cassidy said. She took a deep breath to keep her cheeks from turning red with embarrassment. There were reasons she wasn't on top of wolven tradition, Snow had made that clear. It didn't help the feeling of failure as she was forced to reckon with her shortcomings to strangers. "I didn't know what the lines of communication were like or even that they existed. I've been trying to keep the pack together since I took over from MacTavish."

"There are others who should have known," the female Wolven said.

"Briella." Hammer shook his head, and she subsided. "I'm glad you've reached out now. You've recently lost pack members as well, I take it."

Cassidy nodded. "Two. They just didn't come home from their jobs. Disappeared within a couple of weeks of each other. Harold was near the end of January. Blair only a few days ago."

The South Shore wolven looked at each other. "We lost Arabella on February first," the other female wolven said.

The male wolven nodded. "Marquis went a couple weeks before that."

"That's getting pretty close to one a week," Snow said quietly. "There are a few gaps. I wonder how the other area packs are faring?"

"I don't know," Hammer said. "I haven't heard from the Gary pack for a bit. They reach out on occasion, but it's been since before Christmas."

"Is that unusual?" Cassidy asked.

"Getting there. We usually get together every month or two." Hammer plucked at his lower lip.

Snow leaned forward, not meeting anyone's eyes as usual. "I've heard of disappearances from other packs over the past six months. Those I know of firsthand are in Los Angeles and Portland. I've heard through others that wolven in Texas have gone missing. A bunch of them, by the sound of it. Some in Georgia and New York, as well. But that's all secondhand."

"So why is it only happening here now?" Briella asked. "That doesn't make any sense."

"We lost a bunch of wolven here too," Luther said. "Only ours weren't picked off one at a time. MacTavish was responsible for us losing half the pack. More, if you count his wolven."

Cassidy drummed her fingers on the table. "Is it possible the events are related?" There was a pattern here, there had to be. "What happened to the packs in those other cities, Snow?"

The lone wolf shrugged. "Atlanta apparently pulled together after a bit. The trouble almost set the packs in New York to warring, but they managed to get their differences handled. LA and Portland clamped down hard, like North Side is doing. No one goes out by themselves, or at least they still weren't when I left the West Coast. That was a few weeks ago, so things could have changed." She sighed. "Dallas was the epicenter for things going off the rails in Texas. They came to all-out war between the packs of Dallas and those of the suburbs. Then it spread to other cities as allied packs got involved. That started this past summer. Last I heard, it had gotten a bit better, but not before a lot of blood was shed. The situation is still unsettled."

Hammer leaned forward and drove his finger into the table. "How much more do the vamps know about this?"

"I passed on some," Snow said. "Carla didn't seem very surprised."

How could Snow tell that? Cassidy filed the question away for later. "So there's more to be gotten there. I bet the price for that information will be steep."

Hammer's face didn't change, but Cassidy could smell the disgust on him. "I'm willing to pay some of the price, but South Shore won't take on the whole burden."

Cassidy closed her eyes. The idea of giving up blood to Carla was terrifying, if strangely exhilarating. She'd been hoping to save that bargaining chip to find out more about what might be going on with Mary and Ruri, but the bigger picture here was only getting more alarming and muddled. She had to trust that wherever her sister and Ruri were they would be fine. Neither was defenseless, and as long as the tiny point of light that represented Ruri continued to shine in her mind's eye, then she had to do what she could for those who depended on her here.

"I'll take on North Side's portion," Luther said as the silence stretched on.

Cassidy shook her head. "Out of the question. It's my burden to bear."

"You can designate someone else to take it," Naomi said quietly.

"We'll talk about this later." Cassidy leaned forward, staring straight into Hammer's eyes. "We should get the other Alphas together. I don't want to sit on this."

"Agreed," Hammer said. "We don't need a repeat of what happened in Texas."

"We sure don't." Cassidy looked around the table, meeting the gaze of anyone who would look up. "To that end, I'm prepared to pledge that my pack will stick to its own boundaries and to unclaimed territory. Until whatever is going on is over, we won't be expanding our territory." She ended up holding Hammer's gaze again. "Will you promise the same?"

"If we can get the other Alphas to think about standing down on expansion, then South Shore will agree." He looked back at her, his scent steady, showing no signs of doubt. His Beta, or so Cassidy assumed her to be, smelled less certain.

"So we agree not to try anything in each other's territories while we get the local Alphas together," Cassidy said. She kept half an eye on Briella, to gauge her reaction. "We find out what we can from the vampires, share it with the other Alphas, and come up with a plan everyone can agree on."

"That seems reasonable," Hammer said. "I'll reach out to the packs in Gary and Joliet."

"And we'll do…" Cassidy looked over at Naomi and Luther for help.

"There's a small pack in Kenosha," Naomi said.

"And one that's pretty established in Aurora." Luther raised one eyebrow. "How far afield do we want to go with this? Peoria used to have a pack, but I haven't heard anything from them for a few decades. Indianapolis definitely has wolven, so does St. Louis."

"Don't forget Milwaukee and the Twin Cities," Naomi said.

"Ugh, this would be so much easier if there was an Alpha group text or something," Cassidy said. How far from Chicago did it make sense to go? The more packs they pulled in, the safer they'd all be, as far as numbers went. Her wolf bristled at the idea of interacting with so many other Alphas. Cassidy couldn't disagree with the sentiment.

"Group text." Hammer laughed, his teeth flashing white against his dark skin. "You're lucky to find an Alpha who will give you their email address."

"What's your email?" Cassidy asked. It would be better than nothing.

The male wolven in the booth's corner snickered.

"I don't have one," Hammer said with great dignity. "If you really want to get hold of me that way, you can have Rocky's." He jerked a thumb at the wolven who had just laughed.

"Is telegraph more your speed?" Cassidy asked.

"It's a good thing wolven don't get upset about age jokes," he replied.

"So carrier pigeon, then." Cassidy couldn't help needling the other Alpha. The adrenaline from their fight hadn't completely subsided, and the flash of irritation across his face and through his scent was extremely satisfying.

"I think we have a decent plan," Hammer said. He slid out of the booth, forcing his wolven to move out of his way. "We get the other Alphas of the named packs—"

"If they'll come," Briella said.

"If they'll come." Hammer smoothed the front of his shirt. "Two weeks?"

Cassidy looked over at Luther, who nodded. "Two weeks. Here?"

"No," Hammer said. He raised his gaze to the catwalk. There was a flicker of movement as someone drew away from the edge and into the deepest shadows where Cassidy couldn't make them out. Her wolf growled at the intrusion, and Cassidy snarled in agreement. The deal with Carla had been for a private meeting.

"Point taken." Cassidy waved a hand at Naomi and Luther. They slid out of their side of the booth with alacrity. "Then where?"

"Email Rocky," Hammer said. "The less said here, the better."

The wolven slid a piece of paper across the table to Snow.

Cassidy nodded and stepped toward the other Alpha. "It was good to meet you, Hammer."

"Likewise," he said. "I'm pleased to find out the North Side Pack isn't in terrible hands."

"And I'm glad to open lines of communication with an Alpha who isn't too frightened of technology to use it to his advantage." Not that email was cutting edge, but it was better than running back and forth across the city. Were they going to have to do the physical showdown thing every time they met? That had implications for their big Alpha meetup.

"Desperate times," Hammer said. He inclined his head, then swiftly left the room, the rest of his wolven on his heels.

Cassidy stared up at the walkway that overlooked the room.

"Do I take it up with Carla?" she asked her own wolven.

"It is a breach of the agreement," Luther said. "We can't afford to look weak to her."

"She should be willing to scale back on the favor she's going to ask of you," Naomi pointed out.

Snow didn't look at them. "Or you could barter this into getting some information," she said.

"More information." Cassidy narrowed her eyes at the shadows. "I like the sound of that."

CHAPTER FIFTEEN

Cassidy finished off a second bag of beef jerky in the passenger seat as Snow drove them down the interstate. Luther and Naomi sat in the back of her van, side by side on the narrow bed she slept in whenever she wasn't crashing with one pack or another.

"What is it?" Cassidy asked. "You keep looking at me." She licked her fingers of whatever dried meat flavor was left and stuffed the empty bag into her pocket.

"Did Carla have anything to add?" There had been no sign of vampire bites on the Alpha when she'd emerged from her office. Not that there necessarily would have been. Their kind healed so quickly that anything less than a major injury could have been gone in minutes. Her clothing showed no sign of blood, so it was possible that she'd managed to keep Carla's fangs out of her skin.

"Nothing helpful." Cassidy slapped the dashboard in frustration. "She likes to hint and hint, but when I pushed her on where Mary and Ruri might be, she had nothing. Not a damn thing."

"Vamps are good at that." Snow stared out the windshield at the Chicago skyline passing on their right. "At least you were able to pin her down. Was she alone this time?"

"I didn't see anyone behind the screen, but I couldn't come up with a good reason to justify checking."

"Stuffy in here." Snow cranked down the window on her side. The night air thundered in. She leaned over toward Cassidy. "You're the Alpha of a local pack who had their meeting crashed on her watch," Snow said quietly. "Learn to flex that. First off, you're Alpha. Second, she owed you. *Owes* you."

Cassidy closed her eyes. The scent of her disappointment assaulted Snow's nostrils. Beneath it was a layer of frustration.

"You'll get there," Snow said. "I thought you handled yourself pretty well with Hammer, all things considered."

Cassidy's grin was crooked and didn't quite reach her eyes. "All those group projects in college were good for something after all."

"Whatever it was, hold on to that. We have a plan now."

"Yeah." Cassidy pinched the bridge of her nose. "And all I have to do is face down another four Alphas."

"You took care of Hammer perfectly. Taking him down was the quickest way to his respect, but you also proved you could think on your feet. He appreciates that."

"You think so?" Cassidy's cheeks reddened slightly. She seemed starved for approval. Still, it couldn't hurt to give it.

"I do. It was a good move."

"Thanks." Cassidy reached over and patted Snow on the arm, then left her hand there.

Snow looked down at it for a second, then focused on the road again. The contact felt good. She liked the weight of it, the warmth of skin on skin. The only thing better than that was fur on fur. But that was where Snow's interest in touch ended.

"Is this not okay?" Cassidy squeezed her arm gently.

"It's fine." The reassurance was a little too loud to be completely believable. "I don't mind," Snow repeated more quietly. She didn't. It was the implication that bothered her. What else would the Alpha want from her? Still, there was no denying how good it felt to be connected to one of her kind by touch, especially one she was coming to admire.

"Good." Cassidy shifted along the bench seat and settled down next to Snow. She closed her eyes and let out a long sigh. The tension drained from her body.

Snow lifted an arm, letting the Alpha snuggle in against her side, then settled it over her. They were going to have to talk. Until then, she would enjoy the opportunity for some uncomplicated touch.

* * *

Cassidy woke when the old van came to a stop. While the sound of the motor had been on the loud side, it had also been strangely soothing. Even more comforting had been Snow's presence and the arm she'd casually put around her. It wasn't often that she felt protected by one of her wolven. They looked to her for safety and reassurance, but who did Cassidy have at her back? It had been nice to set aside the weight of everyone else's burdens and expectations. It was no surprise that she'd fallen asleep.

She reached out for Snow, but the lone wolf already had the door open. She slid her arm out from around Cassidy and hopped out of the vehicle. The adrenaline from the confrontation with Hammer had settled into a very different type of excitement. The sun's rays caught Snow, outlining her dark skin in gold against the blue sky. Sunlight played through the coiling twists of her hair, taking Cassidy's breath away. A twist of arousal coiled through her gut.

Luther and Naomi had pushed their way out the side door and were already halfway to the hotel's back entrance. Snow wasn't far behind them.

"Hold up," Cassidy said, pitching her voice so it would reach Snow's ears only.

"What is it?" Snow turned in place but kept walking backward toward the den.

"Wait for me." Cassidy jogged up next to her and linked her arm through Snow's.

The lone wolf stiffened for a second, then relaxed.

"Is this all right?" They'd been so cozy in the van. Cassidy had assumed Snow would be receptive.

"This is fine." Snow smiled, but it didn't quite reach her eyes. "Nice even."

"But?"

"But." Snow sighed. "Let's go up to your rooms."

"All right." When Cassidy tried to draw back her arm, Snow held it against her body. It wasn't tight enough to trap it, but enough to indicate she didn't want to let go.

The lone wolf didn't smell disgusted or upset, though her scent was a swirl of conflicting colors. The best Cassidy could make out was that Snow was sad, but there were also currents of anger and contentment. The mix was so odd, she kept expecting to be overtaken by a sneeze, but none was forthcoming. Her wolf was no help. Like Cassidy, the wolf needed release, but she didn't seem overly concerned about the turmoil of Snow's emotional state. In her opinion, if Snow wasn't interested in mating, there were others who would be.

The stairs forced them to disengage. Wolven might be quicker and better coordinated than humans, but mounting stairs arm in arm was still going to be a challenge.

"Race you," Cassidy said and bounded ahead, taking the stairs two or three at a time, depending on how much momentum she'd managed to gain. Snow's steps echoed up the stairs behind her. She was more or less keeping pace with Cassidy but was making no real attempt to catch her. Cassidy grinned. She liked to win, and it looked like she was going to. It wouldn't be the same triumph she'd felt when she dumped Hammer on his ass, but it would still feel good.

Sure enough, she was the first one to the top of the stairs. Her breath came in short, happy pants.

"I won," she announced a couple of seconds later when Snow joined her.

"I'm very happy for you," Snow said gravely.

"Don't even try to suck all the fun out of this," Cassidy said. She pushed on the door to her rooms. "I'm enjoying my victory, and you can't do anything to stop me."

"Is that so?" Snow's quirked eyebrow spoke volumes.

"It is." Cassidy flopped down onto the couch. "I don't want to know that you weren't trying." She patted the cushion next to her.

"Then I won't tell you that." Snow sat down carefully at the couch's far end.

"Thank you." Cassidy stretched out toward Snow, worming around so that her head was next to the other wolven's leg. She made sure not to touch her. "So what's going on? What's with your but?"

"My butt?" Snow looked behind herself.

"Not your behind. Not that there's anything wrong with it. You have quite a nice butt, I've noticed. But we were going to talk about your other but. Not your sitting-on one. Oh god, I'm babbling." Cassidy clamped her mouth shut.

"A little bit, but that's all right." Snow closed her eyes and took a deep breath. "Cassidy. Alpha. I appreciate your interest in me, but I…" She gripped her hands together tightly in her lap. "I can't be with you that way."

"Oh." Cassidy sat up. "You're into guys. I understand. I mostly am too, but since being turned, I'm a little less discriminating. When I was human, I was like ninety percent straight, but now it's closer to seventy-five percent."

"You're bi. I get it. I'm not straight, Cassidy. I'm not really anything."

"Wouldn't that make you bi? Or pan maybe?" She didn't really think of herself as bi, though she supposed technically she was. Mostly she thought of herself as interested in men, but willing to be distracted by women.

"I don't like sex," Snow said. "I have no physical sexual desire to speak of."

"Oh, so you're ace." Cassidy mulled the idea around. "I have a friend at school who is demisexual. Well, they're more of an acquaintance, really. We don't hang out much. Didn't hang out much." She wasn't in college anymore. One of these days she might even remember that.

"I'm familiar with the term, and that's not quite me. There's no halfway to my feelings about sex. The idea of *that* with someone else really doesn't do it for me. I am firmly on the asexual side of things."

"How does that work with the wolven? I swear we're even more highly sexed than humans, and I was in college less than six months ago. Half the people I knew were ready to sleep with anyone who showed any interest."

"It doesn't, at least not very well." Snow's face was so devoid of emotion that it was nearly blank, but sadness wafted off her in a blue cloud. "It's one of the reasons I don't settle down with any pack for long. Sooner or later, someone makes a move." She half-smiled in Cassidy's direction. "Sometimes they take getting turned down well, and sometimes they try to convince me that they're the one who can suddenly make me like this thing that I'm aggressively indifferent toward."

"Oh god." Cassidy scooted back to the far side of the couch. "I would never do that." Shame filled her at the thought that Snow could think she might push herself on anyone like that, especially the lone wolf. "I never meant to make you feel like you had to defend yourself from me. I didn't realize…"

"It's just…" Snow reached out toward her. "I don't like sex, but I do like being with somebody. I miss having someone to hold and who will hold me. Most wolven can't do that without sex getting in the way."

The sadness emanating from her crested close to despair. Cassidy reached out and grabbed her hand, holding it tight.

"I would never," Cassidy said. "I'm happy to have you as a friend. I don't have anyone like that here. Everyone either looks to me to take care of them or wants to mate, then be done. I like what we've had over the past few days. It's weird, but I don't think I've become such good friends with someone since I was a kid. I'm sorry I thought that meant something else was going on."

"I like this." Snow squeezed her hand. "I even liked having my arm around you in the car. But I can't give you anything more."

"That's all right." Cassidy squeezed back. "I like having you around, and this means more to me than a quick roll in bed could." Now that the talk was out of the way and her shame was starting to diminish, her wolf reminded her of the tension that still twisted in their guts. It hadn't gone away, it had only become less important for a time.

"You do need that roll with someone though," Snow said.

Cassidy's cheeks heated. "A little bit. Would you be okay hanging out until I come back? We have some things to discuss, plans to set in motion, and I'd like your take on them."

Snow looked around the room. "If you're sure. I don't want to impose. I'm not one of your pack."

"I'm sure." Cassidy grinned despite the lurch her stomach gave when Snow disavowed any attachment to her. "I'm happy to have you in my home."

"Then go." Snow gave her hand one more squeeze, then shooed her toward the door. "I'll be right here."

"I'm glad to hear it," Cassidy said. The promise loosened the tightness within her. Something about the words made her want to grin as widely as she could. Her wolf stirred approvingly beneath her skin, demanding to feel Snow's touch. Cassidy indulged her briefly by running her hand up Snow's arm in a caress she hoped came off as companionably as she meant it. "See you in a few."

CHAPTER SIXTEEN

The room felt much larger without Cassidy in it. As was the case with so many Alphas, her presence had a tendency to fill places. Her smell permeated the space, however, so it was impossible to feel like she was gone completely.

The conversation had gone reasonably well, which was surprising. So often, whenever Snow would open herself to someone who was interested in her in ways she knew she couldn't reciprocate, everything fell apart after she let her wishes be known. It was early, though. There was still plenty of time for Cassidy to decide she would be the one to win Snow over.

She flopped back onto the couch, letting Cassidy's scent wash over her. More than anything else, she wanted someone to be close to. She had her wolf, and that was often enough, but how often had she laid awake at night, missing the company of someone she could trust next to her as they slept?

Wolven were especially bad at separating sex and romance. She liked the closeness that came with a romantic relationship, up until that closeness threatened to become more.

Maybe Cassidy would be different. She laughed out loud at the thought. *Maybe* hadn't worked out well for her so far. It would be better to keep her firmly on the side of friendship. When they wrapped up whatever was going on in Chicago, Snow would move on, and Five Moons would become one more in the long line of friends she'd made in different packs across the Western and Midwestern states. She would be someone to drop in on when Snow was around, but any touch would be accidental and glancing. It would have to continue to be enough.

Her eyes filled with tears as she allowed Dean's absence to fill her. She'd had two people she'd been able to share the bonds of touch with. Mama had been killed at the hands of her own pack during a shift in leadership. As Beta to the old guard for an Alpha not interested in descending into rum-running, Mama had come out second best when a challenger had come for the old wolf. Dean had been so young still, nowhere near old enough to ask her to initiate the change. In her memory's eye, the gap where his front teeth had fallen out was gone, but he'd had the too-large adult teeth which looked out of place next to his remaining baby teeth.

They'd been out of the way, overlooking the large warehouse room from a balcony. Snow had made sure Dean was far enough from the edge that he couldn't see what was going on, but she hadn't been able to resist watching. Her wolf had pushed her, insisting that they needed to know who their new enemies were, even if they were the same packmates who had looked out for them as recently as that morning. She and her wolf had watched the Alpha go down. Their mama hadn't lasted much longer beyond that. Her eyes, brilliant and white had met hers above the muzzle of the wolven who was ripping out her throat.

She'd scooped Dean up and scrambled out a window and onto the roof. They'd scampered across hot corrugated iron, then down the side of the building. They hadn't stopped for their possessions but had headed straight for the docks along the river. Stowing away on a barge heading north had been easier than she'd expected. There were times when she deeply regretted that they hadn't had the time to grab something of their mama's, a blanket or a sweater. Something that would retain her aroma for a long time.

Snow couldn't remember how Mama smelled. Her memory of Dean's scent was also fading. The same couldn't be said for the remembered warmth of his arms around her as they slept. That she could bring to mind whenever she pleased. How much longer would that memory last once she lost what he'd smelled like? She would have to see if anyone had held on to any of his things. From what she'd been told of MacTavish's takeover, that seemed unlikely, but it was certainly worth the effort of checking.

Wallowing in her own maudlin thoughts wasn't going to change anything. Snow pushed herself up from the couch. Mama and Dean weren't going to come back just because she missed them. Five Moons would be back when she was done with whatever worked to get that arousal out of her system. The opportunity to poke around the North Side Alpha's space was one she should take advantage of now.

Most wolven didn't keep as much as most humans did, but they weren't immune to the habit of collecting items. They might spend part of their time in wolf bodies, but their human sides still needed practical things like can openers and pants. Other items would be sentimental. Those were what Snow was hoping to find.

She started with the low shelves on the edge of the living room. There were some books on them, college-related by the look of them. Five Moons had picked up a lot of textbooks in her time in university. There were books in French also. Snow didn't speak that language, but she could recognize it. The effect was a strange mishmash of topics. Books on economic theory shared shelves with coffee-table books of fashion plates. The French books got their own shelf. Sprinkled among them were a few history and English short story collections.

What had Five Moons been studying? Nothing here seemed connected with doing field work in Honduras. Not that Snow was one to turn her nose up at a varied academic career. She'd been auditing classes at colleges and universities all over North America for decades. Her own interests ran the gamut from folklore to genetics. Maybe Cassidy also had problems focusing on only one area of interest.

A plastic and cloth fern graced the top of one of the bookcases. It would have been reasonably convincing, except for the dust and the fact that it didn't have the green smell that Snow associated with plants. It was an odd thing to hold on to.

The kitchen area held an assortment of pots and pans. It looks like Five Moons used the skillet most often. The saucepans were shiny and bright in contrast to the scratches and dings on the frying pan. The fridge was mostly bare, except for some soft drinks. That made a certain amount of sense. Dean's wolven had dined together when they hadn't gone out for a hunt as a group. Members of the pack took turns preparing food.

A small dining area was mostly untouched. Five Moons had a table and chairs in there, but the tabletop was quite dusty. A painting hung on the back wall. It showed a church under a sunny sky. She hadn't noticed that Five Moons was particularly religious. Wolvenborn tended not to be so much, but some of those who were changed as adults held fast to those beliefs. There were exceptions, to be sure. One of the packs Snow had spent time with in the Navajo Nation held quite strongly to the customs and traditions of the humans on the reservation. She'd spent a long time with them. Their pack structure had been subtly different from that which usually came about in other North American packs.

Her time there had ended like it had in so many places, however. Someone had gotten too close and pressed for more than she could offer, and she'd left rather than deal with the inevitable conflict and fallout that would follow.

There wasn't much else to snoop through in the common areas of Five Moons' rooms. All that was left was her bedroom and bathroom. Snow hovered in the doorway. If she'd been a member of the pack, spending time in the Alpha's rooms without her wouldn't have been much to comment on. Or at least it wouldn't be in a more functional pack. Wolven liked to spend time with their Alpha. That Five Moons had set herself up here, alone, had concerning implications for how integrated she was with her packmates.

Five Moons' scent was stronger out in the living room, and there lurked the scents of other wolven as well. It wasn't like she'd cut herself off completely, so there was hope.

Snow lingered a little longer as she took in the bedroom. A massive king-sized bed took up much of the space. An old dresser was crammed up against one wall next to a small pile of discarded laundry. Her wolf urged her to head over there and bury their nose in one of Cassidy's—no, Five Moons'—shirts. Snow shook her head. Five Moons was a friend. She wouldn't entertain the notion that somehow this wolven could be different from all the others and allow them to have that closeness without crossing Snow's boundaries. Smothering themselves in her smell would blur the line between friendship and relationship, and she wasn't going there again.

The wolf whined but didn't press her. She didn't care for sex any more than Snow did. Their heat was a monthly occurrence that was tolerated, a set of physical motions they went through on their own to release the uncomfortable pressure to mate, and then it was over. That didn't mean the wolf didn't also miss the touch of a close companion.

As she dithered in the doorway, the door to the hall opened behind her, and Five Moons stepped through. The reek of sex came through the door with her.

Snow wrinkled her nose. "Better now?"

"So much." Five Moons shook her head. "I was about ready to peel my own skin off. Thanks for sticking around."

"No problem." The opportunity to look around had been a good one. If Snow hadn't spent a bunch of time in her own head, she probably could have scoped out the bedroom too. Hopefully, she would have another opportunity.

Five Moons crossed to the kitchen and pulled open the refrigerator. "So what did you think of our meeting with Hammer and his folks?"

"It went well enough," Snow said. "I have concerns about the direction the situation is headed given what I've seen and heard from around the country. I thought maybe Chicago wasn't going to have the problems the others have had, but it seems you're not immune. Your troubles seem to have started off differently."

"Do you really think MacTavish was part of a larger pattern?"

"Could be." Snow shrugged. "We need to talk to the other Alphas, find out if they've had anyone disappear or a takeover attempt."

"I wish Mary was here." Five Moons opened an orange soda with one hand while pushing the fridge door closed with the other. She leaned against the counter and took a long pull from the can.

Snow cocked her head. "Do you think the government is involved?"

It was Five Moons' turn to shrug. "Maybe. If my sister was here, she could touch base with the other Hunters and find out what's going on in their cities."

"What other cities are they in?"

"I have no idea. Mary doesn't talk about her job much. Like not at all, unless I really press her for it." The smell of annoyance prickled Snow's nostrils. "It's not like I'm asking her to give up state secrets. All I want is to know more about how she interacts with us and what the other supernatural creatures are like." Five Moons sighed, then continued more quietly, "And how many of us she's killed. And what she'd do if she got orders to take out me or a member of the North Side Pack."

"That's a hell of a conflict of interest," Snow said. "Do you know who the Hunters even work for? I've heard it's the CIA."

"Some flavor of Fed, that's all I know. I met one of the other Hunters once." Cassidy shuddered. "She was intense. Unpleasant too. Mary didn't get along with her for the most part. They worked together long enough to take down MacTavish."

"I thought you did that."

"No. We, that's me, Ruri, and the rest of the pack who escaped the takeover, we came at MacTavish's 'pack' while he and some of his wolven were lured into Mary and Stiletto's trap."

"I see." Snow blinked. That wasn't what she'd expected. "What about talking to Stiletto?"

"Not without a Ouija board." Five Moons' lips twisted into a humorless grin. "She didn't survive taking out MacTavish and his dogs."

"So Hunters aren't invincible. That's good to know."

"Mary doesn't need to be taken out," Five Moons said. "She wouldn't attack us. I'm pretty sure."

"Pretty sure isn't a hundred percent certain."

"If she attacks us, I'll fight her myself, but I don't think it'll come to that."

"If you say so."

Five Moons nodded decisively. A faint glow emanated from each eye, one crimson, the other electric blue. "I do."

"So we have nowhere to go for extra intel, except the vamps," Snow said. "We have a meeting with the local Alphas in a couple of weeks. Carla wasn't helpful on the information about your sister front. Did she have anything else to offer?"

"No." Five Moons shook her head, her shoulders slumping a bit. "I wish I'd thought to take you with me. It was all I could do to keep from letting Carla take my blood. She's very appealing and not at all my type. That didn't seem to matter, though."

"You are Alpha." Snow would keep repeating the phrase until Cassidy understood what it meant. "You don't ask permission, not from those outside the pack." Bad Alphas didn't ask permission within the pack either, but Snow would be damned if she allowed Five Moons to become one of those. "Carla can't roll me like she does those of you who are more interested in...matters of the flesh. Start thinking strategically. Those in your pack are resources for you. Learn to use them."

"Does that include you?"

"I'm just here as a favor." Snow grinned. "You can ask me if you need help, but I'm not going to feel bound to help you."

"So I need to keep being nice." Five Moons shared her smile. "Got it."

"So, back to thinking strategically. Where are we going to meet with the other packs?"

CHAPTER SEVENTEEN

The next week passed with little drama. Cassidy made sure to model good behavior and never left the North Side Pack's den without being accompanied by another wolven. That her companion was usually Snow didn't seem to raise too many eyebrows. Even Luther had few objections. She made sure to spread the time she was in the hotel among her wolven, making sure no one felt neglected.

When she did leave the den, it was to continue the search for their missing packmates. Snow's assistance was invaluable when it came to new ideas of where to look. After Blair's scent had completely dissipated near the gas station where she'd worked, Cassidy scoped out lone wolf hangouts within the city. When those didn't pan out, she gave the area around Faint a strong once-over, searching for any sign of Blair's or Harold's scents.

In desperation, she'd also checked out unclaimed land outside some of the other Chicago-area packs' territories. With every search, she was careful not to come in contact with other wolven or to cross over into their turf. She didn't need to start an incident. If she'd had any lines of communication with the packs, things would have been easier. Once she'd met up with the other Alphas, she would be certain to keep in contact, but to seek them out before their meeting felt premature.

Closer to home, she'd started building a roster of tasks that would keep the pack safer and more fulfilled. It was a task she'd been dreading, but Snow helped her through the worst of it. As she spoke to her wolves and delved into the many talents they brought to the pack, she was becoming more comfortable with her role. It helped to understand that being Alpha didn't mean she had to be everything for all members of the pack. That one had taken a little while to permeate, but with Snow's gentle if determined insistence on getting the concept through her skull, she was starting to feel like she'd made a breakthrough.

Looking at the pack like a group project had been Snow's idea, and it was starting to pay off, as long as she didn't think too much about the consequences of failure. She couldn't deny that it was easier to keep all the pieces and parts of maintaining a pack going when there were more to spread the burden among.

It was also nice to get away from the responsibility and expectation every now and again. Threading her way through the narrow green space along the Chicago River definitely wasn't the best way to do so, but it helped. She would have preferred an open lope through one of the larger parks, but she didn't dare be so far from her pack, not in the troubling times they found themselves. Graceland Cemetery might have been an option, but not for a few hours yet. The grounds were too open for anything but an extremely late-night jaunt. The slightest bit of daylight could mean being discovered, even if it was only the remaining slivers of light that accompanied the currently setting sun.

Her wolf yawned, levering their jaws wide and popping their eardrums. Now was not the time to be dwelling on what could be or might be. There was small game to be had here, and the wolf preferred they spend their energy tracking the rabbit they'd scented a while back rather than in worrying about things that may or may not come to pass.

Cassidy agreed. It was the reason they were out for a run and not back at the hotel, after all, but she was finding it difficult not to dwell.

The pale form of Snow's wolf materialized out of the bushes and slid past them, giving them a quick bump of the shoulder. She looked back at them, her tongue lolling from the side of her mouth and her eyes sparkling in the dim light.

Cassidy and the wolf sprang after her. Snow was so much more willing to play in furform than in skinform. Cassidy's wolf had made it known to Cassidy that she liked having Snow around. The wolf relaxed around her in a way she didn't around most of the others, not even

Naomi or Luther. Cassidy didn't disagree, but she was trying to be respectful of Snow's boundaries. It was difficult, more so in skinform. The same rules didn't seem to apply when their wolves were in full ascendance.

Snow grinned, then disappeared into the tall grasses that opened in front of them. This late into winter, the blades that stuck through the snow were brown and withered. For a wolf whose fur was so light, that was to Snow's benefit and she took full advantage. Cassidy growled as she dived into the grass behind her. Snow's scent danced its way between grassy hummocks, tantalizing her and teasing her onward. The scent of rabbit forgotten along with the cares of being Alpha to a struggling pack, Cassidy and her wolf gave chase.

The wind whistled past them, carrying the scent of snow and river water mostly covered with ice. The faintest hint of mold lingered on the breeze. They'd had a few warmer days, and the sun had melted the snow down to the ground in a number of places. It had gotten warm enough for decomposition to start in the underbrush. They sniffed the air, their ears pricked forward at the promise of warmer days to come. They weren't too cold now, but it was reassuring to know that winter never lasted forever.

It was as close as the wolf got to acknowledging the future. Cassidy wondered if that was why the wolven seemed so ageless. Was it something about the wolf within each of them that allowed them to simply ignore the passage of time? The thought was as soothing as it was terrifying. The moment she was in was pretty awful, with someone pulling and tugging at the pack and its borders and her sister having disappeared. If she didn't know it would one day end, how could she get through it?

Warm amusement filled her. A flash of a mouth agape in a canine grin, tongue lolling flashed into her head, then was gone. Winter wasn't only a season, her wolf seemed to say. It was also a state. One could always look forward to winter ending.

Their shoulders eased, the tension that had filled them evaporating as Cassidy considered the wolf's explanation. There was value in looking forward, but not at the expense of where you were at the moment.

It was all very New Age, but also comforting. Cassidy allowed herself to drop back into the wolf's state of mind. Their body moved under the direction of one mind, of one heart.

The stretch of grassy area along the river ended at a chain-link fence. Snow's scent followed along it, then continued. The wolf stuck their nose under the fence and lifted up. The fencing shifted out of their way. Someone had cut through the links to get to the larger area of trees and shrubs beyond. In summer, they might have happened upon a tent or two as the city's homeless population braved the elements, but those largely disappeared in colder months, or so Luther had told Cassidy.

They hurdled a downed tree and bounded around its stump. A scent floated in front of them, grey with decay, but recent. The wolf shifted toward it, homing in on the scent trace like a laser. There might be some good meat left on whatever carcass that was from. Scavenging had turned Cassidy's stomach the first few times the wolf had indulged, but no longer. They were merely stopping for an easy meal. It was like a fast-food cheeseburger. Maybe not the best meal you could get, but it filled your stomach nonetheless.

Snow must have had a similar instinct. Her scent led along the same path as that of the decay, a bright trail in contrast to the leaden pall of death.

As they wove their way through the underbrush, the trace intensified. It was a relatively recent death, but something about it wasn't right. Cassidy couldn't stop unease from prickling through her. They slowed from a lope to a walk. The way through was choked with young growth. The last bits of sunlight disappeared from the sky as they slipped between saplings and forced themselves through small branches that snapped easily to let them past. The noise they were making was disgraceful, but they couldn't let Snow's trail go cold. While it was never truly dark in the city, the shadows were growing denser as they pushed on.

They pulled themselves out from under a particularly bramble-laden patch and almost ran into the lone wolf. She was flattened along the ground, half under a less prickly bush. One ear twitched back at them, but she stayed facing forward.

They plopped down next to Snow, their head cocked in question.

An errant breeze brought another whiff of dead meat to them, but along with it was something else. It had been covered by the scent of death, of meat ripe for the taking.

They would not take this meat.

It was wolven.

A whine rose in the back of their throat as they sank to the cold ground, broken branches and dead plants prickling through their thick fur in places. The wolven had been dead for long enough that it no longer smelled fresh. Whatever or whoever had put it there was likely no longer around. Still, something that could take out even the weakest wolven would be a challenge to tangle with.

They had to see who it was, there was no question of that. With two of the pack missing, they had to know if it was one of theirs. A chill prickled along their spine, lifting the fur in its wake until it stood like a bristling mohawk.

It could be a lone wolf, yet another who had chosen not to announce themselves to Cassidy as tradition demanded. This was one reason why such conventions existed. How could they protect their people when they didn't know who was within their boundaries? The land on both sides of the river was claimed by the North Side Pack. They came through frequently on the way to and from their den. It was perfect for blowing off steam close to home.

They crawled forward, the twin aromas of wolven and death growing stronger in their nostrils and on their tongue. Snow followed at their heels, so close that her breath bathed the pads of their feet.

All they needed was a quick check to make sure the wolven wasn't Blair or Harold, then they could figure out what to do next.

The breezes played about them, cramming the smell of dead wolven deeper into their muzzle. No animals darted through the tangled briars and shrubs. Their previous lack of caution in chasing Snow had probably cleared out any small prey.

The way was slow, each step careful and precise. The chance that the killer was still around was slender, but not so slight as to be ignored. So they avoided dead branches and shriveled leaves to the best of their abilities. Keeping so close to the ground also allowed them to bypass the worst of the bushes. Thorns had to be very long to penetrate all the way to their hide, but they could and did snag on their fur. A shaking briar patch would give them away as surely as stepping on a dried stick.

It was farther to the carcass than they had expected. The body lay on top of packed snow, naked flesh having gone dark purple-grey and mottled from exposure and decay. The trees grew close, which had helped screen it from eyes along the river. Something had been snacking on it. Crows, probably.

They skirted the body as widely as they could, not wanting to intrude on its resting place, but needing to get a look at its face. This close, the wolven's scent should have been recognizable, but they couldn't place it. Hunkered as low as they could get, they slunk closer and closer, trying and mostly succeeding in watching both the remains and the ground.

Long dark hair splayed out from the head in twisted hanks. They shifted further to see beyond it. Their ears swiveled, listening for any sound that might indicate the killer was still around and had made them.

Nothing.

When the face came into view, Cassidy wanted to howl with relief. She didn't recognize the man. He wasn't one of hers. They kept their muzzle clamped on the exultation, which quickly turned to shame. There was no rejoicing to be had with the death of a wolven who had done nothing to her or hers.

There was work yet to be done. Someone had killed a wolven within her boundaries. If one of her wolven had done the deed and hadn't reported it, they would have a problem. If it was a loner... Well, that was a different problem, but it felt infinitely more solvable.

Hammer had lost wolven also. What if this one belonged to him?

CHAPTER EIGHTEEN

Snow kept close to Five Moons as they loped back to the den in the dark. The same wind that had brought the smell of dead wolven to them was clearing out her nostrils as they put more space between them and the body. The scent she caught from Five Moons was one of concern. Snow hadn't noticed any sign of recognition when they'd found the body, but the Alpha was spooked.

Compared to their leisurely trip up the river, the way back was much quicker. Snow made sure to stay as close to Five Moons' heels as she could manage. It was difficult. The other wolven was fast, and Snow couldn't shake the feeling that the Alpha was holding back so as not to lose her.

They burst out of the trees behind the hotel. The ground turned from earth to broken concrete; Snow's claws skidded on slick patches covered with dead leaves and snow. Five Moons widened the distance between them. Her legs started to stretch and distort between one stride and the next. By the time Five Moons hit the doors at a full sprint, she was in human form.

"I need Naomi and Luther," Five Moons hollered as she disappeared deeper into the hotel without bothering to stop for the clothing she'd left by the back door.

Snow shouldered her way through the doors and came to a full stop. A curious pack member stuck her head around the corner. When all she saw was Snow shuddering through her change, she withdrew. Whether it was a courtesy or not, Snow was grateful to shift without an audience. More than a hundred years was a long time to carry the shame of her weakness. It had been with her for so long that she'd come to accept it, like a despised packmate, one she couldn't abide, but that had been there for so long she couldn't conceive of life without it.

Her skin pebbled into instant gooseflesh when the last of her fur receded in a slow wave. The fluid on her skin cooled rapidly in the chill air from outside. She gave herself a hasty once-over with one of the towels that hung by the door for exactly that purpose, then wasted no time in shrugging into her clothing.

Snow kept her ears open as she mounted the back stairs. There were some sounds of movement down the halls. She put her shoulders back, carried her head high, and made no attempt to muffle the sound of her footsteps. The pack all knew her by now, though some made no effort to hide their suspicion of her.

No one came out of their rooms to check on her as she made her way to the stairs to the penthouse. She heard rustles as wolven moved behind doors, likely in response to her presence, but no one came out to confront her.

That wasn't surprising in itself. Five Moons was in a highly agitated state, and it was impossible that her pack couldn't sense it. She was worked up enough that Snow could dimly feel her concern, though she'd made it clear she had no desire to be a member of the North Side Pack. Five Moons had offered a few days ago. The offer had felt more like a formality than something she'd expected Snow to agree to. To her own surprise, Snow had considered it. Not for very long, to be certain, but that she'd paused at all before demurring had been unexpected.

We're fine on our own, Snow thought to the sister of her soul. She pushed open the door to the stairwell, then loped upward, taking the steps two at a time. In a few moments, she was at the open door to Five Moons' rooms. Luther's and Naomi's scents spilled out through the doorway.

Five Moons pulled a shirt over her head, then met Snow's eyes. "Good, you're here."

Snow steeled herself, then stepped into the room.

Luther looked over at her. "We've had some...interesting news from the Alpha," he said quietly. His scent had less anxiety to it than

Five Moons' and Naomi's. Tight anger was doing a lot to cover that stench.

"I didn't recognize the wolven," Snow said. "Was it one of yours?"

"Thankfully not."

"That's not good."

"Not good?" Luther glared at her. "How is not having lost one of our packmates not good?" His voice raised on the second question.

Snow's skin prickled as she became aware that every eye was on her. She looked up and met Five Moons' gaze from across the room.

"If it's not one of yours, and it's one of South Shore's, how are you going to tell Hammer?" Snow asked quietly.

"Do we tell him at all?" Naomi asked from one of the couches. She directed the question at the ceiling as if she was setting it free into the room.

Luther's face darkened. "If we want to continue to have him as an ally, we should."

"And if he thinks we did it?" Five Moons asked. "The easiest solution would be to pretend we never found it."

"The body won't stay undiscovered forever," Snow said. "With you as the one to let him know, you control how Hammer finds out. Besides, the dead wolven could have been a lone wolf. Or he may have belonged to one of the other local packs. Aurora Pack territory isn't so far."

"You're right," Five Moons said. She paced back and forth along the living room windows that overlooked downtown Chicago. The lights on the skyscrapers were barely visible through the dense clouds that had rolled in with dusk. "You're all right." She sighed. "We can't do anything without more information, and the best way to get it is to bring Hammer in. If the vampires are the ones to break this to South Shore, they'll lose all confidence in us."

"They might anyway," Naomi pointed out.

"That's true. But I have to believe that bringing them in on this is the only way we have of convincing them we're on the level."

"Whatever you're going to do, you need to do it soon," Snow said. "The longer we wait, the more chance that someone finds that poor wolven and lets him know."

Five Moons didn't answer. Instead she pulled out her phone and swiped the lock screen open. Everyone waited as she tapped at the screen for a minute, then she pocketed the device.

"I emailed our contact and told him to have Hammer call this number. Hopefully, they check their inbox regularly." She straightened up and looked Luther and Naomi in the eyes, before turning to watch Snow. "So what are our next steps?"

* * *

"We set a couple of our wolven to watch the body," Luther said. "I should be one of them."

Cassidy nodded. That made sense. "Who're you taking with you?"

"Bring Phoebe," Naomi said.

"Phoebe?" Luther raised an eyebrow. "She's a little timid, don't you think?"

"No one will see her unless she wants to be seen."

"Good call," Cassidy said. "Take her with you." She didn't know Phoebe very well. The wolven wasn't one who sought her out regularly. They'd mated once, during Phoebe's heat a month and a half ago, but that had been it. The wolven had left after Cassidy had fallen asleep.

"Yes, Alpha." Luther bowed his head then stood. "We'll go right away."

"Do that. Head south on the west side of the river. He's in that patch of scrub before the Damen Avenue Bridge."

Luther nodded, then slipped out the door.

"When Hammer gets back to me, I'm going to suggest that he and I head to where the body is."

Snow lifted her head. "It's your territory. You get to set how many of his pack he brings with him."

"Will he go for just himself?"

"Doubtful," Naomi said. "Would you go by yourself into his territory?"

Cassidy thought about that. It didn't seem very safe. Her wolf definitely didn't like the idea. "Probably not."

"I'm going to have more freedom to move between your territories," Snow said. "I'm no threat."

"You spend much more time here, that could change," Naomi said. She angled herself to watch Snow out of the corner of her eye. "You going to finally take the plunge and join us?"

"You don't have to answer that," Cassidy said. It would have been nice if the answer was yes, but she wanted Snow to get there on her own. Anything that smacked of coercion on Cassidy's part would probably scare Snow away for good. It was just like Naomi to be the one to ask the question. Cassidy liked Naomi and sought out her company on a regular basis, but the wolven had a way of pushing.

She was always looking for the weak spot, for the chink in someone's armor. It was one of the reasons Cassidy valued her counsel, but she couldn't let her guard all the way down around her. Not like she could with Snow.

"That's all right," Snow said.

When she didn't elaborate, Naomi turned her attention back to the ceiling. She chewed on her lower lip. Something was bothering her, which was probably why she was going after Snow like that.

The vibration of Cassidy's phone had both Snow and Naomi focusing on her again.

"That was fast," Cassidy said as she pulled out the phone. Her heart dropped as she took in the number glowing up at her from the phone's face. It wasn't an unidentified number as she'd been expecting. This one was all-too familiar. With its New York City area code, Cassidy knew it even better than her own. She also knew the woman's face that grinned up at her. She swiped her thumb across the lock screen to answer it.

"Mom," Cassidy said, lightening her voice so the concern didn't bleed through. "What's up?"

CHAPTER NINETEEN

"It's all gone."

Cassidy had to strain to make out her mom's quiet voice over the phone.

"All of her things." Sophia's voice gained in strength. "Who would take everything she owns?"

Mom was in town. Now. When everything was going wrong. Of course she was.

"Why are you wandering around Chicago at night?"

Naomi appeared at Cassidy's back. The warmth and tacit support helped. Cassidy took a long, deep breath. She reached up and behind, clasping the back of Naomi's neck, further grounding herself.

"Your sister's phone won't let me leave new messages. It stopped a few days ago. You can't do anything about it." Sophia's ragged laugh fluttered down the line. "God knows I tried."

Cassidy winced. "We can't leave you there by yourself, not in the dead of winter. Did you book a hotel?"

"I thought I'd stay at Mary Alice's place. I have keys. The one for the front door didn't work, but no one changed the back."

"I'm coming to get you," Cassidy said.

"How? You're in Honduras."

"I mean I'll find someone to get you." She glanced over at Snow, who was watching Cassidy's side of the conversation with raised eyebrows.

Snow hesitated for what felt like eternity before nodding. Discomfort rolled off her in a blue haze shot through with veins of sickly red.

"Okay." Sophia went silent.

"Are you still there? Mom?"

"Yes, I'm here. Why is this happening?"

"We can talk more when you're somewhere safer than a Chicago industrial district."

"Will you stay on the line until my ride gets here?"

The request was so quiet and shaky that Cassidy's chest felt like it was compressing in sympathy. She wanted to stay. The last thing in the world she wanted to do right that second was to hang up on her mom, but she had to. Hammer would be calling, or so she hoped. If she couldn't get that mess taken care of, there was the potential for so many people to get hurt. People who looked to her for protection. Her mom's situation definitely needed to be handled, but this was one she had to delegate.

"Cass? Are you still there?"

"I'm here, but I have to go. I need to call someone to come and get you. Where are you, exactly?"

"I'm on the sidewalk in front of your sister's building."

"But you can get inside?"

"Yes."

"Then head in. I'll have my friend honk three times when she gets there."

"Okay." Her mom's voice regained some of its normal strength now that they had a plan.

"We'll talk again soon."

"Yes. Goodbye, Cassidy."

"Bye, Mom." She waited for her mom to disconnect first, then stowed the phone back in her pocket.

"That's a complication we don't need right now," Naomi said. Despite the harsh words, she slid her arms around Cassidy's waist in a loose embrace.

"It's a complication we have," Cassidy snapped, even as she relaxed into the comfort of Naomi's closeness.

"Are you prepared to tell her who you are?" Snow stood and moved toward Cassidy, her eyes uncharacteristically holding her gaze.

"I don't—I can't—" Cassidy took a shuddering breath as Snow wrapped her arms around Cassidy's shoulders from the front. "I don't know."

"Then you need to decide before I get back with her," Snow murmured into her ear. There was no judgment in her tone; it was simply a statement about what needed to happen.

"We can keep her from finding out you're here," Naomi said. "This is a big place."

"It is," Snow agreed. "If you're supposed to be in…Honduras, is it?" She shrugged. "I couldn't make out everything she was saying."

Cassidy nodded. "Mary came up with it as a cover story. A reason why I wasn't going to be around the way Mom expected me to be." It was scant explanation, but it was all she was prepared to give.

"I can stick to your cover story if you want." Snow gave her a final squeeze, then stepped away.

Cassidy desperately wanted to reach out to her, to draw her back in where she could feel the lone wolf's touch, where Snow's scent would dominate the smells in her nostrils. She covered the urge by placing her hands over Naomi's and pulling her packmate tighter against her, then she let Naomi go.

"Have someone set up a room for my mom," Cassidy said to Naomi. "Let's call ourselves an artists' collective for now."

"The old commune story, got it," Naomi said. "That'll be fine. It's been a while. Some of our older packmates will appreciate trotting out an old classic."

"I don't suppose we can keep her relationship to me secret?" Cassidy asked. Having their closeness be generally known felt like a massive vulnerability, like going for a run in skinform without her shoes.

Naomi shook her head. "I mean, you can, but the second anyone gets close enough to smell her, the jig will be up."

"Then just let everyone know they should be discreet, both to Mom about me and to others about her."

"Yes, Alpha." Naomi bowed her head slightly, then left the room.

* * *

Snow watched the Alpha closely as she paced the length of the living room and back.

"I don't know what to do," Five Moons finally admitted in a strained whisper.

Despite her recent resolution to be more distant with Cassidy, Snow couldn't help but reach out for her again.

"I know," she said, pulling Cassidy to her. "So many of our kind go through this. Those of you with human families all have to make this decision at some point. You aren't the first to grapple with it."

"Is that what Naomi meant?" Cassidy asked, her words muffled in Snow's shoulder.

"It is. A lot of newly made wolven bring family to meet the pack." Snow didn't tell Cassidy that they usually only did so once.

"Do they tell them about the wolf?"

"No. It's typically more of a 'come meet the cool people I live with now' kind of a situation. It doesn't tend to go over well. The families have a hard time with the whole situation. I think most of them think their loved ones' pack is nothing more than a weird cult. If they're lucky, there's a split with the family and they become estranged."

"How is that lucky?"

"They don't have to watch their family members grow old and die while they stay young. A clean break is easier."

"Oh." Cassidy sagged against Snow. "I was waiting until my control was perfect, then the plan was to visit Mom in New York."

"That's another way to do it."

"Mary being gone is fucking everything up."

"It certainly seems to be."

Cassidy laughed, a little wet burble that contained more pain than joy. She pushed away from Snow and mashed the heels of her palms against her eyes for a moment. "You'd better go get her," she said.

"You're not coming?"

Cassidy shook her head. "I don't know what I'd say to her. Maybe by the time you bring her back, I'll have figured something out."

"Then I'll keep the details of your activities sketchy."

"Thanks." Cassidy looked up at her through the curtain of hair she'd allowed to flop in front of her face. "I owe you."

"If you say so."

"I do."

"See you in a bit," Snow said as she turned and made her way out the door to the hallway.

She took the stairs two to three at a time, depending on her stride and how far it was to the next landing. Was the Alpha going to try to live a double life or bundle her mom back on the plane to New York and out of her life? She had no judgment for either option. Each had its advantages, or so she'd heard. With her family being all wolven, she'd never had to contend with outliving those she loved.

That wasn't really true. She'd outlived both Mama and Dean. It was a little different, since they'd died from violence. At least she hadn't had to watch them age while she stayed looking young.

Snow had plenty of time to ponder Cassidy's plight while she drove toward the Hunter's home to pick up Cassidy's mom. The Hunter's mom too. She couldn't forget that. It was doubtful the human woman knew any more about her other daughter's activities than she knew about Cassidy's.

Halfway to the pickup point, Snow realized she'd left the hotel without a buddy. Cassidy hadn't mentioned anything about needing one, and Snow had been so wrapped up in what she needed to do and the implications that she'd completely forgotten. By the time she pulled up to the darkened building, she was watching the cars behind her more than those in front. Her heart tripped in her chest every time a vehicle turned a corner after her, only to subside a minute or so later when they turned again or pulled in somewhere to park.

She sat in the dark, watching for headlights moving too slowly, or worse, cars with their lights extinguished. The side streets were quiet, and she allowed herself to relax.

The knock on the driver's side window would have had her jumping two feet into the air, if not for her seat belt.

"What?" she snarled through the cracked window.

An older white woman jumped away from her, pale skin going even paler at the strength of her reaction.

"Oh no." Snow scrambled to undo her seat belt and open the door. "Mrs. Nolan, is that you?" Her face was certainly reminiscent of Cassidy's. The cheekbones and jawline were only a little blurred by age, and they shared the same look in their eyes.

"Are you Cassidy's friend?" Mrs. Nolan took another step back, then stopped when she bumped into a large rolling suitcase.

"I am." Snow gave Cassidy's mom a wide, if tight-lipped, smile. She'd never been so glad that she wasn't strong enough to shift quickly. Even so, her teeth had started to change. If her eyes had flashed white, hopefully the human would chalk it up to a trick of the light. It was hard to trust your own eyes in the dark, or at least that's what humans seemed to think. "Weren't you supposed to wait until I honked?"

"I couldn't wait in there any longer," Mrs. Nolan said. "It's so eerie without any stuff in it. Empty buildings are so much creepier than full ones, don't you think?"

"Oh, sure." Not in the least. Her eyes could pierce the gloom with relative ease. She would have taken an empty building over a cluttered one any day. It was a lot harder to hide in the open than behind furniture. Snow gestured for Mrs. Nolan to pass over her bag. "I'll put that in the van for you," she said. "Why don't you get in?"

"Thank you so much." Mrs. Nolan rolled the suitcase over to Snow, then walked around the front of the van.

"Cassidy said I should pick you up and take you back to my place," Snow said as she buckled herself into her seat. "You okay with that?" Why had she asked that? Treating the situation like it was optional was no way to proceed. She hoped there would be no issue. Somehow, kidnapping a middle-aged white lady off a Chicago street seemed like a terrible idea.

"If it's no trouble. Any friend of Cassidy's is a friend of mine. Where do you live?"

"It's an artists' commune on the North Side." Snow smiled brightly. "You'll love it, Mrs. Nolan." She pulled away from the curb.

"Please, call me Sophia." Mrs. Nolan's eyes glittered in the streetlights. "So how do you know my daughter?"

And apparently Sophia was going to be chatty. "I guess you could call me an advisor," Snow said. The best lies held a grain of truth.

"Really? Like at Northwestern."

"Sure." Snow took a deep breath and prepared to lie her pants off all the way back to the North Side Pack's den. Cassidy owed her one. A really big one.

CHAPTER TWENTY

"Go on, Alpha," Beth said to Cassidy. "We can handle this. I promise."

"Are you sure?" Cassidy cast another look around the room, seeing it the way she thought her mom might. It was on the smaller side, which wasn't unusual for an old Chicago hotel. Hopefully that wouldn't count against her. It was clean and well-maintained. If it had been affected by the destruction she'd seen in areas of the hotel after they'd moved back in, she couldn't tell. "I'll just check on the bathroom."

"I'm sure." Beth shifted to intercept her. She placed her hands on Cassidy's shoulders. "Trust us. This isn't the first time we've put up human family."

"So I've heard." Cassidy grasped Beth's wrists. "This is really important to me."

"I know..." She tilted her head over toward the other wolven in the room. "Gene and I got you covered."

Gene nodded vigorously, his long red hair with its loose curls flopping into his face. "We do, Alpha."

They seemed eager to please, but then Gene always did. As part of what had passed for MacTavish's pack, he did his best to be indispensable to her. That seemed to be the way with those who had belonged to MacTavish before Cassidy wrested them away from him. Either they were eager to please like Gene, or they were always trying to climb the dominance rankings within the pack. Most of the climbers had perished in the North Side Pack's transition to Cassidy. A few of those had chosen to strike off on their own, but some had come over. Gene's mate Jimmy was one who was always trying to rise in the ranks, in contrast to the more placid Gene. They might have been mates, but a more different pairing couldn't have existed. Cassidy had to figure out what to do with Jimmy. He kept pushing buttons, trying to pick fights with more dominant packmates who would then thrash him.

"All right, all right," Cassidy said. "I hope you won't be offended when I come and check on your work in a bit."

"Of course not," Gene said.

Beth rolled her eyes but kept her mouth shut.

Cassidy pointed at Beth. "I promise it won't be in five minutes."

"I'll believe it when I see it," Beth said, her voice dry enough to wither plastic plants. "Or rather when I don't."

"Promise." Cassidy let herself out into the long hall. She checked her phone. It was 7:32. No stopping back in until 7:38 at the earliest. She considered setting the phone's timer, then shook her head. What she really needed was a distraction. Walking the rest of the hotel to make sure nothing was too obviously out of place should eat up at least five minutes of her time.

As she headed toward the lobby, Cassidy opened up the mail app on her phone. Still nothing from Hammer. Why couldn't the South Shore Alpha have his own cell? That wasn't a fair gripe, she realized. Even among her own pack, the only other wolven with phones needed them for work. She resolved to ask Snow what was going on with the wolven aversion to technological progress.

Heading down the main stairs, she slipped her phone back in her pocket. From her vantage, the common area looked reasonably put together. The furniture was beat to hell, but she wasn't going to be able to change that before her mom got there. Not that she knew when that would be either. Snow also didn't have a phone. She'd left around ten minutes previous. If traffic wasn't too bad, and by now it shouldn't be, that gave the lone wolf twenty or thirty more minutes to get to Mary's place and then maybe forty minutes to get back. So an hour and a half on the outside. Nowhere near enough time to fix the scratches on the cushions. Hopefully, those didn't look too much like claw marks to the untrained eye. She had some throw pillows up in her rooms. They might help camouflage the worst of the damage.

Oh no, you're not trying to distract yourself at all, Cassidy snarled at herself as they took the stairs a few at a time to the penthouse.

Her wolf stirred, disturbed at the venom Cassidy was directing at her own self.

"I'm not mad at you," Cassidy said aloud.

The wolf settled down within her but heaved a reproachful sigh that echoed in her mind.

"I guess it won't hurt to be a little easier on myself." She knew the source of her harshness. What did she do when her mom got here? Cassidy had been lying to her for months. The reason for the lie had been a good one, but how did she explain it? "Sorry I didn't tell you I was turned into a werewolf. Hallmark doesn't have a card for that," would not go over well. All the decorative pillows in the world weren't going to gloss over that fact. So what did she say?

Gathering up an assortment of pillows from her living room and bedroom didn't get her any closer to a reasonable story. She did have to leave behind a distressing number of them because of the ripped seams and long rents through them. She only had four that were in any shape to pass her mom's muster. The others had seen too many sessions of being chewed on by her wolf or by her packmates in wolf form. She crammed the rejects into one corner of the walk-in closet. Cassidy made a note to grab a vacuum cleaner and get rid of the accumulation of wolf fur tumbleweeds in the corners.

Tidying up her space and the other common areas kept Cassidy busy for far longer than the five minutes she'd promised to Beth and Gene. Other wolven started to appear to give her a hand with the public spaces. Cassidy suspected Naomi was the one to thank for that. And so it was that forty minutes later, Cassidy was alone in the room that would belong to her mom for the length of her stay, however long that might be. It looked great. Gene and Beth had brought in a number of small personal touches. She didn't know whose art was on the walls, but she made a note to inquire. The small collages looked like they'd been done by the same artist. Cassidy wouldn't have minded having one or two of the pieces in her rooms. Her walls were devoid of art; she hadn't realized how much she'd missed the ornamentation until she was leaning in, trying to get a good look at the details of one of the pieces.

The room was perfect. Her mom wouldn't be able to find fault there, that was for certain. All she had to do now was figure out how to explain…well, everything. Time was ticking down. It was likely there was not much time before Snow returned. Cassidy checked her phone again. And still nothing from Hammer or his wolven.

Frustration welled up inside her, but she clenched her fists and pushed it down. Getting angry at someone who was an hour away wouldn't help anything. Never mind that it was her wolven who were exposed and watching over the body of someone who might turn out to have been part of Hammer's pack.

Cassidy stomped out of her mom's soon-to-be room. She quartered the hotel until she picked up Naomi's scent, then followed it to the room of one of the other wolven.

"Come in," was the answer to her diffident tap at the door.

Cassidy opened the door, then stuck her head through. Naomi was on the bed, curled up with Jamieson and Carlos. The male wolven were shirtless, and Naomi had stripped down to her just her shirt and some underwear.

"What is it, Alpha?" Jamieson asked. He rolled over, exposing his naked belly to the air.

"Figured we'd get some skin-on-skin time in before we have a human guest," Naomi said.

Cassidy stepped into the room. "That's fine." She would have dearly loved to crawl into the pile. With her level of anxiety, the presence of her pack was sure to calm her. "Can you have someone meet Snow and get her and my mom directed to my mom's room?"

"Of course." Carlos rolled off the bed. "I'll do that right away." He padded past her in his bare feet, taking a moment to trail his fingers over her bare forearm, then was out the door.

Cassidy closed her eyes at the touch. "Thanks." Her eyes popped open. She looked around the room, trying to think of her next task.

With a lazy swing of her arm, Naomi beckoned Cassidy over. "There's a cold spot in the bed. You might as well keep it warm until he comes back."

"If it's to keep you from catching a chill…" Cassidy pulled off her top, leaving herself as shirtless as Jamieson. That was another thing to remember before Mom got there. Time to find a bra.

"Come on." Fed up with Cassidy's sudden hesitation at the bedside, Naomi grabbed her arm and pulled her down onto the mattress.

Cassidy couldn't strangle the undignified squawk, but after Jamieson's and Naomi's laughter started, she found she didn't care. She rolled into their arms, allowing their closeness to drive away the dark jumble of her thoughts. They wouldn't have time for much more than a cuddle, but she would take this one last bit of respite before it was time to face her demons.

* * *

When they pulled into the small lot behind the pack's hotel, sweat was rolling down the small of Snow's back. Five Moons' mom could have made a hefty sum as an interrogator for the cops, and she would do it all with a smile on her face. The human woman had zeroed in on every inconsistency in Snow's story, and despite not wanting to outright lie to her, Snow found herself making up answers just to get herself out of a conversational bind.

"Let's get you inside," Snow said cheerfully. "I'll get your bag, go on in through the doors."

"Oh, I'll wait," Sophia said. "I do appreciate you getting that for me." True to her word, she popped out of the van and looked over the back of the building as Snow snagged her bag. "Is this a hotel?" she asked as soon as Snow came around, luggage in one hand.

"It was once," Snow said. "It was converted a while back." By her brother, but she kept that detail to herself.

"Looks pretty old." Sophia carefully skirted the packed snow and ice on the way from the small parking lot to the hotel's back entrance. "Is it Art Deco?"

"Maybe?" It was certainly possible, but art history wasn't Snow's strong point. "Here you go." She held the door open for Five Moons' mom.

"Thank you." Sophia kept looking around as she entered the building with Snow right behind her.

Now that they were back, Snow wasn't certain what to do with the human, but she didn't have to wonder long. A shadow detached itself from the wall and resolved into the figure of Carlos.

"Oh my." Sophia jumped as he appeared in front of her. Humans' lack of awareness always took some getting used to.

"We have a room set aside for you," Carlos said. He grinned widely, flashing the dimple that disarmed most women.

Sophia was no exception. "Well, thank you so much." Her Brooklyn accent strengthened as she smiled back at Carlos. Her hand lifted, perhaps instinctively to fiddle with the ends of the hair that fell down below shoulder length. It was an unlikely auburn shade. The color itself wasn't off, but that she should have hair without the slightest bit of grey seemed unlikely, even at her age. Snow supposed it wasn't completely impossible. Whoever did her hair did a good job.

"Well, all right then." Carlos allowed a bit of the South to seep into his voice. "I'm Carlos."

Snow blinked at that. She'd always assumed he was from the Midwest. There was so much she didn't know about these wolven. She would need to get their stories before she left.

Sophia took the elbow Carlos offered her, leaving Snow to trail along behind them. Already, they were chatting as if they'd known each other for decades. Carlos inquired about New York City, with an impressive grasp of the landmarks, though occasionally he would land on one that Sophia had no knowledge of. It was a masterful redirection, and Snow was elated to have the human's attention on somebody else. Her skills went to making people less likely to notice her and in convincing them not to murder her if they did. She'd never developed Carlos's brand of easy charisma, the ability to build effortless rapport with a stranger. Hell, she had problems building relationships with those who knew her.

They went up in the elevator. Not many of the pack made use of it, not unless they were moving something that wouldn't fit up the stairs. A metal shelving unit packed with cleaning supplies and chemicals took up the back wall. Sophia seemed not to notice it or that a few of the overhead puck lights were out.

"So this is a commune?" she asked incredulously. "You must do yours differently in Illinois than we do back in NYC. If you hadn't told me, I wouldn't have known. Not enough murals. And the smell isn't right."

"Not enough weed?" Carlos asked, his eyes twinkling.

"Not nearly enough. Don't tell my daughter I said that. She'd die if she found out I know what marijuana smells like. How long have you known her?"

"Only a little bit," Carlos said. "And this is our floor." He gestured Sophia forward with an extravagant hand motion, then followed her. "You're up here on the right a ways." Carlos led her to the room, then leaned forward and put a key to the door's lock and gave it a turn.

"Thank you." She looked back at Snow. "Do you know when Cassidy will call?"

Snow shook her head. "I'm sorry, Mrs. Nolan. Sophia. I don't know." For all she knew, Cassidy had decided to spend her mom's time at the hotel in her room.

"I suppose I'll just have to wait then." She smiled at both of them, then held out her hand for the suitcase. "You've both been very gracious." She opened the door and walked through. Her sharp intake of breath was audible out in the hall. "Cassidy Anne Nolan. What on earth are you doing here?"

CHAPTER TWENTY-ONE

"Surprise," Cassidy said, holding her arms wide and pretending with everything she had that there was nothing terribly unusual about her presence in an old Chicago hotel room. Surrounded by werewolves. With her sister missing. When she'd been telling her mom for months that she was in Central America.

"Cassidy Anne." Her mom let go of her suitcase, allowing it to tip forward and hit the ground with a thud. She put her hands on her hips and glared at her errant daughter. "Are we somehow in Honduras? What are you doing in this 'artists' commune'?" She tilted her head to observe her youngest daughter.

The move always made Cassidy feel like she was on the wrong end of a vulture about to have a very nice lunch. Did she really want to do this? Was there any way around it? If there wasn't she was going to need someone to block her mom's path to the door.

She lifted her head and inhaled. Yes, that had been Snow's scent she'd picked up as her mom came through the door.

"Snow, do you mind sticking around for a bit?"

"Don't think I'm going to take it any easier on you because you have a friend here." Somehow, Sophia Nolan's flinty gaze got even harder.

"Yes, Mom. No, Mom."

When Snow stuck her head around the corner, Cassidy motioned her inside the room. Reluctance colored her scent, but Snow joined them, closing the door behind her.

"So assuming we haven't traveled through some magical sci-fi portal to the rain forest, maybe you can fill your mother in on what's going on here. On what's been going on."

"It's a bit of a story," Cassidy said. "I'm not sure where to start." *I'm not sure what you'll buy.*

"Cassidy Anne." Sophia Nolan's gaze hardened further. "I don't want to hear stories. I want to hear the truth. Have you been in town this whole time?"

"Yeah, I have." The words came out a shade more petulant than Cassidy would have preferred, certainly sulkier than she'd intended. She was the Alpha of the North Side Pack, for crying out loud. How was her mom making her feel like a wayward five-year-old?

"And is your sister hiding out somewhere in this hotel too?"

"No." Cassidy shook her head emphatically. "I don't know where she is. Last I heard she was heading to Wisconsin, but that's it, I swear."

"And why should I believe anything that comes out of your mouth? Does Mary Alice know you've been shacked up here instead of going to classes?"

"Uh, yeah, Mom. It was her idea. Well, telling you I was in Honduras so you wouldn't get on me for dropping out of school was her idea." Becoming the leader of the local werewolf pack hadn't been her intention. It had been partly Mary's fault or at least a result of her actions.

"Really. So both of my daughters are seeing fit to get up to mischief behind my back."

"It's not like that." Cassidy uncrossed her arms. "We didn't want to do this, and believe it or not, it's not because of you, Mom. Mary and I are just trying to get through a weird situation without imposing on you. That's all."

"Maybe. I don't understand why you couldn't tell me what was going on if it was so bad you had to drop out of school."

Cassidy opened her mouth to answer, but her mom kept going.

"And now Mary won't answer my calls. What did I do to have you both cut me out of your lives?" Her eyes welled with tears that she made no attempt to keep from spilling down her face. "I've tried to be nothing but a good mother to the both of you, and now I don't know what to think."

"It's not about you, Mom." Cassidy speared the fingers of both hands through her hair. Her mom's anguish was twisting her own guts into knots.

"I need to talk to Mary."

Cassidy sighed. "Me too." If only to have a united front against their mom's pain and disappointment. She didn't remember much about when her dad died. Most of what she could recall was her own sadness and getting to watch way more TV than normal. Mary had always been around, but their mom had barely left her room for days at a time.

"I thought you said you knew where she was."

"No, I said last I knew she was in Wisconsin. I haven't talked to her or her girlfriend in a few weeks. It's a big place. I can't just walk up to the state line and ask to see her."

"So you're all right with her cutting communication with both of us?" Sophia sniffled, then started searching through her purse. After a moment, she produced a small package of tissues. She blew her nose lightly, then offered one to her daughter.

Cassidy shook her head. "I'm not all right with it, but I know…" How did she tell her very human mom that she could still sense Ruri?

"Know what?"

"I know they're in one piece. Don't ask me how, I just know, okay?"

"Okay?" Her mom's eyes sharpened once more. "How in the name of god's green earth am I supposed to be okay with that? They're okay, but I should take your word for it. Your word. The word of the girl who's been lying to me for…How many months has it been, anyway? When did you throw your sister's money away and drop out of college?"

"I don't have to tell you that." Cassidy wrapped her hands around the back of her neck. "I shouldn't tell you." And there she was, stuck at a crossroads as her mother looked on with eyes both accusing and deeply betrayed. She dropped into a crouch as her wolf sidled restlessly within her. She could complete breaking her mom's heart by kicking her out. Pretending nothing was happening was an option so far gone she didn't even think about it beyond dismissing it. So which one would it be? Break ties with her mom or sink her into a world she had no knowledge of and little ability to survive in.

"Mommy." Cassidy looked up at Sophia, who regarded her with a mix of anger and now concern. "Mommy, I don't know what to do."

"Oh, baby." Unable to resist her youngest, Sophia hastened over. She levered herself down to crouch next to Cassidy and wrap her up in her arms. "Whatever it is, you can tell me."

"I don't know about that." Cassidy looked around for Snow. It took her a moment to find the lone wolf. She'd managed to make herself so unobtrusive she was almost invisible in the far corner of the room. Cassidy tilted her head toward the door. "Watch the door, would you please, Snow?"

Snow crossed the room and reached for the doorknob.

"From the inside." Cassidy closed her eyes. "Mom, you need to promise me you won't freak out."

* * *

"Cassidy?" The Alpha's name was out of Snow's mouth before she could take it back. Neither the question nor its formulation were what she would have said if she'd only taken a moment to compose her thoughts. "Are you certain about this?" She wracked her brain, sifting through memories of stories told to her over more than a century. Precious few of them were about a wolven who broke the truth of their existence to their human family, and all of those ended badly. She didn't know if they were true stories or fables concocted to keep newly-turned wolven from endangering their packs by bringing humans into the mix. For Cassidy's sake, she hoped it was the latter. Either way, the implications were frightening. Either it had happened so rarely there were almost no stories or the outcomes were so disastrous there had been few left to tell about it.

Five Moons' laugh was so bitter Snow's tongue curled. "I have no idea what I'm doing, Snow. I never have, I don't know why I'd start now."

"Cassidy?" Sophia Nolan's face twisted in confusion. "What are you talking about? And why are you taking off your shirt?"

"You wanted to know what was going on." Five Moons pulled off her shirt, then folded it and placed it at the end of the bed. She pulled down her sweatpants. "This is the only way to show you."

Snow backed up until she could feel the wooden door to the hall behind her. She crossed her arms and did her best to look imposing. Fortunately, her submissive nature didn't extend to humans. If Sophia made a break for it, Snow would be ready to stop her.

"Sweet pea, put your clothes back on," Sophia said, holding her hands out entreatingly as Cassidy dropped to all fours. "We can talk this over. Whatever it is, we'll get through it. I promise."

"I love you, Mom," the Alpha said, her voice dropping in register even as her muzzle started to distort. She was taking her time with the change. Snow understood her reasoning; Sophia wouldn't be able to explain away what was happening. Her brain would have time to keep up with what was unfolding. Seeing the transformation unfold so graphically would also be infinitely more terrifying.

"Cassidy!" In contrast to her daughter, Sophia's voice went up an octave and a half. "What's happening to you?" She whirled and glared at Snow. "What did you do to her? What's going on?"

Snow shook her head. "You should watch. She's doing this for you."

"For me? Are you insane?"

"It's true." The words were recognizable, if barely, around an elongated muzzle and long teeth. Cassidy's back legs snapped and re-formed. The mottled pelt that was unique to the Alpha was a shadow against her skin, then it swept over her in a wave, as if a switch had been thrown. Fluid dripped from the ends of her fur to be absorbed into the carpeting. Moments later, her transformation to the in-between form peculiar to the strongest wolven was complete. She pushed herself to a standing position, towering above the human and the human-shaped wolven. Cassidy was easily a foot taller than she'd been in skinform.

Sophia looked up the length of Five Moons' body slowly. Her mouth dropped open as she took in the powerful, if unfamiliar, form in front of her. "What did you—" She launched herself toward Cassidy. "Where is my daughter you...you monster!"

Apparently, Cassidy had misjudged her own mother. Knowing what she did about the Alpha, Snow wasn't too surprised. Someone who ended up with one daughter becoming a Hunter and the other the Alpha of a pack was not going to be a shrinking violet.

Cassidy's shoulders dropped at her mom's response. She half-turned, trying to hide her face.

"Mrs. Nolan," Snow said. "She's still your daughter."

"How can she be?" Sophia raised a hand in a loose fist and brought it down on Cassidy's upper arm.

"Mom, stop," Cassidy rumbled. She caught the next blow with ease. Even from across the room, it was evident she was being very careful with her mom. "It's me, your sweet pea. Your Cassie-bean."

"It's not right," her mom sobbed. Tears streamed down her face, dripping off her chin onto her shirt. "I don't understand any of this."

"It happened in the fall." The Alpha dropped her mom's hand. "Some wolven, what you would call werewolves, did this to me."

"W-werewolves?" Sophia shook her head. "That's impossible."

"Are you going to deny what's right in front of you?" Cassidy asked.

"This has to be a dream. A nightmare. My little girl..."

"Is right here." Cassidy reached out her hands, being mindful of the claws, and grasped her mom's face with the gentlest of touches. "I'm still me, Mom. I'm just more."

"More?"

"That's right."

"Why didn't you tell me?"

"Why do you think?" She looked down at her fur-covered torso, the legs with their heavy thighs and the knees in the wrong spot. At the claws that poked out the end of a thickly furred foot with toes more massive than they had any right to be. "How was I supposed to explain this to you?"

"Is she—" Sophia looked over her shoulder at Snow.

Cassidy met Snow's eyes. She cocked her head as if to say the decision was up to Snow.

"I am," Snow said after a moment. Outing herself felt like the right thing to do. She might not be the one to stand shoulder to shoulder against all comers, but she could damn well support her friend.

"And the others I saw on the way here? What about Carlos?"

Cassidy nodded. "They're my pack."

"Pack?"

"Like family. We take care of each other."

"So that's why you stopped calling." Sophia's mouth wavered as she fought back another wave of tears. "You don't need me anymore."

"If she didn't want you around, she wouldn't have shown you her wolf," Snow said. "Don't you realize how much she trusts you?"

"Really?" Sophia watched her daughter through watery eyes.

"Yeah, Mom. This is the hardest thing I've ever done." Wolven didn't cry in their furforms. Snow hadn't known they could cry in betweenform, but Cassidy's eyes were as wet as her mother's.

"Harder even than when you told me you were leaving New York for university?"

"Harder even than that. I was so worried about…" Her voice trailed off.

"Your sister knows." It wasn't a question.

"Yeah," Cassidy whispered.

"And she's a werewolf too?"

Snow cringed at the term.

"We call ourselves wolven. And no. No she isn't. She's…" Cassidy laughed. "She's got her own deal going. It's why she had to go to Wisconsin."

"I see," Sophia said in such a way that indicated she really didn't.

"It's her damage to let you in on. I can't be the one to betray her secrets. Her girlfriend is wolven. It's how I know they're okay. Well, alive, anyway."

"I see," Sophia said again. She walked away from her daughter on not quite steady legs. It wasn't far to the bed, and she sat down heavily on the edge. "Sweet pea, this is a lot. I'm going to sleep on it." She smiled, managing to include both of them with the shaky expression. "See you tomorrow?"

"Yeah, Mom." Cassidy took a deep breath. A moment passed as she wrestled her wolf back inside. The fur receded in fits and starts and her limbs cracked and popped as she reverted to skinform. "I'll find someone to clean the carpet." She retrieved her small stack of clothes.

"That would be nice, dear."

"I love you very much, Mommy." The words were a statement, but the tone a question, naked and vulnerable, longing for return validation.

"I love you too, Cassie-bean."

A terrible weight lifted from the Alpha's shoulders. She stood up straight and gestured to Snow to open the door.

Snow complied and preceded Cassidy into the hall. It was silent. There was no way to tell that others lived there except for recent scent traces of some of Cassidy's packmates.

"It's all right, everyone," Cassidy said as she shut the door behind her. At first there was no change, then small shifts of movement could be heard in nearby rooms.

"That was a choice," Snow said.

"Was it?" Cassidy cracked her knuckles, then looked over at Snow shyly. "I'm exhausted, but I don't want to be alone. Will you come up with me?"

CHAPTER TWENTY-TWO

"As you ask," Snow said. It made sense that Five Moons could use the comfort of other wolven. What she'd done had to have been draining.

"Thank you," the Alpha said quietly.

They made their way down the hall to the stairwell up to the penthouse. Snow tried to close her ears to the muffled crying coming from behind the door they'd just left. There were times when excellent hearing was a curse. Five Moons' shoulders stiffened until they could no longer hear the sobs, though she didn't relax until they were back in her rooms.

The Alpha stared glassy-eyed around the living room before gesturing vaguely toward half the apartment.

"I don't know what that means," Snow said.

Five Moons snorted a half-laugh. "You know what, neither do I." She dropped onto a small couch, landing like her legs had given out under her.

Snow hesitated. The Alpha smelled like despair. "Should I get Naomi and some of your other wolven? You should be surrounded by pack right now."

"Oh god, no." Realizing how harsh the response sounded, Cassidy shook her head hard enough to send her hair flying about her shoulders.

"Okay." Still Snow hovered by the doorway.

"I can't be...They make me..." Cassidy buried her face in her hands. "You're the only one I can be straight with about how fucked I am. This whole thing is a shitshow, and I'm actively making it worse for everyone here."

"Oh no." Snow flew across the room and slid onto the couch next to Cassidy. She threw her arms around the Alpha and held her tight. "You're not the one making things bad."

"Really." Cassidy relaxed into Snow's embrace. "I don't see that I'm improving things. And now I've made my mom cry."

"You are in a hell of a situation." Snow squeezed Cassidy. Her wolf moved inside her, until it felt like she too was settled against the Alpha. "Very little of it is your own making."

"Very little? I see how you are." The words might have been meant to be joking, but there was a little too much venom lurking behind them.

"If I'd told you none of it was your fault, you'd have blown me off completely. Cassidy Anne Nolan, Alpha of the North Side Pack, you have a problem with responsibility."

"What?" Her voice cracked in distress as Cassidy tried to push Snow away.

"You do." Snow loosened her hug but didn't let the Alpha go completely. "You take on too much of it, even when it doesn't belong to you." When Cassidy tried to interject, Snow kept talking. "You are responsible for the welfare of your pack and yourself. You aren't responsible for the actions of those outside the pack. Not whoever is taking your packmates, not your sister and/or whoever made her disappear. Not even your mom."

"But—"

"You do the best you can with the tools and information at your disposal," Snow said. Cassidy still smelled of deep sadness, but it was starting to lighten. Snow would be damned if she was going to allow this wolven to self-destruct before her eyes. "I wasn't sure you had what it takes to be Alpha when I showed up here."

"You made that plenty clear," Cassidy said dryly.

"And wouldn't you have smelled it if I lied?"

"Well, yes."

"I thought so. You still have a lot of learning to do, but I don't know that you're handling this situation any worse than Alphas with years of experience would. South Shore hasn't figured out what's going on. None of the Alphas I knew on the West Coast have either. So yeah, there's room for improvement, but show me a new Alpha who doesn't need that. You're not making things worse. You're doing what you should be: you're protecting your wolven."

"Then why does it feel like I'm stuck in quicksand? Like the harder I flail, trying to get things handled, the further down I sink?"

"Because things suck right now. There's no way around it. But they don't suck because of your actions."

"I guess."

"And you keep trying, don't you?"

"Yeah."

"Then what else can you do?"

Cassidy allowed her head to fall back against the back of the couch, trapping Snow's arm behind her neck. "I wish I knew when it was going to end."

"I know." Snow allowed her other arm to fall away. "There's only one way through, though. That's forward. Keep putting one paw in front of the other." She shrugged. "That's all you can do. Well, mostly."

"What do you mean mostly? Are you keeping some nugget of wisdom from me? Something that'll make all of this make sense."

"Yes, because I am the wisest of all wolven." Snow made no attempt to tamp down the sarcasm in her voice. "You could do what I do and take off when things get tough. There's always that."

"Oh." Mild shock colored Cassidy's scent at her blunt words, but the despair was mostly gone. "I don't think I'm going to do that."

"And that's why you're Alpha, and I'm not. That and I couldn't win a fight to save my life. Literally."

"For someone who keeps talking about how submissive she is, you don't back down to me."

Her wolf twitched again, doing her best to stay near the Alpha, even as Snow moved away. "You're different." Somehow. If Snow could figure out how Cassidy was different, she might be able to leave, but this Alpha kept drawing her back, despite her best efforts. Her instincts vacillated between wanting to get as far away from the situation in Chicago as she could and wanting to be closer to this wolven she had resolved to distance herself from.

"Lucky me." Cassidy grinned up at her.

Snow's heart gave an odd little flip. "That remains to be seen."

"I guess so. You can stick around for as long as you want."

"Have you run that past Luther?"

"He can deal with it. I'm Alpha, remember?"

"I'm just glad when you remember."

"Thanks, Snow." Cassidy snuggled down against her. "I'm so glad you're my friend."

"Me too." But how long would they stay that way? How long until Cassidy decided she needed a physical commitment out of Snow? Before the Alpha's urges ruined a perfectly good relationship? "So what made you decide to tell your mom, anyway?"

* * *

"Were you surprised?" Cassidy asked. She was glad her face was tucked against Snow's shoulder. She didn't want to look her in the eye during this chat.

"A little bit." Snow paused for a moment. "Okay, more than a little bit. A lot."

"Doing it your way wasn't working for me." Cassidy snuggled in deeper against Snow. "I couldn't leave her out in the cold. My dad died when I was little. Mary's missing. She has no one else, and I'm supposed to just turn her away? Not gonna happen."

"You have the advantage of her living in a different city. I've seen other wolven who've made that work with their families."

"Except she's already caught me in one lie. Pretty sure this isn't Central America."

"No. Not humid enough." Snow smelled faintly of disapproval. "There isn't much precedent for pulling what you just did. What you're trying to do."

"Doesn't mean it can't work."

"True." Snow's rib cage expanded with a large sigh. "You do have advantages those other wolven didn't."

"Yeah, I've got you in my corner." Cassidy risked grinning up at Snow. She was being cheeky, but she knew the lone wolf would smell the sincerity behind the smartassery.

"I think your sister is a stronger backer than I am. A Hunter to look out for you is a card a lot of non-humans could wish for. It's definitely better than being on their hit list."

"Do you know wolven who have been hurt by other Hunters?" Cassidy hoped she wasn't about to learn something new about her sister.

"I know of others who have been killed by Hunters," Snow said. She spoke slowly as if she was picking her words with great care. "They were in different cities. One of the packs that got taken out was a piece of work. I wasn't really sorry to see them go, but some of the others that went weren't so clear-cut."

Her neck was developing a major twinge. Cassidy shifted to give herself some relief. "That doesn't sound like Mary."

"I haven't heard as much about your Malice," Snow admitted. "When I started hearing whispers about what happened to Dean, everything was pretty jumbled. Each detail I picked up was more awful than the last one. But it always ended the same way, with a Hunter popping up to finish things."

"Well, she helped. Stiletto too, though if she hadn't died in that last fight I'm pretty sure I would have ended up in the back of a dark van, trussed up like a birthday gift for her bosses."

"Talk out of Atlanta had her more interested in vamps than us. She took out a couple of nests of demons too. No one cried too much about that one."

"Wait, what?" Cassidy stared at Snow. "You're telling me demons are real?"

"Of course they are." Snow lifted an incredulous eyebrow. "So-called werewolves are real, so are vampires and the fae. Why would you draw the line at demons?"

Cassidy spluttered as she tried to find the argument that would convince her new friend that she wasn't an idiot. "Well, what about angels then? If we have demons, there must be angels too."

"Actually, no." Snow's scent shaded into vaguely puzzled, as if she'd never really considered the possibility before. "Demons yes, but I don't know any stories of angelic types. Well, not recent ones. The ones I know about are way old, oral tradition-type stories, you know?"

"That's weird."

"I guess it is. Still, I think it says something about our world that demons are a thing, but angels aren't."

"Why do you think we exist?"

Snow blinked. "You mean wolven specifically, or are you taking a hard left into philosophy?"

Cassidy chuckled. "Wolven, silly. I wasn't the most philosophical person before being turned. Becoming wolven has made me even more practical."

"We are a pragmatic bunch. I blame the wolves. Mine thinks I get far too worried with petty human concerns."

"Yours does that too? Even after…"

"You better not be about to ask what I think you are."

"Oh hell, no. I know better than to ask someone's age. That's a taboo that carries over from humans." She stared off at the ceiling for a moment. "Huh." Cassidy glanced over at Snow.

"What huh?"

"Just thinking about taboos and what carries over."

"Like what?"

"Well…" Cassidy hesitated.

When the silence had gone on for a while, Snow smacked Cassidy lightly on the shoulder. "You might as well ask. I'm not going to bite your head off."

"It's about race." Cassidy spat the phrase out before she could come up with something else. It was something she'd thought about a couple of times, only to have her wolf imply that she was being incredibly silly to be concerned about it.

"Okay." Snow's face went still. "What about it?"

"Wolven have a lot more people of color living in a pack than I'm used to." Cassidy waved a hand. "I'm not racist, I promise."

"It's very hard to stay a bigot when you're wolven, or so I've been told." Snow still smelled cautious, as if she wasn't sure where Cassidy was going with the line of questioning.

"I'm making a huge mess of this." Cassidy pushed herself up so she could be face-to-face with Snow. "I've noticed that our pack is much more diverse than I would expect. Humans tend to stick with those they're most comfortable with. And if you're white…"

"You stick with white folks." Slowly Snow nodded. Her scent thawed a bit, though not completely. "I think I see where you're going with this."

"I'm just wondering why." Cassidy laughed. "I wonder why a lot these days."

"This is only my opinion, but I think it has everything to do with the ability to shift. I'm not saying that people don't hang on to their various bigotries once they become wolven, if they weren't born that way, but I think it's a lot harder." Snow became more animated the more she talked. "Sure, there are always rumors that somewhere out west is an enclave of skinhead wolven. But then you get out west, and you're told that it's a pack to the south. The wolven to the south all tell you that they heard there are white supremacist wolven in the rural Midwest. I've been around the country a bunch of times, but I've never heard more than rumors when it comes to race-based bigotry."

"That's a relief."

Snow gestured down at the dark skin of her arms. "Especially looking like I do. I get hassled by cops and rednecks from time to time, but those have all been humans. Think of a pack like a smaller reflection of the human community it's in. We tend to pull new members in from around us. Even packs that go strongest for the 'born is best' mentality still end up with members who are made. They come from those they see and know every day."

"Born is best?"

"The idea that the best wolven were born that way." Snow laughed hollowly. "My family is living proof that's not the case. I'm pure wolven, was born wolven. My mama was born wolven, my daddy was born wolven. Dean's daddy was human. There's some genetic fuckery involved. I have some theories, but no way to prove any of it. Anyway, there was a chance Dean could have been born wolven, but he came out pink and mewling without a lick of fur on him. I turned him on his eighteenth birthday."

"So what does that prove?"

"I'm one of the weakest wolven out there, Cassidy." Snow's eyes caught hers and held them. "By any measure the wolven have, I am always going to be at the bottom of the pile. Dean was Alpha."

"Weak?" Cassidy stared at the lone wolf. "I think you're one of the strongest people I know."

Snow patted her on the cheek. "That's sweet of you to say, but I know what I am."

"I don't think you do."

They sat for a few seconds, staring at each other. Cassidy wondered what Snow saw in her, whether it was as far off from reality as what Snow saw in herself.

She decided she didn't want to think too much about it. "Thank you for the talk. You've given me a lot to think about. I'm pretty wrung out, though. I'm going to head to bed. Do you want to come?" She lifted a hand to forestall Snow before she could object. "Only for sleep, I promise. The only way I'll ever try anything more than the most platonic of touching is if you initiate it. You have my word on that."

For a second, Snow looked like she might start to cry. Her scent spiked orange and red, but she took a deep breath. "I appreciate that," she said simply. "I'm going furform. It's been a long day, and I won't really relax until the wolf does too."

That was a fantastic idea. Cassidy rose to her feet, then stuck a hand out to Snow. "My lady," she said with grave attention.

"You're a dork," Snow said with a grin, but she still took Cassidy's hand.

"Maybe," Cassidy said. She tugged on Snow's arm, then stepped to catch her before she went flying. She'd put a little more muscle behind the tug than she'd realized. "Sorry. I was trying to be gallant."

"Might want to work on that," Snow said. She stuck her tongue out for a second, then extricated herself from Cassidy's arms and headed for the bedroom. As she walked, she untucked her shirt and pulled it over her head.

Cassidy waited to give her enough space. They'd spent very little skinform time together naked. While the wolven Cassidy spent her time around put little stock in nudity, she didn't want to make Snow uncomfortable. She'd been serious when she'd said she wouldn't try to pressure Snow into anything remotely sexual. Until they figured out those boundaries together, she would give Snow as much space as possible.

A minute or so later, she entered her room. Snow's clothes were in a somewhat tidy pile at the end of the bed. Snow herself wasn't there, but Cassidy could hear the unmistakable sounds of a wolven shifting in the bathroom. One of the amenities of each room was a walk-in shower. Cassidy's was nice and spacious. Showers made so much sense for the wolven. Each individual had their own preference for how long they spent in furform or skinform. No matter how much time they preferred to walk on two legs versus four, there was a good chance they would be shifting at least once a day. The change was not a clean process. Having somewhere that was convenient to rinse off made an incredible amount of sense. Cassidy certainly took full advantage of the showers. Sometimes, she even used hers to clean herself, but it saw far more action as a place to change from human to wolf and back.

Snow's change took a while, so Cassidy disrobed while she waited. She folded and stacked her shirt and pants neatly, then gave Snow's stack of clothing the same treatment. As she was finishing up, Snow came out of the bathroom, her head and tail held high. The breath caught in Cassidy's throat as it had when she'd first beheld Snow's wolf form. There was no denying the lithe beauty of Snow's wolf. Not like her own wolf, who was patchy and broad.

Her wolf shifted at the thought, then sent her an image of strong jaws snapping the neck of a scrawny coyote. Cassidy smiled ruefully. There was no sense in being down on herself for something she couldn't control, any more than Snow could control her wolf's looks. It was a silly thought, one that would be swept away when the wolf became ascendant. After the day she'd had, she was looking forward to something simple, which the wolf offered and more.

Cassidy nodded to Snow, then padded past her, trying to ignore the cool draft from the windows on her bare skin. Her change started as soon as her first foot hit the tile of the shower. By the time she'd walked all the way in, she was halfway through the transformation. When her forelimbs hit the floor, it was paws, not hands, that made contact. She took a moment to wait for her muscles and bones to settle themselves and for her head to clear from the agony of the change. The spike of pain receded as quickly as it had come on.

There was fluid stuck to their fur, as usual. The wolf gave them a thorough shake, then trotted out of the shower to the bedroom. Glowing white eyes watched them as they made their way over the carpeted floor. Snow flopped over onto her back, exposing her belly when Cassidy and her wolf jumped onto the bed. They gave the underside of her chin a quick sniff, then settled down next to her. The scent of Snow's wolf—similar to her human scent, only more concentrated—filled their nostrils. They breathed in deeply and exhaled. Only then were they able to relax and put the events of the day from them.

There would be other things for their human half to concern herself with when they got up, but until then, this was heaven.

CHAPTER TWENTY-THREE

The warmth of her brother at her back welcomed Snow back to wakefulness. She panted, tongue fully out of her mouth, from the joy of waking up next to kin again, then stopped. Panting brought another wolven's taste to her tongue, deep into her nostrils.

Cassidy. Familiar anguish took hold as she remembered that her only brother had been torn from this life and for what? So a psychopathic wolven with no idea of his place in society could have a pack to try and call his own. That MacTavish had failed brought no solace. His failure didn't return Dean to her.

The other shape on the bed moved, flopping over to rest her massive and shaggy head on Snow's flank. This was definitely not Dean. He'd been as sleek as she was. Cassidy was powerfully built as a wolf.

The contact was nice, her wolf reminded her. She stretched, then snuggled into Cassidy's form, letting it wrap around her.

Light streamed in through the windows. From the angle, it was still early, but they'd slept the entire night through. That was unusual. Snow was a light sleeper. Too many nights sleeping alone in a van, she supposed. It wasn't the most restful of locations.

Cassidy's head snapped up, and she grumbled deep in her chest. Her entire body tensed, then she was gathering her legs under her and bounding out of the bed. Snow jumped up after her, ears pricked for whatever had set her off, but there was nothing she could hear. A quick sniff revealed nothing amiss.

From the bathroom came a quick wolf growl, followed by a very human intake of breath. Seconds later, Cassidy strode through the door, toweling herself off vigorously before heading to the old dresser in the corner.

"Phoebe's coming," she said when Snow whined a question at her. "She's worked up."

She was? How did Cassidy know that? Maybe she'd gotten a call on her cell phone. No, that made no sense. Phones required thumbs to use, and Cassidy had been in furform when whatever had set her off came through.

Cassidy pulled on a pair of dark pants. "I'm going to meet her downstairs." She dragged a shirt on over her head, then headed for the door.

Snow jumped off the bed and followed at her heels. Five Moons was in full Alpha mode. If Snow hadn't seen it with her own eyes, she would never have known the doubt and anxiety under which Cassidy was laboring. There was no one else to see it but her. She'd judged Cassidy for choosing to make her personal den so far from the rest of her pack, but it made sense now. The facade she'd been maintaining had to be exhausting. The pack would have understood, but how could Cassidy have known that? Perhaps when things had calmed down a bit, she might be convinced to open up to her packmates. Snow made a mental note to suggest it when the opportunity presented itself.

That time was certainly not now, as they flew down the stairwell, steps blurring past beneath them. Five Moons straight-armed open the door at the ground floor, and Snow darted out before it could close. A couple of wolven who'd been lounging on the furniture in the lobby looked up as they arrived. The one in skinform half stood, while the other turned their furry head to inspect the front doors.

"No need to worry," Five Moons said, holding up one hand. "Phoebe is almost here, and I wanted to meet her quickly."

The explanation seemed to satisfy them, though they didn't question the source of Five Moons' information.

Sure enough, only a few moments passed before Phoebe's silhouette appeared on the other side of the frosted glass of the front doors. As soon as Phoebe stepped through the second set of doors, Five Moons was right there to greet her.

"Alpha," Phoebe said. She stopped in her tracks but leaned in to bury her nose in Five Moons' neck.

Five Moons wrapped her in a quick embrace, breathing in her scent, then letting Phoebe go. "What is it?" she asked.

"There are humans along the river," Phoebe said. "They're cleaning up garbage and other debris. They were on the other side, but we assume they'll be crossing at some point."

"Did they see you?" Five Moons asked.

Phoebe shook her head. "Luther stayed with the body. He sent me to tell you. What should we do?"

Five Moons pulled her phone from her pocket and ran her thumb across the front screen. She tapped it twice, then shook her head. "Still nothing." She scowled and speared her fingers into her hair, taking a moment to think.

Snow walked up and pressed the length of her body against the back of Five Moons' legs. Whatever she was considering would be the right move, as long as she was confident about it. She tried to will the thought through her pelt and into Five Moons.

"Go back to Luther," Five Moons said. "Keep an eye on the body. If the humans get too close, keep them away. Try not to do anything that'll get the cops called. Or animal control." She looked down at Snow, and her face softened for a moment. "We have a trip to make, and I'm going to need your help."

* * *

This was a terrible idea. Cassidy had recognized that even before Snow let her know at length just how awful her plan was and why. It didn't change anything. She knew, with a certainty she hadn't felt for months, that if Hammer didn't come and see the body for himself, the situation between the packs would be blown wide open. It was already tenuous enough. Her attempts at contacting the other packs were going slowly. Bogging it down even further was leaving Luther to babysit a corpse. He had a meeting today with the Aurora Beta. She needed him there.

They crawled along the packed Tri-State. Even the open windows in Cassidy's car couldn't relieve the feeling of oppression and powerlessness.

"You sure you won't change your mind?" Snow asked from the passenger seat. She fiddled with the locking mechanism, tracing the raised plastic with her fingertip while her knee bounced up and down.

"If I had any other choice…" Cassidy leaned forward, her eyes on a gap in traffic. She drove the accelerator to the floor and yanked on the wheel, then stomped on the brake. They slotted neatly into the space between cars. Their exit was coming up, and they needed to get over.

"So send someone else."

"Who? Luther is on body patrol."

"What about Naomi?"

"I need her at the hotel to watch the pack." Traffic was a slow-moving mass. It was tempting to sit there with her foot on the brake until another gap opened, but that was an urge best to be avoided. She'd learned a few years back that when driving in Chicago traffic you had to think like a shark. Never stop moving. Don't alert others of your intentions. It hadn't been like this in New York, but then she had never driven there, only taken the subway and the occasional cab. Mary had taught her to drive once she'd moved to Illinois.

"You could do one of those things."

"Do you think either of them could convince Hammer to leave his den for such a suspicious reason?" She inched to the right, aiming at the gap between the front and back bumpers of the cars there. If she was implacable enough, someone would let her in. It was a tactic she hated to employ, but dire times called for insane solutions. "I know I'd be skeptical."

"Maybe not." Snow shook her head. "I wish you'd brought someone a little beefier with us."

"We need to convince Hammer we aren't trying to pull anything. You're the best one for the job."

"Gee, thanks."

"It's nothing." A trailing car had to apply its brakes as Cassidy continued to creep into its lane. She waved her thanks at the other driver, checked over her shoulder, then made for the exit lane. It felt so good to finally get up to speed again, but that was short-lived as they hit the traffic light at the top of the ramp.

She was keenly aware of the passage of time as they made their way through the South Side's surface streets. It pressed in on her at every stop sign and light. When they pulled up to the house, she was ready to leap from the car, but Snow reached over and put a hand on her forearm.

"They need to come to us," she said. "How would you react if Hammer burst through the front doors of your place?"

"You're right." Cassidy stayed put but couldn't help craning her neck to peer out the side windows. The neighborhood was quiet under the weak winter sun. Water dripped off icicles on roof edges. Small puddles of water formed on the sidewalks.

"It's that one." Snow pointed out a heap of a house that had started life as a simple bungalow. Some architectural Dr. Frankenstein had grafted additions, floors, and wings onto the home until it squatted in the middle of the block, a strange mélange of architectural styles and time periods.

The front door opened and two wolven emerged. They sniffed the air, then looked straight at them. Cassidy recognized one as the Beta. She made her way down the steps. With a start, Cassidy realized Hammer's Beta was barefoot. The lack of shoes didn't seem to slow her as she crunched her way over packed snow to the side of Cassidy's car.

"Five Moons," she said. "Snow."

"Briella." Cassidy nodded to her. "I know it's unconventional, but I need to speak with Hammer. I sent an email, but no one's gotten back to me. It's incredibly urgent."

"Urgent, is it?" The Beta leaned her head into the car, paying Snow no mind, her gaze locked aggressively to Cassidy's.

"Literally life and death."

"Why should I care about the life or death of a North Side wolven?"

"Because the wolven in question isn't one of mine."

That got her attention. She was nearly halfway into the car now, her nostrils flared as she tasted the air for the truth in Cassidy's words. "Is it one of ours?"

"I don't know," Cassidy said with exaggerated patience. "That's why I'm here."

She inhaled once more, then gave a decisive nod. "He'll see you for that." Briella extricated herself back through the window.

"I should hope so." Cassidy pushed open the driver's side door and joined Snow in the narrow channel that had been cut through nearly waist-high snowbanks.

"I'll watch your back," Snow murmured as Cassidy passed her.

Hopefully, it wouldn't be necessary. How well they could protect themselves if the entire pack turned on them was questionable.

"Wait there," the Beta said when they mounted the stoop. She disappeared inside the house.

The wolven who'd stepped onto the stoop with her leaned against the wrought iron railing. He might be pretending to ignore them, but he twitched every time Cassidy moved. Oddly, he didn't seem particularly attuned to Snow's movements.

Cassidy could feel him, like a star veiled by clouds, barely twinkling at the edge of her eyesight. Snow was also there, brighter, but not shining as strongly as Cassidy's wolven did. As they waited, she wondered what it would be like to reach out toward him. Her mind stretched in his direction, sweeping the haze out of her way until he shone nearly as brightly as the wolven she claimed as her own.

He watched her now, all pretense gone. His eyes were so wide they showed the whites all the way around his iris.

"What are you doing?" he whispered.

"Alpha?" Snow asked. "What's happening?"

She ignored the questions, concentrating as she reached out to this glittering star. She was so close, with only a little more effort, she'd be able to pull it into her orbit.

The door opened behind him.

"There had better be a good reason why you're on my doorstep, trying to filch one of my wolves out from under my nose." Hammer's voice was deceptively quiet. "Is there a good reason I shouldn't pull your arms out of your sockets right here?"

CHAPTER TWENTY-FOUR

Cassidy jumped at the voice coming from right behind her. The surprise, along with the unpleasant feeling of snapping back into her body, sent her nearly a foot into the air. She managed to get turned around right after hitting the ground.

"Nice to see you too, Hammer," she said. "When's the last time you checked your email?"

"Email?" Hammer cocked his head, then leaned back to shout through the open door. "Rocky! Check the emails!"

Cassidy plastered a wide smile across her face to keep from snickering. Hammer looked like he was in his late twenties. She still hadn't gotten used to the fact that while a wolven might look like her contemporary, they could be her senior by decades or even centuries.

"That doesn't answer my question, Five Moons," Hammer said. Soft malice entered his voice as he leaned toward her. "Why are you messing with my wolves?"

"I didn't mean to," Cassidy said. She refused to look away from him and wouldn't have even if her wolf hadn't insisted on standing their ground. "I wanted to see if I could…"

"If you could what?"

"Touch him. Not physically." Cassidy held up her hands, the palms facing out. "I don't know how to explain it."

"Whatever you were doing, I would suggest not trying it with wolves who don't belong with you. If I wasn't such an agreeable Alpha, you might be fighting for your life right now." He grinned wide, displaying already pointed teeth.

"I'm sorry. I didn't know what would happen. I was curious, that's all. I haven't spent much time around wolven who weren't mine."

"If you're not here to hassle South Shore wolven, why did you come?" He shook his head, his dreads swaying ponderously with the movement. "It's highly unorthodox for you to show up at my den unannounced."

"I know. I was told." Cassidy glanced around, taking in the quiet residential street. "Look, I know it's odd, but I'd rather not talk about this out here. Can we go inside?"

Hammer hesitated, clearly not happy about the idea of having her in his home.

"I wouldn't ask if it wasn't important. It's just the two of us, I swear. We won't try anything."

"All right." He pushed the door open completely, then led the way into the dark interior.

Cassidy sneezed as her nose was assaulted by the smell of so many wolven she didn't know. The aromas mingled together in a visual display of colors that should have clashed but didn't. Somehow, they swirled around each other in a brilliant whole, with Hammer's deep purple threading through it all like a thrumming bassline.

"Rocky," Hammer called as he made his way deeper into the house. "Where are you?"

"Coming, Alpha." The wolven she'd seen at Carla's nightclub came bounding down the stairs, clearing the last three to land in a crouch at the bottom. "What is it?" he asked as he bounced to his full height.

"Five Moons says she sent you an email." He jerked his thumb back at Cassidy.

"Yesterday. Did you see it?"

Rocky frowned. "There was nothing new this morning."

"Maybe it went to spam? Or I got your account wrong."

"I'll go check." He took off back up the stairs.

"We'll be in the den," Hammer said to his departing back. "Through there." He pointed at a partially open door. Golden lamplight spilled out through the gap. "I'll join you in a moment."

Cassidy reached back and took Snow's hand, drawing her along as they walked down the narrow hall. The gesture was as much for her own comfort as it was for Snow's. While she didn't sense any specific animosity directed their way, they were still in a place she knew could turn hostile. Her heart thundered in her ears, and her wolf was on high alert. Cassidy didn't dare unleash her. She knew deep in her bones that the effort would be seen as aggressive.

"Make yourself comfortable," Briella said as they entered the room. Rumpled furniture filled the area, much of it with the same heavy use and wear as that in the hotel. "Didn't think we'd let you have the run of the place on your own, did you?"

"Of course not." Cassidy chose to sit on a battered armchair. Snow pulled her hand away, but stayed next to the chair, leaning against it.

Hammer entered a moment later, a metal tray with steaming mugs on it. "Tea?" he asked as he placed the tray on the edge of a large desk. Briella got up from her seat and crossed the room to stand next to them.

"Yes, please," Cassidy said.

"Not for me," Snow said a moment later. She sniffed at the air but didn't seem alarmed at what she smelled.

Hammer nodded. "How do you take it?"

"What kind is it?" There was a mug of coffee on the tray, and Cassidy couldn't make out the type of tea past its acrid scent.

"Earl Grey."

"A spoonful of sugar, then." Cassidy took a deep breath. "What are we doing?" Urgency beat within her. She wanted out of the house with its smells of strangers. She wanted to make sure the dead wolven by the river deep in her territory wasn't from the South Shore Pack. She wanted her own wolven back to the safety of their den. This pretense of domesticity was the last thing she needed.

"Hmm." Hammer passed her the mug. "So it's not good."

"Yeah. Bad enough to send me to your doorstep. That should have been enough to convince you I mean business." Cassidy blew on the tea then took a sip. She needed something to do, if only to keep from grabbing Hammer by the scruff of the neck and dragging him to that lonely spot along the Chicago River. The tea wasn't the usual Earl Grey she was used to. The taste of bergamot was partially obscured by a strange bitterness. She smacked her lips at the tingling on her tongue.

"There's a lot you don't know." Hammer inclined his head at the mug in her hand. "Including the flavor of wolfsbane."

At her side, Snow wrenched her arm from Briella's grip, then slapped the mug out of Cassidy's hand.

"What are you doing?" Cassidy jerked her leg back to keep from being sprayed by hot liquid, then leaped to her feet. She reached out to her wolf, straining to let her through. There was no response.

"Wolfsbane puts the wolf to sleep," Snow said. She struggled against Briella for a moment longer. When the South Shore Beta let go of her arm, she stumbled.

"What's wrong with you?" Cassidy snarled at Hammer.

"You're the one in my den," he said calmly. "I'm doing what I must to keep my wolves safe from you." He waved a hand at both of them. "Calm down, it was a small dose. You'll be able to reach your wolf in fifteen minutes or so. Wolfsbane doesn't stay in our systems long. Consider this a free lesson in the many dangers that exist for the unprepared."

"There's a fucking dead wolven along the banks of the Chicago River," Cassidy growled. "It's in the heart of my territory. He wasn't one of mine, and we didn't put him there."

"The hell, Five Moons?" Briella said.

Hammer shot her a quick look, and she subsided.

"That's why I sent you an email," Cassidy said. "I wouldn't be here if we had some other way of getting hold of each other."

"The vamps will run messages," Hammer said quietly. He closed his eyes and tilted his head like he was listening for something.

"For a price," Snow said quietly.

"Like I would trust them with something like this." Cassidy couldn't help trying to reach out to her wolf but wasn't able to find so much as a whisker.

"What does he look like?" Briella asked.

"We didn't get close enough to see any defining marks. He is—was a Black man with a goatee and dreadlocks."

"Could be Marquis." Briella's face hardened, but beneath the touchy exterior, Cassidy smelled deep pain.

"This is definitely a problem." Hammer shook his head and opened his eyes. "You're sure it's not one of the loners, I take it. You wouldn't be here otherwise."

"I didn't recognize him." Cassidy lifted her shoulders in a defeated shrug. "We haven't had any loners come through, not until Snow. If he's one of yours…"

"You want me to find out from you, not from the vamps." Hammer clapped his hands together. "I'd have done the same thing. Well, mostly." He cast a sideways look at Snow.

"We can take you to where he is." Cassidy stretched an arm out in the vague direction of the river. "There's not much time. A group of humans are picking up garbage on the opposite bank. If they get involved, this could get messy."

"And it could prevent us from bringing one of our own home," Briella said. "I hope it's not him."

"Me too," Hammer said. "No point in mourning until we know. We should head there with all haste."

"Then maybe next time don't poison the messenger," Cassidy growled. She tried reaching for her wolf again, but there was still nothing to catch onto, no sign that she'd ever existed. For the amount of time Cassidy had spent wishing she'd never been changed, this felt like missing a huge chunk of her very being. The presence of the wolf hadn't been what she'd objected to, not really. Having someone there who knew every bit of your darkest self, but still stood steadfastly by, was an immense comfort, even if that someone didn't understand why you worried about this or that. The wolf championed her, pushed her to be better, and now that she was gone, Cassidy desperately wanted to be whole again.

Before Hammer could respond, there was a quiet knock at the door. "Come in, Rocky," the Alpha said.

Rocky stuck his head through the door, then quickly looked down. "There was a message from Five Moons in spam, Alpha. Don't know why it got routed there. Her first message wasn't."

"Well, there you go," Hammer said to Cassidy. "Spam."

Cassidy took a deep breath, trying to throttle the anger out of her voice, knowing it would still be laced through her scent. "We need to get going. My wolves are putting their necks out. I want to get them home before something happens."

"Agreed." Hammer looked over at Briella. "Get me three others to match North Side's numbers. You stay here. This stinks, and I won't leave the den unprotected right now."

Briella nodded and scooted past Rocky, who was still in the doorway.

"It's not a setup," Cassidy said. "I promise."

"I'm not worried about you." Once again, Hammer glanced at Snow.

"Which didn't stop you from drugging me."

"No, it didn't." Hammer fixed Cassidy with a level stare. "We will all, every single Alpha you meet, be willing to do whatever we have to do to keep our packs safe. This isn't a glee club, we're not goddamn Junior Birdmen. We are predators." He stabbed one finger into his palm to emphasize each of the last three words. "We protect our own and we tolerate those who don't cross us. That's it."

"And that's why they'll be able to take us out," Cassidy said quietly. "You don't think they know that?"

"Who? We don't even know that something is being done to us!"

"I bet they thought the same thing in Dallas." Cassidy glanced over her shoulder at Snow, hoping for some conversational backup.

"I don't know what they thought in Dallas," Snow said. "There wasn't anyone left from the affected packs to talk to. Anyone who survived scattered."

Not quite the support she'd been hoping for, but Cassidy would take it. "I don't want to become one of those packs, do you?" She met Hammer's eyes, glare for glare. "Maybe there's no one out there picking us off one by one, but can you afford to be wrong? If we open up communication between our packs, what's the worst that happens? Aside from having to deal with my stink on the reg?"

He kept his eyes locked on hers, not willing to look down, to be seen to back down, here in the heart of his power. "You show me an enemy to stand against, and I will stand with you," Hammer finally growled. "Asking for more…" He shook his head.

Cassidy looked away. He'd made his concession, now was not the time to force him to bend his knee as well. "Maybe your tech wiz checks his email more often, then. Including the spam folder."

"That's reasonable." Hammer stepped back and turned away from her. "You heard Five Moons, Rocky. Keep an eye on the emails."

"Yes, Alpha. Alphas." Rocky took a tentative step into the den.

As he did, Cassidy realized she had no idea where Snow was. She cast around for the lone wolf, heaving a small sigh of relief when she caught sight of her lounging against the wall. It would have been easy to dismiss her as casually hanging out, but somehow she'd managed to completely withdraw from everyone's attention. Snow caught her searching and gave her a tight smile.

"And here are the others," Hammer said. Two more wolven stepped into the room. Both were women, one a Latina with tan skin and blue-black hair in a short bob that stopped at her chin. The handle of a knife stuck out of her boot. Cassidy hadn't seen a wolven who carried a weapon before. Most of them seemed to rely on the gifts of their wolves. The other was a white woman whose pale skin was spattered with freckles. Her long blond hair was pulled back into a severe bun which displayed her ears, one of which had quite the notch out of it.

"We're to take Rocky too," the black-haired wolven said.

"Veronica." Hammer indicated the first wolven with his chin. "And Ginnie." He indicated the blonde. "You know Rocky already." He sighed. "It's time. Let's see if Five Moons found our missing packmate."

CHAPTER TWENTY-FIVE

The breeze was chilly, but the sun was strong enough to bring some warmth to her shoulders, even through her jacket. Snow ghosted along behind Cassidy as they worked their way through the tangled undergrowth. It had been easier to access the place where they'd found the body from along the river. Of course, having to drive and park made for a much different proposition. No one wanted to be out in furform, not with humans along the banks, but skinform had so many disadvantages.

From the stench of decay, they were nearly there. Though the day was warm enough to speed the decomposition process further, the body had been hidden among trees where the sun would have trouble reaching. Hopefully, it would stay that way. At some point, even humans would notice and come looking for it, if they didn't stumble across it from blind luck.

"Too much death," Rocky whispered next to her. "I can't smell who it is."

Hammer grunted. The sound could have meant anything. His face was set in an expressionless mask, and the surrounding scents were doing a good job of obscuring the fragrance of his mood. His body language was incredibly easy to read, especially since he'd foregone a coat.

"Almost there," Cassidy murmured from the head of the group. "Luther should be meeting us soon. Or Phoebe."

Frankly, one of them should have made their presence known earlier. Though they weren't as loud as a similar sized group of humans, they were putting up a hell of a ruckus to Snow's ears. Skinform didn't lend itself well to stealth. Snow's skin itched with the urge to shift.

She quickened her pace as much as she could without making even more noise.

"Where are they?" Cassidy whispered as Snow caught up to her.

"I don't know. I'm surprised you don't either." Five Moons had an odd way of keeping tabs on her wolves, and Snow hadn't seen its like. It wasn't unusual for Alphas to have a close bond with the wolven they protected. The lack of a bond generally meant the group wasn't a true pack. Five Moons knew the location of her wolven to a degree that couldn't be explained by her senses. When they had time, Snow would have to ask her about it. Her list of questions for the North Side Alpha had gotten so long she'd started writing them down. There were too many to keep in her head.

"They're both around, but not here." Cassidy shook her head. "This isn't what I told them to do."

"We need to be careful."

"Agreed." Cassidy dropped into a crouch and picked her way forward, keeping an eye for dead branches and leaves that could give away their position.

It didn't take long for the others to follow suit. The already tense group grew even twitchier. Snow allowed the wolf to expand her senses, letting her ride closer to the surface. She would have to deal with the prickling at the tips of her ears and the ends of her fingers where the change threatened to begin. It wasn't a state she could hold indefinitely. Sooner or later, she would have to either let the wolf through all the way or push her back down, but for now, the discomfort was manageable.

Their progress dropped to a mere fraction of what they'd been making, but the group was nearly soundless now. Snow still felt exposed. The hairs on the back of her neck lifted, sending a cold chill down her spine. If someone had wanted to set up an ambush, they had the perfect time and place. They could take out two Alphas at once, and the wolven of Chicago would be leaderless.

Cassidy dropped into a crouch and pointed between the trees ahead. The body was close, not even ten yards away. Hammer nodded and led his people toward it.

"We're outnumbered if Hammer decides to attack," Cassidy murmured once the South Shore wolven had moved past them. "What do you think? Keep close, or let them do whatever they need to, whether it's their packmate or—"

A high-pitched yelp, nearly a yip stopped the Alpha midsentence. It was followed by a low whine, which, though quiet, held all the emotional weight of a howl of despair.

"Well, there's one question answered," Cassidy said. "I really wish…"

Snow shifted her weight. She desperately wanted to get out of there. The situation was highly volatile, and the tiniest thing could spark it into violence. But she was starting to believe in this Alpha. "If we take off, we would be answering any questions they might have about whether or not we're responsible for his death."

"And we don't want that."

"No."

"Damn it. Where are Phoebe and Luther?" Cassidy gnawed at her lower lip. "Let's leave South Shore some space. I want to see if there's anything that might tell us where our wolves have gone."

Your wolves. Snow kept her mouth shut. The Alpha already had enough to worry about without Snow correcting her. Plus, it was nice to be included among Five Moons' wolven. Not that she would ever claim a place in the pack, but maybe they could come to some sort of pack-adjacent arrangement.

"I'll check along the river," Snow said instead.

"Keep out of sight." When Snow fixed Cassidy with a look telling her she wasn't a cub on her first stalk, the Alpha half-grinned and shrugged. "I'll take the fence line. Do a perimeter sweep and meet back here."

Snow nodded, then got as low to the ground as her human legs would allow. Save for garbage, the river's edge was as empty as it had been the previous day. The same detritus they'd run into yesterday littered the frozen ground. The city had driven an ice breaker through the packed snow and ice, pushing some of the flotsam that had been caught on the frozen surface up over the edge. No wonder the humans had a detail working to clean the banks. If not for them, the place would be choked with debris come spring.

She made her way around, keeping a watch for anything that seemed more disturbed than it had yesterday. She also sniffed the air regularly to parse through the scents of the area. Faint whiffs of Phoebe hit her nostrils. Her scent was fresh in Snow's mind, since she had interacted with her earlier that morning. Luther's scent wasn't as strong. Either he hadn't been around as recently as Phoebe or he'd stayed further away. Snow tried to isolate his aroma to a particular area but couldn't. It had had longer to disperse.

When she got back to where she'd parted ways with Cassidy, the Alpha was already waiting, crouched behind a bush that afforded her cover from being seen from the river.

"Anything?" Cassidy asked.

"Phoebe was here more recently than Luther, but that's all I've got."

"It looks like Phoebe came and left along the river. I didn't see any sign that Luther left that way."

"He's not here now." Snow drummed her fingers on the ground. "He doesn't strike me as the type to hide as a gas."

Cassidy cracked a quick smile. "No. Luther is many things, but a joker isn't one of them."

"Now what?"

Cassidy looked over her shoulder at the group who were barely visible through the trees. "We finish what we came to do, then head home."

"They've had some time." Snow slunk over to the South Shore wolven. She made no effort to hide the sound of her movement through the underbrush, but she did take care to use the greenery to screen her from passersby. The Alpha followed her closely, so close at times that the vapor from her breath steamed past Snow's vision.

Hammer looked up at their approach. "Alpha. Snow."

"Alpha." Five Moons bowed her head. "This is Marquis, I take it."

"It is." He indicated the body, his people standing by it, though he was a step from them. Ginnie still had the dead wolven gathered to her, tears streaming down her cheeks.

"I'm very sorry," Five Moons said. "I wish…"

Hammer smiled, which did nothing to diminish the pain in his eyes or his scent. "As do I. We will take him with us and run to remember him. If we're lucky, his spirit will join us one last time."

"We didn't want to disturb him," Five Moons said. "Not until you'd had the chance to confirm who he was. Did you smell anything when you came here? Any sign of who could have done this?"

Hammer shook his head. "All I could smell was death and carrion birds."

At the mention of birds, Snow looked up toward the tops of the trees. No birds remained, which wasn't unexpected, given the sudden appearance of live wolven in their feeding ground. "What about that?"

"What about what?" Cassidy asked as she too looked upward. "Oh."

Tree limbs were snapped and bent downward as if something heavy had come through them. Something that had landed where the dead wolven now lay. She and Cassidy hadn't gotten close enough to take note of his wounds, but now she could see that his skin had been lacerated in multiple places. There was very little blood on the snow around his body. He'd been dead before he hit the ground.

"How does a wolven fall out of the sky?" Cassidy asked.

Rocky shifted back from the small group around Marquis and looked up. "Helicopter, I'd say."

"How could you possibly know that?" Cassidy eyed him closely.

"This isn't the first body I've seen tossed from one." Rocky shook his head and looked away.

"'Nam," Hammer said.

"Ah." Snow nodded in understanding. For some reason veterans and other military folks were easy to find among their ranks. They tended to get bitten, probably because the armed forces messed with their self-preservation instincts. Even so, a surprisingly large number of Vietnam vets had ended up as wolven. She didn't pretend to be a sociologist, though she'd taken some classes. The reasons so many wolven had experience, and trauma, from that particular war eluded her. Come to think of it, she'd noticed a number of packs who were starting to pick up veterans of the recent wars in the Middle East.

"So the real question is who's throwing wolven from helicopters?" Hammer asked.

"I have some suspicions," Five Moons said. "I wish Mary was here."

CHAPTER TWENTY-SIX

The smell of dead wolven lingered on her hands; Cassidy rubbed one against her thigh in a vigorous attempt to exorcise the smell, but to no avail. By some miracle, they'd gotten Marquis's body back to the South Shore Pack's car without being seen by humans. Hammer and his wolves were heading south even as she and Snow were on their way back to the hotel. Hopefully, Phoebe and Luther would both be there. Not for the first time, she wished there was a way to carry a cell phone with her paws. She'd left hers behind, figuring she might have to shift. It would have been so nice to be able to check in to see if there was any sign of either missing wolven.

Well, if wishes were wheels, her grandmother would be a trolley, or so her mom would say.

Mom. Cassidy's heart sank into her stomach. One more course on her overflowing buffet of problems.

A warm hand dropped on her thigh. It landed lightly, as if unsure of its reception. When she did nothing to move away from the touch, Snow relaxed, allowing it to lie comfortably against her.

"You all right?" Snow gave her thigh a light pat. "You're getting tense, and the speedometer is rising."

"Is it?" Cassidy glanced down. They were doing almost eighty-five. "Shit, it is." She eased up on the gas. She took a deep breath through her nose. There was no point in getting all worked up, and besides, if there was a worse time to get stopped for speeding, she didn't know it. "No, I'm not all right. Worried. Really worried."

"About anything in particular or…"

Cassidy barked a laugh she didn't feel at all. "You know, I would love it if I had only one thing to freak out about."

"At least Hammer doesn't seem to think you killed his wolven."

"That's true. So one thing has gone right for me lately. Of course, if he had any way of connecting us to a damn helicopter, then he'd probably be looking at us sideways."

"I've met exactly one wolven copter pilot," Snow said. "Since most of us don't do so well when cooped up, she piloted one with an open cockpit design."

"Really?" Cassidy turned her head for a moment to regard the lone wolf. The amount of people Snow had met was insane. It seemed like she always had a story or knew someone. "She's not from around here, I hope."

"Oh no. Lives outside of Portland. Oregon."

"That's a relief. No chance she was moonlighting in our neck of the woods?"

"I would be very surprised."

Cassidy let out a dramatic sigh of relief. "Then that's one suspect we can cross off the list."

"It is indeed." Snow went quiet, but Cassidy could tell she had more to say so she allowed the silence to stretch. "So what is your theory? You mentioned your sister, but I don't think Hammer made the connection."

"You think so?" That was an actual relief to hear. She'd wished she could have taken back the statement as soon as she'd said it. Everyone in the North Side Pack knew Mary as Malice and as Chicago's Hunter. It didn't sound like the larger community was aware of Cassidy's relationship to the Hunter, and she really wanted to keep it that way.

"You said she's not in town, so how do you think she's related to all this?"

"I'm pretty sure she isn't, not directly." Cassidy gripped the steering wheel tightly and made sure to ease off the gas pedal. "I don't have the same confidence about her bosses."

"Ah." Snow nodded. "What are we going to do against the Feds?"

Cassidy shook her head. "Hope I'm wrong? And I easily could be. It's a hell of a conclusion to jump to based on someone maybe being thrown out of a helicopter."

"It might have been the police. They have copters too."

"Now that's an idea." Cassidy reached over and grabbed Snow's hand. "Surely we have some cops among the various packs in the area. One of them could look into it for us. I'll send Hammer an email."

"Hopefully Rocky's keeping a better eye on it this time."

"Fingers crossed." She shook her head. "I hate this. I hate it so much." Cassidy was suddenly conscious of the small space they were in. If something happened, there was nowhere to go. She opened the windows, trying to relieve the creeping claustrophobia, but the wind across her face didn't help as much as she'd hoped.

Snow kept her hand on Cassidy's leg, and she was glad for it. The warmth and comfort that radiated from the simple touch was enough to keep her grounded for the rest of the drive. Her wolf didn't help much; she wanted out of the car as badly as Cassidy did, but she was willing to be distracted by Snow's presence.

Despite the flow of traffic being reasonable for that time of day, the trip home felt like it was never going to end. When they finally pulled into her parking spot, Cassidy wanted to sob with relief.

Snow must have felt it also, because she hopped out of the car as soon as Cassidy shifted the car into park. She stopped and waited for Cassidy by the back door.

The river called to her. The chance to shed her human cares and stretch her legs was almost impossible to resist, but she did. The matter of Luther and Phoebe still needed to be cleared up. They were close enough that it felt like Phoebe might be in the den, but Luther's star remained distant.

She had responsibilities. She and the wolf trudged toward their den, Snow trailing along behind her.

CHAPTER TWENTY-SEVEN

Though Snow had waited for Cassidy, she was craving some time alone. Something had changed in the car, and she needed to worry at it for a bit. The Alpha continued to give her a lot to think about and in a direction she hadn't allowed her thoughts to travel in years. Decades even.

"I'm heading upstairs," Snow said to Cassidy as they headed toward the lobby.

"Are you all right?" Cassidy asked.

"Tired." She patted Cassidy on the elbow. It wasn't the Alpha's fault that Snow needed to sort things out. "It's been a busy day."

"You can say that again." Cassidy's scent betrayed a deeper sadness and concern.

"I'll be by after I get a nap in, okay?"

"I'd like that." The sadness lightened a bit and Snow didn't try to stop her responding smile.

"Good."

"I'll let you get Phoebe and Luther figured out." She probably should have stuck around to help figure out what was going on, but how was she supposed to concentrate? No, it was better to head to her room and see if she could unravel some of her conflicting thoughts and emotions on her own. Because that always worked well. She shook her head as she mounted the steps to the second floor.

Her wolf swirled restlessly within her, mirroring her turbulent emotions. *What troubles you so?* she seemed to ask.

"It's not going to work," Snow said, pulling open the door to her room, a room she hadn't been spending much time in, truth be told. It barely smelled like her, and even here, there were faint notes of Cassidy's unique scent. She closed the door, then strode across the room to throw open a window. How could she be expected to think about the situation dispassionately with reminders of Cassidy in there with her? It felt like the Alpha was sitting on her shoulder, watching. Judging.

Judging? The word felt wrong to both Snow and the wolf. Weighing, maybe, but one thing they liked about Cassidy was the lack of judgment. One of many things they liked about her.

"Then what's the problem?" Snow collapsed backward onto the bed and let the cold air from the window wash over her. "Why do I feel like being interested in Five Moons, in Cassidy, is the worst thing that could have happened?"

Why indeed? Her wolf settled within her, leaving her with one point of relaxation among the tightness of her muscles.

"Well, there's the simple fact that this has never worked out for us before."

A warm glow of agreement washed away a little more tension across her shoulders.

"There's the part where she's the Alpha of a very broken pack, one that's being held together with little more than grit and twine."

But it is being held together, the wolf's continued approval seemed to say.

"I guess that is a point in her favor." Snow flopped over onto her front and stared at the pillows at the head of the bed. "She could have left all of this, but she's stayed. We know she doesn't flinch away from difficult paths."

Another set of muscles loosened up along Snow's upper arms.

"So you don't object to her, I take it?"

A phantom sensation, like the memory of a warm tongue along the side of her face bloomed into being.

Snow laughed. "That's good to know."

The sense of warmth cooled somewhat as the wolf demeanor changed to be more serious.

"But I have to be okay with her too, I get it." Snow crossed her arms and laid her chin on them. "I just don't know if I'm ready to go there. The timing is terrible. It literally could not be worse." Of course, without the terrible timing, Snow might not have been seeing the traits in Cassidy that she was coming to admire. The sticking point was the sex. Was Cassidy going to be all right not having it with her, and was she going to be all right with Cassidy having it with someone else?

When the second half of the question didn't provoke a pang of jealousy, Snow relaxed a bit. That was a trade she could make. Cassidy could hypothetically seek physical comfort with other hypothetical wolven, as long as she actually shared emotional intimacy with Snow. Hypothetically.

She liked Cassidy a lot. Seeing her in action with Hammer had cast her in a very different light. She might not be a perfect Alpha, but her instincts were good. She was a good protector, and Snow felt at ease with her in a way she hadn't been with anyone for a long time. That this Alpha would accept her comfort, could open a side of herself to Snow that nobody else got to see, made her think that there could be something there. The offered support in the car might have been a small gesture, but Snow hadn't been prepared for the intensity of her own reaction when Cassidy had accepted it. How could one simple act of reaching out mean so much to her? And she'd been the one doing the reaching.

The wolf made a surprisingly good therapist, but a real one would have been even better. None of the wolven she knew in Chicago could serve in that capacity. A couple out in Navajo country could, and there were a number on the West Coast who were excellent at talking through matters of the heart. A couple of them were even licensed to do so or had been at one time. There was a point at which you had to let your license lapse; certification boards started to get suspicious when the paperwork showed you'd been practicing for going on fifty or sixty years.

So she was on her own to pick out the threads of this mess. Why was she so scared, and what was she going to do about it? And would Cassidy want a relationship with her if it didn't include a physical component? Was this all because she gave some decent advice, and the Alpha wanted to keep her in that capacity?

She flopped over to stare at the ceiling. Nothing about the situation was getting any clearer.

* * *

Snow's aroma lingered through the first floor and into the lobby. Cassidy stood at the bottom of the stairs, considering her next move. While Snow's scent was starting to tatter into a fraying silver ribbon, traces of Phoebe's still lingered. That was a relief. Less reassuring were the barest notes of Luther's presence. He hadn't been here for a bit.

Cassidy gnawed at her lower lip as she made her way into the lobby. Her mom needed to be taken care of, but she had more pressing matters. The timing of everything was a complete mess. Every time she thought they might get one fire handled, another popped up.

As if her thoughts had summoned her, Sophia turned around on one of the overstuffed chairs.

"Cassie-bean!" She stood, a notebook held between her hands.

Naomi lounged on the couch next to her mom. She tried not to smirk at the pet name, but the curl at the edge of her lips was unmistakable.

"Hi, Mom." Now was not the time

"I've been doing some research." Sophia held up the notebook. Sure enough, it was covered with handwritten notes. "Naomi has been very helpful with giving me ideas for finding Mary." She moved around the chair and closed the distance between them.

"I'm glad to hear it." Cassidy forced her lips into a smile and carefully did not glare at the other wolven.

"You've been here longer than I have. Do you know anything about these investigators?"

When her mom tried to press the notepad into her hands, Cassidy held them up. "There are like ten million people in the Chicago area. I don't know anything more about them than you do."

"You could at least look at the names." Her mom's brows drew down into a hurt frown. "Don't you want to find your sister?"

"Of course I do, but she's not the only one missing." Cassidy leaned around her mom to fix Naomi with an intense look somewhere between "we have important things to talk about" and "help me out of this mess now."

The amused look slid off Naomi's face, and she sat up out of her relaxed slouch. "Cassidy? Is this about Phoebe and Luther?"

"Yes. Where are they?"

"Cassidy Nolan." Sophia stood up straight. "Are you going to help or not?"

Cassidy screwed her eyes shut and took a deep breath. Then another. "We can talk as soon as I get some things figured out first. Why don't I meet up with you in your room? I'll be up soon."

Despite her mom's glare, Cassidy held her ground. The force of Sophia's disapproval felt like it went on for hours, but she was probably only being stared down for a few seconds.

"Fine," her mom said. "I'll continue my research while you take care of the so-much-more-important things than your sister who's been missing for weeks."

"Thank you, Mom."

When Cassidy didn't rise to the bait, her mom strode across the lobby to the bank of elevators. She turned on her heel and pointedly didn't look at Cassidy while she waited.

Another eternity passed before the elevator opened and her mom stepped into it. Cassidy heaved a sigh of relief and turned back to Naomi.

"Sorry, what were you going to say?"

"Phoebe is in her room. She came back a couple hours ago. Nothing from Luther." Naomi gave her Alpha a side-eyed glance. "She said he wasn't there when she got back to the site. Didn't want to be there without a buddy."

"I told them to stick together," Cassidy said. She wrapped her hands around the back of her neck, trying to squeeze out the tension that was setting up permanent housekeeping there. "Where the hell is Luther?"

"Phoebe thought he met up with you." Naomi was on her feet.

Cassidy shook her head. She closed her eyes to better concentrate on the stars that made up the constellation of her pack. Those in the building shone strongest. Snow was off on her own, veiled somewhat by the fact that Cassidy hadn't claimed her. Those who belonged to the pack or to Cassidy but who weren't in the den were still there; Luther was shining among them. Wherever he was, he was alive. Out of force of habit, Cassidy looked for Ruri's star. It still twinkled, the light strong, if removed. So at least Mary was probably all right too. She could only hope.

It really was too bad that she couldn't use the stars as a wolven-finding device. She had to be so close for them to register as anything other than distant. Proximity of other pack members helped somewhat, but that only went so far.

"He's alive," she said as she opened her eyes.

"You're sure?"

"Of that." Cassidy laughed hollowly. "Not a whole lot else. I need to fill you in on what's happened, and we need to figure out our next steps."

"Yes, Alpha." Naomi fell in step with her.

"What's been going on with my mom?" Cassidy asked as they mounted the stairs up to the penthouse.

"She came out for some breakfast. She seems like a nice lady. She's been hanging out with Beth. And Carlos."

"That's good." Cassidy considered the situation for a moment. "Please tell Carlos that I don't want to hear about him seducing my mom."

"Does that mean no sleeping with her? Or just keeping it under your radar?"

Cassidy squeezed her eyes shut and waved a hand at Naomi. If she answered the question, then all her plausible deniability about her mom's dating life would go straight out the window.

"Got it," Naomi said. "I think," she whispered barely loud enough for her Alpha to hear.

"Thank you." Cassidy pushed open her door, then started pacing in her usual spot in front of the living room windows. It wasn't enough, so she opened one of the windows and stepped out onto the flat roof.

Naomi ducked through the window and joined her.

For once, the wind wasn't off the lake, so the temperature wasn't completely freezing. Mounds of snow endured in shadowed areas, though much had melted wherever the sun could reach it. They were due for a storm soon; with her recent luck, it would be one that would dump a foot and a half on the city. The stiff breeze scoured away the smells that remained in her nostrils: traces of dead wolven, Hammer's suspicion, the grief of his pack. She filled her lungs with fresh air, then exhaled.

"So, the dead wolven was Hammer's," she said, not taking her eyes off the Chicago skyline. "That's the bad news. The good news is he doesn't seem to blame us. Going to get him was the right move."

"I'm glad that panned out." Naomi came and stood right next to Cassidy, who wrapped one arm around her shoulder and pulled her in so they stood without even a fraction of an inch between them.

"Mm hmm. I wish I could say it gets better from these, but it doesn't." Cassidy snorted loudly. "Because of course it doesn't. Seems Marquis—Hammer's wolven—was thrown from a helicopter, so now we have to examine those implications. The Alphas are meeting in a couple weeks. It would be good to have a theory to bring to them, but so far I don't have anything that sounds even close to reasonable."

"That's not good."

"It really isn't. Also, we definitely need to track down Luther. He was liaising with the Aurora pack. He's met with them once, and I'd rather not have to send someone else out to them." She hated herself for having to think of the practicalities around Luther's disappearance. A better person than she would have been concerned simply because someone she cared for was missing, but she couldn't afford to be that person right now.

"I'll get a few of ours on the search. Jimmy has a good nose."

"Can we trust him?"

Naomi shrugged. "If we send him out with Zoya, I think so. She'll put him in his place if need be."

"Good plan. I'll come with you to send home how really important this is." Normally, Cassidy hated giving out assignments directly, preferring to delegate through her Beta or Naomi, but this was too crucial to allow a miscommunication to mess it up. She was simply going to have to get past the voice that whispered that there was no reason for these people to take her instructions, not when they were so much older and more experienced than she.

"And if we don't find Luther?" Naomi stared right at her as she asked the question. Usually, the wolven's directness was welcome, but Cassidy wasn't ready to consider those implications.

"Then we keep moving forward," Cassidy said. It was the right move, no matter how ill-equipped she felt about it. Luther was a huge part of her support and possibly losing it felt like an insurmountable obstacle. "I'll reach out to Aurora if we haven't tracked him down by the end of the day."

"I can do it."

Cassidy chewed on the inside of her cheek. Unknown Alphas reaching out directly to other packs was full of pitfalls, as she'd discovered with the South Shore Pack. She also didn't want to dump the job on Naomi, not when she wasn't Cassidy's Beta. If Luther didn't reemerge from wherever he'd gone, that would have to change.

"Alpha," Naomi said. "I'm happy to do it. Things are going smoothly with Kenosha."

"That's another bit of good news, then. I'll take every bit I can." Cassidy nodded. "If you're sure you can handle it. I'm counting on you to bring me in if that changes."

Naomi grinned. "Of course. I know my limitations."

"At least one of us does."

Naomi's scent sharpened with curiosity. "I don't get that vibe from you."

"Fantastic. I can hide my neuroses from my wolven. Awesome."

Her scent slid right past curious into concerned. "Are you all right? You've been off since you got back from meeting with Hammer the first time."

"So everything going wrong that can go wrong and my mom showing up without notice aren't enough for you?" Cassidy bared her teeth in a dangerous grin. How far did Naomi want to push things?

Naomi turned to look toward the lake, not that it was visible from where they stood. "That's more than enough. For most people." Her own grin was crooked. "But you're not most people."

Cassidy leaned her forearms against the half-wall around the roof's perimeter. "There's nothing else to say. I'm doing what I can with what I have."

"And you're doing a good job of it or as good a job as anyone can do. Things will look better when we track down Luther."

"I'll be happy when everyone is home." Maybe then she could finally relax, with Snow would be best. The idea of curling up in furform with the lone wolf was incredibly appealing, even more than heading out for a run with her.

"We're not going to find him up here," Cassidy said, pushing herself away from the roof edge. "Let's get Zoya and Jimmy out on this. They aren't to leave each other's sight, mind. If Luther had come back with Phoebe…"

"I'm on the same page, boss," Naomi said. "I've got you covered."

"I'm glad," Cassidy said simply. It was true. She couldn't remember Naomi having said those words before, not so explicitly. The other wolven had never done anything to make Cassidy question her commitment to her or the pack, but it was nice to hear it put so starkly.

Finding Zoya didn't take long. During the week, she would have been at work, but since it was a Saturday, she was in her room. Her shaggy head lifted from the round bed that had been installed in front of the window. The window opened a crack to let in the outside air. It had been a while since the pack had gone out for a communal run, and Cassidy wasn't the only one feeling the lack. After they found Luther, she resolved that they should all go out. It would do them good to get some dirt and grass under their feet and to feel the wind through their fur.

Zoya's head cocked in question at the appearance of the Alpha and one of the most dominant wolven. Brilliant green eyes the color of new growth considered Cassidy and Naomi with frank curiosity.

"I have a job for you," Cassidy said. "Meet us in the backyard. You can keep to furform."

The wolf rolled off the raised bed and onto the floor with almost no sound. She shook herself, fluffing out russet fur that had gone flat where she'd been lying on it. She headed for the open door as Cassidy and Naomi went in search of Jimmy.

He was more difficult to track down. They finally found him in one of the hotel's empty basement rooms.

"Naomi," Jimmy said, rolling to his feet. "Alpha." The room was in a state of disarray. Carpeting had been pulled up and gathered into a messy roll along one wall. The windows were covered up with cardboard and blackout curtains. Twin banks of lights ran the length of the ceiling.

"Jimmy, are you installing a grow-op in here?" Cassidy asked.

"Depends," he said. He shifted his weight from one foot to the other. "How much trouble am I in if I am?"

"Oof." Cassidy perched on the counter at the small kitchenette. "I really don't have time to deal with this."

Jimmy cringed, and a ruddy flush spread across his cheeks until they nearly glowed red, his pale skin doing nothing to hide his embarrassment. "I thought we could bring in some extra cash. It's no secret we've been a bit strapped lately."

Naomi stalked across the room and grabbed him by the scruff of the neck. "We don't do that here. You want to bring the cops down on us?"

"What? It's legal now." He struggled in Naomi's grip but couldn't shake free.

"Is that so? You applied for your grower's license, did you?"

"Well. No."

"Then it's not legal, is it?"

"Even if it were legal, what have you lined up for distribution?" Cassidy asked. "It's not like you can just sell it on the street. Not legally. And how are we going to explain the uptick in our electrical and water needs? If you wanted to try this, you could have come to me. We could have put together a business plan, looked to secure funding, figured out the ROI..."

"But, Alpha—"

Cassidy chopped her hand down to cut him off. "We don't have time for this. Meet us out back. Shift to furform."

"Got it, Alpha." Jimmy bobbed his head when Naomi let him go. He reached for the waist of his pants and shoved them down. "I'll be right there."

Cassidy had no words for him, at least none that were constructive. She turned on her heel and headed for the nearest stairs.

"That's a boneheaded move, even for Jimmy," Naomi said as they took the stairs two at a time. When Cassidy checked over her shoulder to see if Jimmy was in earshot, Naomi laughed. "If he didn't know it before, he does now. MacTavish might have allowed, hell, even encouraged, illegal money-making schemes, but Dean never did. I'm glad you've kept that up."

"It's an unnecessary risk," Cassidy said. She shrugged. Being compared to Dean made her almost as uncomfortable as comparisons to MacTavish. "There are ways of doing this right. Besides, I've seen the books. We're fine as long as we don't spend beyond our means. I wonder where he got the idea we're low on funds?"

"MacTavish had his wolven turn in whatever cash they had, so he could sit on it like some asshole banker. Maybe he's concerned that since you don't do the same thing, we have no nest egg." Naomi shrugged. "I don't think anyone's gone over the pack finances with MacTavish's wolves."

"Maybe it's time."

"Do we trust them?"

Cassidy considered the question until they hit the top of the stairs. "To a point. They haven't tried anything yet, and if they haven't by now, I don't know that they will. Jimmy's heart seems like it's in the right place. Besides, it's not like we're going to tell them names and account numbers. I'd rather not have anyone else doing anything iffy because they think they're being proactive and helping out the pack."

"You're the Alpha," Naomi said.

"That I am." They were at the doors to the backyard, and the sound of paws on carpet and the smell of wolf in furform let Cassidy know that Jimmy was right behind them. She pushed open the door to let him past, then turned to Naomi. "I'll get them headed in the right direction. Can you get Phoebe and bring her to my rooms?"

"Will do." Naomi took off at a jog while Cassidy followed Jimmy's dark brown tail out into the overgrown backyard.

The day was chillier in the shade. Cassidy rubbed her arms briskly through her shirt and tried not to shiver.

"Follow the river south to the green space by the Damen Avenue bridge," she said to the waiting wolves. "You'll know you're in the right place when you smell dead wolven."

Both sets of ears perked up, but Jimmy's tail dropped low between his legs.

"He wasn't one of ours. He belonged with South Shore, and they've taken him back." Cassidy let out a deep breath. Her breath steamed in the cold air. "Luther and Phoebe were watching the body while I got Hammer. Phoebe came home, but Luther didn't. I need you to check out the area. See what you can find about Luther's disappearance. If you can track him out of there, that would be great. He's still alive, I know that much, but I don't know where he is, and we really need him right now."

Zoya stood from her seated position and whuffed once in what Cassidy knew was agreement. She stalked around Jimmy, then bumped him with her shoulder and bit him on the top of the flank hard enough that he yipped in protest. He jumped up to face her, but Zoya took off toward the river's banks.

Cassidy watched the two wolves go. Their brown fur blended quickly into the dead trees and vegetation at the back of the property. All the wolven knew the narrow green spaces that had been allowed to remain along both sides of the Chicago River's north branch. They were as familiar with Luther's scent as they were with Cassidy's or their own.

Phoebe might help shed some light on what had happened, but she wasn't especially confident that the wolven would be able to do so. Still, Cassidy had to keep moving. If she stopped, the consequences weren't going to be good, not for her and not for her wolves.

CHAPTER TWENTY-EIGHT

The room had darkened when Snow opened her eyes. The shadows didn't bother her too much, not while in furform. Wrestling with the question of Cassidy had exhausted her, and late in the afternoon she'd decided it was time for a nap. She must have been more tired than she'd thought, as not a trace of color was left in the sky, what little of it she could see through her window.

A slight twinge of guilt pulled at her. She'd said she would head up to Cassidy's rooms, but the lure of sleep had been too much. Hopefully the Alpha would understand. Five Moons had more than enough on her plate to keep her occupied.

Her stomach growled, a rumble the wolf echoed. While food wouldn't help her decide what she should do about the North Side Pack's Alpha, it would certainly improve her outlook. She got up and stretched, pulling way back on her haunches and digging her paws into the soft covers of the bed until her spine popped from her shoulders to her tail. After a quick shake to settle her fur in place, she jumped down and headed for the door. Cassidy's mom knew about the wolven now, so traipsing around the hotel in furform probably wasn't off-limits. Cassidy hadn't said anything against it.

Would she have known to? Snow twitched her ear in the wolf equivalent to a shrug. It didn't matter. If a human was going to stay with wolven, it was bound to happen. It probably had already.

The door popped open when Snow pulled down on the handle with one massive paw. She trotted down the hall, her head and tail held high. The scents of the wolven who lived on this floor were strong, but there was not a whiff of Cassidy's smell, beyond the faint traces that indicated she lived in the building and occasionally came to this part of the hotel.

The kitchen would have both cooked and uncooked food. Saliva coated the inside of her mouth at the thought of a nice juicy haunch of beef. Venison would have been better, but no one had been out on a true hunt for a bit. Beth had been making do with what she could get freshest at the local butcher shop.

It didn't occur to the wolf to check what time it was. She had the information she needed: it was dark and her stomach had declared it was time to eat. Snow kept an eye out for a clock, however. She sensed the wolf's faint sense of amusement. When she finally passed a working clock, Snow was surprised to see it was nearly 7 p.m.

She vaulted down the stairs, glad that someone had seen fit to carpet them. That had probably been Ruri. Dean's Beta was quite handy and paid attention to all the details. That all the doors in the hotel could be opened either in wolf or human form was because of her foresight. Trying to scrabble down the steps without something for nails to catch hold of would have been a disaster. Not that the wolven ran the chance of being hurt too badly from a tumble, but if a situation arose where they'd have to take the stairs in a hurry, they would be severely hampered.

Her thoughts on the ease with which she could mount the stairs in wolf form were interrupted by raised voices from the first floor. She veered away from the basement kitchen and decided to check on the commotion instead.

She skulked through the stairwell door and into the lobby where three wolven were gathered around the entrance's double doors. All were in skinform, and all were yelling, one complete with wild gesticulations and another leaning back with crossed arms. The third was a little further away. He too was hollering, but he'd kicked off his shoes and seemed to be preparing to take off his clothing. Anger and distress poured off the group in jagged waves.

Snow slunk forward, working to stay hidden from everyone involved in the altercation that was definitely brewing.

"I *will* see your Alpha." The voice that cut through the combined hubbub of angry wolven was familiar.

Oh no. Snow moved more quickly, still staying to the periphery, but confident of who she would see when she rounded the final piece of furniture. She hadn't been able to smell this person, nor would she ever be able to.

Framed against a backdrop of darkness speckled with white flakes was Carla, Chicago's vampire lord. She stood directly outside the threshold to the building, drawn up to her full height. Despite being several inches shorter than the shortest of the wolven who confronted her, she still managed to seem like she was the one staring them down.

"Cassidy 'Five Moons' Nolan, Alpha of the North Side Pack, owes *me* a favor, and I have come to collect." Each of Carla's words hung in the air like a razor blade, poised and ready to draw blood at the slightest misstep.

"Bull fucking shit, vamp," Carlos said. He sneered down at her, revealing full wolf teeth in a mouth that had never been designed for them. His eyes gleamed brilliant red.

"You tell her," the now-shirtless wolven said from behind him. Snow thought perhaps it was Jamieson.

Tall Alicia, who was broad-shouldered and imposing without the benefit of starting the shift to furform, stood directly behind Carlos. Her eyes burned a deep violet that almost disappeared against her nearly black skin. She said nothing and simply stood with her arms crossed. She had an air of implacability. Nothing would move her if she didn't want it to. Of course, most things weren't vampire lords who could destroy those in her path before they realized she was there.

On top of it, Carla was right. Five Moons owed her. The North Side wolven might not believe her, but it was true. Only Five Moons could defuse this situation before it deteriorated too much further.

Snow hunkered, her mind tripping five hundred miles an hour, weighing the variables behind her safety and those of the wolven at the door. The stories said vampires couldn't enter an abode without an invitation. She'd never had the opportunity to see if that was the case, but Carla wasn't making any effort to rush the door, despite her obvious irritation.

The vampire held herself still, which wasn't unusual. What didn't add up was the stiffness. Something was wrong. Snow couldn't help but sniff at the air for some inkling of the source of Carla's irritation, besides being stymied in her demands to enter the den.

Where was Cassidy? Could Snow get to her quickly enough that they could return to the lobby before something irrevocable happened? She ran the calculus on the time it would take to get to Cassidy and back. Even if she was able to find her right away, it was still too long.

Snow scooted out from her hiding spot, deliberately drawing the attention of the group at the door, including Carla. She braced her feet on the carpet.

I need to take this one, she explained to the wolf. To her relief, the wolf agreed and withdrew, though slowly. The wolf kept an eye on their surroundings through the eternity of her change, ready to come rushing back into her body if anyone showed the least bit of inclination to attack.

No one did, and why would they? The move was insane. If Snow had been one of them, she would have been among the least in power, if not the very lowest. Perhaps if the pack had had cubs, she would have taken precedence over them in terms of dominance, but that certainly wasn't a given.

Four sets of eyes were on her when Snow finished trembling her way through the change. She pulled herself up, paying no mind to her nudity even when the frigid air from the door threatened to freeze her where she stood.

"The vampire is right," she said. "Five Moons owes her. She should be allowed inside."

As the last word left her mouth, Carla jerked forward, no longer straining against the force keeping her from entering the hotel.

Snow's words had just broken the barrier.

Carla took a stumbling step into the lobby, sending Carlos and Jamieson flinching away from her. Alicia simply continued to stand, though she too watched Snow.

"Isn't that interesting?" the vampire Lord of Chicago said. "It would seem you've found a home after all."

* * *

"So you found yourself a PI?" Cassidy lounged on her favorite couch, trying not to see its shabbiness through her mom's eyes.

"I did. I ran my list from the Internet through Angie's List. Had to sign up for an account and everything. He comes highly recommended." Sophia stood in front of her windows, watching the twinkling lights of downtown. "You have great views from here."

"I like it."

"Seems a little lonely. You getting out and seeing people?"

"I see plenty of people, Mom. I'm fine." Cassidy tried not to sigh too audibly. Sophia didn't apologize. Apparently, she preferred to go back to doting on her children as if nothing had happened. While she was happy for the reprieve, Cassidy knew her mom hadn't forgotten their earlier argument. "Tell me about this investigator."

"His name is Alec Gunn. Apparently he's a retired police detective." Sophia turned enough to watch her daughter out of the corner of her eye. "He was surprised no one filed a missing persons' report."

Cassidy grimaced. That had never occurred to her. The unease in her belly told her it was a bad idea. Was that her own discomfort with the idea, or was the wolf worried it could lead back to the pack? "Did you file one?"

"Alec suggested I pull together as much information as I can, then go down to Mary's local precinct tomorrow. Until then, he says I should put out some notices on as many social media accounts as I can."

Cassidy's grimace turned into a full body cringe. "How is that supposed to help? You know Mary doesn't have anything like that."

"Her gallery does. And other people might have seen her."

"She's not going to want you to throw her personal business up for everyone to see." Cassidy tried to find a more comfortable position on the couch. Her wolf was prowling within her. Inviting the attention of potential predators was a terrible idea.

"He's the expert, Cassidy." Sophia's voice was sharp. "We're already two weeks behind. What do you want me to do?"

"Just be careful. Try not to blow Mary's life up too much." *Try not to shed too much light on my life while you're at it.*

"Will you give me a ride to go to the precinct and meet with Alec tomorrow?"

"I don't know if I'll be free." Sophia opened her mouth to protest, but Cassidy raised a hand. "I can find someone to take you, though. That won't be a problem."

"Good, because I told Alec I'd be at the station at nine sharp."

"Sure, su—" Cassidy stiffened. A shock pulsed through her system, and she started in her seat.

"Are you okay?" her mom asked. "You look like something just bit you."

"In a manner of speaking, I guess," Cassidy replied absently. It had felt more like what she could have expected had she decided to stick a fork into an electrical outlet, but the source was clear. It was Snow.

The lone wolf blazed suddenly at the center of the mental star field that made up Cassidy's pack.

That in itself was curious enough, but on the heels of the unexpected sensation was an unmistakable feeling of rage, strong enough that Cassidy's muscles tensed in sympathy. Her wolf did more than tense. She jumped up within Cassidy and dug her claws deep into the underside of Cassidy's rib cage, demanding to be released.

Cassidy couldn't contain her gasp at the pain from the wolf's insistence. She waved her mom away when she started across the living room to check on her daughter.

Well, she tried to wave Sophia away. That became awkward quickly when Cassidy tried to stand up just as her mom was pressing a hand to her forehead.

"Mom!" The word came out with more force than she'd intended. Cassidy gentled her tone. "I'm fine. There's a problem with the wolven. The other werewolves." Although they'd been talking for a couple of hours now, she hadn't yet gone into the intricacies of how the wolven viewed themselves versus how the rest of the world saw them. Hell, she hadn't even told her mom about being the one in charge.

"You feel a bit warm," Sophia said.

"You need to…" Out of options, Cassidy gently took her mom by the shoulders and lifted her out of the way. She took care not to tear her mom's sweater with the claws that had already emerged from the tips of her fingers. For every second she delayed, the wolf kicked up a bigger fuss, until it felt like she might just punch her way through Cassidy's skin.

Sophia scoffed at the contact, but whatever she saw in her daughter's face put a stop to the protests.

Cassidy took advantage of her mom's pause. "I'll be back when I can."

She left the room without looking back. Her teeth gritted to keep from shifting in the corridor, and she looked within to see if she could determine who was involved. Three other wolven were showing signs of distress. They pulsed erratically on her inner starscape, a light show she could no longer ignore. A short while back, she'd made note of some feelings of mounting aggression among them but had discounted them. Such things happened regularly, and Cassidy had learned not to interfere unless it seemed like they were going to lead to actual bloodshed. Those feelings had now escalated to the kind of tension that preceded an outburst of extreme violence.

She reached for the lights of the three as she trotted toward the stairwell closest to her mom's room. They belonged to Carlos, Alicia, and Jamieson. Carlos had been set to keep an eye on the hotel's lobby for the evening. The other two were in close proximity to him, both physically and in rage.

Snow was there too, but her initial outburst of incandescent anger had now been completely eclipsed by anxiety that bordered on panic and showed no sign of receding.

Cassidy broke into a headlong dash down the stairs. Fur erupted through her skin in a smooth wave as muscles cramped and shifted. She grimly clamped her mouth against the pain caused by surfacing the wolf so quickly. She refused to allow the wolf to take over completely, keeping them in betweenform. If the three wolven were attacking Snow, the sight of Cassidy in her Alpha form should warn them off. If it didn't…

Her mouth hung open as she grinned a lupine smile that promised death to those who might defy her. Saliva dripped from her jaws, but she didn't care. The wolf was truly ascendant for the first time in days, and for once, Cassidy was in complete agreement with her lupine counterpart's instincts.

They burst through the doors to the stairwell with so much speed that they used the momentum to career off the walls. A quick plant of the feet and a push-off hard enough to dent the drywall sent them rocketing toward the top of the grand stairs.

When they emerged at the top of the wide staircase, five heads turned to take them in as they towered, claws out and eyes burning. Tattered clothing hung from their frame, the seams no match for their body's abrupt change.

They raked their eyes over the gathered wolven. No, the gathered beings. Not all of them were pack.

There were no marks upon Snow's body. Naked as she was, the smallest wound would have been immediately visible. Her eyes widened at Cassidy and the wolf's sudden appearance, but the mental echo of her distress faded immediately.

The other three weren't menacing Snow as Cassidy and the wolf had feared. Instead, they were arrayed in a loose semicircle around the small woman whose presence filled the first-floor lobby, despite the distinct lack of scent she brought with her.

"Hello, Cassidy," Carla purred. "I've come to collect."

"What's going on here?" Cassidy forced the words past a muzzle and tongue poorly formed for human speech.

"Your wolf was kind enough to let me in," Carla said. Her teeth had descended and were easily visible against her delighted grin. She turned her head to indicate Snow, but her eyes never left Cassidy's.

"I didn't mean it," Snow said softly. As she looked away, her star seemed to recede. A shiver struck through Cassidy and her wolf.

They descended the stairs slowly, watching everyone for signs that the standoff was about to deteriorate further.

"Regardless of intent, here I am," Carla said.

"What I want to know is why," Cassidy snarled.

Carla turned in place to keep facing her as they crossed the lobby to oh-so-casually stand between Snow and the vampire. Judging by the faint smirk on Carla's face, her choice hadn't gone unnoticed.

Before Cassidy could open her mouth to reiterate her demand, a gasp from the top of the stairs pulled everyone's attention away from her and Carla. Cassidy didn't need to look; she recognized the voice. She'd been hearing it all her life, after all. Carla's eyes flicked to the stairs and back so quickly Cassidy wouldn't have seen them move if she hadn't been watching for it.

"Cassidy Anne," her mom said in shocked tones. "What is going on here? Why is Snow naked? And why isn't anyone doing anything about it?"

CHAPTER TWENTY-NINE

"Not! Now!" Cassidy roared. She tried not to notice the flinch that turned into a stumble on her mom's part. "Get back to your room." She turned to face Carla. "You…"

"Yes, darling?" Carla made a show of considering the nails on her left hand. She glanced up, pantomiming surprise that Cassidy was still there. "If we're going to talk, let's do it somewhere a little more private." She reached out as if to touch Cassidy.

The wolf growled, the sound echoing deep inside their chest. She dearly wished to tear this vampire upstart into very small pieces, but Cassidy had made her a promise.

Carla withdrew her hand slowly. "Or we can talk here, but my business is sensitive. You may not want prying ears to overhear things that might make them a target." This time Carla's eyes tracked slowly over to Cassidy's mom.

The wolf didn't take kindly to the vampire lord's implication. Cassidy's legs threatened to buckle as the wolf attempted to claw control away from her. She leaned forward, her muzzle inches from Carla's face.

"Do not. Do that. Again." She forced the words past the wolf's urgent efforts to break the rest of the way free. She could almost taste the vampire's blood on her tongue. It would be so satisfying, and the struggle before the kill would be exhilarating. She felt it in her bones.

"The conference room is free, Alpha." Naomi had joined her mom at the top of the stairs. She had one arm around her mom's waist and was trying to guide her away. Sophia wasn't cooperating, but Naomi was gently overpowering the resisting human.

"Good. Idea." With supreme effort, Cassidy wrestled down her wolf, then stepped away from Carla. "Lead us," she snarled at Alicia, who had the misfortune of being the closest wolven.

Behind her, Jamieson had gone full wolf. His light brown fur stood on end, and emerald eyes glowered at Carla from beneath a brow furrowed into a snarl that promised pain to whatever ended up in his jaws. Alicia cocked her head at him in wordless communication, then she headed around the main stairs and deeper into the building.

"Go," Cassidy said to Carla. She tried to glance Snow's way but couldn't immediately find the lone wolf. Snow was close by; she still shone in Cassidy's mind. That was fine. The less attention that she brought to herself, the safer she would be. Her mom was gone from the top of the stairs, though her voice was still raised in confusion as Naomi escorted her back to her room. That problem of her mom was merely being kicked down the road a little farther.

Satisfied that everyone was where they should be, Cassidy turned to follow Carla, who was sashaying along next to Alicia and speaking in tones low enough that even Cassidy couldn't hear. The vampire reached out and placed a dainty hand on Alicia's forearm, then pulled it back, making sure to trace her fingertips over muscles that were bunched up beneath the wolven's skin. Fury poured off Alicia in a cloud of crimson that seared the insides of Cassidy's nostrils. Jamieson prowled along behind them, emitting a growl so low it was nearly inaudible. It thrummed along Cassidy's bones, stoking her wolf's fury.

The conference room looked very little of the sort. While it might once have been used for business meetings or the like, these days the pack typically used it to watch movies on the large monitor mounted to the far wall. The recess in the ceiling hid the projection screen that went with the old projector that stood in one corner. A mismatched group of chairs and sofas took up the middle of the room. If the lobby's furniture looked battered, the furniture here tottered only a few steps from complete destruction. They were all comfortable, as Cassidy could attest, but they looked on the edge of collapse.

Carla glanced around, the bridge of her nose crinkling delicately. That was fine. If she was so much better than the surroundings, why had she even come here?

Cassidy threw herself down on one of the taller-backed chairs. She considered the vampire as Carla perched herself on an armchair with fewer rents in the cushions than the others. She had very little sense of how the vampires operated, having decided early on that she needed to concern herself with keeping her pack together. Vampires hadn't figured into that equation. Did Carla make house calls? It seemed unlikely that she visited many wolven dens, not judging by the disdain with which she surveyed her current surroundings.

Alicia stood by the door, Jamieson at her side. Two sets of jewel-toned eyes glowed at them.

This was going to require a different kind of backup. Cassidy closed her eyes and reached out into the star field of her pack and grabbed Naomi's star, giving it a gentle tug. She eyed Snow's star as well. It would have been a great comfort to have the lone wolf there, not only because she made Cassidy feel better, but because Snow saw things Cassidy missed. She cupped Snow's star in imaginary hands, allowing her warmth to wash over her, slowing her heart rate. Her head cleared and the wolf subsided in her demands to be set completely free.

They would stay in betweenform. If Carla attacked, they would be better equipped to defend the pack.

"So, Alpha."

Cassidy held up one finger, watching with interest as a flicker of rage passed over the vampire's face before disappearing as smoothly as a ripple easing back into the surface of the water.

"One moment, if you please." She could get the words out now that her anger had subsided somewhat. It was easier to think away from the smell of Snow's anxiety.

"Of course." Carla leaned back and crossed her legs slowly. The flash of pale flesh at the top of her stockings was designed to capture Cassidy's interest.

Even knowing as much, Cassidy couldn't help but look. The vampire oozed attraction from every pore. Could she even help it? Was Carla always hunting for her next meal without being aware of it? Only moments before, she'd made some sort of attempt with Alicia, and here she was trying something with Cassidy.

"If you're going to stare at it that closely, you might as well take a taste," Carla said quietly.

"I'll pass, thanks." Cassidy lifted her lips in what would have been a sardonic smile if she'd been in skinform. The display didn't deter Carla, quite the opposite. A shiver seemed to run the length of her body. Cassidy had no doubt that if the vampire could emit a scent, she would smell of arousal.

"Ah yes, young love." Carla gave her a slow wink. "Who am I to get in the way of that?"

"If that's what you want to think." Cassidy looked away in a show of unconcern. Maybe she and Snow would come to an understanding, but she doubted the vampire lord had come all this way to gossip about the North Side Alpha's love life.

"Oh, so it's like that, is it?"

"Sure." Her feelings for Snow were a confused tangle, one she wasn't interested in unraveling with this vampire. She wasn't even that interested in women. She'd assumed that her change into a wolven was responsible for her increased sex drive and the fact that she would occasionally dally with female partners. When her heat was on her, it didn't matter too much to her or the wolf where they got their satisfaction. Other times, it was as much a matter of closeness and physical connection as it was sex.

And none of it mattered now, not with a vampire leering at her like she knew exactly what loops Cassidy's mind was taking her through.

"Alpha?"

It took everything Cassidy had not to run to the door and embrace Naomi.

"There you are." She locked eyes with Alicia, then with Jamieson. "Make sure no one interrupts us."

Alicia nodded. "Not even—"

"No. Not even." Chances were good the wolven was going to ask about her mom, and there was no way she wanted Sophia within a hundred yards of Carla.

"Very good." Alicia preceded Jamieson out the door. He gave Carla one last dark look, his hackles raised so high he appeared to have grown a hump across his back.

Naomi waited by the door, then closed it. She pressed an ear to it, then came to join them.

"This is as private as you're going to get," Cassidy said. "What the hell are you doing in our home?"

"Ah. Yes." Carla produced a crooked smile that held a sliver of discomfort. "It's interesting you should use 'our' when talking of home. I am currently without mine and in need of a place to stay. You owe me a sizable favor, so I've decided to stay with you until I can iron out this little…wrinkle in my current situation."

The request and confession shocked Cassidy into frozen horror.

"The hell you say," Naomi said in awed tones.

"Indeed." Carla sat back in her chair, her chin raised as if daring them to think any less of her than they had seconds ago.

"So what happened?" Cassidy asked. "Did they come for your people too?" If someone was after wolven, it wasn't too big a stretch to think they might go after the vampires also.

"My troubles are more...internal." Carla's smile twisted further into pain.

"And if you stay here, how much of those troubles can we expect to find at our door?" Naomi asked.

"Not that it matters, as you *owe* me a favor," Carla said, with emphasis. "No one knows I've come here. Unless one of your people talks, it should stay that way. Surely, I can count on the Alpha to keep her people under control?"

"Like you kept yours?" Naomi asked.

Carla's eyes flashed red and her mouth gaped in a sudden hiss. She lurched forward in a blur and was suddenly looming next to Naomi. Her teeth were nearly as long as the wolven's, and when she moved as she had, Cassidy had no trouble imagining the kind of damage she could wreak, even on one of the wolven.

"Enough," Cassidy said quietly. She meant the command for Naomi, but Carla subsided as well.

Confident her point had been made, Carla reseated herself demurely on her chair.

"I owe you a favor," Cassidy said. "That much is true. However, my pack owes you nothing. How can I be sure someone didn't follow you here? You weren't exactly subtle about your request for entry."

"I sacrificed a lot to make sure I escaped Faint without a tail." Carla smoothed her skirt over her legs. "And no vampire may enter unless invited. It's one of the more irritating myths about our kind that happens to be true."

"What are the others?" Naomi asked.

"You can ignore that." Cassidy stared at Naomi long enough for the wolven to back down. "How long will you be staying with us?"

Carla straightened at the implied acceptance of her request. "Two or three weeks. A month at most. There are designs in the works, contingencies, backups, and the like. Those who deposed me have no idea what is now aimed at them. They'll reconsider." She assumed a languorous smile. "I'll have back what's mine."

Cassidy stood. "One month, then your favor is paid, whether or not you're back in charge of Chicago's vampires." She turned to Naomi.

"We can put her in Jimmy's grow-op room. It should be well protected against light."

"Yes, Alpha." Any doubts Naomi had about the wisdom of taking in a fugitive vampire lord were absent from both her voice and her scent.

"Oh, and Carla," Cassidy said.

"Yes, Alpha," Carla replied, her tone mockingly similar to Naomi's.

"Stay away from the human. If I hear you've so much as touched her, I will rip out your throat, favor or no favor."

CHAPTER THIRTY

"Are you all right?" Snow approached the Alpha from the side, making sure to give her a wide enough angle to see her coming. Cassidy was radiating stress. That she hadn't yet put a fist through a wall was impressive.

"Fine." Cassidy ground the words out past gritted teeth. The lobby had emptied, except for Alicia who lounged in an overstuffed chair within view of the front doors.

Snow stepped closer and lowered her voice. "Then maybe try acting like it. I'm not one of your wolves, but even I can feel you're upset." She ran her hands over her forearms, as if the movement could do more than temporarily keep her arm hair from standing on end. "It's nearly...tactile."

Cassidy expelled a snort but closed her eyes. It took nearly a dozen breaths before Snow felt the Alpha's presence recede.

"Thank you," she said.

When Cassidy's eyes opened, the red and blue shine of her eyes had diminished, but they still lurked within the depths of her retinas. Someone who didn't know better might have mistaken the glow for a trick of the light. No one in the building was likely to make that error, not even Cassidy's very human mother.

"How are you doing?" Cassidy asked, her tone level.

"I'm well enough." Snow looked down at herself. She'd found some clothing during the commotion with Sophia Nolan. It wasn't much, a pair of sweatpants and a T-shirt that were both too large. It wasn't unusual to find caches of clothes in odd spots in a wolven den. Fortunately, someone had left these in the drawer of an end table. "It'll take more than a little nudity to shake me."

"I owe you one." Cassidy shook her head. "What the hell am I supposed to do with her?"

"Your mom? Or the deposed vampire lord who's come to stay?"

Cassidy expelled a genuine, though startled laugh. "More the vampire problem, but both, I guess."

"You did the right thing by allowing her to stay. If word had gotten out that you walked back a favor you owed, even to a vampire…Well, a lot of folks would know not to trust you."

"I got that, but she's here, in the same hotel as my mom. There's no way Carla doesn't know we're related and closely."

"I picked up on that too."

"There were wolven on the top floor who picked up on that."

When Snow shot Cassidy a look, the Alpha shrugged and looked away.

"I can't just stand around and give a goddamn vampire unrestricted access to my mom."

"So set one of your wolven on your mom as a chaperone. Beth would be a good fit. Or Carlos. Sophia seemed to be getting along fine with him."

Cassidy shook her head. "Carlos is a little too smooth for my tastes. I don't want to end up with him as a stepfather."

"Then Beth it is." It seemed simple enough to Snow, but she could tell Cassidy wasn't so certain.

"Could you do it? Would you? Please." As far as begging went, it was on the dignified side. Snow bit her lower lip. Getting entangled further with Cassidy and her family was not her intent. She and Cassidy had gotten closer, and she was in danger of becoming the Alpha's go-to, before even her Beta, had he not been missing. While Snow enjoyed Cassidy's company, more than she was really comfortable admitting, they were straying into familiar territory. Soon would come the veiled hints, then the veil would be pulled aside. When Snow didn't bite, there would be cuddles. Those were the worst. They felt so good, and Snow would allow herself to believe that maybe it could work. And then everything would fall apart. There would be a kiss that wouldn't be returned, or the snuggles would get more intimate, more sexual.

"Hey," Cassidy said. "Earth to Snow. You still with me?"

Snow nodded, smiling wide though she didn't know how to feel. Saying no to Cassidy was so hard. Did she really have to? Her wolf shifted, leaning toward the Alpha. She didn't seem conflicted at all. Snow took a deep breath to shut down the question, but before she could say anything, two wolven skidded into the foyer.

"Alpha!" Zoya called out to them.

Cassidy leaned over the railing. "What did you find?"

Zoya shook her head.

"It's no good," Jimmy said. Snow didn't know the wolven well, but from the few interactions she'd had, he seemed the type who could turn anything into a joke. There was no sign of anything but deadpan seriousness to him now.

"What do you mean?" Cassidy asked.

Jimmy grimaced. "He was taken."

Cassidy leaned back from the railing, her face a still mask, but her scent spiked with fear. "Well, shit," she whispered.

"Maybe take them upstairs?" Snow murmured.

"What do you mean taken?" Alicia's strident voice filled the hallway. A door opened down the hall, then another. From the sounds of movement in the rooms around them, other pack members had also heard.

"Too late," Cassidy said. "They need to hear it now. Better from him now than later on from me." She poked her head back over the railing. "Head to the ballroom. I'm calling a pack meeting."

It was the right call, though not an easy one. A few weeks ago, Cassidy probably would have taken Snow's suggestion. The Alpha was definitely evolving. It would be interesting to see what kind of leader she developed into.

* * *

The buzz in the room was oppressive, with an edge that set her bones to vibrating. Fear rose off the gathered wolven in a pale blue miasma. Cassidy paced at the front of the stage, conscious that every eye in the room was on her. There had been a time when she'd loved being the center of attention, but this was too much. The same old concerns clamored at her from the back of her mind. What if she made the wrong call and people died? What if she died because of her own fuck-ups? Why couldn't someone else do this?

She stalked off the twelve steps from one end of the stage to the other, then swiveled on her heel and marched them out again. Her wolf counseled her to ignore the words of her own brain. They were little more than biting flies. Hadn't they kept this group together when it was set to fracture? They'd done that. Were still doing that. This was simply one more obstacle to be overcome, and the wolf was certain they would rise to this challenge as they had all the others.

Snow sat in the front row, the weight of her gaze added to that of the pack. She didn't lean over to whisper with her neighbor, as so many of Cassidy's packmates did. She caught Cassidy watching and gave her a tight smile. It seemed genuine, even if some strain shone through.

Looking past the lone wolf, Cassidy saw the chairs were not quite half full. It would be a long time, if ever, before every seat would have a body in it. Cassidy had made the choice to leave the seats there, as a promise that one day the North Side Pack would be back to the strength it had enjoyed before MacTavish decimated it. Now, it seemed more a reminder of how many of their packmates were gone. Cassidy hadn't met most of them, but it didn't matter. Her heart ached for each empty spot.

Everyone was here. She gestured for Zoya and Jimmy to join her in front of the pack.

"I set these two to find out where Luther could have gone," Cassidy said to the gathered wolven. "I'm hearing what they have to say for the first time. From what little I already know, it's important for you all to be here."

Shuffles among the chairs met her announcement as wolven turned to look at their neighbors. There were a few muted whispers between the handful of mated pairs, but beyond that nobody said a word. The grim stares as they refocused on the little group at the front said enough.

"So what did you find?"

Zoya glanced at Jimmy. He didn't seem interested in speaking up, so she opened her mouth to speak. She hesitated.

"Go on," Cassidy said as gently as she could manage. "I won't bite."

"We didn't find much at first," Zoya said, her voice gaining strength as she continued. "There were so many scents, so many wolven overlapping."

"The location is where we found the South Shore Pack's dead wolven," Cassidy said. "We contacted Hammer, the Alpha, and he came to inspect the body and take it back if it was one of his." She closed her eyes as the memory of South Shore's raw grief rolled through her. "It was."

"Yeah, that muddied things a lot," Jimmy said. "I was able to find Luther among the mix and track him around. He spent a lot of time there. Him and Phoebe."

All eyes shifted to the shy wolven, who shrank back into her seat.

"They were there at my request," Cassidy said. "Someone had to keep an eye out while we got in touch with Hammer. Phoebe came to let me know humans were cleaning up along the riverbank."

After a glance from Jimmy, Zoya picked up the recounting. "We don't know when Luther was picked up. We found human scent traces. There was a fight, but a little ways from where the body was. We think they picked Luther up and carried him to a waiting vehicle."

"A Hummer," Jimmy said.

"Hummer?" Cassidy cocked her head. "How do you know that?"

"They peeled outta there right quick," Jimmy replied. "Left a good amount of rubber on the road. Those treads were wide. And chunky." He nodded with quiet authority that was out of character.

"Jimmy did a tour in Iraq," Naomi said from the front row. "He's got a good grasp of American military equipment. If he says something was a Hummer, I'd believe him on that."

It was a narrow endorsement, but if Naomi was willing to vouch for him, then Cassidy was willing to believe her.

"We tried following the Hummer," Zoya said, then raised her shoulders in a helpless shrug.

"Once the burned tire smell faded, we lost them pretty quick." Jimmy shook his head.

"So we've lost our Beta," Cassidy said. "And it seems like he was taken by the military?"

"Could've been cops," Alicia said from the back row. "They have all sorts of military surplus equipment."

"Or some rando who likes to cosplay soldier," Carlos offered.

"I don't think a civilian could have taken down Luther," Cassidy said. "He's a tough one."

There was a combined sound of agreement from the wolven.

"A group of civilians wouldn't have the coordination needed to take him down either," Jimmy said.

"So we're left with military or police." Cassidy grasped the back of her neck.

Jimmy nodded grimly. "Or ex-military, mercenaries, that kind of thing."

"Someone organized and with a grudge." The cultured tones came from the back of the room. The voice was familiar and unwelcome.

Cassidy met Carla's steady gaze from the last row of chairs. No wolven sat near her, but there was one human. Her mom was managing to look both uncomfortable and filled with beaming pride at the same time. She was going to have to put a bell on each of them.

It was time to wrap up the meeting. "Here's what's next," Cassidy said. "Obviously, we're sticking with the buddy system for the foreseeable future. Let me or Naomi know if you see any humans acting oddly, especially if they're part of a group. Keep an eye out for military and military-type vehicles. Add helicopters to that list. And cop cars. Lastly, Naomi is Beta until we get Luther back." As with the other missing pack members, Cassidy felt it best to operate under the assumption that they were only temporarily separated from the pack. They all still registered on her inner constellation. Until that stopped, she had to assume they were recoverable.

Without waiting to hear if there were questions, Cassidy hopped down from the stage. She stopped in front of Naomi.

"Meet me in my rooms in fifteen," she said. "I have some loose ends to wrap up, but then let's talk."

Naomi nodded. Her expression was inscrutable and her scent a confused mix of anxiety and pride. That wasn't unexpected. Cassidy had just dropped the Beta announcement on her. Maybe she should have given her new Beta a heads-up first. Well, there was no going back now.

She paced up the aisle toward where her mom and a vampire lord were quietly chatting. Events were moving out from under her. Things were coming to a head, but she had precious little clarity about which direction they were going. Two weeks was too long to wait until getting the Alphas together. They had to move now before whoever was massing against them could get wind of their plans.

If they hadn't already.

"You were so great up there," her mom said when she stomped to a halt by their chairs. "I had no idea you were in charge."

Cassidy closed her eyes and took a deep breath. "Thanks, Mom. I'm going to take Carla for a private conversation now."

Carla made a delighted moue with her mouth. "So very commanding."

Sophia scooted to the side to allow the vampire to pass. "We can catch up later."

"Of course," Carla said.

Cassidy tried not to glare. "I think she was talking to me," she said in perfectly level tones.

"I'm sure she was," Carla said. "Try not to pout." She reached out to pat Cassidy on the cheek.

"Can you not?" Cassidy batted her hand away. She turned on her heel and headed for the door. "We'll talk in your room."

CHAPTER THIRTY-ONE

Cassidy waited, foot tapping against the bare concrete of the basement room's floor. The vampire was taking her sweet time getting down there.

The room wasn't at all swanky, but at least someone had removed the tables and the UV lights. A made-up bed sat against the wall farthest from the covered-over windows. No one had yet seen fit to lay the carpeting back down. This was a considerable step down from the furnishings Carla must be used to. They couldn't hold even the weakest candle to the decor and layout Cassidy had seen at Faint. Still, here there was no chance the sun would accidentally get to her while she slept. There were no homicidal vampires out to get her either.

With no more warning than a change to the air and a blur, Carla Sangre, the former vampire Lord of Chicago stood in front of Cassidy. She held her chin high, trying to appear as though she was looking down at Cassidy from a great height.

"Nice of you to join me," Cassidy said, her voice dry.

"With such an invitation, how could I resist?" Carla smiled languidly. "To what do I owe the pleasure of your attention?"

"What do you make of Jimmy and Zoya's report?"

"It's news to me. I'm unaware of any police activity relating to our community."

"Our community?" Cassidy raised an eyebrow. "Do you mean vamps or…"

Carla waved a hand. "The wider non-human community."

"If you can call it that."

"Why, whatever do you mean?"

Cassidy snorted. "It seems to me like we're all just our own little islands, doing our best to get by."

"There are avenues of communication. It really is too bad you haven't had anyone to show them to you." Carla smiled demurely. "I would be happy to offer you what I know. You've been so good to me already. With a few more amenities, I think you'll find I can be very helpful. Once I'm comfortable."

"This was a little last minute," Cassidy said. "If you'd called first, we could have done some upkeep ahead of time. I trust this will be adequate for today, at least."

"Yes, yes. Of course." Carla turned away from her and perched on the edge of the bed. "There is the matter of…sustenance."

Cassidy leaned against the wall across from the vampire and folded her arms across her chest. "Didn't pack yourself a blood juice box before running away from home?"

"I barely made it out. There was no time to plan beyond contingencies already in place." Carla looked up at Cassidy. A dark red spark lurked in the depths of her eyes. "I fed well yesterday. The hunger won't rise for a day or so yet. At least not in such a way that I'm forced to bow to its call."

"I'm glad to hear it."

"But I will need to feed." The crimson mote intensified. "Gaining sustenance before I lose control over the hunger will be much less… messy than allowing it to take over."

"You're not feeding on my mom. Or my wolves. Or me." Cassidy shrugged. "Whatever else you do is fine, as long as you don't attract any unnecessary attention."

"The blood of your kind will go a long way to keeping the hunger at bay," Carla said. "You may find there are those among your pack who don't mind being fed upon."

"I've made myself clear," Cassidy said mildly. "My wolves are off-limits."

"Even those who have frequented Faint before?"

Cassidy's eyes snapped up to meet Carla's.

"Even those who have been fed upon before? Those who have enjoyed it?"

Carla's eyes filled Cassidy's vision. She hadn't seen the vampire move, but there she was, so close that Cassidy could feel her presence like a cool pressure along the front of her torso. It should have been unnerving. Cassidy was used to the heat of the wolven, who ran warmer than humans. That was not the case for the vampire.

With more effort than it should have required, Cassidy tore her gaze away from Carla's, even as the vampire leaned in farther. She became aware of Carla's hands, one at her waist, the other across her shoulder, using it as leverage to pull herself up the couple of inches it took to cover Cassidy's lips with her own.

Her mouth was as cool as the rest of her, but not unpleasantly so. No, it was refreshing, exciting even. Cassidy's eyelids slid closed, and she gave herself over to the kiss. This was what she'd wanted, wasn't it? Someone to take charge so she no longer had to assume the burden of binding the pack together. They would have fractured without her, and she was keenly aware that she was the only thing keeping them from dissolving completely. But what if someone else could carry that weight or, even better, carry her?

She allowed her mouth to fall open when the tip of Carla's tongue delicately traced the edge of her lower lip. A shock, electric with desire and pent-up frustration sizzled between them as their tongues twined around each other. This was so much more satisfying than rolling around with those animals who blindly looked to her for a firm hand.

Animals? Cassidy stiffened in shock at the direction her thoughts were taking.

No, that wasn't right. She jerked her head back, just as the needle-sharp points of Carla's teeth grazed the edge of her tongue.

"Hell no." Cassidy gave Carla a hard shove.

The vampire slid back, before alighting on the bed as if it had been her idea all along.

"Stay the fuck out of my head," Cassidy said, her voice rough. Was it anger at the vampire's underhanded tactics or pent-up desire that screamed to be satisfied that was eating at her?

"You wanted it, darling." Carla shook her head. "Don't try to tell me you didn't. I could feel your desire. Taste it as if it were my own." She licked her lower lip.

Cassidy snarled. The desire might have been there, but it had been provoked. And yes, it burned within her, demanding release so strongly that her wolf prowled the confines of her body, but it would never be satisfied by the likes of this vampire.

"Very impressive, Alpha." Carla smiled coquettishly.

"You. Will. Not. Touch. Anyone. Under. My. Protection." With each word, Cassidy stepped closer to the exiled vampire lord until she was nose to nose with Carla. If the vampire could breathe, they would have shared the same air. "Is that clear?" she whispered.

"If you say so," Carla responded, with no indication she had been cowed in any way. "I would suggest that you assign one of your wolves to me when I go out for my own hunt. Buddy system, remember?"

"I'll send you out with two." Cassidy drew herself to her full height, allowing herself to loom over the vampire. "I don't trust you to watch out for them."

"Very well." Carla inclined her head.

"And I need you to talk to your sources. Figure out what this group is that's hunting us." She glared at the vampire. "I'm sticking my neck out for you. If my head gets lopped off by someone else, your protection evaporates."

"I take your point. I will be reaching out to my contacts to consolidate what power I have left anyway. If the topic comes up while I tend to my own matters, I'll make sure to pay attention to it."

"Don't put yourself out too much. Just remember, for the moment, our fates are linked. If I get taken down, I'm making sure you're coming with me."

For the first time, Carla smiled without a trace of artifice. "There you go."

"There what goes?"

"There's the Alpha edge you're going to need to get through this. I wasn't sure if you had it, but I suspected it was there. You're too young to be taken seriously, but there's something to you. Something that's going to keep me alive long enough to return to my rightful place in this godforsaken town."

"That is the worst compliment I've even gotten." Cassidy shook her head and turned to leave.

"There's some Malice to you," Carla said.

"And now it's the second worst compliment I've gotten." Cassidy headed out the door, almost running into Beth. She grabbed her by the shoulders to keep Beth from toppling over.

"Alpha," the wolven said. "I'm so sorry. I didn't know what to do when you called the meeting, so I left her. I tried to find Luther to explain, but…"

"It's all right, Beth." Cassidy shrugged. "I ended up with an opportunity to make sure Ms. Sangre and I see eye to eye." She bared teeth gone pointed during her face-off with Carla. "There's no chance for misunderstandings now."

"Yes, Alpha." Beth nodded.

"If she wants to go out, you're to go with her, but not without one of our packmates. And if we have any more all-hands-on-deck type situations, I'll make sure to have specific instructions for you. The misunderstanding was all on me."

Beth relaxed in Cassidy's grasp. She leaned into her Alpha, tilting her head to one side in the gesture of submission Cassidy had grown accustomed to. It was funny, but Snow rarely did that, for all her protestations about her low dominant status.

Cassidy leaned her head over until her cheek touched Beth's. The acknowledgment of her submission seemed to lend strength to the wolven. She took a deep breath and straightened.

"I won't fail you, Alpha."

"I know." Cassidy cupped Beth's cheek for a second, allowing her confidence in her packmate to flow through the bond between them. Then, knowing Beth was as prepared to wrangle Carla as she could make her, Cassidy turned and headed up to her rooms.

Naomi wasn't yet there when Cassidy arrived, which suited her fine. The stress she'd been holding in through sheer force of will loosened a bit. Her wolf twined itself around her, radiating comfort and strength. She believed in Cassidy with everything she had, and as long as Cassidy didn't think too hard about things, she was able to trust that she was worthy of the confidence. Sometimes.

For now, she was content to drop into the nearest chair and try to relax. She leaned her head back and closed her eyes, paying attention to her breathing. As much as the long breaths helped slow her racing heart, it gave her something to concentrate on that wasn't the long list of concerns she held.

A dry laugh escaped her lips. "Concerns." The word sounded so innocuous. It was too bad English had no term for "things going on that were terrifying, but that you had to put on a good show about in order to keep others in the pack from panicking." No, that was a mouthful. Better to stick with "concerns."

And her breathing was picking up again. Cassidy did her best to go back to concentrating on it, but her brain was insisting on coming up with plans of action to address the various concerns. It wasn't doing so in any organized fashion, either. That would have been too easy. No, it was throwing out half-formed ideas, then dismissing them almost as quickly.

Cassidy groaned and sat forward, burying her head in her hands.

"Problems?" Naomi's voice asked from the door.

"D'you think?" Cassidy swiveled around to view her second-in-command.

The crooked grin on Naomi's face perfectly reflected Cassidy's tangled emotions.

She laughed again, as humorlessly as Naomi was smiling, then indicated the chair across from her.

"Sorry to put you on the spot with the Beta announcement," she said.

Naomi waved the apology away as she plopped herself down into the armchair. "It makes sense."

"I'm glad you think so. Still, in other circumstances, I would have run it past you first. You know, make sure you actually want that kind of responsibility."

"It's okay, Cassidy. I promise. I figured it might happen sooner or later. There's no way Luther was going to stick around as Beta long term."

"Really?" Cassidy cocked her head in question. "He seemed up for it."

"For now. He's a bit set in his ways, though. You two were going to butt heads eventually. Besides, I don't know that he wants to be here forever."

"What do you mean by that?"

"Well…" Naomi leaned back in her chair. "He hasn't been the same since he lost his mate a couple decades back. I'm kinda surprised he stepped up at all, instead of disappearing into the nearest wilderness."

"I'm glad he stayed. I don't know what I would have done without him." Cassidy's eyes were growing suspiciously moist. She discreetly wiped at them while trying to get herself back in hand. Sure, they'd been arguing a bit more than usual lately, but Luther's absence had left a massive hole in her life. She was suddenly having to face up to how much she'd relied on her Beta.

"I've got you," Naomi said quietly.

Cassidy laughed. Or tried to. It came out as more of a damp burble. "Thank you."

Naomi clapped her hand over Cassidy's knee. "No extra charge. Well, except the increase in my salary now that I'm officially management."

"I'll double what you're making, and you don't have to clock in and out anymore."

"Excellent. Now, when do we discuss stock options?"

Her voice was so serious that Cassidy had to look up to see if Naomi was joking. The only crack in her serious facade was the dancing merriment of her scent. It didn't completely overshadow the dark anxiety that lurked beneath it, but it did lighten it.

Naomi kept up her straight face for a few seconds, then allowed it to dissolve into a deep belly laugh that Cassidy couldn't help but join her in. They sat in their chairs laughing like idiots for far longer than the joke really warranted, and when they finally subsided into quiet giggles, Cassidy's sides ached. She wiped tears from her face and took a deep breath.

"Stock options are on the table when we go public," Cassidy said.

"Ah, so never." Naomi nodded sagely.

"Exactly." Not sure what to say next, Cassidy allowed the silence between them to grow before finally breaking it. "We need to move up the timeline."

"You mentioned as much at the pack meeting," Naomi said.

"I mean it. There's too much going on, and a lot of it seems aimed at us, both the pack specifically and the wolven in general. I still want to get the Alphas together. My gut says that our strength lies in numbers and North Side is too small to hold out on its own."

Naomi nodded, her eyes intent.

"Besides," Cassidy continued. "Someone's going to a lot of trouble to rile things up between us and South Shore. They wouldn't be doing that if we weren't a bigger threat together than separately."

"Agreed."

"Great." Cassidy clapped her palms down on her thighs. "So what are our options? I'm pulling together whoever will show up for the night after tomorrow, but I don't know what to offer the other Alphas."

"We do have a fallback territory," Naomi said. "Dean bought the land back in the 1940s. It's not too far from Danville and butts up against Kickapoo State Park. We can evacuate our pack that way. It's a big plot, so we could temporarily take on a few packs."

"If they're willing."

"If they're willing." Naomi shrugged. "You'd have to be pretty persuasive. Most Alphas won't want to share territory, even if it's for a short time."

"Is that a normal thing for packs to do?"

"I don't know. We only have the land because Dean liked the idea of having somewhere to get away to. We took vacations there regularly when the pack was bigger. It was a big hit with the cubs." The tension around her eyes softened as she recalled better days for the pack.

The lump that appeared in Cassidy's throat was so large she had to swallow twice to clear it. She knew the pack wasn't operating at full capacity, but she hadn't considered the absence of children as an indicator of exactly how messed up the situation had become.

"That sounds nice," she said. "I think we could all use some time away, somewhere we can stretch our legs. And who knows, we might even be closer to wherever our packmates have been taken."

"That's an interesting spin," Naomi said. "What do you need me to do now?"

"Contact the Alphas from Aurora and Kenosha. I'm going to talk to Hammer so he can let his contacts know." Cassidy took a deep breath. It felt good to be making concrete plans. "Let the rest of the pack know that we're heading to the fallback location in a few days."

"Yes, Alpha." Naomi stood. The instructions seemed to have revitalized her as well. She rubbed her hands together. "Once we get our ducks in a row, whatever asshats are coming after us won't be able to make a dent."

"That's the idea," Cassidy said. Now all they needed was enough time to pull it off. She took a deep breath and her wolf stirred. They needed to release the tension Carla had wound within them. A quick roll might do the trick, but who they really needed was Snow.

CHAPTER THIRTY-TWO

Snow lay on her back, staring up at the ceiling. If she'd been able to see through the floors between her and the penthouse, she knew she would be staring directly at Cassidy. The Alpha was too much in her head these days. Hell, she was more than in her head. She was starting to burrow her way into Snow's heart.

The need to go to her pulled at Snow's body. She clenched her hands with each wave, bunching up the bed's covers into tighter and tighter bundles. The pinpricks of pain in her palms with each squeeze kept her grounded in the moment and, most of all, in her own head. Cassidy was not her Alpha. She had no Alpha, had no pack. Didn't need one, didn't want one. It was a familiar litany, usually a comforting one, but it no longer held the same assurance it had those weeks ago before she decided to make the trip to the Windy City. And here she was, being blown into the pack of her dead brother.

She couldn't feel the other pack members, so that was something. But Cassidy… Even though she was refusing to heed the call to go to the Alpha's side, the urge to do so was only increasing. The pressure of her presence was growing stronger and stronger.

Snow screwed her eyes shut and held on for dear life. This wasn't what she wanted. Or maybe it was. She wanted what she wanted.

Cassidy wasn't going to want the same. She would need things Snow wouldn't give her. Couldn't give her. The Alpha's eyes, intense with desire, floated in the darkness behind Snow's closed eyelids. They shifted to sadness, then anger as that desire was thwarted. Then they looked away.

A knock at the door startled Snow straight up in her bed. Her claws ripped through the bedsheets. Cassidy was here.

"Snow?" Cassidy's voice filtered through the heavy wooden door. "Are you all right?"

Of course. If she could feel the Alpha as clearly as she did, the Alpha would feel her as strongly. Given Cassidy's strange strength, probably more.

"Yes." She didn't elaborate, hoping Cassidy would take the hint and go away.

"I know you don't want to talk," Cassidy said. "But I need your help." The heavy door couldn't completely muffle her self-deprecating laugh. "Because of course I do."

Snow went back to looking at the ceiling, only now it was more of a glare. "Fine." She pushed herself up in bed but refused to stand. "You can come in."

"Thank you." Cassidy cracked open the door and stuck her head in. "Are you sure?"

"For now. How do you need me to save your hide this time?"

"Save my…" Cassidy came fully into Snow's room and closed the door quietly behind her. "It's not just my hide you're saving."

"I know."

"What's wrong?" Cassidy asked. "Aside from…" She waved one hand vaguely as if the easy flip of her wrist could somehow convey all the crap that had been raining around the North Side Pack for the past few weeks.

"It's nothing." Snow turned to stare out the window. The darkness beyond was broken by points of light from far-off windows. There were no answers there either.

"It's not nothing." Cassidy leaned against the wall next to the door. "You don't have to help, you know. I don't expect it of you. You don't even have to stick around."

The breath in the back of Snow's throat hitched sharply. "You want me gone?"

"What?" Cassidy stood up straight in shock. "Of course not. I most definitely want you here, more than anything, but I won't stand in your way if you want to go."

"Are you sure?" She swiveled her eyes to watch the Alpha closely, alert for any change in her stance or any shade to her scent that would betray if Cassidy was lying.

"Of course, I'm sure. I could not do this without you, Snow. I'm a little ashamed that I'm not strong enough, and I'll never admit that to anyone but you." A weight seemed to lift off Cassidy's shoulders, her stance loosening almost into a comfortable slouch. "I'm sorry if that means I lean on you too much."

"I don't mind being leaned on," Snow said grudgingly. Her breath no longer caught each time she inhaled. "I don't know what to do with you."

"Whatever you want." The grin on Cassidy's face was sharp with wicked humor, then it softened into something more genuine. "I mean that however you want it to mean. Let me keep hanging out with you. Give me your opinion whenever you want. Parade around naked in front of my mom."

"Ah." Snow's cheeks heated slightly. "I'm sorry about that."

"I'm not. It gave her something to worry about that isn't where my sister is and why I won't tell her what Mary's deal is."

"Then I'm glad to be of assistance." Snow pushed herself up against the headboard and patted the mattress next to her. "And how else can I help today?"

Cassidy's face lit up, and she plopped down on the length of the bed. She arranged herself loosely around Snow's form, throwing one arm across Snow's lap and snuggling down into her body heat with a deep sigh.

"This is a good start."

"You came all this way for a cuddle?"

"What?" Cassidy's voice was muffled. "This feels good."

It did. "I was assuming what you needed was more urgent than hugs."

Cassidy squeezed Snow around the waist, then sighed. "A little bit, I suppose. I do appreciate the chance to clear my head. Next stop is Mom."

"Oh dear."

"I'll tell her you say hi." The wicked grin danced around Cassidy's lips for a second before she rolled over onto her back. "I was hoping you'd run a few errands for me."

While privately mourning the loss of the snuggles, Snow nodded. "Check in with the other Alphas?"

"We need to move the meeting up. It's the only way. There's a well-trained and motivated group out there who's hunting us. I don't plan on giving them an easy target."

"Who do you need me to talk to?"

"The Alphas in Gary and Joliet. Naomi is touching base with Aurora and Kenosha. I'm going to handle Hammer."

"Oh. Gary, huh?"

"Is that going to be a problem?" Cassidy craned her neck to eye Snow curiously.

"No. Maybe?" It had been a long time since she'd seen the Gary Pack's Alpha. She hadn't heard that pack leadership had changed, so she assumed Bone or Marrow would still be in charge.

"I'm sure Naomi would switch if I get to her before she takes off."

"No, I'll handle it." Thirty years since her last attempted romance was enough time for the awkwardness to dissipate. Surely. "What am I saying?"

All business again, Cassidy sat up. "Let them know we're meeting the night after tomorrow and find out what ideas they have for a meeting place. And for god's sake, get some sort of email or cell phone number, even a landline, so we can communicate quickly about where we're going to end up."

"Night after tomorrow is awfully close to the full moon."

"It is. I don't see that we can afford to wait until after."

"If you say so. Everyone's going to be on edge."

"I trust the Alphas to be able to hold their shit together, even a couple days out. They're Alphas after all."

"I only need to know what to say if someone asks."

"Maybe don't tell them to keep their shit together. I'd go with it's too important to wait. Tell them about Luther's disappearance, the death of Hammer's wolf, and the involvement of an organized group, possibly military or police in nature. If that doesn't terrify them, I don't know what will."

The thought plainly disturbed the Alpha. The scent of fear, cold and sharp, coalesced around the bed.

Snow wormed an arm around Cassidy's shoulders and pulled her in tight. "I'll get it handled."

Cassidy melted into the embrace. "I know."

* * *

As she shut the door quietly behind her, Cassidy rolled her head on her neck. She felt lighter than she had in days, weeks even. Probably months. Too bad it wouldn't last. She had one more stop to make before she could head back to her room to drop Hammer an email informing him of the change of plans. It turned out it was a good thing they hadn't settled on a meeting place. With input from the other Alphas, they could choose a location where the likelihood of discovery would be low.

Maybe she should head up to her room and take care of that now. Letting the South Shore Alpha know sooner rather than later had to be a priority, right?

The idea was tempting, but Cassidy knew she was only trying to delay the conversation she had to have with her mom. It was silly to reach out to Hammer without getting the other Alphas to weigh in, anyway.

Her mom's room wasn't far from Snow's. She squinted down the hall, trying to get up the courage to get moving. How impressive she was right now, how reassured her own wolves would be over her courage and daring as she hesitated, scared to death of a conversation with her own mother.

The wolf bristled against her harsh tone. She didn't like it when people spoke ill of Cassidy, even when the sharp little voice that never failed to remind her of all her flaws came from her own brain.

"I get it," Cassidy murmured. "I'll be better."

The wolf subsided and wrapped herself around Cassidy's core, projecting the feel of fur and warmth. The job at hand might be difficult, but she wasn't alone.

It shouldn't have been so reassuring. It wasn't like the wolf could talk to her mom for her, but support was support, even when it was silent.

She squared her shoulders and took a deep breath.

The rooms might be on the same floor, but they were on opposite ends of the building. By the time she made it to her mom's door, she was full of anxiety. Good thing her mom wouldn't be able to smell it.

She raised her hand and knocked on the door with a confidence she definitely wasn't feeling.

"Is that you, Cassie-bean?"

"It's me, Mom." Cassidy dropped her hand to the door handle. "Mind if I come in?"

"Mind if I get to spend some time with my favorite youngest daughter? Of course not."

Cassidy tried the door, but the handle refused to turn.

"Hold on a second," Sophia said. "Your mom doesn't move as fast as she used to."

Footsteps approached the door and were followed by the successive clicks of the deadbolt being thrown, the handle unlocked, and the chain being removed.

"Can't be too safe?" Cassidy asked pointedly when her mom finally opened the door.

"Oh, you know," Sophia said vaguely as she motioned her daughter into the room. "It feels like a hotel, even if it's your 'den.'" She hooked her fingers into quotes on the last word.

"It's what we call it, Mom." Cassidy pulled the chair out from under the room's small desk and sat in it. "It has meaning."

"So does home." Her mom's tone was acerbic, emphasized by the prickliness of her scent. "Which is where I wish your sister was."

"Me too."

"Then why haven't you done something about it? You're in charge of these people, aren't you? Tell them to go out and find her. Can't they"—Sophia lowered her voice and leaned forward—"sniff her out?"

"That's kind of insulting, Mom." Cassidy caught her mom's eyes and held them for a moment. Maybe some of the Alpha mojo would work on her mother too.

Sophia waved a hand. "I don't know what else to call it. And I see them wandering around as wolves, so why is it insulting?"

So much for her Alpha presence doing anything. "It just is. Besides, if I could do that, I would have already. I'm worried about her too. How much progress has your PI made?"

One eye twitched at the mention of the investigator she'd hired. "You don't seem worried enough to do something about it."

"Mom!" Cassidy's voice was sharp and as soon as her mom's eyes narrowed, she knew she'd misstepped.

"You're the one running things here. I saw you on stage. These people would eat from your hand if you asked them too. What use is being in charge if you can't get what you need from it?"

"I don't do this because of what I need. It's what they need that's important. These people, these wolven rely on me, and I won't repay that trust by sending them into danger on my say-so."

"Danger?" Sophia's eyes widened. "Mary's in danger? How long have you known?"

"That's not what I meant. I don't know if Mary's in danger. Maybe she is, maybe she isn't. How much did you hear at the gathering?"

"Most of it. I didn't think we should go, but Carla thought it would be all right."

"She did, did she?" Cassidy pinched the bridge of her nose with her fingers. She should have known the vampire was the instigator.

"It sounded serious."

"It was. It still is. Mom, someone is coming after my pack. We don't know who and we don't know why."

"Then whoever you send to look for Mary should be safer, right?"

"Not on their own. Anyone traveling alone is in danger of disappearing like the others. And if I send enough wolven to deal with whatever Mary's maybe gotten herself into, I won't have enough left to protect the rest of the pack. I had to make a choice, Mom." Cassidy looked her mom in the eyes again, this time trying to get her to understand. This was a decision born of desperation, not the one she wanted to be making. Mary's disappearance gnawed at her more every day, especially now in light of what was coming to a head. They could have used her. More terrifying was the prospect of someone strong enough to keep her wherever she was without even a way to communicate what was going on.

"And you decided not to choose your family."

"No, Mom. I did choose family."

Sophia's eyes filled with tears. "Oh." The word was more gasp than anything else.

"I have more than one family now. That doesn't mean you're not important to me, that Mary isn't important to me, but you two don't rely on me. You don't need me."

Her mom averted her eyes as the tears spilled over, running down her cheeks. Her anguish was real, rolling from her in blue waves. She braced herself against the edge of the counter as if it were the only thing holding her up.

Cassidy couldn't watch her. She leaned forward, training her gaze on the carpeted floor, giving her mom the privacy to cry as much as she needed to. What she was going to ask next was going to hurt even more. When the quiet sniffles began to subside, she looked up again.

"You should go back to New York." She kept her words quiet and neutral. Surely her mom would see their wisdom.

Sophia's sniffs were replaced by an angry "Ha!" She angrily dashed the remaining tears from her eyes and glared fierce daggers at her daughter. Cassidy felt every inch the younger child in that moment.

"You may not care about your sister, but I do. I'm not leaving this city until I find the answers you've given up on. The answers you've

decided are less important than this mismatched group of…of…
Weirdos!"

Now it was Cassidy's turn to reel back as if struck. "Mom, whether
I care or not isn't the point. But I do. Care. A lot. The point is that
it's incredibly dangerous for you to be here right now. If whatever is
going on with my people spills over onto you, I won't be able to live
with myself."

Shaking her head, Sophia pushed away from the cabinets. "No, it's
fine. You're too busy with your new family. As the only one here who
still cares about your sister, I'm the one who needs to find her."

"And how are you going to do that? You don't know the city."

"I'll get a hotel then. A real one. The investigator will find
something eventually. It's early days yet, but he's confident. And if he
can't, there's the police."

"You can't go to the cops on this one."

"Why not?"

"Mary—" Cassidy clamped her mouth shut before she could blurt
her sister's secret out.

"Mary what?"

"You could get her in really big trouble. And tracking her could
involve me and the pack. How're you going to explain werewolves to
the cops, Mom?"

"I thought they preferred to be called wolven." Sophia cracked her
snide tone like a whip. "Fine. But I meant what I said. I'm not leaving
without knowing what happened to your sister."

"We're leaving the den soon," Cassidy said. "You're welcome to
stay, but I don't know how long pesky things like utilities are going
to be on."

"It'll be fine. I'll make do. I'm not some helpless old lady."

"Mom. Mommy." Cassidy crossed the room to where her mom
leaned against the counter, her arms crossed. She wrapped her arms
around Sophia's waist. When she wasn't pushed away, she lay her head
on her mom's shoulder. "I'm sorry. I wish I could choose you and Mary.
I've spent so much time trying to find a way to take care of both my
families. It's tearing me apart, but I truly think this is the best decision
I can make. I don't love you or Mary any less but come on. Mary was
in the Army. You raised the two of us on your own in New York City."

Warm fingers stroked her hair, smoothing it down on the back of
her head and over her neck the way they had when she'd been a little
girl and her heart had been broken from one scrape or another. Sophia
brushed away her tears, then pulled Cassidy into a hard hug.

"My sweet girl." Her mom's voice was as choked with sorrow as her own. "I understand. You have duties to take care of, but so do I. Don't worry about me. I'll stick around and find your sister. When I track her down, we'll find you and all will be well."

"I hope so. Promise me if you don't find anything in a couple of weeks that you'll head home. Have that detective call you there."

"Okay, Cassie-bean. Okay."

She wasn't going to do it. Cassidy could smell the determination sweeping Sophia's earlier despair before it. There had to be someone Cassidy could ask to keep an eye on her. Hammer would hopefully be coming with them to the fallback den. If he didn't join them, she could appeal to him. The only other one she could think of was Carla, but that would put her in the uncomfortable position of owing the vampire another favor. But if it meant her mom would be safe… Well, that was something she could consider depending on how the Alpha meeting went.

"Thanks, Mom." Cassidy took a deep breath, taking in her mom's aroma intentionally for the first time in her life. She committed it to memory and smiled, content in the knowledge that she would be able to access this scent memory whenever she liked. If that happened to be with Mary, then that would be even better. "Love you."

"I love you, Cassidy Anne. Everything will work out, you'll see."

Cassidy nodded. She wanted to believe, needed to believe, but she'd seen too much since October to take it to heart.

CHAPTER THIRTY-THREE

The hum of the old Volkswagen bus' wheels on concrete was soothing in a way car rides had rarely been in the months since Cassidy was turned. She hadn't minded long cross country trips before. The idea of jumping in a vehicle and driving for one or more hours hadn't made her break out in a cold sweat. From what she'd since learned, very few wolven did well in cars. Snow was the obvious exception to the rule, at least when she was the one driving. She glanced over at the lone wolf who stared intently through the windshield into the darkness.

Snow must have heard her move, as she allowed her eyes to drift off the road and lock with Cassidy's. She smiled, her eyes crinkling with real enjoyment before she turned her attention back to driving.

Cassidy's hand twitched, and she stuffed it into her pants pocket to keep from reaching over and placing it on Snow's thigh. They weren't mated. There was no indication that they might be, not from the wolf, anyway. But Cassidy still felt lighter when Snow was around.

"What are you thinking?" Snow asked.

"Oh, you know…" Cassidy said, then trailed off.

"I really don't," Snow said when the silence had gone on for longer than comfortable. "Worried about tonight?"

"Of course." Cassidy pushed herself up straighter in her seat. "I have no idea how this is going to go. Who's going to show up? Will the other Alphas listen? Are we going to be able to band together?" She shook her head. "I miss Luther telling me that it goes against all tradition to have the youngest, most inexperienced Alpha call together a meeting like this."

"Why didn't you bring Naomi?" The question was quiet, but no less impactful for its lack of volume.

"I get it if you don't want to be here," Cassidy said.

"I didn't say that."

"So you do want to be here?"

"I didn't say that either." Snow heaved a long sigh. "This isn't my usual scene. You know I'm happier on the fringes. You've asked me to get in the thick of all of this, and I'm outside my comfort zone. By quite a lot."

"Ah." There were good reasons, beyond the fact that Snow made Cassidy feel safe. "You know a lot more about the other packs and Alphas than I do."

"So does Naomi."

"True, but it's not the same. Also, you're way better at letting me know exactly what's going on. Like, you've studied us, the wolven. I get it when you break what's happening down for me. Luther and even Naomi tend to make pronouncements as if that's simply the way things are. You give me a handle on why. If you're there, you'll see everything firsthand, and I trust you to let me know about whatever I miss."

"I'm not the best choice for guarding your flank." A whiff of distress rolled off Snow.

Cassidy wrinkled her nose. "That may be, but I'm pretty sure I can handle myself. I took down Hammer, after all."

"This is as many as five more Alphas." The stink of anxiety strengthened as Snow shot her another look. "You don't know if some or all have decided to form an alliance, take you down, and take over the North Side Pack."

"I feel like we have a bigger enemy than each other." Cassidy drummed her fingers on her thigh. "And if they can take the pack away from me, maybe it was never really mine."

"I don't think that's true at all." Snow's concern shaded into anger.

"Hey, I know it's your brother's pack, but you can't be blind to the fact that we're barely limping along right now."

"Maybe, but I see you've got a whole lot more going for you than you think."

Images of Hammer's interactions with his wolves filled her mind. The easy way he lived among them. How they turned to him but were also capable of standing on their own. Her pack had none of that, and Cassidy hadn't realized how bad it was until she'd had the South Shore Pack as a point of comparison. She wanted what they had, desired it more than she'd desired anything in her entire life. The fact was, she didn't know how to give it to them. She was a decent Alpha to get them from one crisis to another, but she wasn't good for the pack's long-term health.

"Anyway," Cassidy continued brusquely. "I needed Naomi to stay back and keep an eye on things. We're heading out on 'vacation' tomorrow. There's a lot to do, and I don't trust that our mysterious adversaries won't try something while I'm gone."

"That seems particularly foolhardy," Snow said. "Even without you there, they're still a whole-ass wolven pack. If anyone is dumb enough to try a frontal assault, they're going to regret it."

"I'm sure you're right, but it doesn't hurt to be prepared."

"Well, I'm glad you asked me, even if I am a little nervous about it." Snow flashed a bright grin over at her. "I'll do my best to keep an eye out."

"And I'll keep my eye on you." Cassidy smiled back.

"How are you going to manage that? I'm good at disappearing."

"That you are." Cassidy shrugged. "But you're one of my stars."

"Stars?" Snow turned her confused gaze on her for a second, before looking back at the road.

"That's how I think of the wolven in my pack. And a few extras." She inclined her head toward Snow. "It's like I'm in a star field, and all the stars around me are my wolven. As long as you're all there, I know you're alive."

"Is that how you know about what's going on with your wolven even if you're not there?"

"Sometimes. They have to be pretty close for me to get an inkling for what they're feeling or what direction they're in. The more of my pack is around me, the stronger the sense is." She looked up at Snow through her eyelashes. "Or if I'm particularly close to them. Emotionally."

"Ah." Snow left the last statement alone.

"Don't all Alphas do that?"

"I don't think so. Or at least, not to the extent you do. I'm sure they all have something going on, but yours is unusually specific. I imagine it has something to do with how you came to be wolven. Again"— Snow smiled in the dark—"all I have are theories. No proof."

"So you're telling me the only way I'll find out more is by talking to the other Alphas." Cassidy snorted softly. "I guess I can send out a survey. By mail."

"Email will go straight to spam."

They shared a chuckle in the darkness. Cassidy glanced down at the phone in her lap. "Looks like we're about fifteen minutes out. You should be seeing signs for Naperville soon."

Cassidy had never heard of the Greene Valley Forest Preserve, but it was a good fit for what they wanted to do. When the Aurora Alpha had suggested it, she'd agreed. Aurora was getting a sweet deal, as the Preserve was minutes from their den, but it was reasonably central for the rest of the Alphas. They weren't headed right for the Preserve itself, but rather some undeveloped land to the north of it. It was nearly midnight, so the chance that they'd run into hikers would already have been low, but this way they didn't have to worry about anyone. Everyone had the coordinates and knew to meet when the moon was at its highest, which wouldn't be long now.

The moon was uncomfortably close to being full. Waiting until their original meeting time would have put them with the moon a few days waning from its fullest point. Snow had reminded her that everyone would be on edge this close to the full moon, but Cassidy hadn't felt they could wait. So the Alphas might be a bit on edge. It was better than waiting to have more packmates picked off. Whoever was after them must have been watching pretty closely to nab Luther the only time he'd been out alone in weeks. She couldn't continue to lose people every time they slipped up the slightest bit.

They navigated the rest of the way in silence that was broken only by Cassidy's quiet directions. They would park at Camp Valley Greene. Snow had confirmed that there would be no campers there, not in the middle of the week in March. Some people enjoyed winter camping, but Cassidy wasn't one of them. Maybe if she was in furform the entire time, but she thought the local Girl Scout troop would have some issues with that. They'd chosen the spot not because of its proximity to outdoor recreational opportunities, but because they needed somewhere to stash the van. From there they would make their way to the meeting spot.

When they pulled up to the shuttered camp, Snow had to come to a complete stop.

"I'll get it," Cassidy said. She hopped down out of the van and considered the chain holding the wooden gates together. The corner of one of the gates was separating, despite someone's attempt to shore up the joint with additional screws. It took barely any effort to pry the pieces apart. Once the chain was free, Cassidy squeezed the chunks of wood back together. The gate would still look whole, at least from the road. She pulled open the gate section and waited for Snow to drive past before closing it and winding the chain with its padlock over the corner.

She had to jog to catch up to Snow, who had decided to park the van at the far end of the lot. Even though her beloved Volkswagen was orange and white, it was screened by a few spindly trees and far enough from the road that it shouldn't be noticed.

Snow waited in the driver's seat until Cassidy was next to the van, then stepped out. "How do you want to do this?"

"You're here to watch and report back once we're done," Cassidy said. "You take on furform and stick to it. I'll shift to talk to the Alphas, but I don't see any reason for you to expose yourself like that. Just keep an eye on the other Alphas and whoever they bring with them. They should each have only one wolven along. That's what Hammer and I told them."

"Sounds easy enough."

Cassidy grinned tightly. "Here's hoping. If you get wind that someone's brought along more wolves than they were supposed to, I want you to nip me on the left hand. I'll know to go back to full furform and kick some tail."

"Tail?" Snow arched an eyebrow.

"I was going to say 'ass,' but that seemed too human-centric."

"I think you're trying a little too hard. And you sound like a refugee from the early 2000s."

"Everyone's a critic." Cassidy held up her hands. "But if it's such an offense, I'm glad I tried it out on you first. It wouldn't do to embarrass myself in front of the other Alphas."

Snow laughed. The quiet sound didn't quite conceal her anxiety.

Cassidy glanced up at the sky. It was a clear night and away from the city's lights, the stars sprayed across the heavens. The moon looked down on them, nearly full except for a thin sliver of darkness on one side. It was nearly at zenith, and it bathed the ground around them in a cool radiance that beckoned. The change would come easily tonight. Her wolf stirred at the thought, rising eagerly and ready to take over.

"I guess getting there a little early to sniff the area out isn't a bad idea." Cassidy pulled her shirt over her head. Her skin sprouted goose bumps the instant the cold night air struck it. Sure, the clear night sky was an advantage for stargazing, but it was damn cold.

She folded the shirt hastily and tossed it past Snow onto the front bench. The lone wolf removed her sweatshirt and T-shirt in one go. She didn't fold it, so much as drape it neatly on the seat before skimming her pants down her legs.

As Cassidy bent over to do the same, her lower legs were already cramping, and the backs of her hands itched as the wolf did her best to muscle her way to dominance.

"Let me get my shoes off, dammit," Cassidy mumbled. She ignored the questioning look Snow sent her way. It was difficult to untie laces with fingers that twitched as the muscles threatened to re-form themselves despite her efforts to keep the wolf at bay. With a snarl of frustration, she snapped the ties on her right shoe, then the left. She kicked them off, pulling her pants down at the same time. It shouldn't have worked, but she managed not to fall over. There was no time to fold the pants. Those, she balled up and threw into the van, followed a second later by the footwear. Hopefully, they didn't end up under the pedals.

"Bring it," Cassidy said. She let go, allowing the wolf to flood over her. The shift was close to instantaneous, and she grunted as skin split and fur grew over muscle and tendon that cracked and popped. Fluids sluiced off her to land steaming in the snow.

They fell forward onto paws tipped with lethal claws. An experimental flexing revealed that though the ground was frozen, they still bit easily into the ground. Clouds of vapor dispersed from their jaws as they panted, trying to catch their breath.

Next to them, Snow had barely started her own shift. They lifted their muzzle, testing the wind for any threats to this wolven who was so important to them. There was nothing beyond the distant smell of human machinery. Headlights on the road marked out a passing car, and when it was gone, the only scents of engine and oil were from the orange van. They caught whiffs of squirrels and small brown birds too small to make a decent mouthful and too difficult to catch to make the effort worthwhile. Something bigger had been through, and they inhaled more deeply, tasting the scent until they understood the shape and color. Groundhog, or at least that was how Cassidy thought of it. To the wolf, it was good eating, but only if caught unawares. One of those cornered and on the defensive would be attempted by only the most desperate wolf.

That was only the immediate area. The wooded areas beyond beckoned, but not until Snow was able to join them. Nose high, then pointed toward the ground, then high again, they circled away from the shifting wolven. Small animals and the scent of the land recently warmed by the sun were all they found. Spring was coming, the ground seemed to say, though the wind slicing through their pelt reminded them it hadn't yet arrived. The woods would provide more cover, both from the elements and from watchful eyes.

By the time they completed their circuit, Snow had finished her shift. Her wolf watched them, her silver pelt seeming to have been carved from the light of the moon. White eyes glowed at them, and they were struck at the power and grace of Snow and her wolf. In that moment, Cassidy realized that this wolven, this woman, was not someone she wanted to live without. The wolf agreed. This one would stand by them and make them stronger.

As they stared, Snow cocked her head, then dipped one shoulder and shifted her weight toward the trees. Her eyes and posture asked questions they were not prepared to contemplate, let alone answer.

They could answer the surface query. They had best be going. The gathering was at their behest. The time to join packs together to take on those who would threaten all of them was now. They inclined their head to Snow, then headed for the trees, knowing, hoping, that she would be right behind them.

CHAPTER THIRTY-FOUR

Packed snow squeaked and crunched under her paws as Snow trailed after Cassidy. Her ears pricked forward then twitched to the sides as she listened intently for any sounds that might be out of the ordinary. It was tricky, as she'd never been to this place, at least not in furform. She'd driven through the area more times than she cared to think about, but being on the ground was very different than being in the car.

So far, all she'd heard was the rustle of the breeze through the tops of the trees. The sound of the wind was different in winter, thinner and sharper without leaves to amplify and twist it. Threaded throughout was the occasional rustle of dead leaves across ice and frozen ground. Once, she'd heard the scrabbling of nails over bark. She'd tensed before the scent of fox hit her nostrils. The animal wouldn't find much tonight. Anything with an ounce of sense was curled up cozily in a den or burrow. Between the cold and the presence of wolven, game would be scarce.

Ahead, Cassidy's form slipped from deep shadow to dappled moonlight, then back to shadow. Her unique pelt allowed her to blend into the landscape so seamlessly that if she'd been trying to hide, Snow wouldn't have known she was there, except by smell.

They wended their way through the wooded edge of the Girl Scout camp, then arrived at a highway. Cassidy sank down next to the lone tree on the verge. Dead grass poked through the snowpack in places and into Snow's fur, some reaching skin and sending up a horrendous itch. She tried to ignore it as they watched the occasional car whiz past.

The expanse of concrete stretched to either side. More snow and ice heaped the top of the median between north- and southbound lanes. This late, traffic was light, but it was harder to track from where they crouched. It wouldn't do to get hit by a car as they tried to cross. The damage wouldn't be enough to kill one of them, not unless they were plowed into by a semi, but it would hurt and take some time to heal. That would put one or both of them at a disadvantage if violence broke out at the Alphas' meeting. Snow didn't really expect it to, not right now, but she hadn't lived this long on her own without assuming that nearly every situation had the capacity to degrade into a destructive physical confrontation.

She definitely didn't want to be the source of rumors that there were wolves in DuPage County. If they were seen, the likelihood was that the human who caught them out would assume they were coyotes, but even the slim possibility was too much to risk. Or so she usually believed. That they were out here on this night without having scouted the new area in skinform first was an indication of how dire things had become.

At least, Dean would have done the scouting, time permitting. She wasn't sure if it was something Cassidy would have thought of. Either way, there had been no time, not once the location had been decided upon and a majority of the Alphas had agreed.

A tickle formed between her shoulder blades at the idea of being so unprepared. For a moment, it felt like hostile eyes were upon her. Her wolf didn't like the feeling any more than she did. At her urging, Snow lifted her head and peered about them, ears pricked, muzzle testing the breeze. A car whizzed past, sending a wash of cold air reeking of a poorly maintained engine their way. She tried to stifle a sneeze, but it refused to stay contained. She let it out, garnering a disapproving glance from Cassidy, which she ignored.

There were no suspicious lights in the trees that might indicate human activity. No click of claws on concrete or boots crunching through snow rimed with a thin layer of ice. The only noise was that of the cars, accompanied by the occasional rattle of an otherwise rumbling engine. Slowly, the sensation of being watched receded as the sounds and aromas around them revealed nothing out of the ordinary.

They waited in silence until there was a sizable gap on both sides of the road. When Cassidy leaped up and dashed across the first stretch of pavement, Snow was quick behind her. They navigated the icy median with only a little scrambling for purchase, then were into the underbrush on the highway's other side long before the next car's headlights could get anywhere near them. The timing had been perfect, and Snow relaxed a bit.

They forged their way through scrub brush and past the occasional stump. The trees here were young, as if the area had only been allowed to return to wilderness a couple of decades previous. They headed toward where the sun had set as the moon climbed further above them. Though she'd been expecting traces of wolven, Snow still tensed when the first tickle came to her nose. She sneezed again, this time to alert Cassidy. The Alpha glanced back at her, odd eyes glowing from within the shadows of the young tree where she'd paused. She lifted her head and sniffed, then shook her head, her shaggy ruff rippling about her. Unlike a skinform head shake, this wasn't a sign of disagreement. Cassidy was settling herself.

The scent trace was old, faded to a pale shell of itself, so much so that Snow didn't know if she would recognize the wolven who had left it if she ran into them right then. It added credence to the Aurora Alpha's explanation that his pack ran these woods on occasion. Her anxiety ratcheted up again. They were getting close, both in time and in place. How would it go wrong? It pretty much had to, didn't it?

Snow's wolf shouldered aside her worries, dismissing them in a scan of the area. How many wolven scents were there? She'd found one, but soon a new one drifted to her muzzle. She sampled it as deeply as she could, testing for age and proximity. It was as old as the first, but another came on its heels. Through the competing smells, Cassidy's fragrance stood out bold and sharp. It was muddled with conflicting emotions. Excitement warred with apprehension; beneath that was simmering rage. The anger had been there since Luther's disappearance, and it was threaded through with a determination Snow hadn't ever before gotten from the Alpha. Cassidy was moving forward now, no matter what ended up in her path.

They forged deeper through the cluttered understory of the young patch of forest. The scents of more wolven overlapped those they'd already found, and they were getting fresher. Very fresh. Cassidy wasn't the only wolven who'd decided to show up early. Snow didn't recognize the aromas, so it wasn't Hammer or one of his wolves. It wasn't unexpected, but she very much wished they'd gotten to the rendezvous first. The extra time would have allowed her to scope out a hidey-hole where she could view the meeting. Now there was no guarantee she wouldn't be watched as she did so.

Cassidy slowed until she and Snow were shoulder to shoulder. Together, they paced forward. Snow took solace in the gesture, understanding that Cassidy was telling her she had nothing to worry about.

They passed an oak that was much older than the scrubby ash and beech trees of the area. Now, the scents of wolven were too numerous to count. Newer traces overlapped and subsumed older ones. A similar note threaded through the scents; they were definitely from one pack. With that note emerging, Snow knew she'd be able to identify the Aurora Pack's Alpha. They stepped into a large clearing not long after. In the center waited two wolven in furform.

Snow sat at the clearing's edge, unwilling to go into the open where she would be exposed to all. She put her back to a larger elm and waited.

Cassidy walked farther into the clearing, then looked back at her. Her unease was betrayed only when she held Snow's gaze a little too long. As much as Snow longed to be able to bound forward and stand side by side with the Alpha, she couldn't. Merely by being there, her position was already precarious. Besides, the other two wolven were massive and stood with quiet confidence. There was little she'd be able to do against them. She had her instructions and would do her best to follow them. She'd been specifically told not to endanger herself.

When Cassidy finally looked away, Snow stood slowly, and as the Alpha moved closer to the Aurora Alpha and Beta, she melted into the underbrush. Without wolven eyes on her, she would find herself a better and safer vantage.

* * *

The wolven waited for her, their gazes weighing every move she made. Cassidy tried to let their judgment roll off her as she and the wolf walked slowly toward them. She felt Snow move back into the bushes and circle to their left. Good, the lone wolf was taking her request to heart. If something happened to her, Cassidy wasn't sure what she would do, but the wolf assured her it would be bloody.

Since the wolf had no qualms about approaching this Alpha and his companion, Cassidy pulled back into herself, allowing the wolf to take over. Usually, even when the wolf was ascendant, Cassidy still retained most of her control. Instinct would serve her better in this moment, so she relinquished it. She wasn't quite an observer in the wolf's body, but it was close. This way, the wolf wouldn't have to filter her reactions through Cassidy's. On the other hand, if the situation shifted to one where Cassidy would need a firmer hand on the reins, it would be much more difficult to wrest control back from the wolf. If the encounter with who she presumed to be the Aurora Pack's Alpha went poorly, everything else was moot.

The wolf had no problem determining which of the waiting wolven was the Alpha. They might be sitting so still that they looked like exceptionally lifelike—if oversized—statues of wolves, but the more dominant one was easy to pick out. His eyes shifted to follow the wolf as she paced closer to him, approaching him so his Beta was on the far side of him. In marked contrast to Snow's shining pelt, the Alpha's fur was deep charcoal, darker even than Hammer's. If not for the brightness of the moonlight, he would have looked black. He was massive through the shoulders and his thickly plumed tail twitched once at her insistence on encroaching on his space.

The Beta wasn't so sanguine. She lifted her top lip in a warning snarl that Cassidy's wolf ignored. Though she was dominant, the wolf knew this Beta ranked far below her. If the Beta tried anything, she would be put in her place. The Alpha was impressive, the wolf admitted as much, but she was certain she could take him with only minor injury. What the wolf considered minor injury would have shocked Cassidy before she was turned. Minor was anything that didn't scar. She'd seen wolven get laid open nearly to the bone and have nothing but unbroken skin only days later. Cassidy had a smattering of scars, most of them left over from the night she was forced down the path to becoming wolven, but she'd picked up a few since then. Nothing like the scars that decorated some of her wolves. Luther had his own sets of deep, long-healed lesions. She'd never asked him about them, but now she wondered if perhaps she should have.

Unfazed by the direction of Cassidy's thoughts, the wolf continued her deliberate perusal of the other Alpha. When he grew weary enough of her inspection to emit a warning growl, fierce excitement flashed to life in their chest. They pushed closer, eyes locked with his. The orbs glowed bright green in their deep sockets, daring them to come in further. That kind of challenge was one the wolf wasn't willing to back down from. She pressed in on him, until they were practically nose to nose. The Aurora Alpha didn't move, but the growl deepened.

Next to him, the Beta was beside herself. She'd hunkered down and her snarl sounded high and wild. The Alpha still made no move, and the Beta nearly quivered with focused rage begging to be unleashed.

There was no warning. One second the Aurora Alpha was as still as he had been all along, and the next he had exploded toward them. His eyes never changed, they still considered and probed, but his jaws snapped at them. In panicked reflex, Cassidy tried to wrest back control, but her wolf wouldn't budge.

Instead, the wolf flowed back and to the side, neatly ducking under the Alpha's attack. They backed up, dodging left and right to keep his powerful jaws from grasping them around the neck. Behind him, the Beta followed, low to the ground, the snarl winding higher still as the Alpha's large teeth clashed together next to their face. They continued moving backward until a tree flanked by thorny briars made further movement in that direction impossible. The Beta's snarl took on a triumphant edge.

By now, the Alpha was low, watching them closely, alert for some trick on their part. Cassidy made one last attempt to take over their body, but the wolf didn't even acknowledge her. Their eyes were locked with the Alpha. The wolf glanced to one side, toward freedom.

The Alpha shifted into the spot, cutting off their escape, but the wolf wasn't moving into it. She sprang up, kicking off the trunk of the tree, and landed on the Alpha's back. For a moment, they scrabbled for purchase, then their claws sank through the dense fur and bit into tensed muscle and flesh stretched taut. The wolf leaned forward and bit down on an ear, her teeth biting through the tough cartilage with a crunch. Blood filled their mouth, the hot iron coating their tongue and sending their already tripping heart into overdrive.

Yes, Cassidy thought. *Pull it off. Give us more.* It would be a simple thing to tear the ear off the other Alpha's head. That would leave an indelible impression upon him. The ear might grow back, or it might not, but either way, every time he touched it or saw it in the mirror, he would remember the moment when the Alpha of the North Side Pack got the better of him. Their triumph was total. Cassidy wanted to howl for everyone to hear, to exult in their primacy.

The wolf let go and hopped down. She licked a few stray drops of blood from her teeth, then proceeded back to the middle of the clearing where she casually sat down. Her jaws stretched in a yawn that Cassidy didn't feel. Adrenaline beat at her, demanding they get up and continue the fight, but her wolf ignored the urge.

Not a sound disturbed the stillness. The Beta's snarl was absent, and the Alpha had ceased his growling. He stared at Cassidy's wolf for a second, his shoulders high around his head, then relaxed, looking for all the world like a human shrug. After a quick shake with surprisingly little blood from his newly pierced ear, he made his way back to the center as well. Without a look at them, he settled into a comfortable sprawl. The Beta came up and slouched down against him. Neither seemed especially concerned that Cassidy and her wolf had come close to ripping one of his ears clean off.

Why didn't we take it? Cassidy asked her wolf.

She received a mental shrug in response. They'd made their point. There was no reason to push it further, not if they wanted to work with the Aurora Pack. Cowing him might have meant he'd go along with whatever they proposed for now, but it would probably mean he'd be open to plotting to take them down. Complete domination of another wolf was rarely an effective tool, especially not with another Alpha. Sometimes a lighter touch was better.

It made sense and gave Cassidy a lot to think about as the three of them panted in companionable silence in the middle of the moonlit clearing. Snow wasn't far, and knowing she was there gave Cassidy and the wolf a boost of confidence.

Are we going to have to do this for every new Alpha we meet? Cassidy asked.

The wolf's answer was ambivalent. Maybe they would and maybe they wouldn't. Either way, they could take out anyone silly enough to come at them head-on.

CHAPTER THIRTY-FIVE

Hammer was the next to arrive. Next to the Aurora Alpha, he didn't look quite as large, but his bulk through the shoulders was as impressive. His dark brown fur was stained nearly black by the moon's cool light. He inclined his head to both of them, then settled himself on the far side of the clearing. Cassidy and the wolf were dimly aware of his companion somewhere in the woods. Occasional scent traces were blown to them when the wind was right. Whoever he'd brought with him didn't register on her internal starscape in the way Snow did. She could have pointed at the lone wolf, as close as she was. She could feel the stars that made up her own wolven. She even knew that they were off to the east, but that was only because she knew which direction the city was in. Hammer's wolf didn't register even as strongly as that.

She wondered what it would be like to tug on one of the Alpha's stars but made sure not to do anything beyond idle speculation. The last time she'd experimented, she'd nearly started an incident with Hammer's pack. Now was not the time to try such things. If the opportunity to talk shop with one of the other Alphas came up, she resolved to ask them how they saw their pack.

They didn't have to wait long before another Alpha showed up. This one was long and lithe without the massive frames of the other two Alphas. Her light grey fur faded darker closer to her body and around her eyes, giving the lavender irises an even more piercing look than they might have had otherwise. She glanced at each of them in turn, dismissing Hammer and the Aurora Alpha before zeroing in on Cassidy. A much smaller wolven darted from the underbrush to her side. The new Alpha dipped her shoulder into the wolven and bounced them to the opposite side of the clearing, then began stepping her way over to Cassidy. She moved with barely reined-in control, giving the impression that she was working hard to keep from dashing across the open space. This new Alpha was on her best behavior. For now.

She stopped a few feet from Cassidy, then raised her head and gave the air a long sniff. She glanced at the Aurora Alpha then back at Cassidy. The wolf didn't move beyond glancing toward her, then back at the edge of the clearing as if completely disinterested.

The dismissive look riled up the female Alpha, but she didn't act on it. Cassidy got a whiff of irritated wolven, but the scent shaded only slightly into red. She probably wasn't angry enough to act on the calculated slight. The wolf didn't think so either.

The female Alpha eyed them up and down for a little longer, the desire to provoke a reaction from them warring with her knowledge that they'd already taken on the Aurora Alpha. After a few moments, she joined the small wolven who'd arrived with her.

A glance into the night sky confirmed Cassidy's suspicion that the moon had passed its zenith and was starting to dip back toward the horizon. The Gary and Joliet Alphas were late. How long should they wait? The wolf didn't think too much of it. Things like punctuality were a human conceit. The Alphas would be there when they got there. Unless they weren't planning on showing up. So when did they know that?

If Cassidy had had her phone, she would have checked it and mentally given them fifteen more minutes. As it was, she marked the moon's position and resolved to get things started after it had sunk farther toward the treetops.

They got to their feet and prowled the clearing's perimeter, the wolf not quite as sanguine as she was doing her best to appear. After a few turns around the edge of the trees, the wolf stopped and stared into the woods. Someone was coming from the north. The wind was at their backs, pushing the scent of female wolven before her. Whichever Alpha this was, she was moving quickly and making no effort to be quiet. By mutual agreement, Cassidy and the wolf decided to sit down on the clearing's south side. All the better to give themselves some space when the newcomer came through. It was a single Alpha, there was no trace of other wolven scent with her.

As she got closer, Cassidy and the wolf realized they'd been mistaken in their assessment. There were two different scents, but they were so similar as to be nearly indistinguishable. When the two wolven burst through the underbrush and into the moonlight, they realized why. The wolven were identical. Their fur was the same shade of pale chestnut verging almost on red. Twin pairs of golden eyes gleamed at them, taking in everyone who awaited, then glancing off to where Cassidy knew Snow was hidden and off to where she wagered Hammer's second had hunkered down. Cassidy couldn't decide which one was the more dominant of the two and found herself feeling vaguely put off that she wasn't able to figure it out. To her surprise, her wolf didn't know either.

The wolven separated, heading in opposite directions as they paced around the edge of the open space. With a chill, Cassidy realized they were in lockstep, even across the clearing from each other. There was no coordination that she could see, they were simply so in sync that they moved as one, without having to watch each other.

As they passed the other waiting Alphas, each inhaled and looked them over, while maintaining the same eerie matched step. The twin wolven ended up in front of Cassidy at the same time. Only then did they break the mirroring, as one went high to sniff around Cassidy's nose, the other shoving her nose toward Cassidy's tail.

The wolf kept up the same appearance of insouciance that she had with the grey Alpha. These two weren't buying it. A sunny scent rolled off them, of humor and skepticism. The smell of the Aurora Alpha's blood still lingered on the air, and the one must have smelled it around Cassidy's face, but neither was worried. If they'd been in skinform, Cassidy wouldn't have been surprised to see them burst into gales of laughter. Instead, one of them shouldered the other as if to say, "Can you believe her?"

The wolf didn't try to stifle the spike of irritation that went through her. Through them. Cassidy also bridled at not being taken seriously.

The smell of humor brightened further, tipping over into outright hilarity.

To her side, Hammer got to all four feet and tensed. His frame blurred, shifting into betweenform with alarming fluidity.

"Enough of that," he said, the words a little distorted by the muzzle that stuck out of his face. "We have business to attend to."

The grey Alpha considered the moon, then shifted to betweenform. Her change was as quick, but with an odd stuttering quality. She gasped in a deep breath, then spoke: "Agreed." Her voice was light and high, but full of no less authority. "Let's get this over with. I don't want to be away from my pack any longer than I have to."

Cassidy stood, not sparing a glance at the twins who still smelled like they were snickering at her. The wolf stepped aside, allowing Cassidy to push her way into ascendance, but taking care not to be completely displaced. They shared the space on the outside of their skin, working to maintain the delicate balance of betweenform. A push from one to retreat from the other would result in completing the shift to skinform or furform. Only the strongest wolven could keep betweenform for more than a few seconds. Cassidy flowed into it between one breath and the next.

"Luna, you're fast," one of the twins said.

The Aurora Alpha grunted. He reached up to finger his ear. The skin had already healed, but there were bald spots in the fur. "And slippery."

"You might do then," the twins said in odd unison as they stood on either side of Cassidy.

"Glad to hear it," Cassidy said dryly. As long as they didn't look too closely at her pack, her secret would be safe.

"We smell your blood but not hers," the other twin said. "I take it she was able to take you?"

The Aurora Alpha didn't dignify the question with a response. With the scent of his blood in the air, it was unnecessary.

"The noisy ones are Marrow and Bone," Hammer said.

The wolven grinned in disquieting unison, displaying long teeth. Cassidy watched them closely, trying to find a distinguishing characteristic.

"Don't bother," the grey Alpha said. "No one knows who is who. I'm Dale, Alpha for the Kenosha pack." When Cassidy opened her mouth, she continued, "That's my Alpha name. I'm not sharing my real name, not until I know you a little better."

"Is that…" She didn't finish the question. If Snow had been there, she would have checked with her, but asking for clarification felt like admitting ignorance, which could be taken as weakness.

"That one is Crag," Hammer said, indicating the Alpha her wolf had tangled with.

"You're from Aurora," Cassidy said.

He nodded once.

"We're from Gary," Bone said. Or maybe it was Marrow.

"Which one of you is Alpha right now?" Dale asked.

"Marrow," they replied at the same time, then smiled as they conveniently didn't disclose which one that was.

Dale let out an irritated sigh. She turned to face the closest twin to her. "Have you seen Hazel?"

The smile slid from her face. "I haven't. They said they were coming."

Hammer scowled. "It's not like them to be late."

Dale glanced at the moon. "We shouldn't wait any longer." She watched Cassidy out of the corner of her eye. "All right, Five Moons. You pulled us together against all our traditions. This better be important."

"Right into it, then?" Cassidy scrubbed her palms against her thighs before she could stop herself. The pads were sweating as much as her armpits would have if she'd been fully in human form. "All right. My pack has lost three in the past couple of months. The latest is my Beta."

"How do you lose a Beta?" Crag asked.

"Doing me a favor," Hammer said. He stepped forward. "I've lost two. The body of one was found at the edge of North Side territory."

"Really?" Bone and Marrow said at the same time. They looked everywhere but at Cassidy.

"It wasn't me," Cassidy said. "We have no beef with South Shore."

"It's true." Hammer nodded firmly. "They also don't have access to a helicopter."

"That you know of," Crag said.

"We barely leave our den," Cassidy said. "No one in my pack has that kind of training or access." She focused on the truth of the statement, trusting it would come out in her scent.

Something must have worked. Crag looked away, but in contemplation, not distrust.

"We've had word that other packs are losing or have lost wolven," Hammer continued. "The Texas packs are in a bad way, especially Dallas."

"I can confirm that," Dale said. "I have ties to a pack in Houston. They've locked down. No one trusts anyone out there."

"Have you lost anyone?" Cassidy asked.

Dale shook her head. "We had an unexpected death, though. Still haven't figured that one out."

"We're down three," Marrow said. At least Cassidy thought it might be Marrow if she was speaking for her pack.

"Two," Crag grunted.

"Someone's nibbling along the edges of our packs," Cassidy said. "Given how Hammer's wolven was planted in our territory and how Luther was taken, my theory is that we're dealing with police or military involvement. Whoever took Luther dragged him out in a Hummer. A military-grade one, not the civilian version."

The chorus of growls that rose from the throats of the gathered Alphas raised a chill down Cassidy's spine. Her wolf added her own displeasure to the combined anger.

"Either option implies government involvement," Cassidy continued. "And the scale…"

"If it's local to our area that's bad enough," Dale said. Crag and Hammer nodded.

"If it's at a national level…" Marrow said.

"…then we're really buggered," Bone finished.

"Could it be international?" Dale asked.

"I don't know," Cassidy said. "My source didn't say anything to that effect."

"Snow's here?" Bone asked. Her and Marrow's eyes lit up.

Cassidy shrugged at the same time that Hammer nodded. She wished he hadn't. She wasn't comfortable sharing Snow's presence with someone she didn't know well.

"I wish Hazel was here," Dale fretted. "They'd know what to do. It's bad enough we're down Velvet." She looked Cassidy briefly in the eye. "Sorry."

"Not as sorry as me," Cassidy said. She got a quick lupine grin in response.

"Velvet's not gonna be here. Hazel could still turn up," Crag rumbled. "Until they do, it's up to us. You called us here," he said to Cassidy. "You must have an idea."

"All I have is getting out of town. We have a fallback property outside of Danville that my pack is heading to tomorrow. It's more defensible than our den. If we join forces and all head out, no one will be able to take us on."

"Strength in numbers," Marrow said.

"We know something about that," Bone said.

"It's going to take some doing for us," Dale said. "We have a mess of cubs to wrangle."

"Same here." Hammer grimaced. "We've been preparing for a couple of days now. We also have supplementary territory. We could take some on."

"The point is for us all to be in the same place," Cassidy said. "We need to have so many wolven that we'd be impossible to overwhelm."

"Sounds like putting all our eggs in one basket," Crag said. "Is it really wise to gather everyone in one place?"

"Two smaller groups are going to be easier to overwhelm than one big one," Dale said.

"If it's the military, they'll have the numbers even for the bigger group," Hammer said.

"Where are the Hunters in all of this?" Bone asked.

"No one has seen Malice for a couple of weeks," Marrow said.

Cassidy kept silent as the other Alphas chimed in about the Hunter's uncharacteristically low profile. This wasn't going how she'd hoped. Hammer was supposed to have been on her side. She'd thought they were in agreement. She clenched her fists in frustration. The wolf counseled patience, but it was so hard not to howl with frustration and throw her hands up and take care of her own pack. Let them figure out their own crap if they weren't willing to listen to her.

CHAPTER THIRTY-SIX

Snow slowly shifted her weight. She'd hunkered down beneath a shrub dense enough to have retained some snow cover. Her pelt would blend perfectly with it, and as long as she moved as little as possible, she would be nigh undetectable. Briella, Hammer's Beta, had passed nearby when she'd made her circuit of the Alphas' clearing, but she hadn't even looked in Snow's direction. It was fortunate for her that the combined scent of the Alphas was overwhelming her own meager scent trace. It wasn't as remarkable as theirs, which suited her perfectly fine.

The discussion had gone on for a while. She could hear what was being said, though her hiding place didn't give her a full view of every Alpha. Their voices were easy enough to single out, and the scent traces that filtered her way gave her a pretty good idea how each one felt about the conversation.

Cassidy was easy to peg. She was getting riled up, though from the tight way she held her shoulders, she was trying very hard not to be. She really wanted everyone to come out to the farm, and it seemed that Hammer's offer of an alternate location was getting under her skin.

Dale seemed convinced, Crag less so. He might still have been smarting from the way Cassidy had handled him. Bone and Marrow were difficult to read. Their main contribution to the discussion was to crack jokes. They were unusual in that while one of them was the Beta, both were speaking. The other Betas kept their own counsel and seemed content to hang out at the clearing's edge. Except for her and Briella, that was. They watched from within the trees.

"Putting everyone in one place is dangerous," Hammer was saying. He punctuated each word by stabbing his finger into his palm. When his aroma came to Snow's nostrils, she inhaled, then sniffed deeper. The animation he was displaying didn't match his scent. He was much calmer than he was doing his best to appear.

At his side, Crag nodded.

"I can't believe you," Dale said. She had shifted closer to Cassidy, though Snow couldn't tell if the movement was a conscious one.

"I can," Bone said.

Marrow grinned widely, chortling softly under her breath.

"So you're fine shoehorning your pack in with this one's?" Crag jerked a clawed thumb in Cassidy's direction. "She has no experience leading, but we're supposed to throw in with her?"

"The plan isn't a bad one," Dale said. "And no one said she'd be in charge."

"Her territory…" Marrow said.

"…her rules," Bone finished.

What was their game? She'd spent a decent amount of time with their pack a few decades back. Bone was as close as she'd gotten to having a romantic relationship with anyone. Their evenings had been filled with cuddles and the occasional kiss. Snow had hoped it would have been different with her, wrapped up as the twins were in each other. It was difficult to tell where one ended and the other began. Even with all the time they'd spent together, she still had a hard time telling them apart. Oh, they would pretend outrage when she mixed them up, but they did nothing to distinguish themselves either. For a couple of beings who enjoyed chaos, they helmed a surprisingly well-run pack.

Reminiscing on her former girlfriend wasn't what she was there to do. Snow lifted her head off the ground a few inches and scanned the area. Her job was to get a read on the Alphas, but she didn't think that meant she should ignore their perimeter.

The local wildlife hadn't resumed its evening wanderings once the wolven had settled in one place. Sure it was a cold night, and the presence of wolven tended to send most creatures to ground, but there should have been something. Some indication of life.

Her stomach twisted as tension roiled within her. The hair on the back of her neck raised, and she cocked her head, listening hard for something. Anything.

She concentrated, trying to hear past the bickering Alphas. There! A crack of a stick echoed through the trees. Snow tensed, her ears swiveling back and forth fast enough to possibly give away her location. The woods were silent, then she barely made out the crunch of boots in packed snow.

Snow barked once, a sharp sound of alarm. The Alphas froze. The sound of boots stopped. Whoever was out there was trying to be sneaky, but they couldn't stop their scent from being blown along by the wind. The stink of human sweat and gun oil pricked at her nostrils.

Snow erupted from her hiding place and sprinted straight for Cassidy. A muffled curse came to her ears, followed by the sound of heavy footsteps running toward them. At first, it was only one set, then more joined in. Snow didn't slow. She grabbed Cassidy by her left hand and yanked her toward the shelter of the trees. A sharp crack rang out over the roar of her pulse in her ears. One of the Betas on the clearing's edge collapsed in a heap, a splash of red on its pelt. More crimson bloomed across it, showing up with shocking intensity against the ice. They stayed down for only a moment, before pulling themselves up on churning legs and flinging themselves across the glade. More reports split the night, and the Beta shrugged off two more bullets, before going down to one that blew a deep hole over their left eye.

It should have been a shocking sight, but Snow let it roll off her. Someone was in the woods, and she needed her wits about her if she was going to keep herself and as many of the Alphas alive as she could manage.

Cassidy lunged forward, blurring in midair and shifting into full furform before her paws touched the ground. Her snarl tore through the night air, a ripping sound that momentarily drowned out human shouts and cracking branches. The forest around them was a bewildering cacophony of gunfire and impacts into flesh. The aroma of iron and gunpowder hung heavy in the air. It was difficult to discern the scent of humans among the competing smells.

A man in full camouflage peeked out from behind a tree, his head swiveling toward them. Night vision goggles obscured his face, so did the iron sights of the rifle he held at the ready. His head tracked to follow Snow as she dodged to one side. It took only a fraction of a second to level his rifle at her, but it was all she needed to reverse course and dodge his shot.

Cassidy was already moving toward the soldier. Snow flung herself in the opposite direction, trying to make herself as big a target as possible. When he turned to follow her, she grinned. Before he could squeeze off another round, Cassidy barreled into him at a full sprint. The human was flung to the side as Cassidy dug her claws into him and climbed his falling body. She grasped his neck in her mouth and pushed off and away from him while biting down hard. The soldier coughed up a gout of blood, then his neck was torn out in a spray of gore. When he hit the ground, his death throes were his only movement. They stopped not long after.

The air around them was still filled with the sounds of battle, but there seemed to be no one in their immediate vicinity. Snow hunkered down. Cassidy took up a protective position above her. She'd known the Alpha would protect her; it hadn't even occurred to her that she might not.

A new sound came to her ears. A rhythmic thumping. Maybe a rabbit sounding the alarm against a log? That was impossible. No animal in its right mind would make itself known, not with the chaos and blood that was radiating out from the clearing. She squeezed shut her eyes and cocked her head to listen for a moment. A helicopter. The back of her throat burned with bile. It had to be there to support the humans who were doing their best to kill them.

Help me, sister, Snow entreated her wolf. They'd been together all their lives and were so entwined as to be one, but there were still times when it was useful to rely on the wolf's senses and how she interpreted them. Her body relaxed as the wolf strained her ears. Through the gunfire and shouts, the engines of the helicopter and the wind that was kicked up by its rotors, there was an area of relative calm. The southwest, Snow thought, interpreting the direction from the wolf's sense of where they were in space. For whatever reason, there were fewer soldiers there.

Snow took back over, blinking and reorienting herself.

"Aim for the limbs," a man's voice shouted out over the din. "Stay away from the head, you asses!"

Snow and Cassidy glanced at each other at the instructions. That put a new spin on things. Though their attackers had demonstrated that they would use lethal force, those weren't their instructions. The thought both cheered and chilled Snow. They had a chance, but why did someone want them alive?

Either way, she wasn't going to allow herself to be captured. Snow reached around and gently grabbed Cassidy's front leg in her teeth and tugged. When the Alpha looked down, she jumped up and started trotting toward the quieter area.

Cassidy followed along without pause, so Snow quickened her pace. Before long, they were both stretched out in a headlong dash, with Snow in the lead. She forded downed logs and eeled her way under dense brush, barely slowing for either. The occasional bloodied and broken body of a dead human was simply one more obstacle to avoid on her way away from danger. With the sounds of the fight passing on either side then behind them, Cassidy raised her head and released a bell-like howl.

* * *

They didn't know who their assailants were, and they didn't care. Cassidy and her wolf were both riding high on adrenaline and the rush of tearing out a man's neck. While their first priority was to keep Snow safe, they hoped someone would dare get in their way and give them the excuse for bloodshed. The other Alphas and their Betas were tearing apart the upstarts who'd dared challenge them. The fight wasn't going to last long at this rate.

Snow seemed to know where she was going, and they'd trusted she would do her best to get them clear. Now that the sounds of battle were beginning to fade, she needed to let the others know. Their continued survival hinged on sticking together, of that Cassidy was sure.

The howl they let out was clear and broadcast "follow me" to all who knew it. They kept to Snow's tail but listened for sounds of pursuit. There was always the chance that the other Alphas and their Betas would draw the fight with them. As long as Snow could stay clear, there was no reason Cassidy and her wolf couldn't take out their bad mood on those who were trying to capture them.

They'd heard the shouted directive, and they knew it was a terrible idea for the humans. The soldiers' only hope for survival was to fight as if they were about to be killed. Holding back would only hasten the inevitable end.

Cassidy and the wolf kept tight to Snow's tail as she careened around a dense group of saplings. The wolf swiveled an ear back, listening for pursuit. They clamped their muzzle shut on a call of triumph when they heard scrambling that could only have come from the human soldiers. Interspersed with the sounds of pursuit were flashes of teeth tearing flesh and voices raised in pain. They wished Snow would slow enough that one of their pursuers might catch them, but the lone wolf was moving as quickly as she could.

The sound of a galloping wolven came up behind them. The wolf was moving as quickly as three legs could take them. Cassidy and the wolf glanced behind them and caught glimpses of grey fur. Dale. The lighter blur behind her was probably her Beta.

They swiveled their head the other way when the sound of panting and the crunch of boots on snow caught their ears from the right. A human male broke out of the trees, a heavy-looking pistol in one hand and a wickedly sharp machete in the other. He was on an intercept course, his knees pumping as rhythmically as possible over the unpredictable terrain. They looked back to make sure Dale was close enough to protect Snow. Their eyes met, and they flicked their eyes toward Snow then back to the other Alpha. Dale put her head down and found a burst of speed. Even with the large wound on her left flank, the Kenosha Alpha was incredibly fast.

Satisfied that the lone wolf would be protected, Cassidy and the wolf veered away to cut off the human still rushing toward them. They kept low, using the cluttered understory for visual cover. He had to hear them, even with his pathetic human hearing; they weren't being subtle. Speed was the objective, stealth a distant second.

Even so, his eyes widened with surprise when they burst through the brambles into his path. He recovered quickly, raising his pistol and squeezing off three shots in rapid succession. Cassidy didn't slow as she and the wolf wove a serpentine path toward him. Two bullets went wide, and they barely felt the third make contact somewhere near their left shoulder. There was no time to dwell on the fact that they'd been shot. The pain was negligible, little more than a burning sensation.

They gathered their back legs under them and launched at the man as soon as they were even remotely within range.

"Stay down, you fucker," he growled as he swung the machete into their path.

He wasn't prepared for how agile they were. They flowed under the blade, then were face-to-face with him. He tried to get a hand up, to get the pistol between them, but it was too late. Foolish, foolish human. Maybe he was only following orders, but it didn't matter. He'd dared to attack their people.

By the time he got the gun up, they'd already ducked down and past him. It took less than an instant to chomp into the soft flesh behind his leg and sever his hamstring.

He screamed as he went down and their pulse roared in their ears. His agony was their balm. They drank his blood in, savoring the fear that came with it. When the soldier threw himself away from them, trying to get up on one leg in a futile attempt to escape them, they took their time closing the distance.

A feeling of disdain filtered through to her from the wolf. It felt like the kind of generally bemused way an elder might observe a cub. The implication was clear. *Stop playing with your food.*

Cassidy sighed. He deserved to pay, and if not him, then who? They closed the distance between them, easily dodging his wild shots. They lunged in, not going for the head as he'd expected, but for the inside of his thigh. With a bite and a tear, they removed a massive chunk of flesh, obliterating a stretch of femoral artery. They left him scrabbling at his pants leg, crying out in pain. He would bleed out shortly. If someone came to his aid in time and he survived, he would be someone else's problem.

They had to return to Snow and the others. They sprinted in the general direction the lone wolf had been headed. Her scent stood out like a glowing silver ribbon in the moonlight. It only took a few moments to catch back up with the little group. Crag had joined them. His front half was covered in blood, though it was impossible to tell if it was all his. He certainly smelled strongly of human viscera.

They fell in toward the back, trusting again in Snow's instincts. The sound of fighting humans and the remaining wolven receded slowly behind them. They were going to make it. Cassidy started plotting how they might come back around and extricate those who still fought.

The plan hadn't quite come together before their vision was wiped out by blinding whiteness.

CHAPTER THIRTY-SEVEN

Snow stumbled, her night vision completely wiped out. The roar of the helicopter overhead and the light told her everything she needed to know. They were being followed, every movement painted by that damn piece of machinery's spotlight. She swiveled, heading to the side, seeking the edge of the patch of brilliance. Behind her, the other wolven had the same idea. Crag uttered a high bark as he separated from the group, racing away from them. Snow could feel Cassidy behind her and knew when the Alpha kept to the same side as her.

Through very bad luck, the light operator above kept the spot tight to her. The patch of ground where she found herself was largely devoid of snow, and she must have presented an easy target.

A high whine cut through the racket from the helicopter, followed by a deep thudding that she felt as much as heard. Small fountains of earth kicked up from the ground in a line toward her. She threw herself to the side as the line cut past her. The caliber of those bullets was higher than anything the humans had been carrying. If one of those hit her, it might take a limb off, if it didn't kill her outright. At the best she'd be incapacitated.

The deeper underbrush was her best bet. She dove for a thicket of brambles that promised pain. The vines had had all winter to dry out and while the thorns might be brutal, they were far better than what the machine gun offered. Cassidy closed on her, braving the despicable line of bullets and somehow dashing through unscathed. Snow dug in deeper, trying to get something thick enough between her and the light to shield her.

To her shock, the spot shifted away from them as Cassidy hunkered down beside her. The feel of Cassidy's body against her own brought a pant of relief that would have been a sob if she'd been in skinform. Cassidy licked the side of her neck, her warm tongue laving away the beads of blood that welled up through Snow's fur. The thorns were as dreadful as she'd expected, but at least she was no longer center stage on the killing field.

Her relief at finding shelter was short-lived. As they peered out from under their frail cover, the spot silhouetted the other three wolven. They milled in confusion for a moment. Flashes of light peppered the trees beyond them. Their pursuers had caught up.

Snow couldn't see deep into the trees, not with the brilliance of the light too close to allow her night vision to reestablish itself. Hoarse shouts of triumph accompanied the staccato pop of firearms.

A man in combat fatigues emerged from cover, inching closer to their hiding place. His attention never wavered from the three wolven who circled, trying desperately to escape the light.

Snow grinned fiercely as a dark shape emerged from the darkness. A shaggy, nearly-humanoid figure stepped out from behind a tree and grabbed the soldier's head, then gave a violent twist. The man spasmed, then dropped into a heap, his death soundless against the background fray. Hammer looked at them, making eye contact with Snow. His eyes pierced into hers, radiating rage such as she'd rarely seen before. It rivaled the anger she smelled on Cassidy, though his was underpinned by a terrible bloodlust. She shuddered when he relinquished her gaze, allowing her to breathe again. Hammer drifted back into the shadows, slouching toward where the other three still weaved and dodged.

They weren't doing well. More spots of bright red blood bled through their pelts on their shoulders and flanks. The Kenosha Beta was starting to flag.

The damn helicopter. They'd had the upper hand until it tracked them down. Snow glared into the sky toward the source of the hated brilliance.

Dale was moving increasingly frantically as her Beta took more shots. Finally, she threw herself down, pressing herself flat to the ground. A second later, she popped back up in betweenform. She pointed toward the helicopter with an emphatic jabbing motion, shouting something Snow couldn't make out.

Crag looked into the light for a moment, then made himself as small as possible. Unfortunately for him, small as possible was still very large. Bullets thudded into him as he completed his own transformation to betweenform. As one, he and Dale lunged toward the Kenosha Beta.

Cassidy leaped up, leaving a cool spot at Snow's side and apprehension twisting in her gut. The North Side Alpha threw herself toward the nearest flashes of light, screaming the whole way. The unnerving sound set Snow's fur to bristling. It should not have been able to come from a wolf's throat. Cassidy skirted the edge of the spotlight, and for a second it shifted to follow her.

Though the light snapped back to the three trapped wolven a moment later, the waver gave Dale and Crag the opening they'd been looking for. They grabbed one of the Beta's legs in each hand, then drew her back. In unison, they swung forward, launching the Beta toward the hovering vehicle. The gambit was ridiculous, laughable even. Snow could only watch as the wolven soared through the air.

Around them, the sound of guns firing stopped as the humans couldn't believe what they were seeing any more than Snow did. The only one still moving was Cassidy. She disappeared into the woods, and the eerie silence was broken only by the abrupt scream of a soldier and the helicopter's rotors.

Snow watched, waiting for the wolven to miss the helicopter and come crashing down to the earth. Seconds stretched, seeming to pass in minutes, hours even as the small grey wolf sailed closer and closer. As she flew, her form blurred, shifting from furform to betweenform. Against all odds, in defiance of all reasonable outcomes, as she finished her transformation, the Beta reached out for the helicopter and touched it. There was nothing for her to grab onto. Her clawed fingers slipped along smooth metal as she threatened to slide past the flying vehicle. With a jerk, she stopped, her claws digging, finding purchase on something. It was too far to tell if she'd found a seam in the metal skin or if she'd somehow managed to punch through it.

An instant later, the Beta grabbed on with her other hand. She swung her feet up and swarmed over the helicopter's side to the top. Her head was dangerously close to the rotors, and she had to slow to push through the terrible downdraft they generated. Snow had no idea how the Beta was managing. Her concentration had to be fierce to keep from losing betweenform, yet her grip on her form didn't waver.

Back on the ground, Crag and Dale had split from each other. The spot followed Crag, which didn't seem to bother him in the least.

The thundering reports of the copter's machine gun rang out. Again, the line of bullets traced a path over red-stained snow toward the massive Alpha. He didn't have Cassidy's agility or Dale's speed. He made no attempt to dodge away from the dangerous spray. A bullet punched through his leg, then through his side, and another chewed up a chunk of his shoulder, but Crag kept going. Aside from a shudder as each round hit his flesh, he didn't respond. He reached between two small trees and grabbed someone, then pulled them forward. The trees bowed apart, but not enough. The soldier clawed at Crag's arm, trying to get him to let go as the Alpha continued dragging him. Small branches tore through the man's fatigues and into his skin. The trees' trunks flexed further, and the soldier came within reach of Crag's jaws. He closed them over the top of the human's head and bit down.

On the helicopter, the Beta had made her way over the top. The side door was open all the way, exposing the machine gun mount and its operator. She grabbed the edge of the opening and flipped down, landing on top of the gunner. The weapon's firing ceased abruptly. Snow couldn't hear what was going on up above, but a moment later a human in blood-streaked fatigues came flying through the copter's open door. They plummeted through spindly branches without ever moving. They were dead before they hit the ground, likely before they were ejected from the helicopter.

A few seconds later, the spotlight gyrated wildly through the trees. Soldiers were lit from above for a fraction of a second before the light moved on. Some were fighting against the wolven who danced among them in furform or betweenform. As the light flashed over them, moments of chaos and mayhem etched themselves into Snow's mind. Each spray of blood, the impact of tooth or claw into flesh sent her scrambling farther back into her hidey-hole.

The helicopter jerked to one side, then to the other. Another body was flung from it, this one taking the front windshield with it. What hit the ground was barely recognizable as human.

The engines took on a curious whining sound, then the helicopter yawed to one side in an awkward swan dive. Snow watched with horrified fascination. Where was the Beta? The helicopter was nearly level with the tops of the trees before righting itself, the rotors shearing branches from their trunks. It balanced drunkenly for a few moments, then lurched to the other side. This time the door through which the Beta had entered was facing up. As the helicopter started another death roll, a wolven shape still in betweenform dodged the wildly swinging machine gun, then launched itself through the open doors.

The racket of the engine was momentarily drowned out as the still spinning rotors shredded trees to bits before flying into pieces. Deadly chunks of shrapnel shot through the air, most of them burying themselves into trees with loud thunks. Those that hit flesh were accompanied by wetter sounds and a sudden increase in screams.

All of that was eclipsed when the helicopter slammed into the ground. A moment later, the night lit up orange around them. The copter exploded in a thunderous shock that blasted her eardrums and washed out her vision in a field of white. Snow hunkered herself down as low as she could, but the shock wave of the explosion pushed her still farther into the thicket. Her ears rang and her vision blurred as it slowly returned.

She wriggled free of her hiding place and stumbled to her feet as the smell of burning fuel filled the air. Fire was to be avoided at all costs. The woods were covered in snow but dry, and burning kerosene had been blasted out in who knew how large a radius. The world tilted on its axis then righted itself. She shook her head.

Where's Cassidy? She couldn't feel the Alpha. Trying not to panic, Snow peered through the smoke to no avail. The clouds sent up by the burning wreckage and trees were too dense to penetrate. Her ears still rang, and she pawed at one, trying to clear it. It was too quiet. That had to be the effects of the explosion. Surely there were other sounds. She couldn't be the only one left alive.

Snow took a deep breath, then coughed as she dragged smoke into her lungs. They'd been heading southwest. She would keep heading in that direction and hope the other wolven who were still alive would make the same choice. Was it the right decision? There was no way of knowing, but staying put would kill her.

Snow put the heat of the fires to her back and pushed forward, her eyes roving for any sign of wolven.

CHAPTER THIRTY-EIGHT

Cassidy came to all at once. She was freezing, and her muscles ached. That might have been from the cold, but it was more likely from the wall of force that had sent her cartwheeling sideways into a tree when it hit her. She scrambled, getting her legs under her and looking around, fingers crooked into threatening claws. No wonder she was so chilly. She and the wolf had lost their handle on furform when they'd lost consciousness.

She glanced around cautiously. When the helicopter had hit the ground, she'd been engaged with two soldiers. They were probably dead, but she wasn't going to assume. It was easier to see with the orange glow that surrounded her. The wolf didn't like it, nor the burning smell that permeated everything. The sound of flames cracking through small branches sent goose bumps up her arms and down her back.

One of her assailants lay in a heap at the base of a tree, his head at an unnatural angle, sightless eyes staring at her. A little farther beyond him was the other, this one a woman with a chunk of metal paneling longer than Cassidy's arm sticking out of her abdomen. It pinned her to the ground. She wasn't moving either.

Satisfied that she wasn't about to be jumped, Cassidy crouched down and allowed her wolf to ascend. The transformation took a little longer than usual; they were both exhausted. By the time she was covered in fur and in a much better form to escape what was promising to be quite the inferno, more of Cassidy's hearing had returned. The fire wasn't a little crackle, it was taking on a throaty roar that frightened her—frightened them—down to the core of their being.

Humans with guns were one thing. A forest fire was another beast altogether, one they couldn't defeat. It would eat them alive. It would devour Snow.

Snow!

Cassidy and the wolf spun in place, reaching out to the lone wolf, trying to get a feel for her using the internal starscape that was her pack. She was still there and had survived the destruction of the helicopter. If she'd been closer, they could have gone right to her, but she was too far away.

Her wolf was screaming for them to leave. There was a patch of trees to her left that looked like it'd escaped immediate destruction. The wind was shifting, fanning small flames into something larger and hungrier but also revealing the night sky and stars in that direction.

They were moving before Cassidy made the conscious choice. Her wolf was making the decisions now. They would run for safety but keep a watch for the other Alphas and Betas and, most importantly, for Snow.

They tried to keep to unburned patches of ground or at least those that weren't actively on fire. Every time they came down on a smoldering surface, pain lanced through their feet and up their legs. Each was worse than any cut or laceration Cassidy had received. Hell, it hurt more than getting shot. They gritted their teeth and forged on toward the tantalizing spot of open air they'd glimpsed.

A crack from above was their only warning. The wolf leaped forward, pushing off with everything she had. They cleared a fallen log that was being consumed by flames just as a large tree branch hit the ground where they'd been only a moment before. The impact sent sparks showering in all directions. The smell of singeing fur hit their nostrils. It was simply one more assault on their senses. Their lungs burned, both from the smoke and the heat.

Fortunately, the smoke was starting to thin. They were treated to eddies of unfouled air, each an opportunity for a deep breath and a clearing of their thoughts. It was in one of these moments that they looked over and saw a naked form lying unmoving at the base of a larger tree. The branches at the top were already wreathed in flames, but the trunk was relatively untouched. They hesitated. The air was clearer here, but for how much longer? And if the wolven couldn't move on its own, did they have enough energy to shift to a form where they could carry them?

The woman was small and completely nude. They couldn't smell wolven over the choking smoke, but no one else would be stripped down to nothing in this burning forest at night.

There wasn't time to think about it. They had to check anyway. Leaving one of their own behind, even if they weren't directly theirs, wasn't something Cassidy would consider.

After a quick look behind to gauge the speed of the fire, which was still frighteningly fierce, they swerved and headed for the wolven. Unless she was mistaken, Cassidy was certain this was Dale's Beta.

They nudged at the small wolven with their nose. She didn't awaken, but she was definitely still alive. The sound of the fire was increasing in ferocity. Cassidy shouldered her wolf partially aside, sharing in her ascendance. It was an agonizing process, every shift of muscle and skin hurt all the more where they were burned. By the time they achieved the delicate balance of betweenform, their legs trembled. Cassidy shoved the pain and the feeling of weakness from her mind, then reached down and picked up the wolven. It was fortunate she was so small. They weren't in any condition to carry someone much larger. If this had been Hammer or Crag, they would have been on their own.

Conscious of the heat growing steadily more intense at their back, they bounded forward, the wolven cradled to their chest in an awkward facsimile of a mother's embrace for her infant. They weren't able to move as quickly as they had, not and balance their burden in a way where she wouldn't slow them down even more. They'd been close to the edge of the area that had been actively burning, though, and it wasn't much longer before they broke through and into mostly smoke-free air.

While putting more space between them and the fire, Cassidy kept looking up, trying to get an idea of where they'd ended up, relative to where they'd started. Snow had been heading in a generally southwest direction before the helicopter had fallen from the sky.

She snickered, a strange half-wheezing snort in her betweenform. Had the helicopter fallen or had it been pushed?

The wolf moved within her in concern, threatening to take over completely if Cassidy couldn't hold it together. She shook her head and tightened her hold on the naked form she was holding. Letting the wolf take over would mean leaving the Beta behind.

Her head had cleared a little bit from what was likely exhaustion with more than a little shock mixed in. She hadn't known wolven could go into shock, but most wolven didn't get a military helicopter dropped on them either. She shambled forward, slower now that they weren't in imminent danger of burning to death. From what she could tell, they were north and west of the clearing where she'd talked with the other Alphas. If they circled south, they might run into Snow, maybe even the others.

The car. That was another potential meeting place. Her steps took on more confidence, and she slung the wolven over her shoulder to give her arms a bit of respite. Now that she had a plan, her mind cleared. It was a matter of putting one foot in front of the other and keeping an eye out for humans. Those closer to the crash hadn't fared well, but who knew how many of them had been deeper in the woods. Not to mention that sooner or later, the burning helicopter would attract a different kind of human attention. They wouldn't be looking for wolven, but avoiding gawkers could get tricky. The faster she met up with Snow, the faster they could get back to the den.

Home. It had never sounded so good. She couldn't wait to see Naomi. To know that her Beta was supporting her with all the little things that she still forgot to consider half the time. Cassidy vowed to check in with every single one of her wolven, to get some skin time or fur time, whichever was their preference. She longed to immerse herself in the comforting embrace of her pack, then to emerge to stand between them and a world that had proven once again it not only didn't care for them, but it would actively hunt them down and hurt them.

She quickened her steps. First Snow, then home. A cuddle pile with as many wolven as wanted in, then maybe a bath. Or the bath could come before the cuddle pile. She would have to make that decision based on how many of her wolves pulled faces when she showed up. She imagined she was pretty rank by now.

It was a comforting fantasy, one she clung to as she skirted the edge of the disaster that had been her Alpha meeting.

* * *

Since making her way from the debris field now burning merrily behind her, Snow had gathered Dale and Marrow and Bone. All bore marks from the fight. The twins helped each other along in betweenform, leaning on the other's shoulder to stay upright. One had a large chunk of upper thigh missing. The top of her femur was partially exposed, though not as much as had been when Snow first happened upon them. The other twin seemed to have had a good part of her left foot shot off. Like her sister, it was already looking better. Dale was as much Swiss cheese as wolven. Like Snow, she was in furform. Her coat was stained with blood; from the scent, it was as much hers as their attackers. Some of the wounds had healed, leaving only dried blood and missing patches of fur. The rest, she ignored as she swung her muzzle back and forth in the wind. If Snow had to guess, she would assume that Dale was looking for her Beta as much as keeping her senses peeled for more soldiers. She was doing the same, except the object of her concern was Cassidy.

There was no sign of the Alpha. Snow had only gotten short glimpses of her dancing among the trees, taking out the humans who'd dared attack them. Then the helicopter had gone down, and there had been no way to know where Cassidy had ended up. She still held hope that the Alpha would find them, but it diminished with every passing second, leaving a hole in her heart that yawned wider and wider.

Their group had passed a few living humans, but they'd been more interested in finding their own kind than in the wolven. They hadn't looked up as the wolven had slunk past, even when one of the twins had stepped on a dry stick. The snap had sounded as loud as a gunshot to Snow, but the humans had been almost aggressively disinterested in checking it out. Bone, or maybe Marrow, had shrugged. It was difficult to maintain one's usual level of stealth when missing half a foot.

How much farther did they go? If Cassidy or the other missing wolven hadn't met up with them yet, chances seemed good they wouldn't.

After a careful listen and a check of the wind, Snow came to a stop. Dale immediately hunkered down next to her. Bone and Marrow leaned against a tree.

Snow regarded each one in turn. Her next thought was to head back to the van. Cassidy would probably think to go back to it. It was a long way back to the North Side on foot, even for a wolven. It was especially far for one who was wounded, as the Alpha almost certainly was.

She met Dale's eyes and cocked her head, then glanced back to where she'd parked. The Kenosha Alpha considered it.

"What's the plan?" one of the twins asked.

Snow stood up and indicated the east with her nose. She wasn't about to risk assuming skinform to talk this out. Not only might they be come upon by humans who weren't as keen on avoiding them as the last group had been, but there was the very real chance she wouldn't have enough energy to resume furform. Getting to betweenform was out of the question. Even if she'd been able to reach the state without great effort under normal circumstances, these were as far from normal as it was possible to get and still be on the same planet.

"What's that way?" The question came from the other twin. The two of them were already staggering forward in the direction Snow was pointed.

"I hope it's a car," the first twin said.

"Never thought I'd hear you say that."

The first twin rolled her eyes, no mean feat in betweenform. "There's a first for everything. Never thought you'd lean on me quite so literally."

"Not true." Their voices were starting to recede as they limped away from where Dale and Snow were still catching their breath. "What about that time with the forklift?"

"You can't count that."

They were being too loud. Snow cringed, listening for the sounds of discovery that must surely be coming. Dale watched her closely, then stood and waited. Her body language indicated that Snow should take the lead.

Snow took a deep breath, then another. No sounds of pursuit. No gunshots to split the night. She got up in a slow crouch.

As soon as her body left the ground, Dale darted after the twins. With a low bark, she admonished them to keep quiet.

One of the twins grumbled in indistinct protest, but the other hushed her.

There was still nothing to indicate they'd been found out. She didn't stop crouching, but Snow slunk forward. At the twins' slow pace, it didn't take long to catch up to them.

Again, the wolven fell into step behind her. It was an exceedingly odd feeling to be the one in the lead. These were Alphas, for god's sake. And one Beta, but Marrow and Bone were so close that they really both rated as Alphas. That one of them would be Beta was more or less a joke on their part, a teasing jab at the pack traditions wolven clung so closely to. They worked the status changes to their advantage, keeping other packs off-balance. Regardless, one of them really should have been in front. Not only did it not feel right for Snow to be the one making these decisions, but she felt horribly exposed. Cassidy wouldn't have put her in this position.

And where was she? There was still no sign of her.

After they'd swung far enough east, Snow led the ragtag group north. The sounds of the highway were audible now, with its cars on concrete. They weren't passing as quickly as they had when she and Cassidy had crossed. How visible was the fire from the road? She glanced back over her shoulder. The sky to the west was still lit up in orange.

This was going to be a problem.

They crept closer until the headlights of cars were visible through the trees. They were parked on the shoulder, and human voices were raised in fretful conversation. Snow wasn't close enough that she could make out the words, but the tone was certainly clear. She stopped, looking at the wolven, then at the road.

"Rubberneckers," one of the twins said.

Her sister nodded.

Dale sat down, watching Snow closely. The implication was clear. This was her mess to figure out. Snow shut her eyes. She didn't want to be in charge, but no one else knew where her car was. It had to be her. She knew it, but she didn't have to like it. Which was good, because she didn't.

But there was nothing for it. No choice. She had to keep moving. With a deep sigh, she turned back south. They would have to follow the road until they found somewhere that wasn't gummed up by onlookers. At least with a massive fire in the distance, no one would be on the lookout for wolves.

By the time they found a patch of asphalt that was free enough of traffic that they might cross, they'd trekked pretty far south. Snow stopped again. This time Dale stepped forward, her scent resolute. She would check if it was all right for them to cross. If Snow had been in skinform, she might have burst into tears. Instead, she flopped down to the ground and tried to relax.

Bone and Marrow also dropped down. Their forms wavered for a second, then each of them shifted, attaining furform in a minute or so. They were as exhausted as everyone else in the group.

The wind brought the smells of the road with it. She wasn't usually this excited by concrete and motor oil, but at the moment it smelled like freedom. Best of all, there were no nasty human scents. It would be a long time before she'd be able to stomach those.

She watched through the trees as well as she could, waiting for Dale's return to let them know that it was safe to cross. They were so close she could nearly feel her van's steering wheel in her hands.

Maybe Cassidy would already be waiting. Five Moons was a strong Alpha. Surely, even if she'd gotten banged up, she would be able to get to the car before them. Her body practically vibrated as she waited, ready to dash and put this place in the past.

Something hit the ground behind her. She hadn't smelled them coming, the wind was coming from the wrong direction. A snarl on her lips, Snow spun to confront whatever had the temerity to come up on them. Fighting wasn't usually her style, but she'd had enough.

CHAPTER THIRTY-NINE

A massive wolven in betweenform growled down at her. She started forward on pure instinct before his scent hit her. It was Hammer. Her body went limp with relief. She slid to a sitting position and looked up at him, tongue lolling from the side of her mouth. Surely he would take charge.

Marrow and Bone ignored him, which Hammer took in stride. He glanced around. Snow trotted back to where she'd been waiting. Soft steps through the underbrush heralded Dale's return.

"What's going on here?" he asked quietly, his voice a low rumble scarcely audible over the occasional passing car.

One of the twins flicked an ear at him, but neither deigned to answer.

With a sigh, Dale made the long shift back to betweenform. "This would be easier if we weren't all Alphas," she groused. "Too many cooks. No one wants to follow."

Snow lifted her head. She would have been happy to follow.

"Is this all you've found?" Hammer asked. "Have you seen Briella?"

Dale shook her head soberly. "I'm missing Jane."

Anguish wafted off the South Shore Alpha in a wave that made Snow want to sneeze. So far, everyone had been smelling of physical pain and determination. Grief was one more marker of distress, one they had no time for.

"And Crag? His Beta?" he asked. "Five Moons?"

"No sign."

"Then what's the plan?"

"Snow has one." Dale shifted to face her. "Don't think she can shift to tell us."

"Hm." Hammer stroked his chin in a movement that was out of place in betweenform. "Do we trust her?"

"She'd set us up?" Dale's voice rose high into incredulity before she modulated it.

Bone's and Marrow's heads popped up and swiveled to take in Dale and Hammer's conversation. Then, with the unison that always creeped Snow out, they turned to regard her.

Four sets of glowing Alpha eyes regarded her in a ring of silent accusation. Snow dropped her head to the ground and pressed her tail around the side of her body. That she could be blamed for what happened hadn't occurred to her. It should have. She made herself as small as possible, trying to convey exactly how scant a threat she was to the wolven looming above her.

Dale shook her head. "I refuse to believe it. If she had it out for us, there's a dozen ways she could have killed us already, starting with not leading us out of there."

"I don't say she'd betray us directly," Hammer said, "but look at her. She's terrified. Leading us is not her position."

"Then what's your idea?" Dale hissed.

"We take this fight back to those who would have destroyed us." Hammer gestured back to where the night sky still held its sullen orange glow. "They're in disarray. Now is the time to make them pay."

"I can't believe this." Dale turned away from him.

Snow tried to press herself even further into the ground. Hammer wasn't completely wrong. In fact, he'd verbalized pretty much every misgiving she had about being in charge of the Alphas, but going back into the woods to take on an enemy they knew little about was about as close to suicide as you could get without standing on the train tracks and staring down the oncoming locomotive.

Something tugged at the ruff of fur around her neck. She looked over and Marrow or Bone had their teeth gently in her fur. When the wolven saw Snow looking, she winked and pulled at her again. Dale and Hammer were still arguing, but the other twin was already skulking closer to where the trees ended and the highway verge began. The Gary Alpha and Beta believed in her. That was something.

She scuttled forward, not daring to intrude upon the Kenosha and South Shore Alphas, who still couldn't come to an agreement.

"Where are you going?"

The whispered question still carried an unmistakable tone of authority, which sent Snow freezing in her tracks. Her tail wrapped even more tightly around her back end, she looked back. Hammer glared at her, and Dale was watching her nearly as fiercely.

The twin with its mouth buried in her ruff kept yanking, but the other circled around Snow to intercept the Alphas' ire. She planted her feet and extended her head toward them, growling the entire time.

"Let her go," Hammer said, "or by god, you'll answer to me."

"You don't have any call on her," Dale said. "Snow is a lone wolf. She can come and go as she pleases."

He drew himself up to the top of his large frame and deliberately stepped into Dale's personal space. "Is that so?" he asked quietly.

"For crap's sake, Hammer." Dale brushed past him. Or tried to.

He dropped a clawed hand on her shoulder with enough force to stop the Kenosha Alpha in her tracks.

Snow allowed herself to be drawn closer to the highway. If Hammer and Dale were about to throw down, she didn't want to be anywhere in the vicinity. Without a common enemy to focus them, the Alphas were dropping right back into their familiar territory of jockeying for position. Their dominance games were going to kill them, and they didn't seem to notice or care about the idiocy of it all.

Hammer shoved Dale to one side, then whirled in the same movement. Before Snow knew what was happening, he was lunging at her. She cringed back into whichever twin was dragging her along.

"What do you think you're doing?" a familiar voice thundered.

If Snow had been in human form, she would have sobbed to hear Cassidy's voice, even distorted as it was in betweenform. As the North Side Alpha strode from the trees, rays of moonlight filtered through the branches to dapple her skin with glowing dots that did nothing to hide the intensity of her eyes. They blazed with fury, one shocking crimson, the other brilliant blue, each a sign of her unusual heritage and an undeniable reminder of the power she held. Her face commanded attention, and she got it from each squabbling wolven, no matter where they stood on the dominance scale. Snow was no exception. She'd made her way halfway to Five Moons, before she realized the Alpha carried a naked wolven in skinform over her shoulder. A tattered piece of cloth hung from her other hand.

"Five Moons." The name was whispered as title by Hammer, who only held Cassidy's gaze for a second before looking away.

"Jane?" Dale pushed past the South Shore Alpha. "Is she…"

"She's alive," Five Moons said. "I found her at the edge of the fire from the helicopter. She's not doing well. We need to get her somewhere to rest."

Her arms outstretched, Dale approached the other Alpha. Without a word, Five Moons relinquished her burden. Dale cradled the Beta to her chest and whispered something to her. When there was no response, she knelt under a scrubby tree and began running her hands over the Beta's limbs, working her way toward her torso as she muttered to herself.

Five Moons turned to face them. "Now, does someone want to tell me what's going on here?"

Tail still tucked firmly against her body, Snow scurried the rest of the way over and pressed herself against the back of Cassidy's legs. It felt so good to have her between Snow and the other Alphas. They were farther away, but Cassidy was there now.

"Hammer has a problem being led to safety by Snow," Dale said.

"We don't know where she's taking us," Hammer said. "She wouldn't shift to tell us."

Dale whipped her head around to stare at him. "She's exhausted from saving our asses. If she could have shifted, she would have, if only to shut you up so we could get on with getting away."

"We're parked across the road from here," Five Moons said. "There's room enough to get everyone out." She walked past Hammer to join the twins at the edge of the trees. "Is that good enough a plan for you?"

"It'll do," he said.

"We're going to need a sizable gap in traffic so Dale can get Jane across," Five Moons said. "I suggest the rest of us take full furform. You'll follow Snow and me to the van. Then we'll head back to the hotel and get you rides back to your packs. Dale, we can have someone look at Jane."

"Or you could take us to our cars," Hammer said.

"It'll be faster if we go to our den," Five Moons replied. She didn't wait for his reply but dropped down to all fours and allowed her wolf to take over.

* * *

Cassidy fumed while the wolf crept them closer to the road. She'd busted her butt to get to the group, only to find Hammer accosting her…her whatever Snow was to her. The lone wolf felt closer to one of

Cassidy's wolves, now more than ever. Cassidy knew she would lay her life down to protect her. Snow had been happy to take that protection. In fact, she was practically glued to Cassidy's left flank.

Hammer was going to have to wait. First thing was to get everyone away from here, then to regroup at the den. Hopefully, the tenuous truce between the packs would last that long.

Traffic on the highway was light, but heavier than Cassidy and the wolf would have liked. Dale needed to be across the road and into the trees on the far side before any headlights could hit her. They were all moving more slowly than was typical, plus Dale was weighed down by her Beta's unconscious body.

They hunkered down on the packed snow and tried to breathe around the stench of the small bundle of fabric they held in their jaws. Cassidy had taken the time to tear the fatigue jacket off a dead soldier with the hope that it might tell them something about who'd dared to attack them. If nothing else, it would be tangible proof of what had happened once their wounds had healed.

Cars continued to whiz past. They could cross after a car had gone by. The driver and passengers would be less likely to look back. It was a gamble, but one that might pay off. There were still human soldiers in the woods, and they needed to be gone before the humans got their shit together and decided to hunt down the wolven who had been so much trouble. Of course, if they hadn't attacked, no one would have dropped a helicopter on them.

Either Bone or Marrow dropped down on the other side of Snow. Their twin plopped herself down next to Cassidy. Their body language was open, each expressing their confidence in them. Hammer lurked behind them, moving his weight frequently and looking to one side, then the other. It was clear that he would rather have been anywhere but there. Dale crouched behind them, her Beta's still form clasped to her chest.

It had been Cassidy and the wolf's intention to have them cross one at a time, but when it was their turn to go, Snow came too. They slowed a bit to make sure the lone wolf had no problems navigating the icy median. Marrow and Bone overtook them and dashed across the road, disappearing into the undergrowth. Despite his harsh words, Hammer hung back to escort Dale and her burden.

Snow flashed Cassidy a quick look accompanied by a definite feeling of appreciation. Cassidy and the wolf were so glad for the softness of the ground beneath their paws. They paused at the edge of the woods on the other side of the highway, watching as Dale made her careful way across the median. Hammer hovered behind her. In the distance, a pinpoint of headlights grew brighter. The road was so flat that it was difficult to determine how far the approaching car was. Not close enough to make out the figures of a massive wolf and a human-wolf hybrid mincing over a concrete median piled with snow. Or so they hoped.

Come on, Cassidy thought.

They would make it or they wouldn't, was her wolf's contention. It would be preferable if they weren't seen, but they would deal with the consequences when they happened.

Except it was more than just what to do with the occupant or occupants of a car who saw them. What if they got away? What if they didn't? Was it better to kill them or to try to turn them? Cassidy had to believe that the wolven weren't monsters, but the steps they would need to take to stay safe could be monstrous. If the choice was the occupants or Snow, Cassidy suspected she knew which one she would pick. She only hoped she would never have to learn for certain.

The car drew closer as Dale stepped down onto the road's concrete. She glanced toward the approaching headlights, then hoisted her Beta up around her shoulders. The small woman flopped into place, and Dale wrapped her arms around the Beta's legs, then broke into a slightly wobbly sprint. Hammer dashed along behind her. They were off the pavement and almost to the woods when the lights swept across them.

Cassidy and the wolf cringed as tires screeched and the car fishtailed to an abrupt stop. They backed into the trees until she was sure she couldn't be seen. Dale dove into the scrub brush, oblivious to how small branches jabbed into her body. Her fur would keep anything but a major limb from reaching skin. She angled her body to protect the vulnerable body of her Beta.

Hammer kept right behind her, as close as a shadow. Cassidy and the wolf waited, holding their breath. What did they do if someone came to investigate? Their heartbeat drummed in their ears. Even a human could have snuck up on them from behind. The other wolven were all past them. They would have to handle anyone nosing around from the road.

Clouds of vapor steamed in the cold air, potentially giving away their location. They moderated their breathing, trying to keep from panting. They lifted their nose, scanning the air. In the distance, a car door opened, then a bright light shone from the driver's side. A cell phone flashlight, if Cassidy had to guess. They backed further into the brambles. At least the snow was so packed down that there were few traces of their passage. The icy surface that had slowed them down might cover for them now.

Whoever stood beside their car shone the light down the edge of the trees then back.

"Hello?" a man's voice called out. It cracked on the last syllable, betraying his nervousness.

The wolf's head snapped up and they started to growl low in their chest. There was no way the man could hear them; the wolf wasn't being particularly loud. They glared in the direction of the car and took a step forward, their head low, their shoulders tense. They felt heavy and menacing to Cassidy.

A moment later, the car door slammed and the tires squealed again, this time as the human sped away. He might not have seen them, but some warning from his lizard brain had told him that his was a very precarious position. Hopefully, he would chalk it up to an active imagination and shadows across the road.

Cassidy and the wolf waited for a moment longer. When they were satisfied he wasn't coming back, they picked up Snow's scent and went to join her. All they had to do was get to the car, then they could head home.

CHAPTER FORTY

The road was dark; the headlights stabbed into Snow's brain as much as they reached into the darkness. She was exhausted and chilly. The heat was blasting through the vents, but she still tried to nudge up the heat slider. It wouldn't go any higher. She'd loaned her sweatshirt to Marrow. Cassidy's extra shirt had gone to Bone. They huddled together on the bench seat that ran the length of the van. Dale's Beta was laid out on Snow's bed, and Dale hovered over her, still in betweenform.

The car was quiet, save for the sound of wolven in skinform snacking on the few morsels Snow had stashed in her vehicle. They were all low on energy, having shifted too much too quickly and having sustained wounds on top of everything else. It was more than a handful of granola bars and some turkey jerky could fix, but it was a start. Snow's throat was dry. The bottle of water she'd had on the drive up had been half empty by the time they parked. It was completely empty now, Dale having poured it down the throat of her unconscious Beta.

Hammer sat cross-legged on the floor in skinform. He gave no sign that the van's interior was anything less than balmy. There were no extra clothes for him, not that they would have fit him, but he didn't seem to mind. Something was on his mind, that much was obvious as he split his time between glaring at Snow in the driver's seat and Cassidy in the passenger's seat. Every time he turned that burning stare on her, Snow had to fight to keep from ducking her head down. Her shoulders ached from the effort of not constantly retreating into them.

"How did that happen?" Hammer finally asked after another few miles had ticked away under their wheels. They were fifteen or so minutes away from where they'd parked.

Snow glanced down at the speedometer and eased off the gas.

"Why are we slowing down?" Hammer barked.

"Don't want to get pulled over," Snow said as mildly as she could. "Don't much want to explain all this to the heat."

"Mm." Hammer exhaled loudly through his nostrils then lapsed back into silence.

"I don't know," Cassidy said eventually. "Either someone talked, or they bugged one or more of us."

"You didn't tell them?"

Cassidy stiffened. When she turned to meet Hammer's bright orange eyes, hers gleamed red and blue. "Of course not." Her voice was mild in contrast with the simmering anger of her scent.

"Who told?" Marrow asked.

"Hazel wasn't there," Dale said. She didn't look up from her Beta.

"No." The simple denial came from three mouths.

Snow shook her head. The Joliet Alpha had been the oldest among the wolven leaders. They'd been the most diplomatic of the group, even more so than Dean. Her brother had looked up to them and had often followed their lead. Working in tandem with Hazel had kept the packs in uneasy harmony, until MacTavish had set his sights on the North Side Pack.

"Then who?" Bone shifted uneasily on the vinyl seat.

"Don't suppose you saw Crag out there?" Hammer said to Cassidy. "Or his Beta."

"Crag's Beta was the first to go down," Cassidy said. "All I saw on my way out was Jane and the occasional human."

"Dead or alive?" Bone asked.

Cassidy waggled her hand back and forth. "A little of both."

The conversation faltered and died. Snow picked at a hangnail, being careful not to jog the van as she fiddled. No one had touched Cassidy's suggestion that they'd been bugged. The implications were frightening, but she didn't see how it was simpler to assume that someone had given them up.

"Maybe we don't drive right up when we get home," Snow said quietly to Cassidy. The others would hear, but the lowered voice should indicate that this was a private conversation. Wolven were usually good about respecting each other's boundaries. When everyone's senses were so sensitive, there was a lot of pretending that something wasn't happening.

"And why is that?" Hammer asked.

Alphas didn't always feel the niceties applied to them, of course.

"What if someone's waiting for us?" Cassidy said, her voice low. "I should have thought of that." Chagrin colored her scent, dropping it down from near rage.

Snow reached over and patted Cassidy on the leg. Next time she would. Hopefully, there would never be another time like this one.

"Ah," Marrow said. "If they could find us in an open forest..."

"...they can find us in our dens," Bone finished. They huddled closer together.

Cassidy sighed. "We'll be careful."

"We need to get home." Hammer leaned forward until his head was between both of theirs. "Go faster," he growled at Snow.

Cassidy put a hand on the top of his head and shoved him back. "If a cop pulls us over, what are you going to do? Attack them as a naked Black man or shift to a massive wolf? How do we explain the unconscious naked woman in the back and the two women wearing nothing but sweatshirts? Or maybe the half-wolf, half-human woman can really scare the pants off everyone."

Hammer snarled and Snow shrunk closer to the window. If he attacked Cassidy, she needed to be able to keep control over the van. The two Alphas locked eyes, each trying to stare down the other. Silence smothered the van's interior. Aside from Snow's small corrections on the van's steering wheel, no one moved.

The silence lengthened, pulling more and more taut until Snow expected it to snap and the fur to start flying.

On a signal no one else could see, Cassidy and Hammer looked away from each other.

"My wolves," Hammer said, his voice nearly inaudible.

Cassidy leaned back and grabbed one of his hands. She pulled it forward and wrapped her other hand around his.

"I know." She laid her head on the back of his hand.

Hammer sighed.

Bone slithered to the floor and wrapped her arms around him. Marrow knelt behind them and hugged her sister and the South Shore Alpha. Dale reached forward and placed a hand on Marrow's back. It was the best she could offer without leaving her place at her Beta's side.

Time seemed to slow down as the Alphas sat, truly united in purpose since the first time they'd met. Snow felt like her rib cage was expanding, as if she'd only been taking shallow breaths until now. The sensation was calming and energizing all at once, and Five Moons sat at the center of it.

Dale dropped her hand, and the moment ended as soon as she removed her hand from Hammer's shoulder.

The Alphas squinted and looked around, as if they'd just woken from a long and fitful sleep.

Snow redirected her attention to her driving. They were halfway into the other lane, and she yanked on the wheel to get back onto the right side of the road.

* * *

Cassidy blinked as she came back to herself. "What just happened?"

Snow gave her a side-eyed stare from the driver's seat, then shook herself and directed all her attention back to the road. "Had to get us back in the right lane. Sorry about that."

"Not the driving…" Cassidy looked over her shoulder at the van full of Alphas. Four sets of glowing eyes met hers. Weirdly, they didn't seem upset, though each one gazed at her through their wolf's eyes.

"That was odd," Hammer said.

"Good odd?" one of the twins asked.

"Or bad odd?" The other cocked her head, then shared a look with her sister.

"Good odd," they agreed in unison.

Dale had bent her attention back to her Beta, but she spared a glance over at Cassidy.

"Odd or not, it's not what we're here for." Unlike his aggressive tone before, now Hammer seemed almost subdued. "Not what we came for. We're in a worse position than the one that drove us to meet, but we still need to make some decisions." He nodded decisively. "We need to meet up. Coordinate."

Cassidy didn't dare say anything. As hard as he'd come out against her plan of joining forces at the meeting, she didn't want to jeopardize his change of heart by speaking out.

"I need to get my Beta back to my pack," Dale said. "And to check on my wolves. Once I know they're safe, I'll be happy to talk this out again."

"Somewhere public," Marrow mused.

"Somewhere they can't hide if they move on us," Bone agreed.

"I'll be there," Cassidy said.

"As will we…" Marrow said.

"…once we find out about our wolves."

"Same," Dale said.

"Good." Cassidy stared into the darkness outside the car's windows. "How about we meet at Harold Washington Library at noon. If you can't make it, send one of your wolves."

"If you or your proxy aren't there, we can only assume you don't want to be included in this partnership," Hammer said. "I will be there. You can count on it."

"Should someone check on Hazel?" Dale asked.

"Best candidate for that would be Crag," Hammer said.

The Alphas lapsed into silence, no one wanting to point out that Crag was probably dead.

"How about once we've decided on next steps?" Cassidy said. She wanted to increase their numbers more than anything, but the idea of following up with an unknown Alpha on their own territory made her anxious.

"I like that." Hammer's eyes held approval for the idea. "It doesn't leave them out in the cold, unless they want to be." He looked around at the remaining Alphas. "It's a plan."

"A good one?" Bone asked.

"Does it matter?" Marrow said almost before her sister stopped talking.

Cassidy sighed. She couldn't tell if those two were going to be help or hindrance when it came to her plans.

"How long until we get to your den?" Hammer asked.

"Forty-five minutes, give or take," Snow said. She checked her rearview mirror, though Cassidy was fairly certain the lone wolf was keeping tabs on the wolven in the van, not the state of the road behind them.

"Mm hm." Hammer shifted to lean back against the side bench where Bone and Marrow were snuggled into a ball. Their tangle of limbs might have looked careless to an outsider, but Cassidy could see that they were going for as much skin to skin contact as they could make happen. Neither of them objected when Hammer slouched against them.

Cassidy watched out the window. The drive went by in complete silence. It wasn't the tense stillness that had permeated the van when she and Hammer had tried to stare each other down. This was more like the stillness between one exhalation and the next. They were waiting to see what came after, and it felt like the entire world was holding its breath with them.

The highway gave way to Tri-State, dark fields giving way to long stretches of concrete bounded by noise barriers on one side and office buildings on the other. The streetlights above the road were harsh. Cassidy couldn't tell if her eyes had been damaged by the explosion or if everything simply seemed incredibly foreign after all they'd been through. She checked the skies periodically, keeping an eye out for helicopters. There was one in the distance, toward the lakefront as they came off the Tri-State and onto the Kennedy Expressway. She stiffened, waiting to see if it was also heading for them, but it flew on in the opposite direction. After that, she couldn't seem to relax. Getting off the freeway helped, but surface streets concealed so many more places for someone to be waiting for them.

It wasn't until they turned onto the hotel's street that she started to unwind a bit.

Through it all, Snow would periodically reach over and pat the top of her thigh or grip her elbow lightly. It was impossible to tell if she was making sure Cassidy was there or trying to reassure her. If Cassidy had to guess, it was probably a bit of both.

What were she and Snow to each other? It hadn't been the time to poke at that question while they'd been running for their lives in the forest outside Aurora. Was now any better? She didn't have anything better to do. From the dueling snores and occasional whimper, Marrow and Bone had fallen asleep. Hammer still leaned against them, but he was staring out the side door window at scenery that flashed past in a second, then was gone. Dale had eyes only for her Beta. And it wasn't like Cassidy could ask Snow.

Could they be something more than wolven who knew each other? She liked to think they'd become friends over these past few frenetic weeks. Something about the lone wolf centered her. Even now, on one of the worst days of her life, each of Snow's light touches lifted her spirits. Now that she thought about it, every time her mind found its way back to that dark place, Snow reached over again.

Cassidy sneaked a look over at the lone wolf. Snow's eyes met hers. They glittered for a moment, the light from the streetlights catching them just right, then Snow winked and went back to watching the road. This time Cassidy was the one to reach over and put a hand on Snow's thigh. Her overture was met by a hand covering hers and squeezing for a second before resuming its place on the wheel.

Maybe there was a path forward here. Snow had been adamant she wasn't interested in a physical relationship with her or anyone. No. She'd never said physical, she'd said sexual. There was a lot more to touch than sex. Cassidy chewed on that for a while. She wasn't willing to forgo sex. She wasn't even sure she could, not when her heat was upon her. But if Snow didn't care that Cassidy had sex on occasion, as long as it wasn't with her, then maybe they could come to some agreement. It would be a non-traditional arrangement, but those didn't seem so taboo among the wolven.

A snicker forced itself past her lips before Cassidy could stop it. At Snow's questioning "Hmm?" she shook her head.

"Just thinking of a completely inappropriate conversation to have with my mom," Cassidy said.

"Is it the one where you tell her she can't sleep with Carla?" Snow asked.

"What?" Cassidy stared at the lone wolf.

"What do you mean what?" Snow looked confused. "You know the vamp is totally going to put the moves on her, right?"

"She won't."

Snow raised a skeptical eyebrow.

"I told her to stay away from my mom," Cassidy said. "If she doesn't, she loses my protection." She grinned nastily. "Mostly because I'll have torn her limb from fucking limb."

"The Lord of Chicago is under your protection?" Dale said from the back. "Did I hear that right?"

"Former Lord," Snow said.

"Well, that changes everything." The eye roll was audible in Dale's voice. "Are you harboring her, Five Moons?"

"For now," Cassidy said. The seat belt was starting to bind across her collarbone. She eased herself down in the seat to avoid the edge rubbing against her skin. "I owed her a favor."

"Maybe that's our mole," Hammer said. "Vamps will sell information to anyone who comes looking for it."

"I don't think so," Cassidy said, trying to keep her voice level. How dare they question her decision to keep to her word? "She only just showed up."

"Still." Hammer tapped the back of their seat for emphasis. "I hear they can communicate telepathically."

"Vamps?" Snow shook her head. "That's an old wives' tale."

"You don't know that for sure." Hammer grabbed the back of the bench seat and levered himself to a crouch. He balanced easily against the bumps and sways of the van as it made its way through the North Side streets. "All anyone knows for sure about a vamp is that you can't trust 'em."

"I'm not trusting her," Cassidy said. "I'm giving her a place to stay while she gets her shit together."

"And how's that working for you?" Hammer pointed out the windshield as the hotel came into view down the block. "Isn't that your den?"

CHAPTER FORTY-ONE

Flashing red lights soaked the neighborhood's buildings in garish crimson and deep shadow. The smell of burning building materials hung heavy in the air. It smelled so different than the forest fire. Even with the addition of kerosene, that inferno had had a much cleaner scent to it. This smoke was heavy and black and it clawed at the inside of her nostrils and abraded her throat.

Snow pulled over and parked as close as she could get them to the hotel. Cassidy threw open the passenger door and hit the pavement before the car had come to a complete stop. Hammer leaped out beside her, not caring at all that he was still nude.

"The library. Tomorrow," was all he said, before dashing for a nearby alleyway.

"We'll be there." Marrow and Bone hopped out next to her as well. They turned and sprinted for a side street.

"Sure. Whatever." Cassidy didn't have time for the Alphas. She had to get closer.

Flames shot out the hotel's windows and through holes in the roof. There had to be half a dozen firetrucks there and as many police cars. She ran up the street, dodging onlookers. A large crowd gathered halfway down the block from the hotel and were so engrossed that no one had noticed the naked and half-naked wolven who'd streaked past them in the night. This was as close as the first responders would allow the rubberneckers. Cassidy elbowed her way through the crowd. She could still feel her wolven, every last one of them, even Ruri. Including Snow.

They were still alive. But not in the building that had been her den. No one could have survived that.

So where were they? Was her mom with them? She hoped so, because if Sophia was trapped in the building... No, she had to be with the wolves. It was the only possible option.

* * *

Snow slipstreamed through the crowd after Cassidy. The muscles in her jaw clenched, the North Side Alpha stared at the inferno that had been her den only hours before.

"Where are they?" Cassidy yelled. She turned wild eyes on Snow.

"I don't know," Snow said. She stepped forward and wrapped her arms around Cassidy's waist. She hoped they'd gotten out of the hotel before the fire broke out.

"I have to find them." Cassidy tried to step out of Snow's embrace. "Let. Me. Go."

The full weight of her Alpha status was behind the command, and Snow found herself loosening her grip. As soon as she realized what she was doing, she tightened her hold on the Alpha.

"Let's get you back to the van," Snow said.

"In a second." Cassidy gave up trying to get free. She went up on her tiptoes to get a better view of the scene. "If we go around back I can get close enough to see if anyone is nearby."

Snow hesitated.

"Only to look," Cassidy said, her voice breaking around the edges with quiet desperation. "I have to make sure they're not near here. We aren't close enough that I can tell."

Fire and police had a pretty tight net around the front of the building, but they didn't know the area like Snow did. They certainly didn't know it like Cassidy.

"We have to make it quick," Snow said. "The other Alphas..."

"They're gone. Heading home."

"Not Dale."

"Then she can watch the van with you." Cassidy shook her head. "You can let me go now. I'm not going to do anything stupid."

"Promise?"

"Promise." Cassidy met Snow's eyes. They glistened. "I'll be able to feel if my wolves are close. But my mom…"

"Your mom…" Snow whispered. Her own mama's eyes meeting hers as she realized her life was about to end flashed into Snow's mind. She squeezed Cassidy tightly then let go.

The Alpha had expected Snow to stay behind, but she kept close to Cassidy's heels. Cassidy might have promised not to do anything dumb, but Snow knew she wasn't thinking clearly.

Free of the hug she probably could have broken any time she'd wanted to, Cassidy headed for a gap between two nearby buildings. The North Side Pack's hotel shared a block with more than its fair share of empty businesses. Humans didn't like to live too close to wolven. Being in the presence of those higher on the food chain made them nervous. Snow couldn't count the number of businesses she'd seen come and go over the decades. They would lie empty for years at a time, then someone would decide the neighborhood was ripe for revitalization. After a flurry of activity, the companies would shutter their storefronts as foot traffic dwindled from little to nothing. It was why Hammer and his pack moved around their neighborhood, to keep from creating dead zones. The buffer had served Dean quite well, only now it seemed that he'd miscalculated. Surely the lack of neighbors had allowed whoever had attacked the North Side den some cover.

Cassidy vaulted up the concrete stoop of an empty building. She grabbed the handle on the metal door and twisted it off. The sound of shearing metal echoed down between the two buildings, where it was swallowed up by the din of the unfolding disaster.

Satisfied that they were still in the clear, Cassidy turned her back to the door and slammed her elbow at the hole. The pounding was somewhat muffled by her back braced hard against the metal door. Snow cringed and moved so she would have a better line of sight on the street. If someone came looking for the source of the noise, she'd be able to alert Cassidy.

It only took a few blows before the door was deformed enough that Cassidy could yank it open. The latch was too warped to give more than token resistance. She disappeared into the building. With one final glance toward the street, Snow followed.

The previous business hadn't bothered to clear out its fixtures or inventory. She dodged around racks filled with old books and magazines, trusting in her nose to follow Cassidy. The Alpha's scent was easy to pick out among the dust and mildewed paper. Ahead, the sound of shattering glass told her that Cassidy had decided to make her own way out.

Snow slipped from the main store to a side office. Cassidy was no longer there, but the prints of her palms were obvious in the dust of the windowsill. Snow followed suit, placing her hands where the Alpha had placed hers and vaulting out the window. She landed on a pile of soil covered with the debris of dead weeds and tree branches. The way to the river was clear.

A pair of glowing odd eyes watched her from the edge of the trees that ran along the river. Cassidy stepped into the light of the moon. It was much fainter than it had been when they'd showed up for the Alpha meeting, but its light traced a silver trail of tears down Cassidy's cheeks. Snow's heart tightened at further evidence of the Alpha's misery. She swallowed to remove the lump in her own throat but was only partially successful.

She broke into a quick dash to meet up with Cassidy. It wasn't as effective as a full sprint would have been, but the ground was littered with refuse that impeded her progress.

"Come on," Cassidy hissed as she got closer. She disappeared into the trees. The Alpha wasn't working to stay silent. The sound of breaking sticks and rustling branches made following her easy. Snow would have preferred to stealth up to the hotel, but she understood Five Moons' desperation.

They didn't have far to go, but Cassidy was much faster than Snow. By the time Snow caught up to the other wolven, Cassidy was crouched at the trees next to the well-worn path from the river to the hotel's backyard.

"Do you smell anything?" Cassidy asked. She put her hands on the ground and bent down to take a deep sniff.

"Smoke and blood," Snow replied. "Human and wolven, but it's being brought down on the breeze. There's nothing close by."

"Human?" Cassidy's voice broke on the question.

"Not Sophia." Snow didn't know who it belonged to, but she didn't taste anything in the scent that reminded her of the Alpha's mother.

Cassidy relaxed for a moment, then refocused on the tracks. "No one's been by recently. We'd be able to tell if they evacuated this way."

Snow nodded. "Are you close enough to feel them?"

"Almost." Cassidy pushed herself back up. "You can stay here if you want."

"I'm coming with you."

Cassidy didn't answer, but Snow had the sense that she appreciated the company nonetheless. With painstaking patience, Cassidy moved up the path. Snow ghosted with her on the opposite side of the trail. The area where the path opened into the backyard was reasonably close to the building. Already, the sounds of firefighters' radio chatter were filtering back to them. With it was the sound of human voices. The scents of blood were stronger, though difficult to separate from the smoke. Snow couldn't pinpoint who had gotten injured.

A thin screen of leafless branches stood between them and the humans trying to put out the blaze. Cassidy settled back on her heels and closed her eyes. Snow crouched next to her, watching the humans. Someone had to watch over the Alpha. She might be a poor choice for it, but she was all there was.

"Anything?" Snow asked when Cassidy opened her eyes.

"No." The relief was stark on the Alpha's face.

"Thank god."

There were shouts from the humans as the wind shifted. A flare of flame and sparks went up from the roof, swirling toward the river. Snow grimaced as the scents of burning and heat seared her nostrils.

"The fuckers came after the pack while we were in Aurora," Cassidy whispered. "We have to get back to the van."

CHAPTER FORTY-TWO

Cassidy's mind raced all the way back to the car. This was all her fault. No, this was the fault of the assholes who'd targeted them, who'd been targeting them. There was no way this sudden disappearance of her entire pack wasn't tied to those who'd gone missing over the past month and a bit.

"What did you find?" Dale asked from the back of the van as soon as she and Snow climbed into the front seats.

"My wolves aren't there," Cassidy said.

"Thank Luna," Dale said.

Cassidy felt her face twist into the approximation of a smile. "They were taken. I'm sure of it. We smelled a lot of my people's blood in the back."

"How do you know they're not..." Dale let the question trail off. She didn't have to finish it.

Cassidy shook her head. "I can still feel them. They're alive, but I don't know where."

"I need to get to my den," Dale said. "The others have left. I don't know where Hammer went, but the Gary Alphas hotwired a car and took off."

"If they came for your wolves..." Cassidy didn't finish the statement. Again, they knew the stakes.

"What are you going to do?" Snow asked.

"I'm going to get some information in the only place I know to go," Cassidy said.

"The vampires." Snow's unhappiness at Cassidy's plan wafted off her in a wave of undulating blue. "Without Carla there. Are you sure that's safe?"

"Only thing I'm sure of is that a lot of wolven are counting on me. I don't plan to let them down."

"None of us do," Dale said, "but I need to get going, and you're my ride. I can't leave Jane."

"Drop me at Faint first," Cassidy said.

"I can take you to Kenosha, Dale, after we drop Five Moons off," Snow said. "I'll help you with her, just in case…"

Dale nodded gratefully. "Just in case."

"At least there's a plan," Cassidy said.

"Such as it is," Snow agreed. "For the next few hours, anyway."

"And when that time is up?" Dale asked.

"Then we come up with another," Cassidy answered. "Until we can stop planning."

"Or until we're dead." Dale's eyes glittered in the dark.

* * *

Snow maneuvered her way through narrow streets at high speed. The light traffic wouldn't last much longer. The wee hours of the morning were becoming not so wee.

Traffic wasn't the only thing they were racing. The vampires' nightclub would be closed soon, making it that much more difficult to get in. Visiting Faint was a different proposition than it had been under Carla's reign. Not knowing who had taken over made it impossible to predict what might be required to get an audience with whoever was now running things. Snow's knowledge of the Chicago vampire community had revolved around her understanding with Carla, so she was no longer much help.

"Drop me off around the corner from the club, please," Cassidy said when they could see Faint's lights down the street. She ran her thumb over the lit screen of her phone. She'd been trying to raise Sophia's phone on the drive over. With each unsuccessful attempt, she tried again. None had gotten through. She stared at the screen for a moment before jamming the phone back into her pocket.

"Don't want to be seen getting out of my van?" Snow asked. "I'm sorry I don't have a nice new SUV like the other moms."

"Very funny." The grin that lurked at the edge of Cassidy's mouth softened her deadpan tone and momentarily lifted her scent out of desperate hope.

Snow shrugged. "I try. But if it's what you want, then…" She took the next left and pulled up next to a fire hydrant. Parking in this neighborhood was always a problem. The vampires made a lot of money from their club, but there were days when Snow was convinced half the profits came from valet fees.

"Thank you." Cassidy turned to face her. She stared at Snow for a long moment, searching her eyes for something.

Snow watched the Alpha in return, trying to memorize her face, the way her hair always escaped being tucked behind her ears, the determined set of her jaw whenever Cassidy was unsure of something but was going to try anyway. There had been a lot of that lately, and the Alpha's jaw was nearly square from how much exercise the muscles had gotten.

Cassidy released her seat belt and leaned forward. "May I?" she murmured.

Her mouth suddenly dry, Snow nodded.

Warm hands cradled her cheeks as Cassidy pulled their faces closer together. For a panicked moment, Snow thought the Alpha was going to try to kiss her. Instead, Cassidy angled her head forward and rested their foreheads together. One hand dropped to wrap around the back of Snow's neck.

The moment didn't last long, but for those few breaths, Snow's pulse rate slowed from a frantic gallop to a more mellow canter. She ceased worrying about anything and reveled in being there with Cassidy. With Five Moons.

When Cassidy dropped her hands, reality snapped back in around them with the painful throb of a dislocated joint being returned to its proper place.

"Remember," she said. "Noon. Harold Washington Library."

"I won't forget." Snow put every ounce of sincerity she had in her body into the promise.

Cassidy smiled. "Good." She opened the door and hopped down to the pavement. The door slammed behind her with a finality that shuddered through Snow's bones.

She scrabbled at the door handle on the driver's side door, then thrust it open.

"Wait," Snow called as she ran after Cassidy.

The Alpha slowed her purposeful stride and turned, walking backward. She tilted her head in question.

"Hold on." Snow grabbed her arms and pulled Cassidy to a stop.

"What is it?" Cassidy asked. She didn't remind Snow that they were on borrowed time. She didn't have to.

"Be careful," Snow said. "Please."

"I'll do my best."

"Do better. I want…" What did she want? Snow hadn't stopped to consider what she would say to the North Side Alpha. She'd felt the possibility that she might never see Cassidy again as a thunderclap within her chest and had reacted.

"What is it?" Cassidy asked gently. Her face radiated interest in the answer and none of the impatience she should have been feeling. There wasn't even the slightest flicker of it in her scent.

"I want you to come back," Snow said. "To me." How would she find out what came next if Cassidy didn't come back? The plaintive thought threatened to send tears coursing down her face. She blinked to keep the prickling in her eyes from becoming more.

"Snow." Cassidy stepped closer until the length of their bodies was pressed together.

The sensation was warm and welcome, and Snow wanted to sink herself into the contact and stay there. Her long shuddering breath steamed in the night air. This was what she'd been missing. How ironic to find it now.

"Snow," Cassidy said again. "I will always come back, as long as I'm able. I will do everything in my power to make sure I return." She grasped Snow's upper arms. "To you."

"Oh." The strength of Cassidy's conviction left her a little breathless. "Well, good." The words were nowhere near enough to convey what the promise meant to her. She believed Cassidy, enough to tune out the little voice in her head that reminded her that they always ended up alone. This was different. It had to be. Cassidy had to be.

Cassidy quirked a tiny grin. "Good. You take care of yourself. I want to come back to you, too."

"Okay." Snow returned the Alpha's grin, goofily she was sure, but she didn't care.

"All right." Cassidy leaned into her, pressing her cheek to Snow's.

Snow closed her eyes and relaxed into the contact. She inhaled deeply, pulling Cassidy's scent inside her and drawing it deep inside her where it could never be taken away. This was one scent she would never allow herself to lose.

Cassidy moved against her. She moved enough to bury her nose in the crook of Snow's neck. She inhaled deeply, pulling Snow's scent deep inside her lungs. She'd done this once before, up on the stage of the building that was probably still burning on the other side of the city. At that time, Cassidy had been learning Snow's scent, now she seemed to be trying to memorize it.

And then she was gone.

When Snow opened her eyes, Cassidy was striding away. She looked back over her shoulder and caught Snow's eye, gave a wink, then turned the corner toward the bright lights of the vampire nightclub.

Did that really just happen? It sure felt like it. Snow hugged her arms around herself, trying to retain the heat where their bodies had been molded together.

Noon. There was work to do before then. She turned and headed back to the van.

"Everything all right out there?" Dale asked as she pulled herself back into the driver's seat.

"As good as it can be," Snow said. "Let's get you home."

CHAPTER FORTY-THREE

Cassidy headed down the sidewalk. Snow's revelation had been unexpected, but not unwelcome. They would have to talk once things settled down, but maybe she didn't have to say goodbye to the lone wolf. She hoped not. Her wolf shifted in lazy agreement. She wanted to stop and wrap herself in the feelings Snow had awakened in her, but there was no time. The softness she felt for the lone wolf wouldn't serve her in a den of vampires. If she'd had anywhere else to turn, she would have done so. Hell, she would have gone to Mary, and they hadn't had a serious and civil conversation since Cassidy had been turned the previous October.

Every step closer to the nightclub resonated up her legs, stripping away the warmth of her feelings, rekindling a burning anger and a resolve to do what had to be done to save her wolves. She would pay back every injury, every death, that her people had endured upon those who would—who had—hurt them.

She checked both ways before she crossed the street to Faint. It wouldn't do to get pasted by a car while heading to beg for support from beings she didn't like or understand. There was no one coming, so she stepped forward, making a straight line for the front doors.

This late, not many waited outside to be let into the exclusive club. She held her head high and stalked up the shallow steps, ever closer to the velvet rope that barred the entrance. She allowed the wolf to ascend a bit, enough for her presence to permeate their skin. In front of her, the humans in line pressed themselves to one side to get out of her way. A large man looked like he wanted to do something about his sudden urge to move. There was always one.

Cassidy looked him in the eyes, daring him to make something of it, while never slowing. He swallowed hard, his Adam's apple bobbing up and down in his neck. She kept going past him, eyes locked until he looked away.

A vampire at the top of the stairs watched her approach with one raised eyebrow. When Cassidy reached the top of the stairs, he nodded to the bouncer who unhooked the rope. He lifted a hand to an earpiece, whispering something Cassidy couldn't make out over the pounding music that suddenly increased in volume as the bouncer scurried forward to open the massive double doors for her.

She didn't stop to thank them, didn't even spare them a look. Cassidy knew where she was going. There was only one place the new head of the vampires could be. She turned down the hall that led to Carla's office. Whispers followed her. What they said, she couldn't make out over the music whose bassline throbbed in time with each step she took deeper into their lair. No one could stop her, but part of her hoped someone would try.

The first vampires along the hall weren't a surprise. By the time Cassidy made it to the stairs, the walls were lined with them. Whatever success Carla thought she might have had with her former subjects didn't seem to have lasted.

She ignored them as she mounted the steps. She disregarded the shadows that deepened unnaturally, that reduced the sconces to barely glowing pinpoints. Each step was one closer to getting her people back. To getting them all back.

The doors to the office swung open on soundless hinges. The room beyond might not have existed for all Cassidy could see. It was a pit of darkness. She felt a pang of anxiety but didn't allow her pace to falter.

She stepped into the shadows and stopped. Her eyes could pierce all but the deepest gloom, but there was nothing to see. She should have been able to see something.

The room sighed around her, an exhalation that skittered down her spine, sending her hands curling into hard fists.

"You came." The words seemed to coalesce from the susurrus that lingered in the room's corners.

A light came on, illuminating a familiar heavy wooden desk. The face the light revealed was also familiar. One she hadn't thought she'd have to see again.

The skittering down her spine erupted into gooseflesh, and her wolf lunged within her, snarling and snapping in a violent demand to be let free. Only a few months ago, this woman had threatened their very existence. She was supposed to be dead. Mary swore she'd watched her die in one final epic fight with MacTavish. Of course she wasn't gone.

"Hello, Cassidy." Stiletto's voice purred at her from every corner of the room. "I'm so glad you've come to visit."

Bella Books, Inc.

Women. Books. Even Better Together.

P.O. Box 10543
Tallahassee, FL 32302

Phone: 800-729-4992
www.bellabooks.com

9 781642 474183